HERGÉ
★
THE ADVENTURES OF
TINTIN
★
THE CRAB
WITH
THE G⊕LDEN CLAWS

L B

LITTLE, BROWN AND COMPANY
New York Boston

This edition first published in the UK in 2007
by Egmont UK Limited
Translated by Leslie Lonsdale-Cooper and Michael Turner
The Crab with the Golden Claws
Renewed Art copyright © 1953, 1981 by Casterman, Belgium
Text copyright © 1958 by Egmont UK Limited
The Shooting Star
Renewed Art copyright © 1946, 1974 by Casterman, Belgium
Text copyright © 1961 by Egmont UK Limited
The Secret of the Unicorn
Renewed Art copyright © 1946, 1974 by Casterman, Belgium
Text copyright © 1959 by Egmont UK Limited
American Edition © 2009 by Little, Brown and Company, NY

Little, Brown and Company
Hachette Book Group
1290 Avenue of the Americas, New York, NY 10104
Visit us at lb-kids.com

casterman.com
tintin.com

Little, Brown and Company is a division of Hachette Book Group, Inc.
The Little, Brown name and logo are trademarks of Hachette Book Group, Inc.

The publisher is not responsible for websites (or their content) that are not owned by the publisher.

ISBN 978-0-316-35944-3
24
Published pursuant to agreement with Editions Casterman.
Not for sale in the British Commonwealth.
APS
Printed in China

THE CRAB WITH THE GOLDEN CLAWS

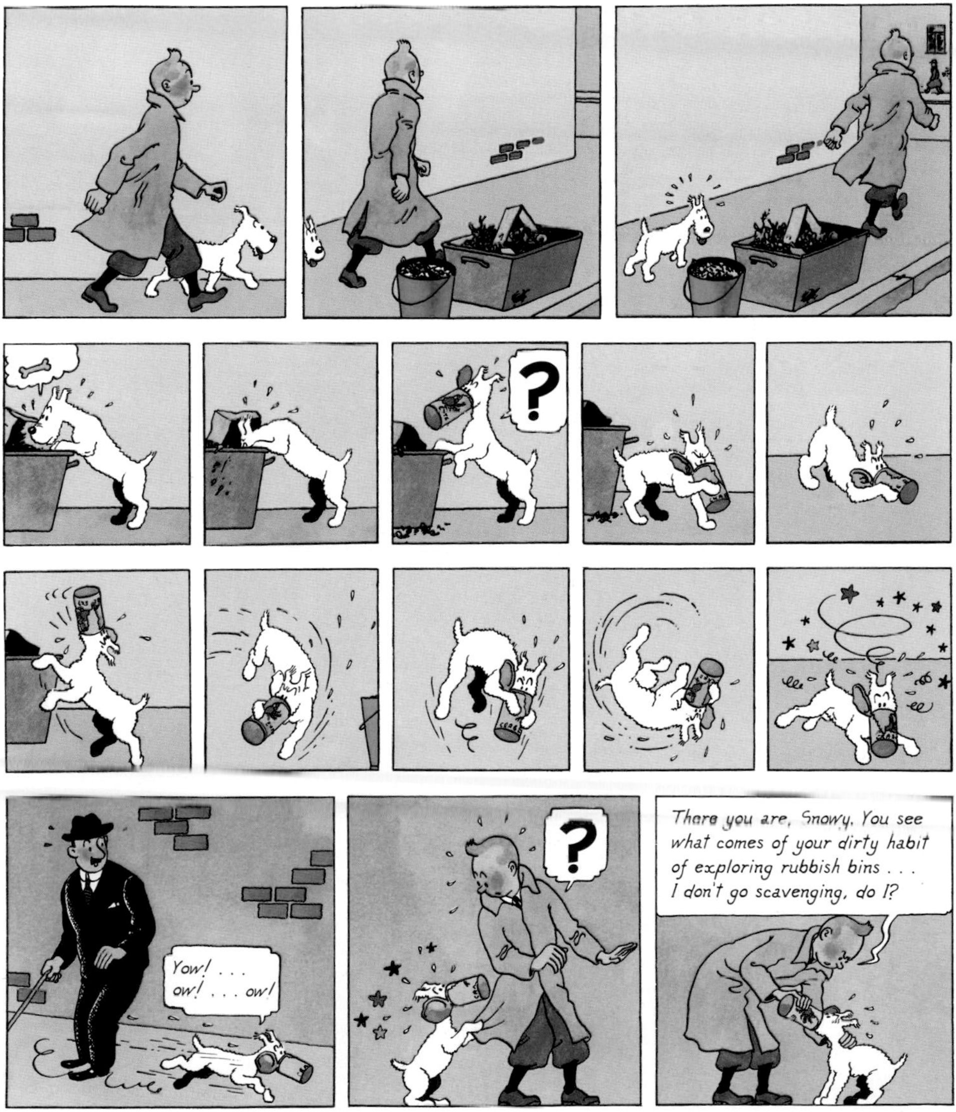
?
?
Yow! . . . ow! . . . ow!
?
There you are, Snowy. You see what comes of your dirty habit of exploring rubbish bins . . . I don't go scavenging, do I?

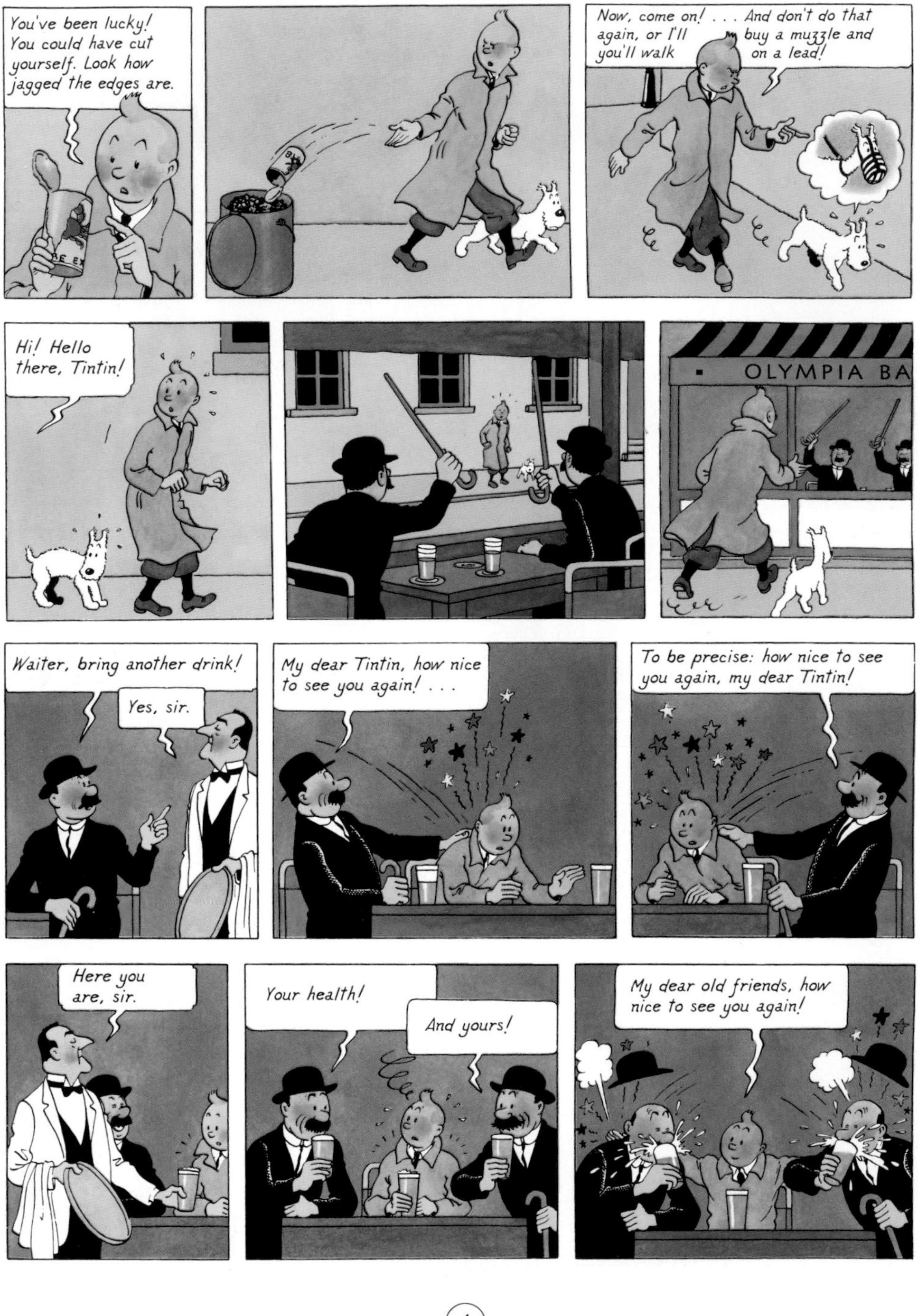
You've been lucky! You could have cut yourself. Look how jagged the edges are.
Now, come on! . . . And don't do that again, or I'll buy a muzzle and you'll walk on a lead!
Hi! Hello there, Tintin!
OLYMPIA BA
Waiter, bring another drink!
Yes, sir.
My dear Tintin, how nice to see you again! . . .
To be precise: how nice to see you again, my dear Tintin!
Here you are, sir.
Your health!
And yours!
My dear old friends, how nice to see you again!

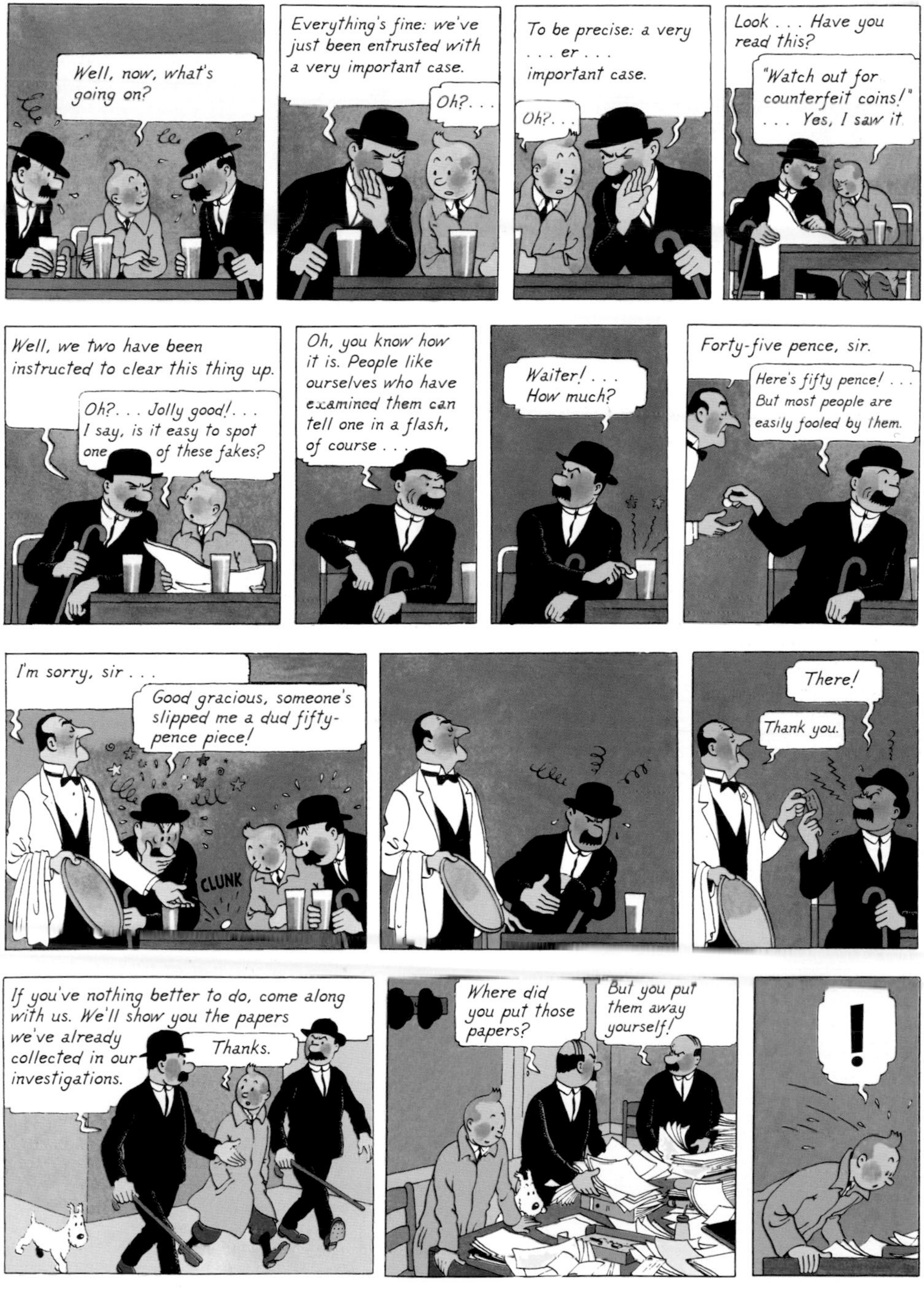
Well, now, what's going on?
Everything's fine: we've just been entrusted with a very important case.
Oh?. . .
To be precise: a very . . . er . . . important case.
Oh?. . .
Look . . . Have you read this?
"Watch out for counterfeit coins!" . . . Yes, I saw it.
Well, we two have been instructed to clear this thing up.
Oh?. . . Jolly good!. . . I say, is it easy to spot one of these fakes?
Oh, you know how it is. People like ourselves who have examined them can tell one in a flash, of course . . .
Waiter! . . . How much?
Forty-five pence, sir.
Here's fifty pence! . . . But most people are easily fooled by them.
I'm sorry, sir . . .
Good gracious, someone's slipped me a dud fifty-pence piece!
CLUNK
There!
Thank you.
If you've nothing better to do, come along with us. We'll show you the papers we've already collected in our investigations.
Thanks.
Where did you put those papers?
But you put them away yourself!
!

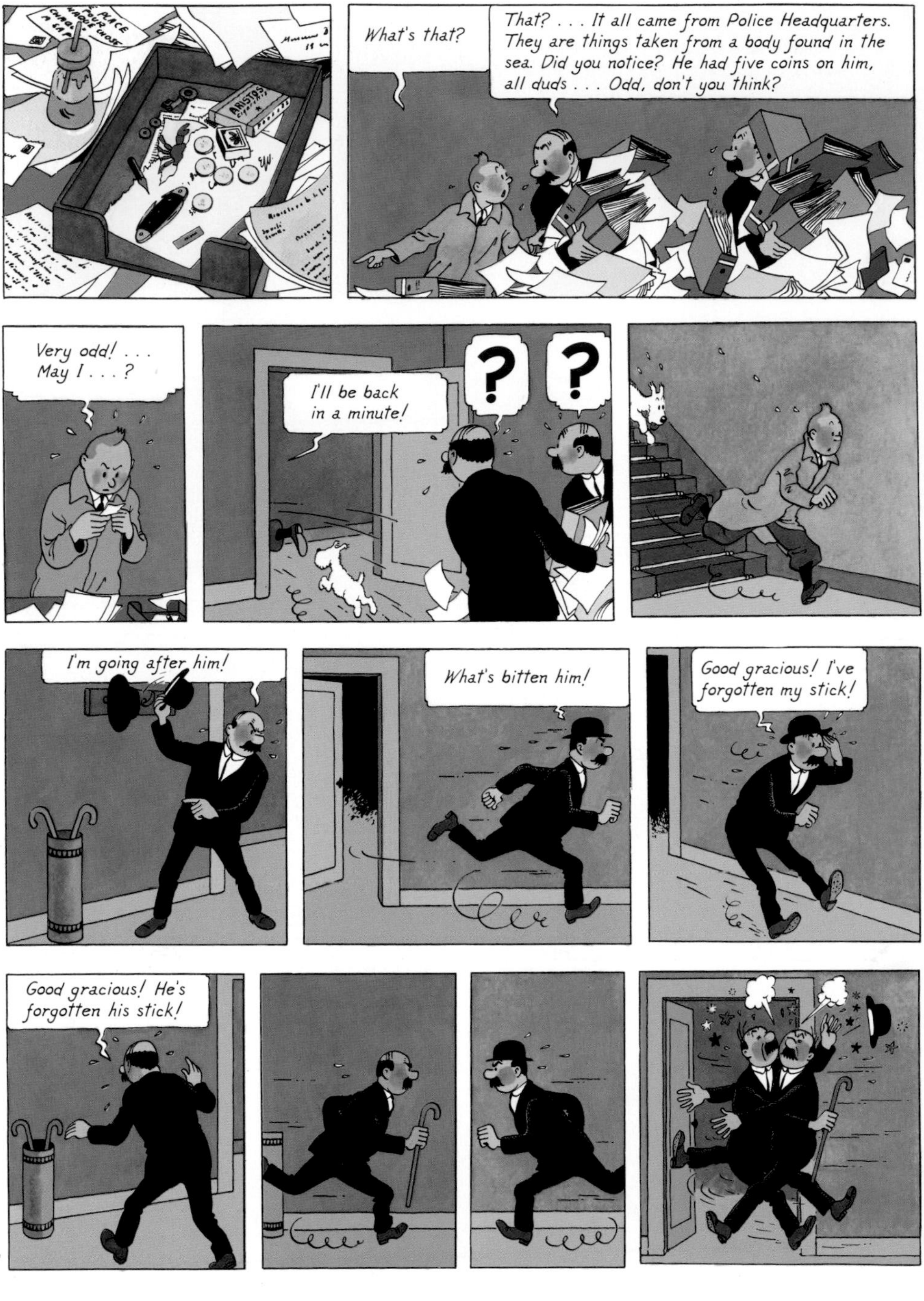

What's that?
That? . . . It all came from Police Headquarters. They are things taken from a body found in the sea. Did you notice? He had five coins on him, all duds . . . Odd, don't you think?
Very odd! . . . May I . . . ?
I'll be back in a minute!
?
?
I'm going after him!
What's bitten him!
Good gracious! I've forgotten my stick!
Good gracious! He's forgotten his stick!

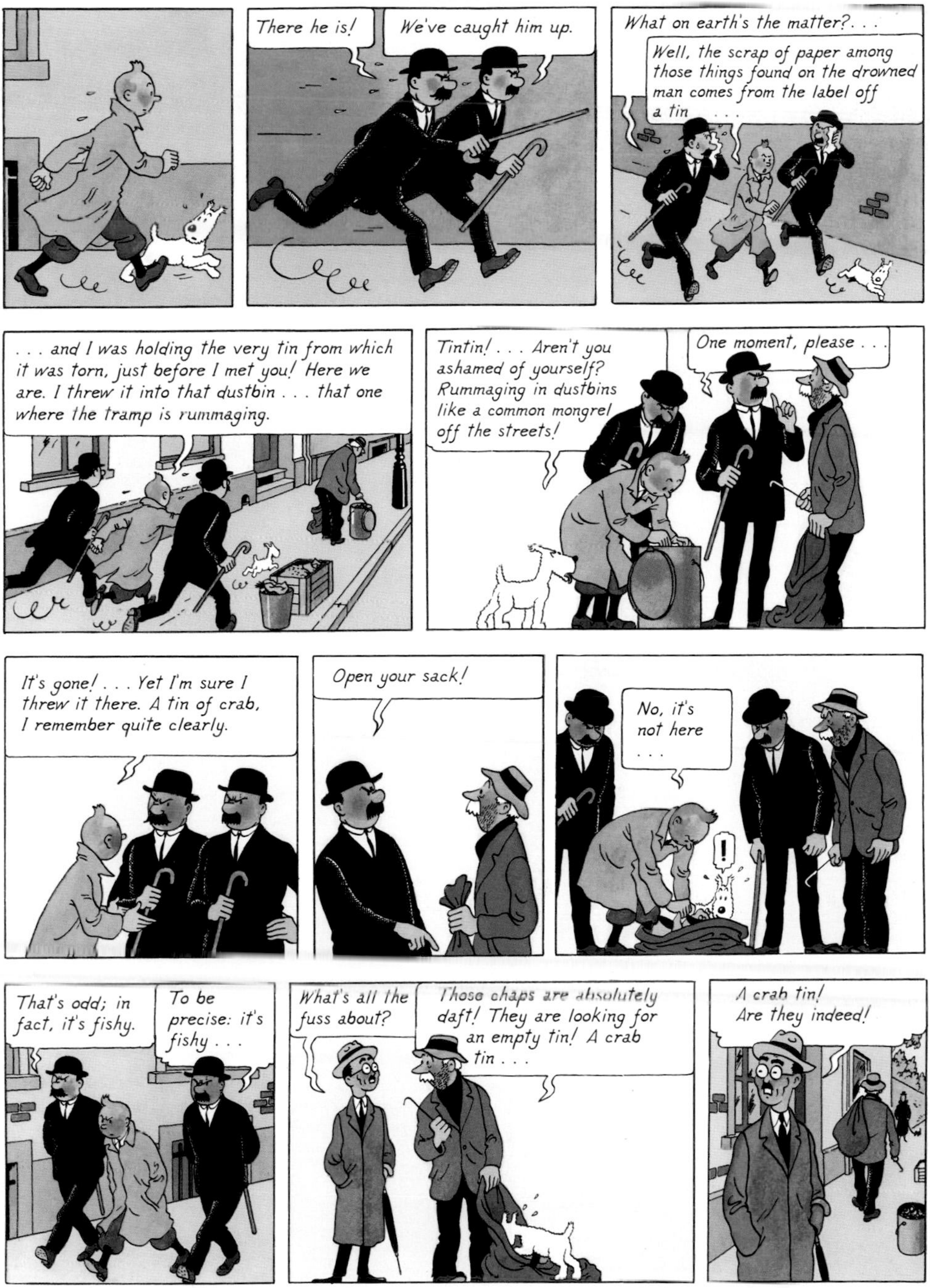
There he is!
We've caught him up.
What on earth's the matter? . . .
Well, the scrap of paper among those things found on the drowned man comes from the label off a tin . . .
. . . and I was holding the very tin from which it was torn, just before I met you! Here we are. I threw it into that dustbin . . . that one where the tramp is rummaging.
Tintin! . . . Aren't you ashamed of yourself? Rummaging in dustbins like a common mongrel off the streets!
One moment, please . . .
It's gone! . . . Yet I'm sure I threw it there. A tin of crab, I remember quite clearly.
Open your sack!
No, it's not here . . .
!
That's odd; in fact, it's fishy.
To be precise: it's fishy . . .
What's all the fuss about?
Those chaps are absolutely daft! They are looking for an empty tin! A crab tin . . .
A crab tin! Are they indeed!

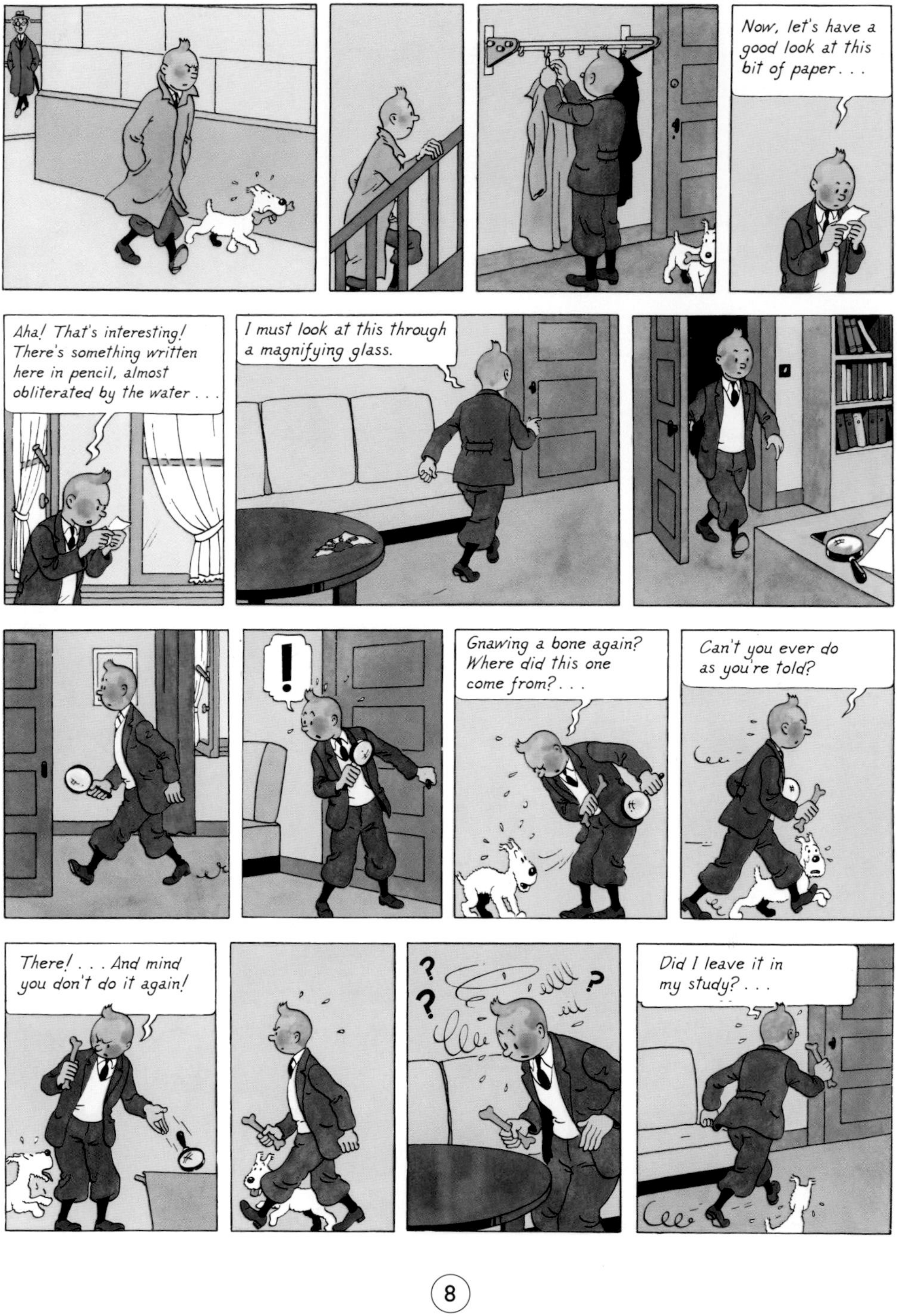
Now, let's have a good look at this bit of paper . . .
Aha! That's interesting! There's something written here in pencil, almost obliterated by the water . . .
I must look at this through a magnifying glass.
!
Gnawing a bone again? Where did this one come from? . . .
Can't you ever do as you're told?
There! . . . And mind you don't do it again!
? ?
?
Did I leave it in my study? . . .

It's not here either!

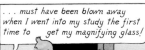

CRASH

Crumbs! That made me jump . . . And it was only the wind slamming the door!

But now I think of it, that bit of paper . . .

. . . must have been blown away when I went into my study the first time to get my magnifying glass!

That's the answer. There it is!

Now let's have a look . . .

Have I gone crazy? I'm positive I put my magnifying glass down here a moment ago!

I'll go over all this in pencil. There's 'K' . . . and an 'A' . . . and that's an 'R' . . . or an 'I' . . . there, I'll soon have it . . .

Karaboudjan

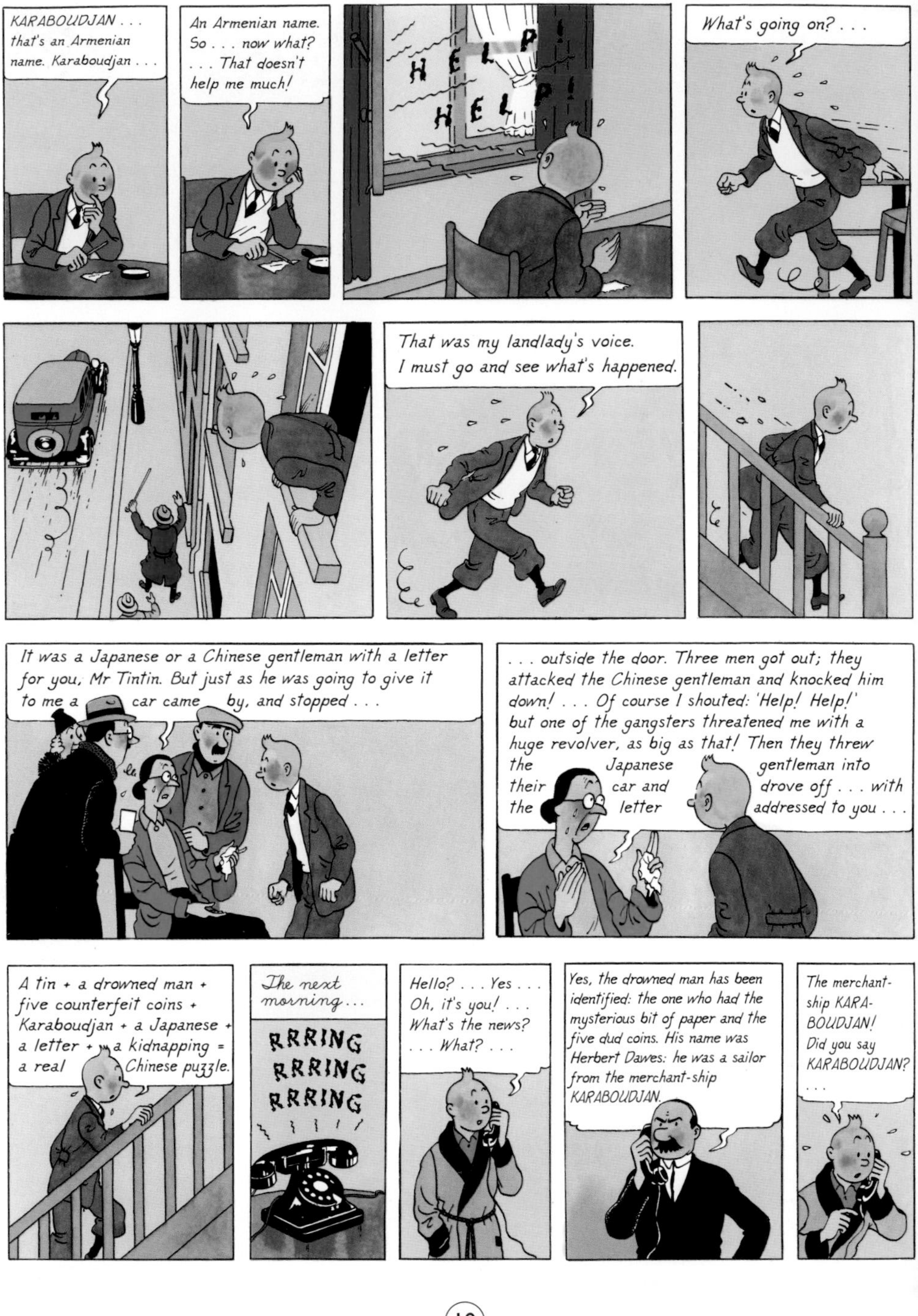

KARABOUDJAN . . . that's an Armenian name. Karaboudjan . . .
An Armenian name. So . . . now what? . . . That doesn't help me much!
HELP! HELP!
What's going on? . . .
That was my landlady's voice. I must go and see what's happened.
It was a Japanese or a Chinese gentleman with a letter for you, Mr Tintin. But just as he was going to give it to me a car came by, and stopped . . .
. . . outside the door. Three men got out; they attacked the Chinese gentleman and knocked him down! . . . Of course I shouted: 'Help! Help!' but one of the gangsters threatened me with a huge revolver, as big as that! Then they threw the Japanese gentleman into their car and drove off . . . with the letter addressed to you . . .
A tin + a drowned man + five counterfeit coins + Karaboudjan + a Japanese + a letter + a kidnapping = a real Chinese puzzle.
The next morning . . .
RRRING RRRING RRRING
Hello? . . . Yes . . . Oh, it's you! . . . What's the news? . . . What? . . .
Yes, the drowned man has been identified: the one who had the mysterious bit of paper and the five dud coins. His name was Herbert Dawes: he was a sailor from the merchant-ship KARABOUDJAN.
The merchant-ship KARA-BOUDJAN! Did you say KARABOUDJAN? . . .

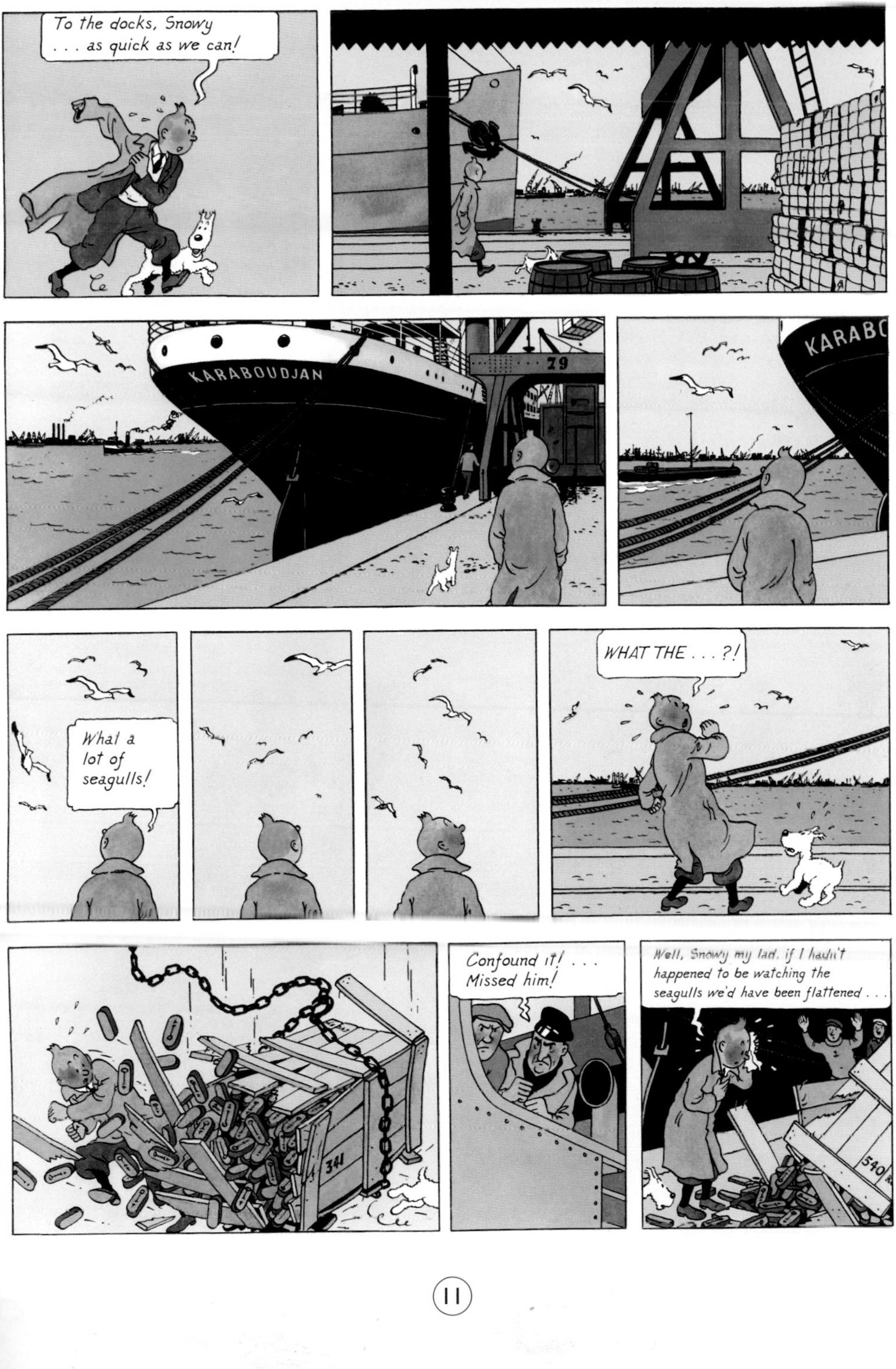
To the docks, Snowy . . . as quick as we can!
KARABOUDJAN
79
KARABO
What a lot of seagulls!
WHAT THE . . . ?!
341
Confound it! . . . Missed him!
Well, Snowy my lad, if I hadn't happened to be watching the seagulls we'd have been flattened . . .
540

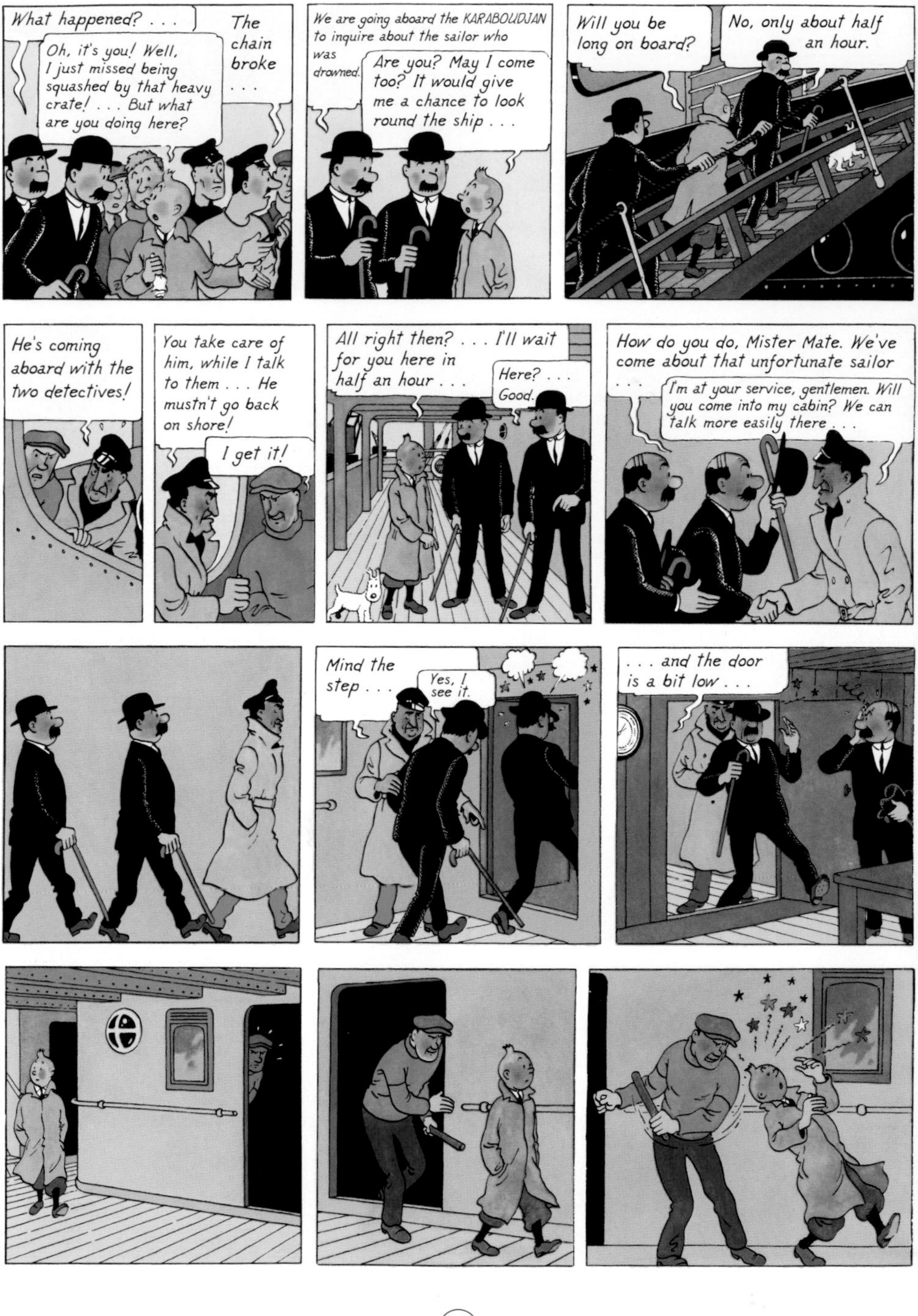
What happened? . . .
Oh, it's you! Well, I just missed being squashed by that heavy crate! . . . But what are you doing here?
The chain broke . . .
We are going aboard the KARABOUDJAN to inquire about the sailor who was drowned.
Are you? May I come too? It would give me a chance to look round the ship . . .
Will you be long on board?
No, only about half an hour.
He's coming aboard with the two detectives!
You take care of him, while I talk to them . . . He mustn't go back on shore!
I get it!
All right then? . . . I'll wait for you here in half an hour . . .
Here? . . . Good.
How do you do, Mister Mate. We've come about that unfortunate sailor . . .
I'm at your service, gentlemen. Will you come into my cabin? We can talk more easily there . . .
Mind the step . . .
Yes, I see it.
. . . and the door is a bit low . . .

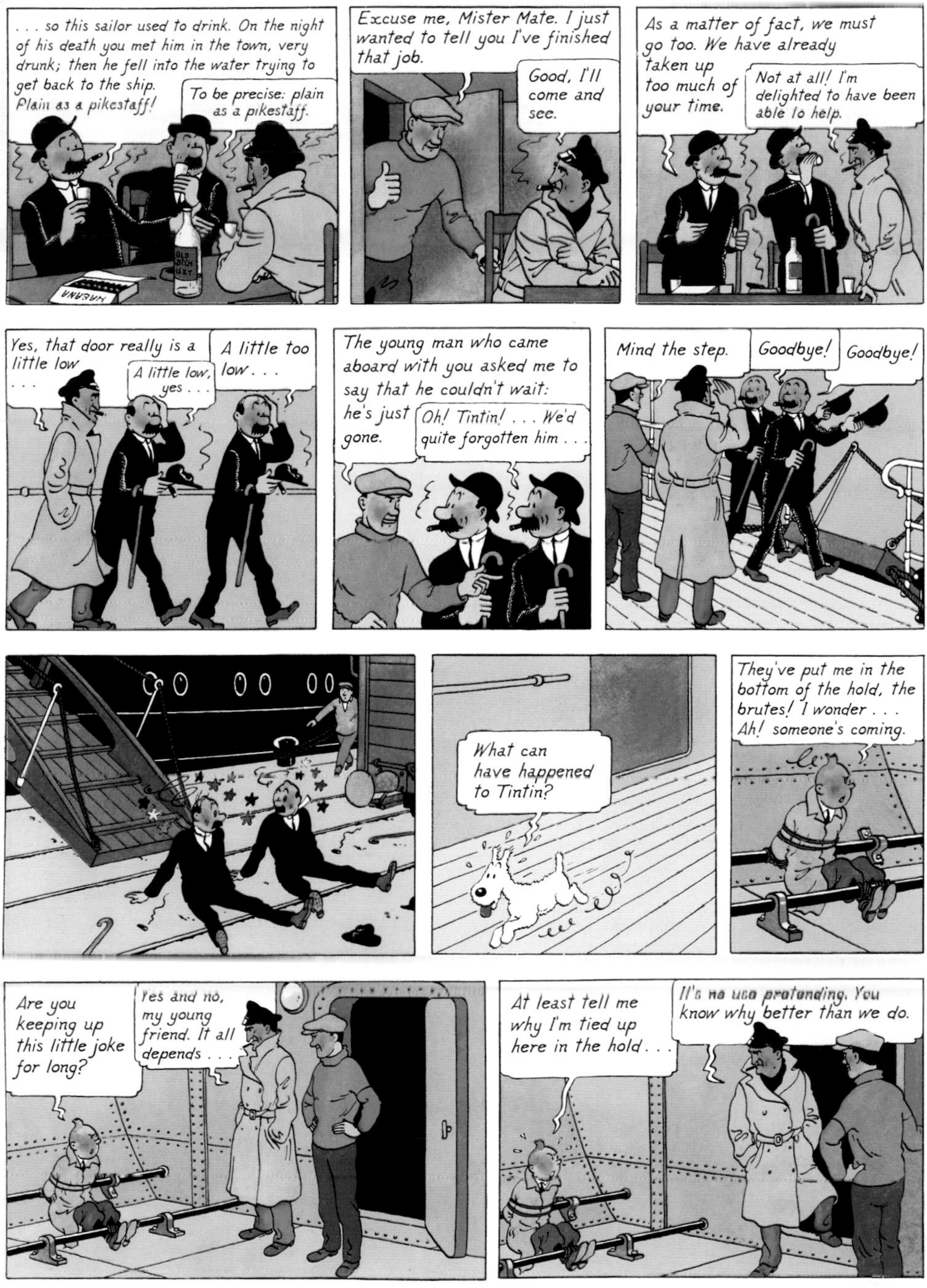

. . . so this sailor used to drink. On the night of his death you met him in the town, very drunk; then he fell into the water trying to get back to the ship. Plain as a pikestaff!
To be precise: plain as a pikestaff.
Excuse me, Mister Mate. I just wanted to tell you I've finished that job.
Good, I'll come and see.
As a matter of fact, we must go too. We have already taken up too much of your time.
Not at all! I'm delighted to have been able to help.
Yes, that door really is a little low . . .
A little low, yes . . .
A little too low . . .
The young man who came aboard with you asked me to say that he couldn't wait: he's just gone.
Oh! Tintin! . . . We'd quite forgotten him . . .
Mind the step.
Goodbye!
Goodbye!
What can have happened to Tintin?
They've put me in the bottom of the hold, the brutes! I wonder . . . Ah! someone's coming.
Are you keeping up this little joke for long?
Yes and no, my young friend. It all depends . . .
At least tell me why I'm tied up here in the hold . . .
It's no use pretending. You know why better than we do.

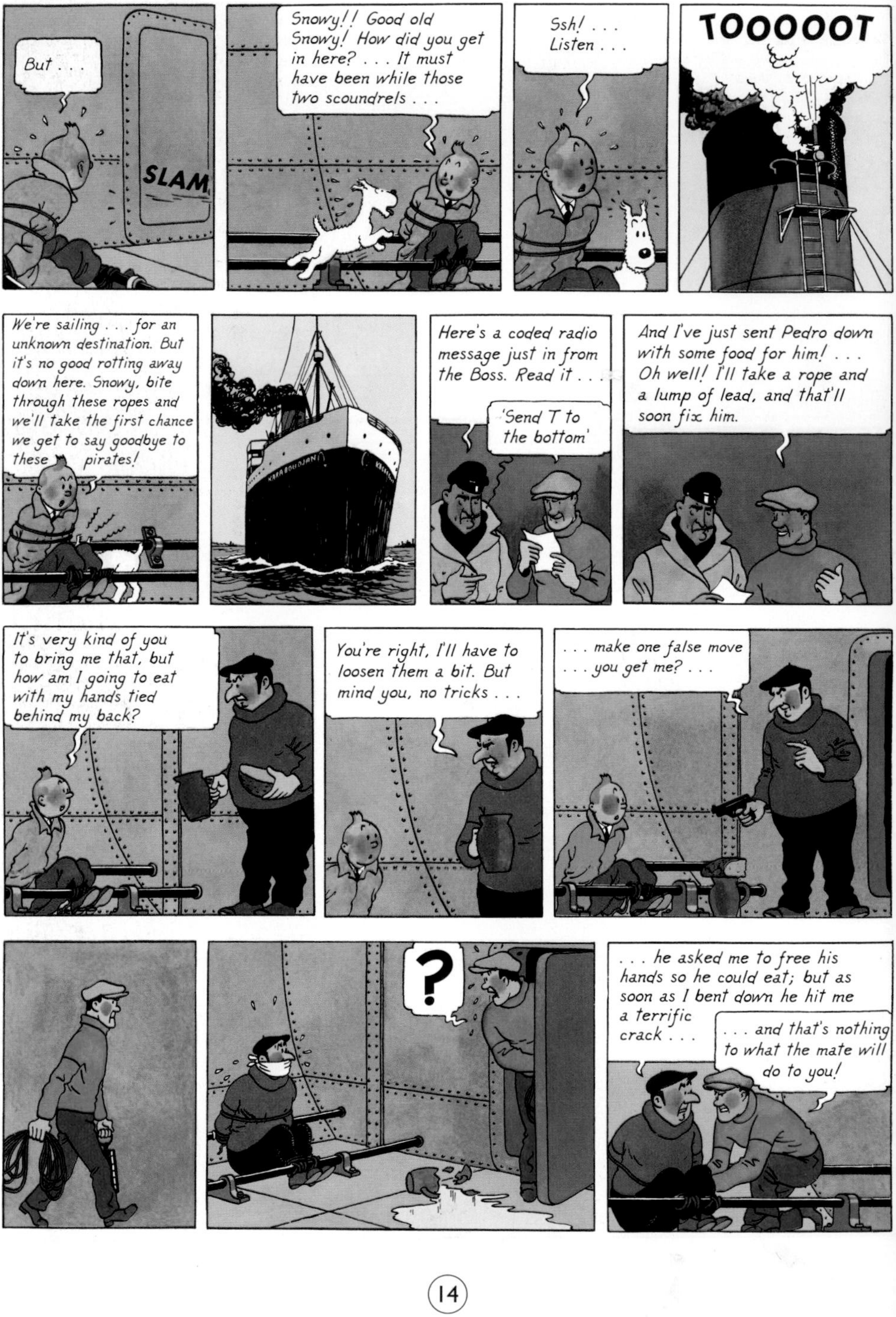

But . . .
SLAM
Snowy!! Good old Snowy! How did you get in here? . . . It must have been while those two scoundrels . . .
Ssh! . . . Listen . . .
TOOOOOT
We're sailing . . . for an unknown destination. But it's no good rotting away down here. Snowy, bite through these ropes and we'll take the first chance we get to say goodbye to these pirates!
Here's a coded radio message just in from the Boss. Read it . . .
'Send T to the bottom'
And I've just sent Pedro down with some food for him! . . . Oh well! I'll take a rope and a lump of lead, and that'll soon fix him.
It's very kind of you to bring me that, but how am I going to eat with my hands tied behind my back?
You're right, I'll have to loosen them a bit. But mind you, no tricks . . .
. . . make one false move . . . you get me? . . .
?
. . . he asked me to free his hands so he could eat; but as soon as I bent down he hit me a terrific crack . . .
. . . and that's nothing to what the mate will do to you!

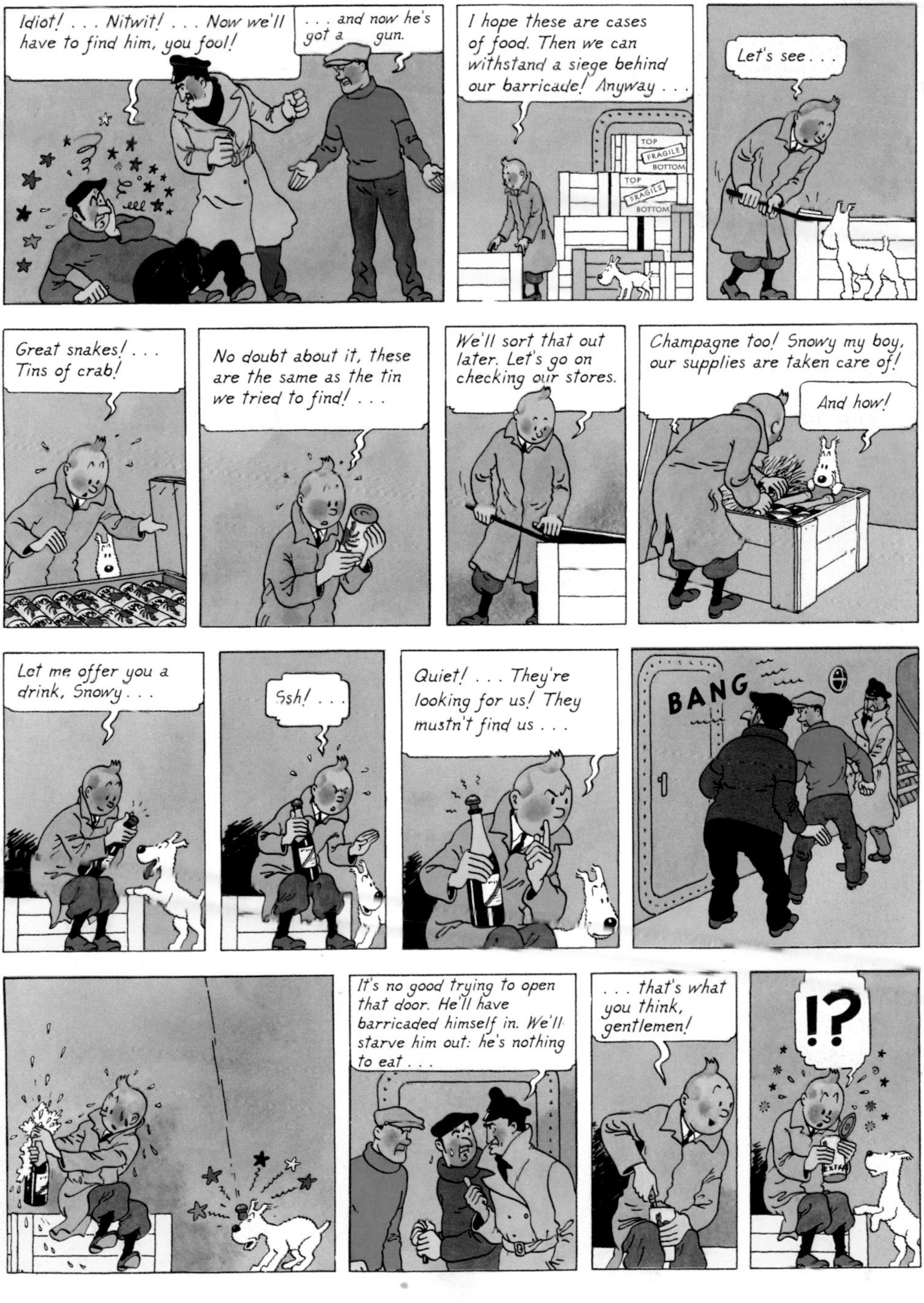
Idiot! . . . Nitwit! . . . Now we'll have to find him, you fool!
. . . and now he's got a gun.
I hope these are cases of food. Then we can withstand a siege behind our barricade! Anyway . . .
TOP
FRAGILE
BOTTOM
TOP
FRAGILE
BOTTOM
Let's see . . .
Great snakes! . . . Tins of crab!
No doubt about it, these are the same as the tin we tried to find! . . .
We'll sort that out later. Let's go on checking our stores.
Champagne too! Snowy my boy, our supplies are taken care of!
And how!
Let me offer you a drink, Snowy . . .
Ssh! . . .
Quiet! . . . They're looking for us! They mustn't find us . . .
BANG
It's no good trying to open that door. He'll have barricaded himself in. We'll starve him out: he's nothing to eat . . .
. . . that's what you think, gentlemen!
!?

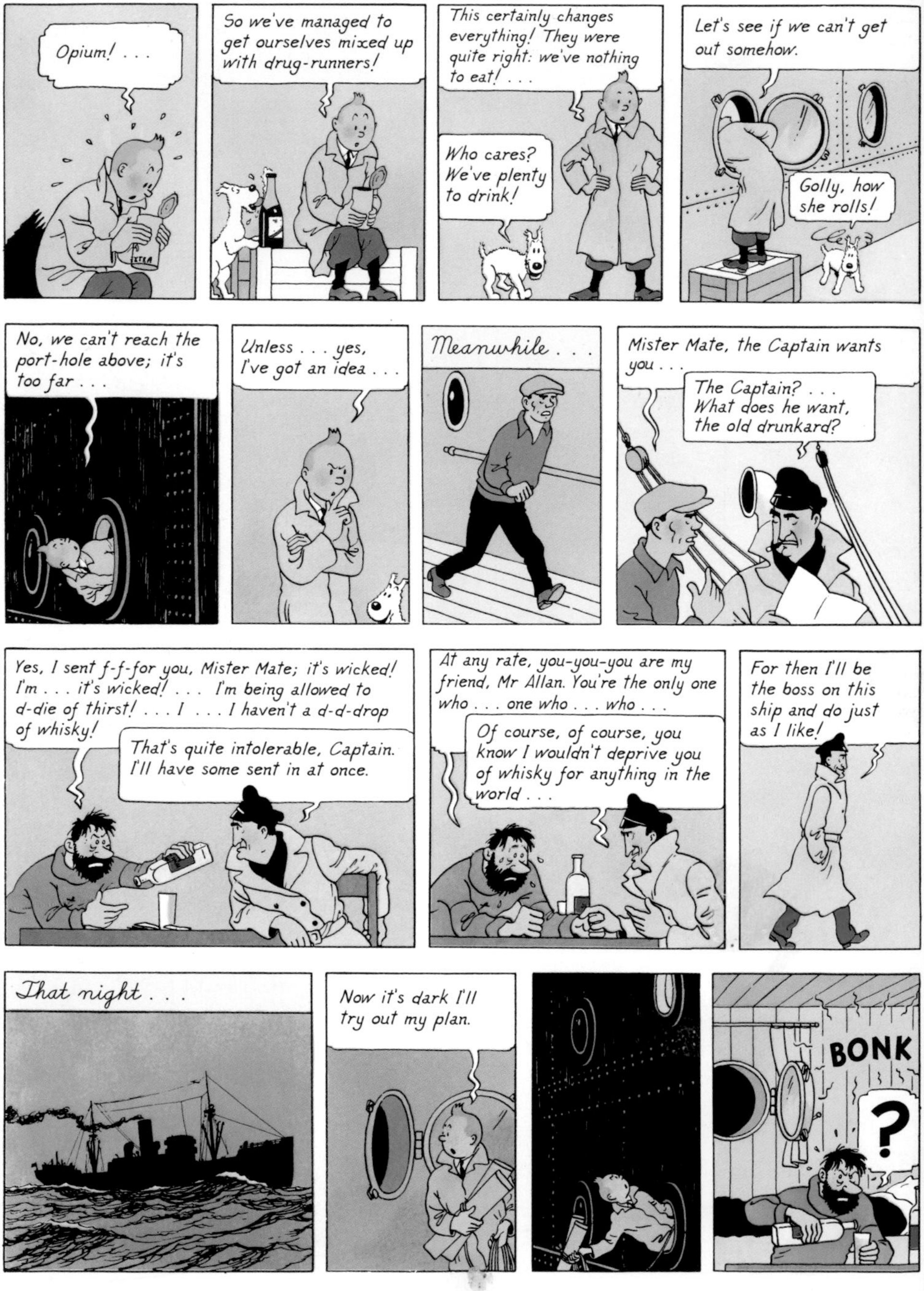

Opium! . . .
So we've managed to get ourselves mixed up with drug-runners!
This certainly changes everything! They were quite right: we've nothing to eat! . . .
Who cares? We've plenty to drink!
Let's see if we can't get out somehow.
Golly, how she rolls!
No, we can't reach the port-hole above; it's too far . . .
Unless . . . yes, I've got an idea . . .
Meanwhile . . .
Mister Mate, the Captain wants you . . .
The Captain? . . . What does he want, the old drunkard?
Yes, I sent f-f-for you, Mister Mate; it's wicked! I'm . . . it's wicked! . . . I'm being allowed to d-die of thirst! . . . I . . . I haven't a d-d-drop of whisky!
That's quite intolerable, Captain. I'll have some sent in at once.
At any rate, you-you-you are my friend, Mr Allan. You're the only one who . . . one who . . . who . . .
Of course, of course, you know I wouldn't deprive you of whisky for anything in the world . . .
For then I'll be the boss on this ship and do just as I like!
That night . . .
Now it's dark I'll try out my plan.
BONK
?

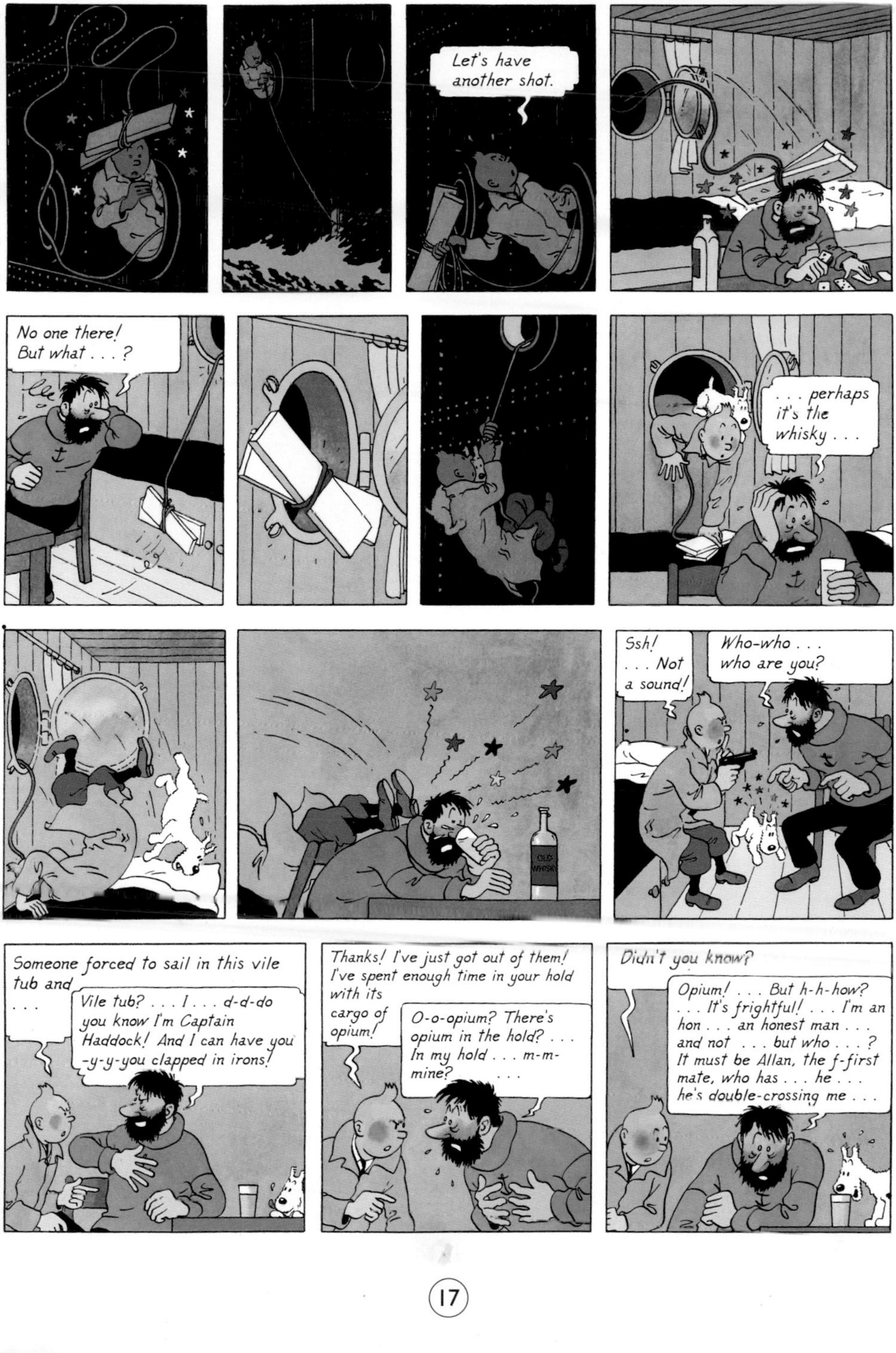
Let's have another shot.
No one there! But what . . . ?
. . . perhaps it's the whisky . . .
Ssh! . . . Not a sound!
Who-who . . . who are you?
Someone forced to sail in this vile tub and . . .
Vile tub? . . . I . . . d-d-do you know I'm Captain Haddock! And I can have you -y-y-you clapped in irons!
Thanks! I've just got out of them! I've spent enough time in your hold with its cargo of opium!
O-o-opium? There's opium in the hold? . . . In my hold . . . m-m-mine? . . .
Didn't you know?
Opium! . . . But h-h-how? . . . It's frightful! . . . I'm an hon . . . an honest man . . . and not . . . but who . . . ? It must be Allan, the f-first mate, who has . . . he . . . he's double-crossing me . . .

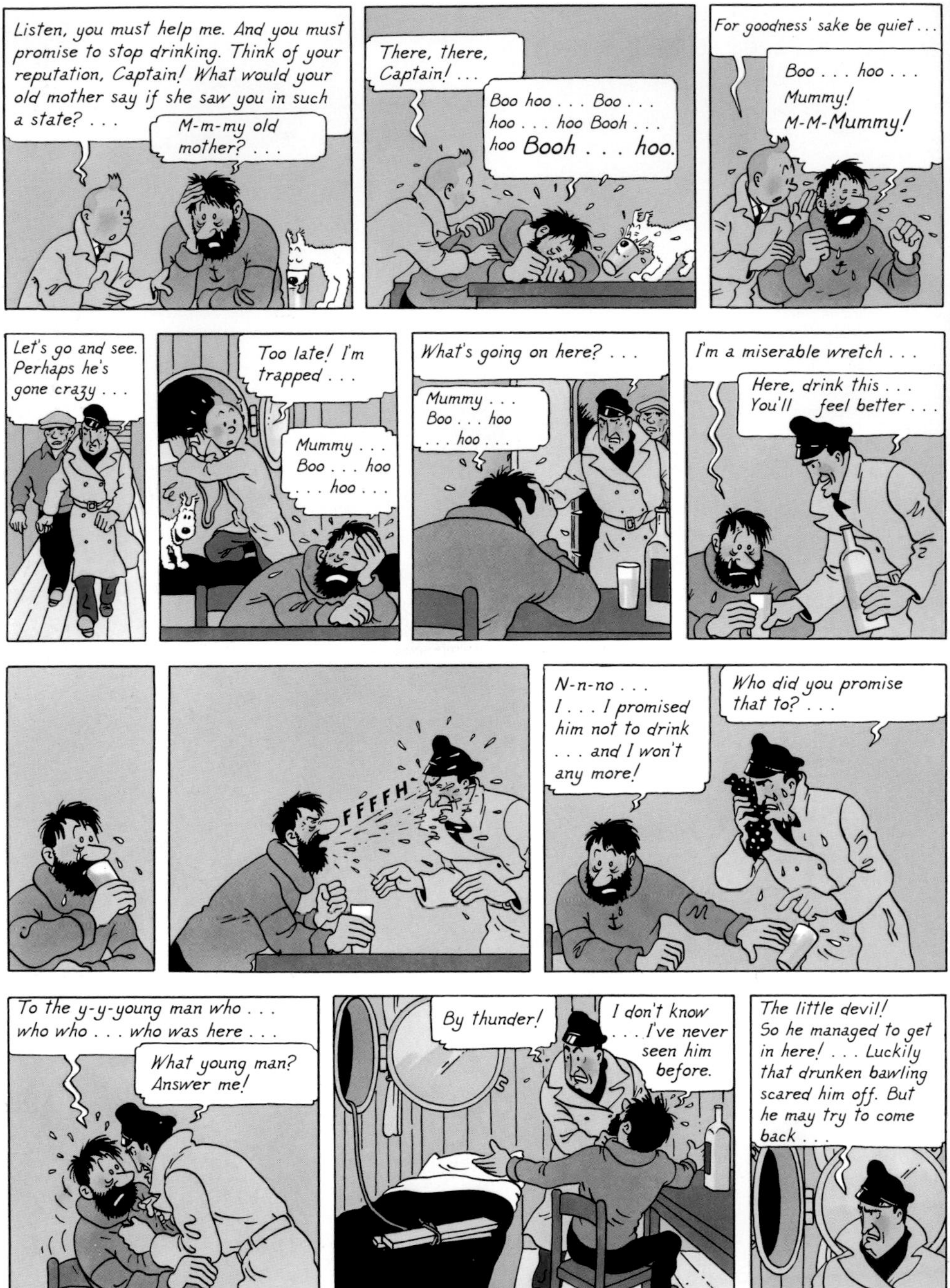

Listen, you must help me. And you must promise to stop drinking. Think of your reputation, Captain! What would your old mother say if she saw you in such a state? . . .
M-m-my old mother? . . .
There, there, Captain! . . .
Boo hoo . . . Boo . . . hoo . . . hoo Booh . . . hoo Booh . . . hoo.
For goodness' sake be quiet . . .
Boo . . . hoo . . . Mummy! M-M-Mummy!
Let's go and see. Perhaps he's gone crazy . . .
Too late! I'm trapped . . .
Mummy . . . Boo . . . hoo . . . hoo . . .
What's going on here? . . .
Mummy . . . Boo . . . hoo . . . hoo . . .
I'm a miserable wretch . . .
Here, drink this . . . You'll feel better . . .
FFFFH
N-n-no . . . I . . . I promised him not to drink . . . and I won't any more!
Who did you promise that to? . . .
To the y-y-young man who . . . who who . . . who was here . . .
What young man? Answer me!
By thunder!
I don't know . . . I've never seen him before.
The little devil! So he managed to get in here! . . . Luckily that drunken bawling scared him off. But he may try to come back . . .

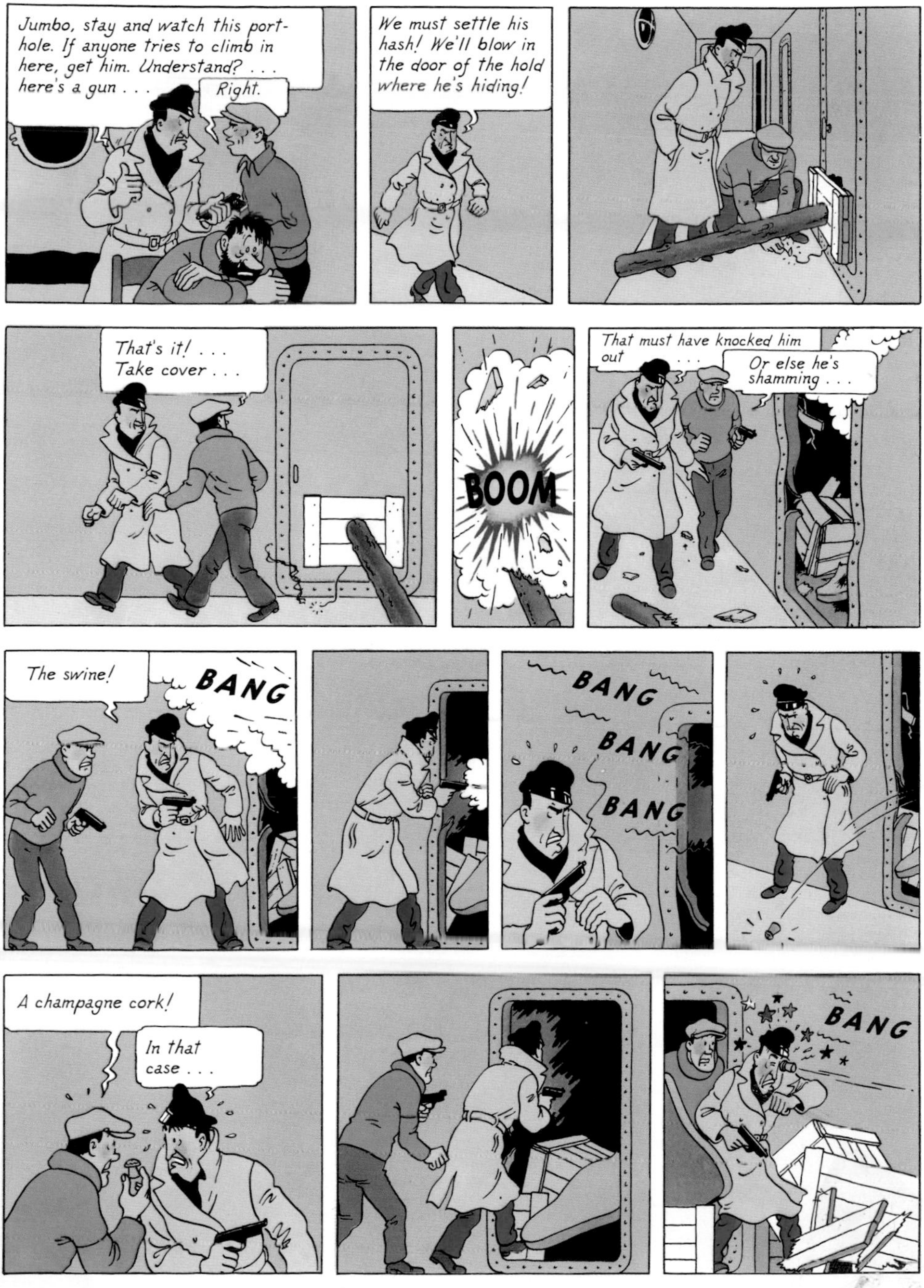
Jumbo, stay and watch this port-hole. If anyone tries to climb in here, get him. Understand? . . . here's a gun . . .
Right.
We must settle his hash! We'll blow in the door of the hold where he's hiding!
That's it! . . . Take cover . . .
BOOM
That must have knocked him out . . .
Or else he's shamming . . .
The swine!
BANG
BANG
BANG
BANG
A champagne cork!
In that case . . .
BANG

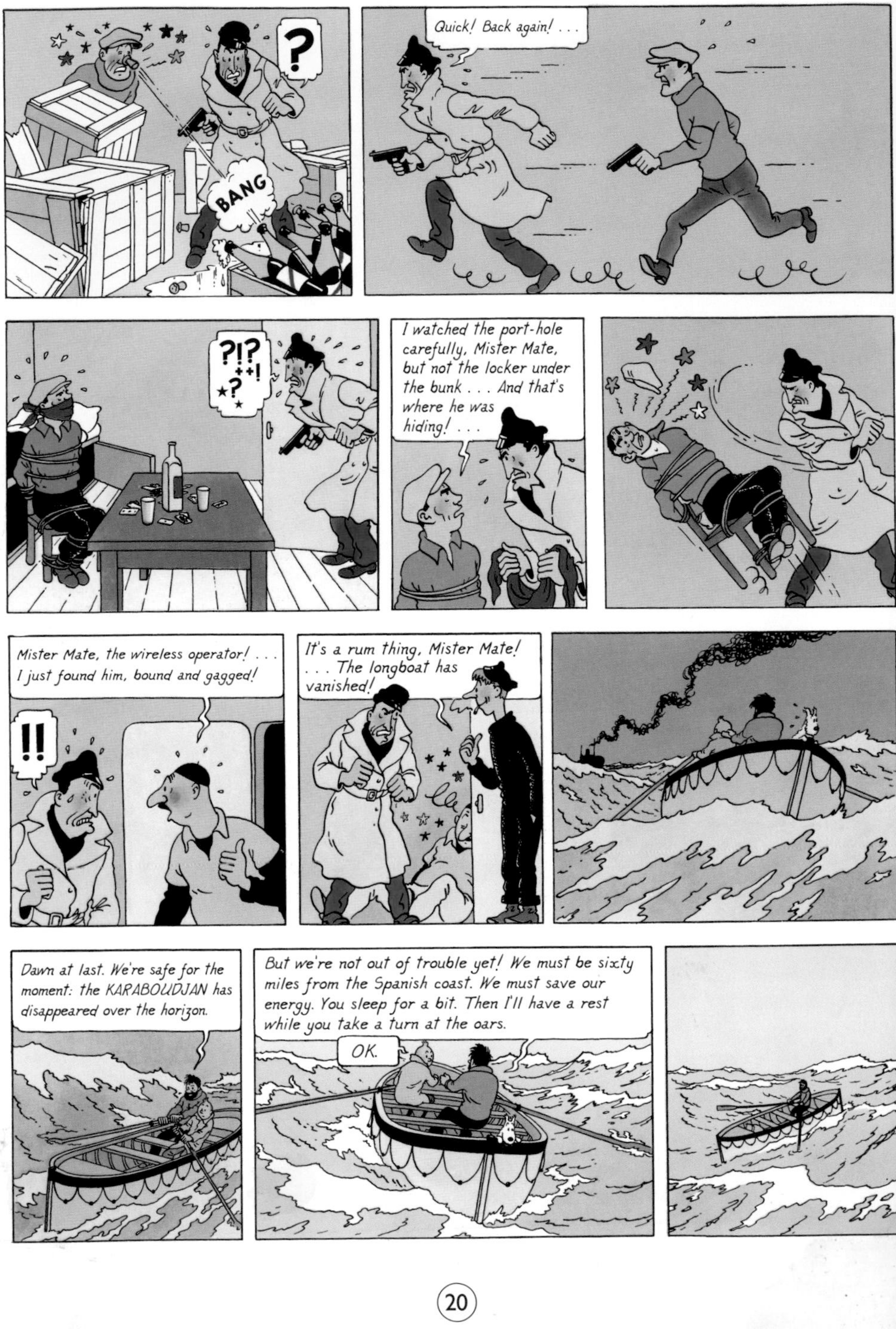
?
BANG
Quick! Back again! . . .
?!?
++!
?
I watched the port-hole carefully, Mister Mate, but not the locker under the bunk . . . And that's where he was hiding! . . .
!!
Mister Mate, the wireless operator! . . . I just found him, bound and gagged!
It's a rum thing, Mister Mate! . . . The longboat has vanished!
Dawn at last. We're safe for the moment: the KARABOUDJAN has disappeared over the horizon.
But we're not out of trouble yet! We must be sixty miles from the Spanish coast. We must save our energy. You sleep for a bit. Then I'll have a rest while you take a turn at the oars.
OK.

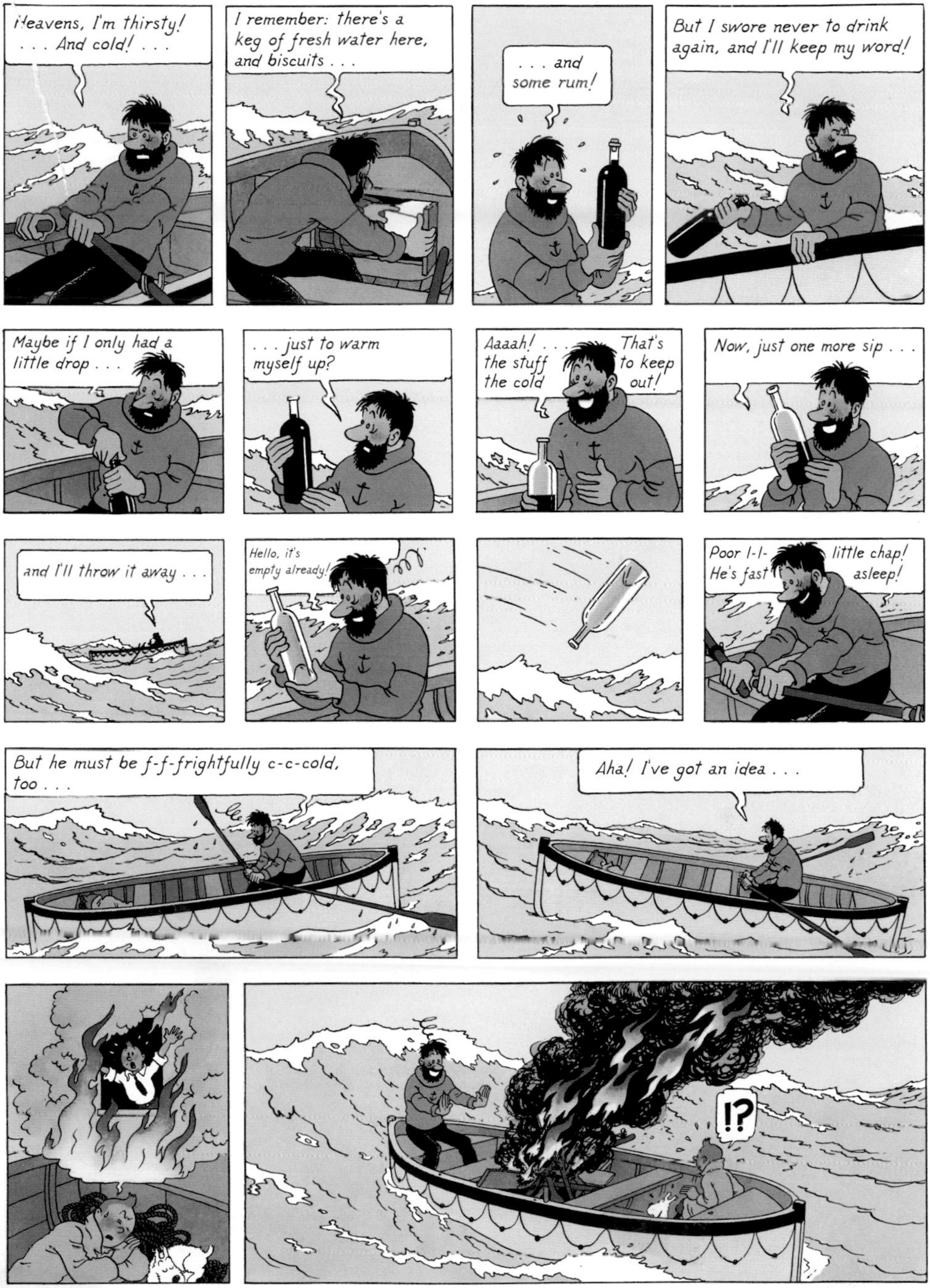
Heavens, I'm thirsty! . . . And cold! . . .
I remember: there's a keg of fresh water here, and biscuits . . .
. . . and some rum!
But I swore never to drink again, and I'll keep my word!
Maybe if I only had a little drop . . .
. . . just to warm myself up?
Aaaah! . . . the stuff the cold
That's to keep out!
Now, just one more sip . . .
and I'll throw it away . . .
Hello, it's empty already!
Poor l-l-little chap! He's fast asleep!
But he must be f-f-frightfully c-c-cold, too . . .
Aha! I've got an idea . . .
!?

Our oars! Hey! . . .
You're burning our oars!
Have you gone mad? . . .

Ah! here's
a bucket!

If . . . if you p-p-put that out . . .
y-you'll have to settle with m-m-me,
you miserable whipper-snapper . . .

Let go of that bucket, you
meddlesome cabin-boy!

?

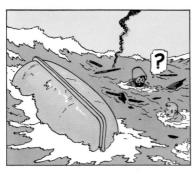

?

What have I done? Oh, Columbus
. . . What have I done!

You've got us into a fine
mess . . .

I'm sorry . . . I'm sorry! . . . I'm a
miserable wretch . . . I drank the
rum from the locker . . . I'm
sorry! . . .

Ssh! . . .

A seaplane! . . .
We're saved! . . .

It's got Moroccan
markings: CN.

RAT
TAT TAT
TAT
TAT TAT
TAT
TAT

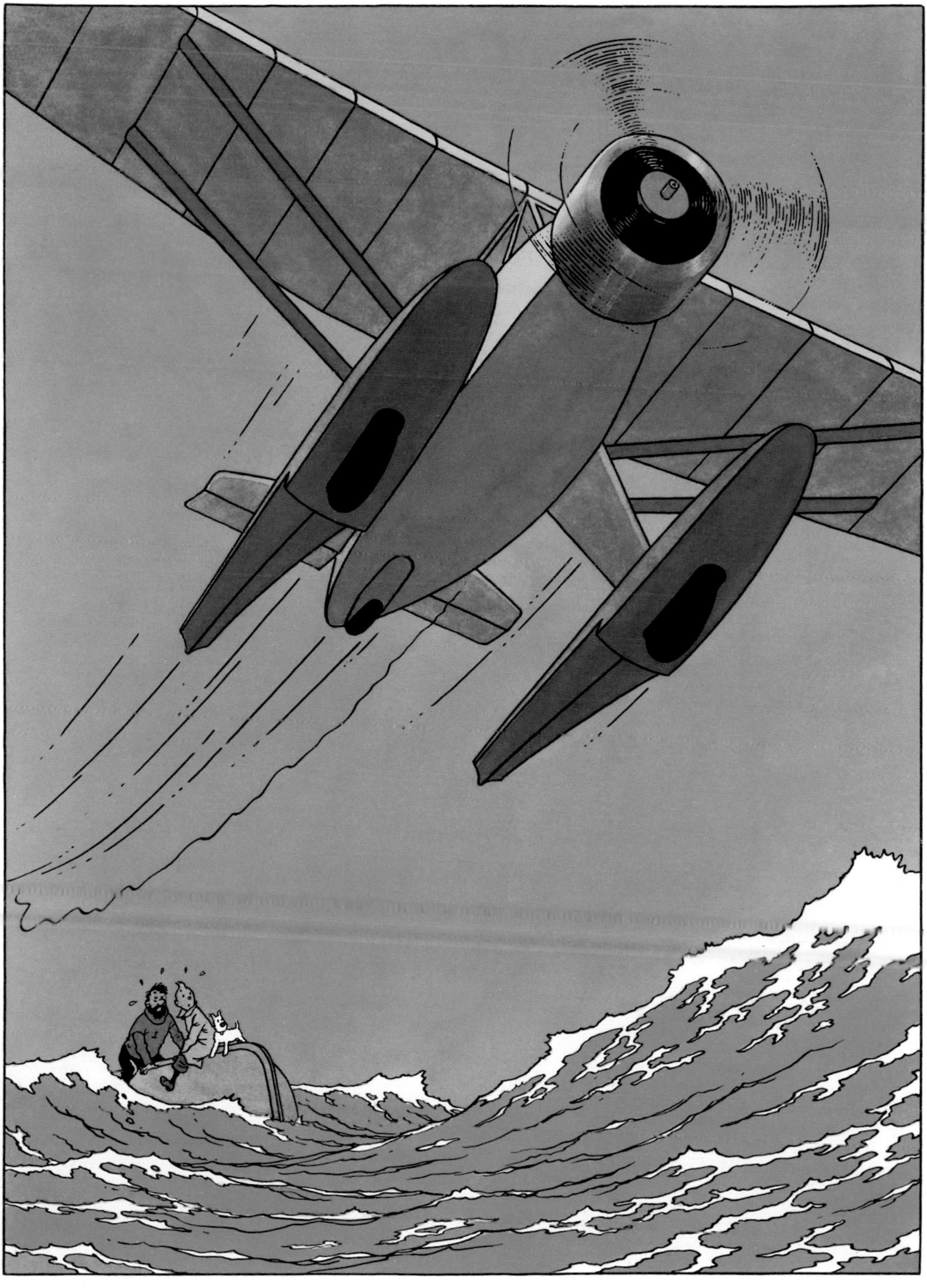

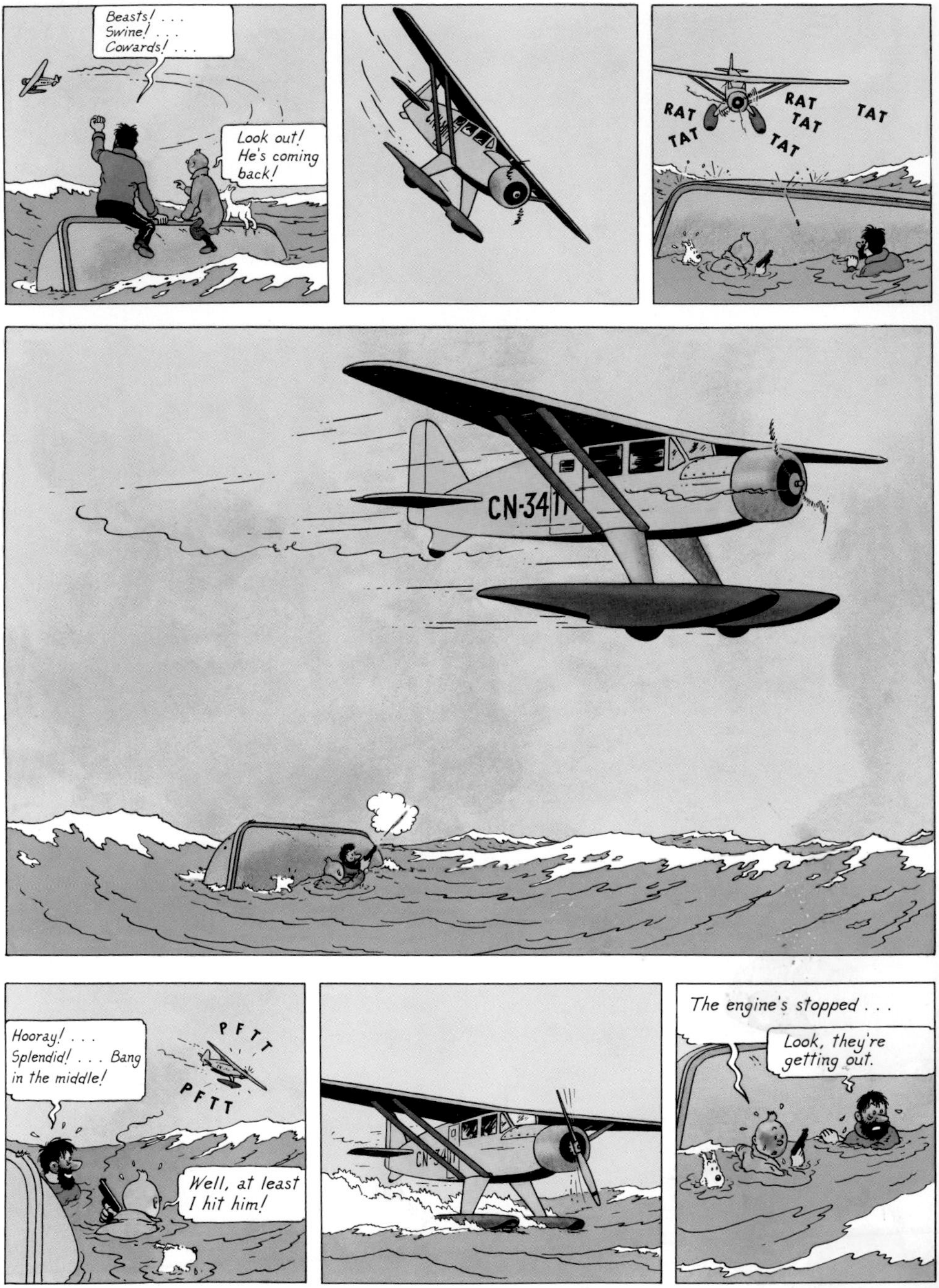
Beasts! . . .
Swine! . . .
Cowards! . . .
Look out! He's coming back!
RAT TAT
RAT TAT
TAT
TAT
CN-341
Hooray! . . . Splendid! . . . Bang in the middle!
PFTT
PFTT
Well, at least I hit him!
The engine's stopped . . .
Look, they're getting out.

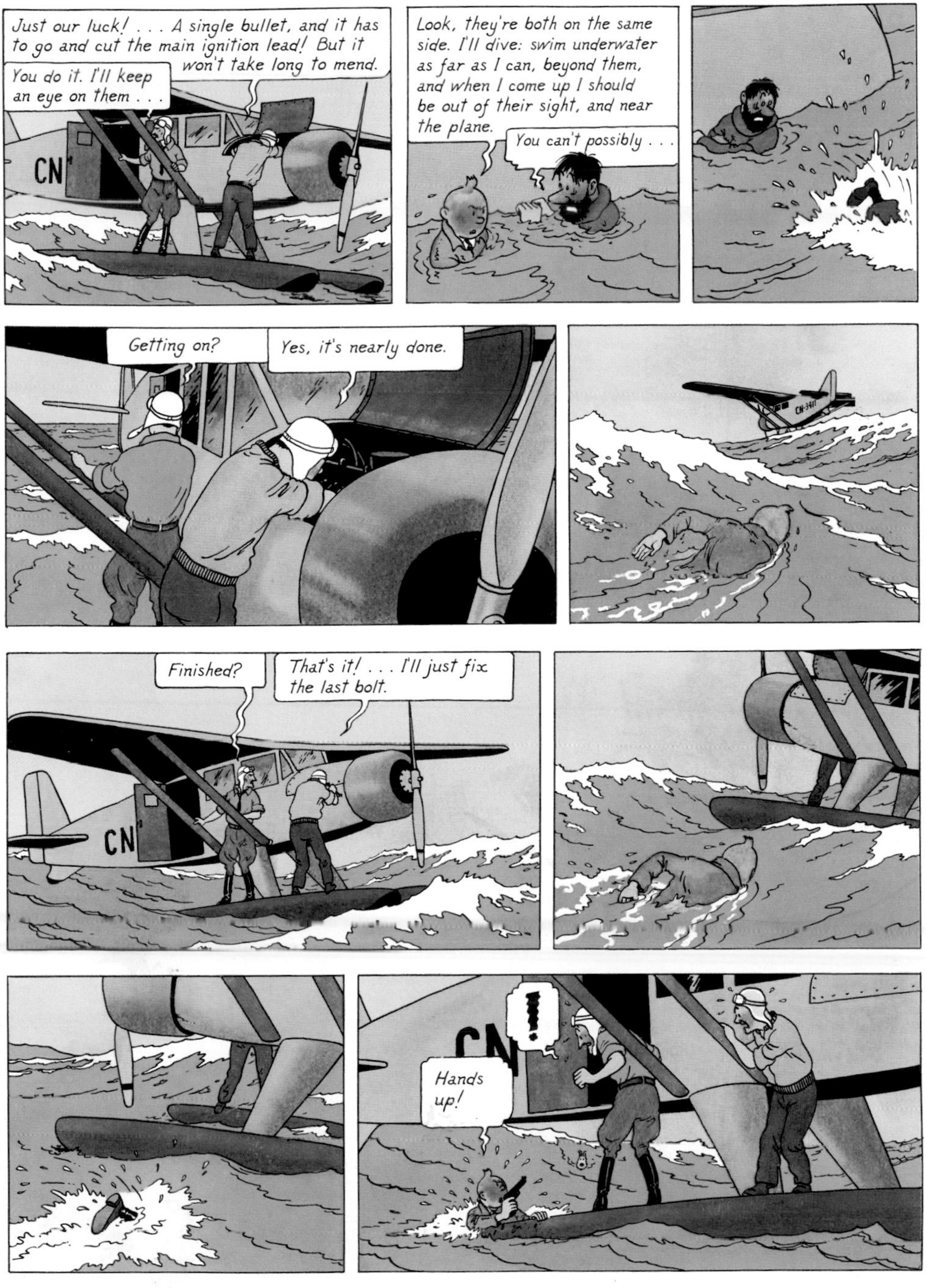
Just our luck! . . . A single bullet, and it has to go and cut the main ignition lead! But it won't take long to mend.
You do it. I'll keep an eye on them . . .
Look, they're both on the same side. I'll dive: swim underwater as far as I can, beyond them, and when I come up I should be out of their sight, and near the plane.
You can't possibly . . .
CN
Getting on?
Yes, it's nearly done.
Finished?
That's it! . . . I'll just fix the last bolt.
CN
CN
Hands up!

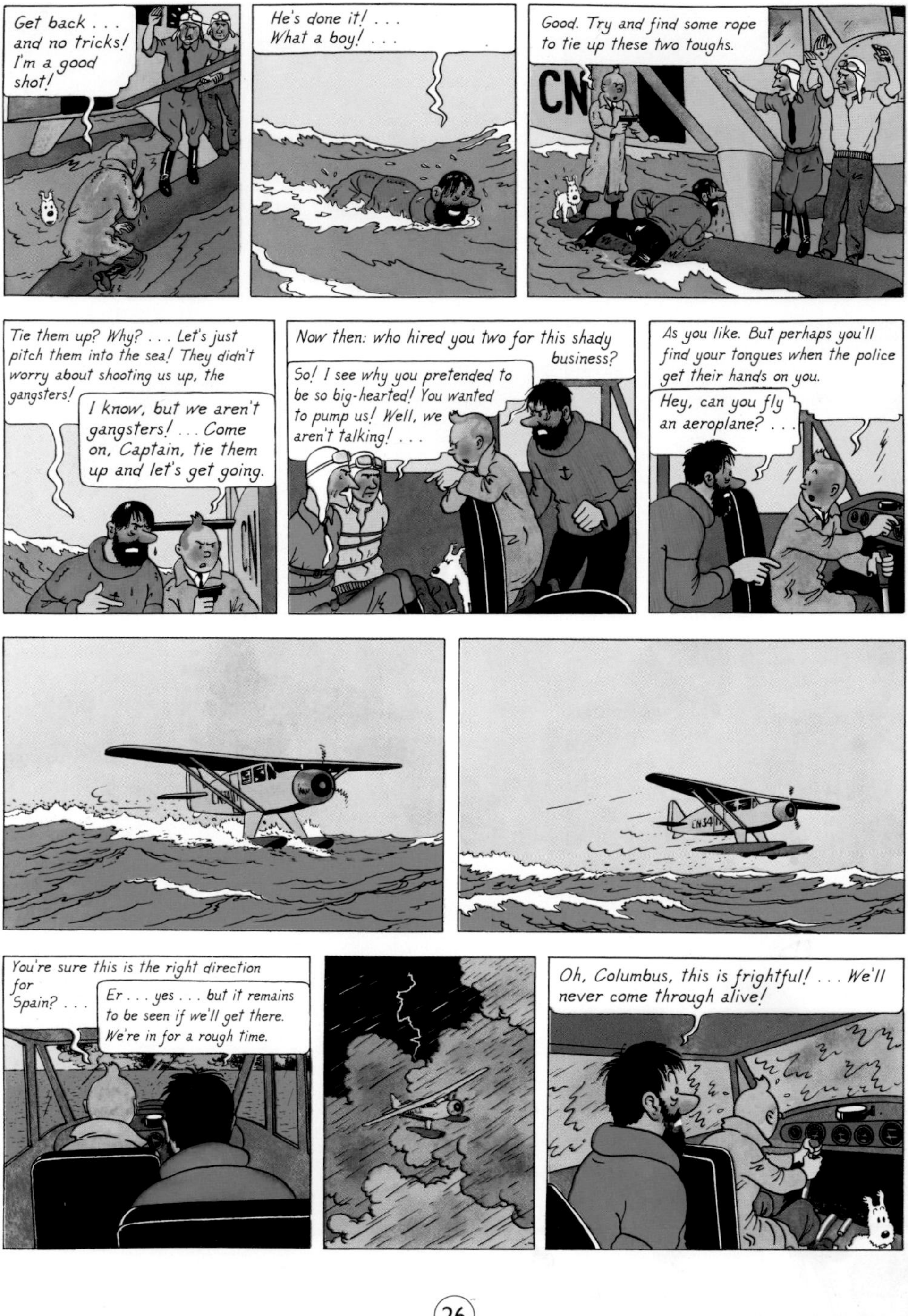
Get back . . . and no tricks! I'm a good shot!
He's done it! . . . What a boy! . . .
Good. Try and find some rope to tie up these two toughs.
CN
Tie them up? Why? . . . Let's just pitch them into the sea! They didn't worry about shooting us up, the gangsters!
I know, but we aren't gangsters! . . . Come on, Captain, tie them up and let's get going.
Now then: who hired you two for this shady business?
So! I see why you pretended to be so big-hearted! You wanted to pump us! Well, we aren't talking! . . .
As you like. But perhaps you'll find your tongues when the police get their hands on you.
Hey, can you fly an aeroplane? . . .
CN34
You're sure this is the right direction for Spain? . . .
Er . . . yes . . . but it remains to be seen if we'll get there. We're in for a rough time.
Oh, Columbus, this is frightful! . . . We'll never come through alive!

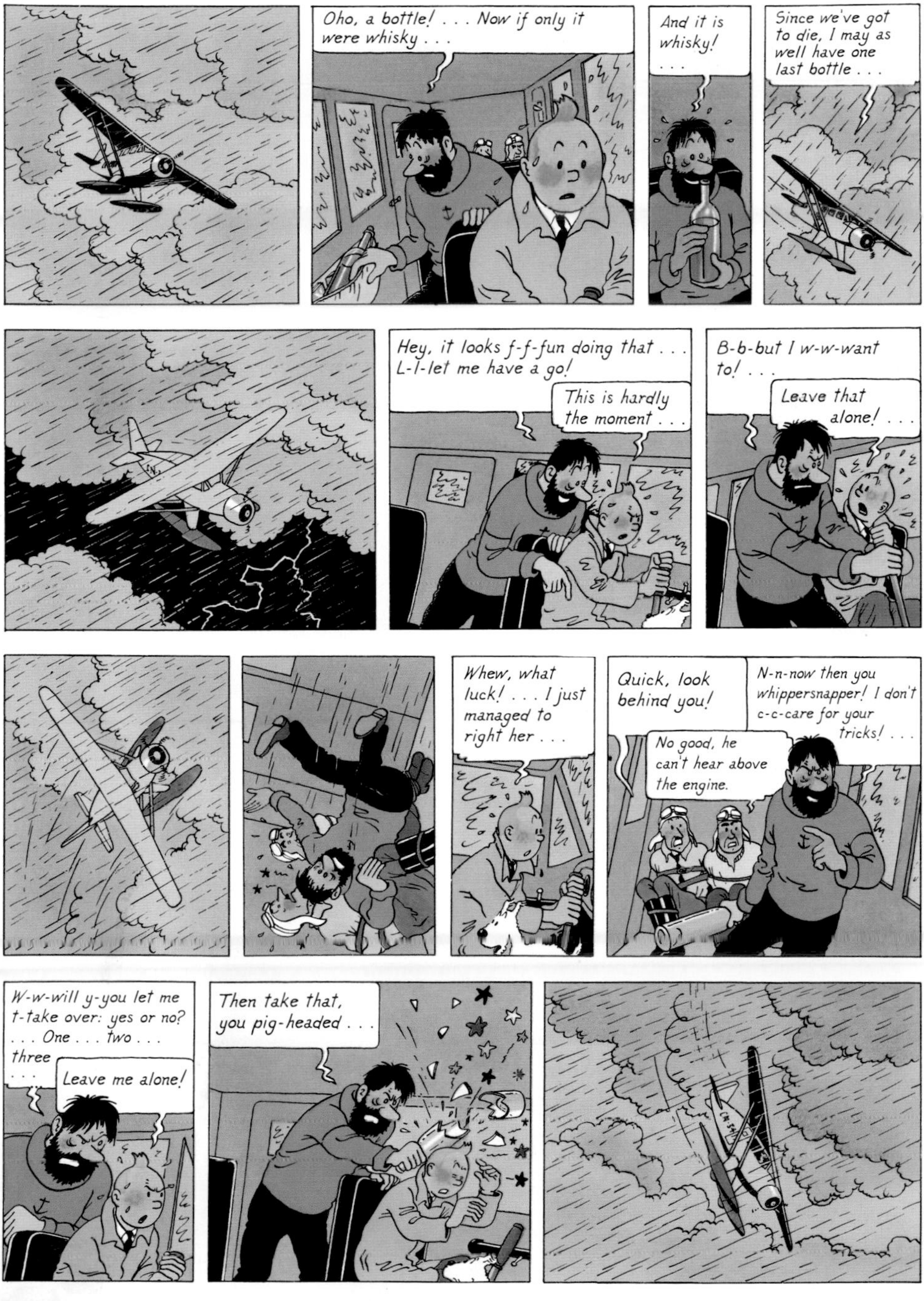
Oho, a bottle! . . . Now if only it were whisky . . .
And it is whisky! . . .
Since we've got to die, I may as well have one last bottle . . .
Hey, it looks f-f-fun doing that . . . L-l-let me have a go!
This is hardly the moment . . .
B-b-but I w-w-want to! . . .
Leave that alone! . . .
Whew, what luck! . . . I just managed to right her . . .
Quick, look behind you!
No good, he can't hear above the engine.
N-n-now then you whippersnapper! I don't c-c-care for your tricks! . . .
W-w-will y-you let me t-take over: yes or no? . . . One . . . two . . . three . . .
Leave me alone!
Then take that, you pig-headed . . .

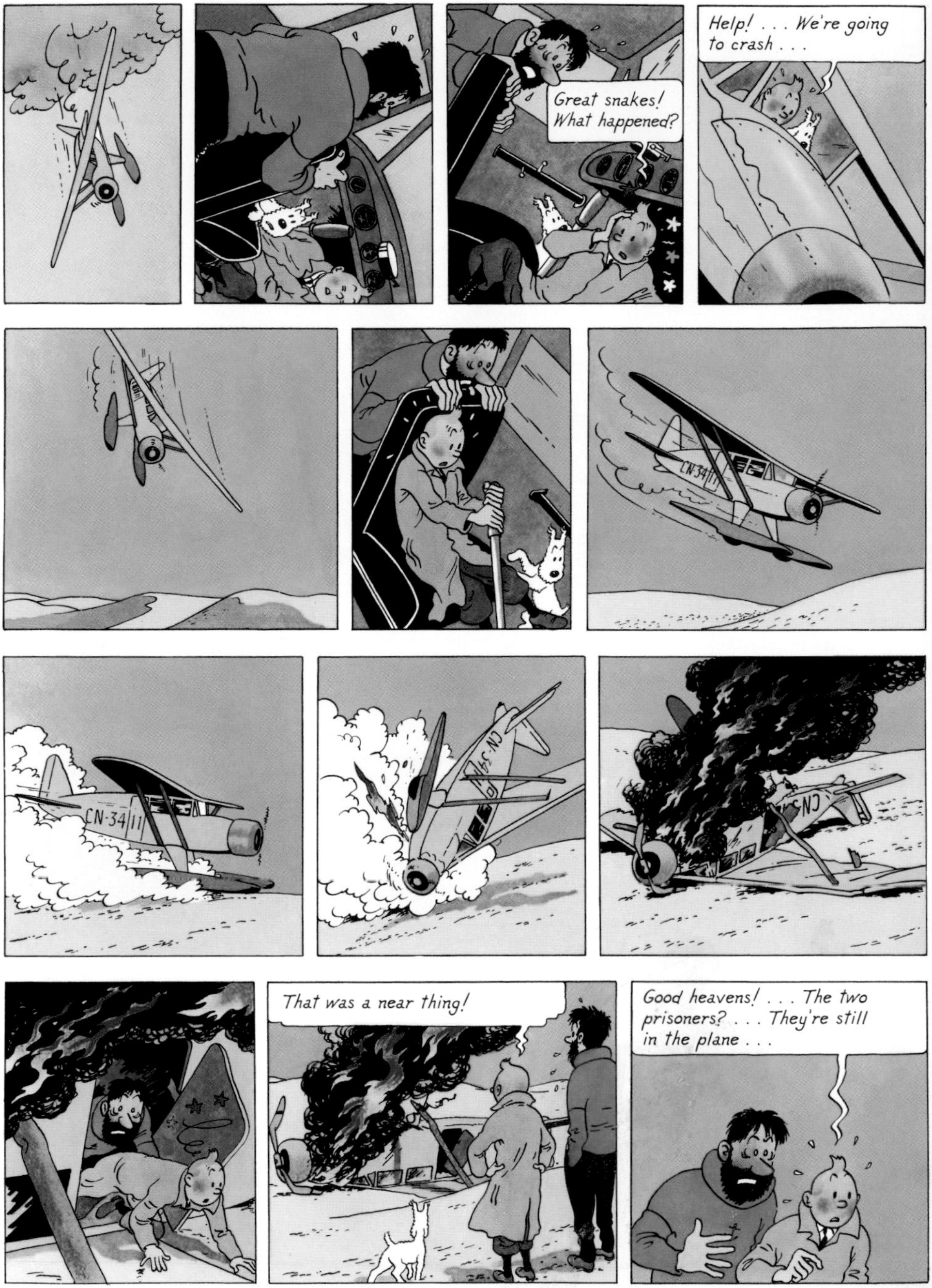
Great snakes! What happened?
Help! . . . We're going to crash . . .
That was a near thing!
Good heavens! . . . The two prisoners? . . . They're still in the plane . . .

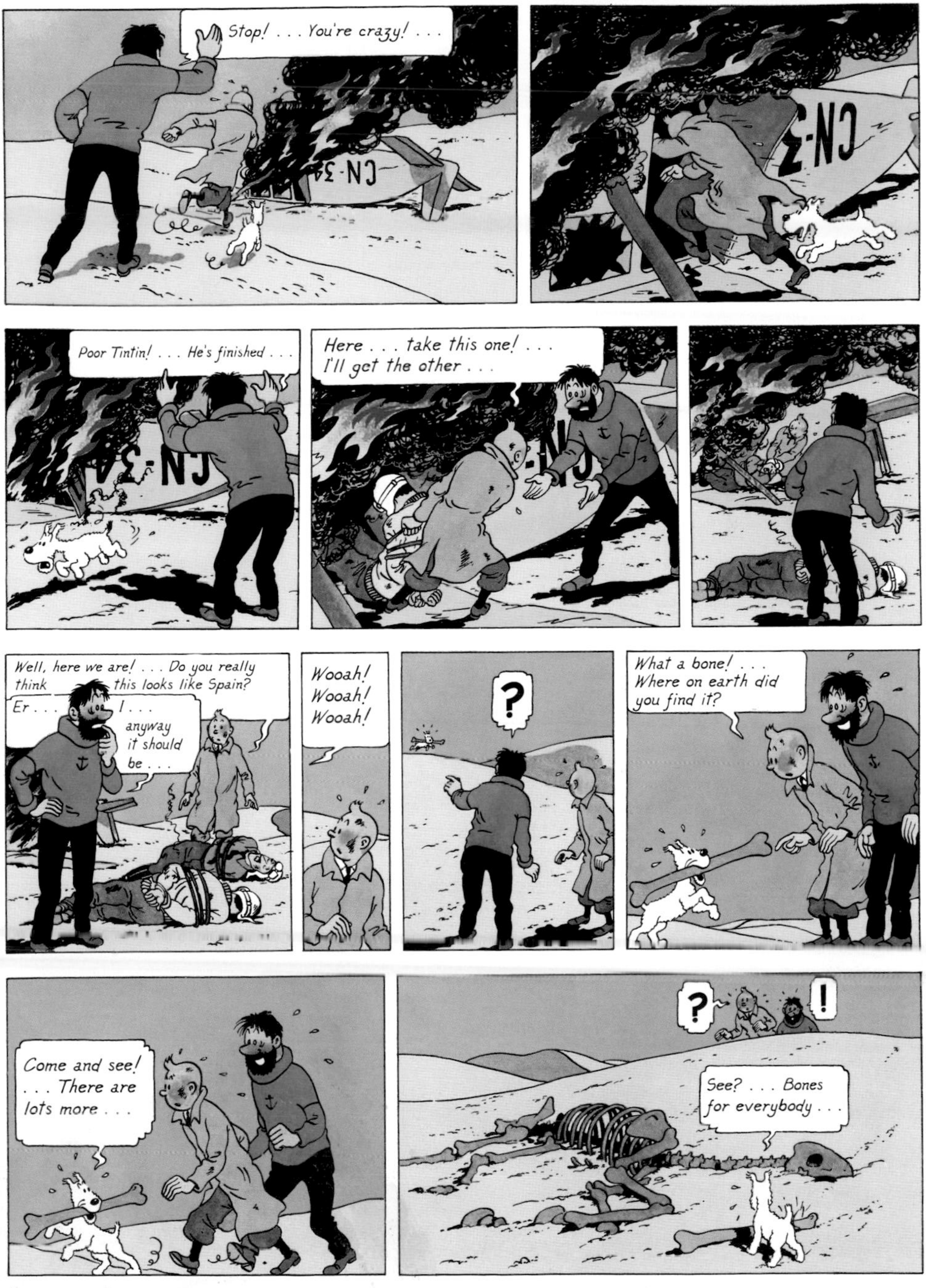
Stop! . . . You're crazy! . . .
CN-34
Poor Tintin! . . . He's finished . . .
Here . . . take this one! . . . I'll get the other . . .
Well, here we are! . . . Do you really think this looks like Spain?
Er . . . I . . . anyway it should be . . .
Wooah! Wooah! Wooah!
?
What a bone! . . . Where on earth did you find it?
Come and see! . . . There are lots more . . .
?
!
See? . . . Bones for everybody . . .

A camel! . . .

A camel? . . . But there aren't any camels in Spain . . .

Unfortunately we aren't in Spain! . . . We're in the middle of the Sahara Desert!

In the middle of the Sahara! . . . then that animal . . . that animal . . . that animal died of . . . died of . . .

. . . died of thirst, of course!

What's the matter? . . . Feeling faint?

The land of thirst! . . . The land of thirst! . . .

The land of thirst . . .

Courage, Captain, courage! We aren't finished yet.

It looks as if he's at the end of his tether.

The land of thirst . . .

The prisoners have gone!

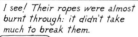

I see! Their ropes were almost burnt through: it didn't take much to break them.

The land of thirst . . .

Look over there . . . they're too far away now for us to catch them up. Never mind . . .

Come on, Captain! Perhaps we shall be lucky and come across a well!

The land of thirst . . .

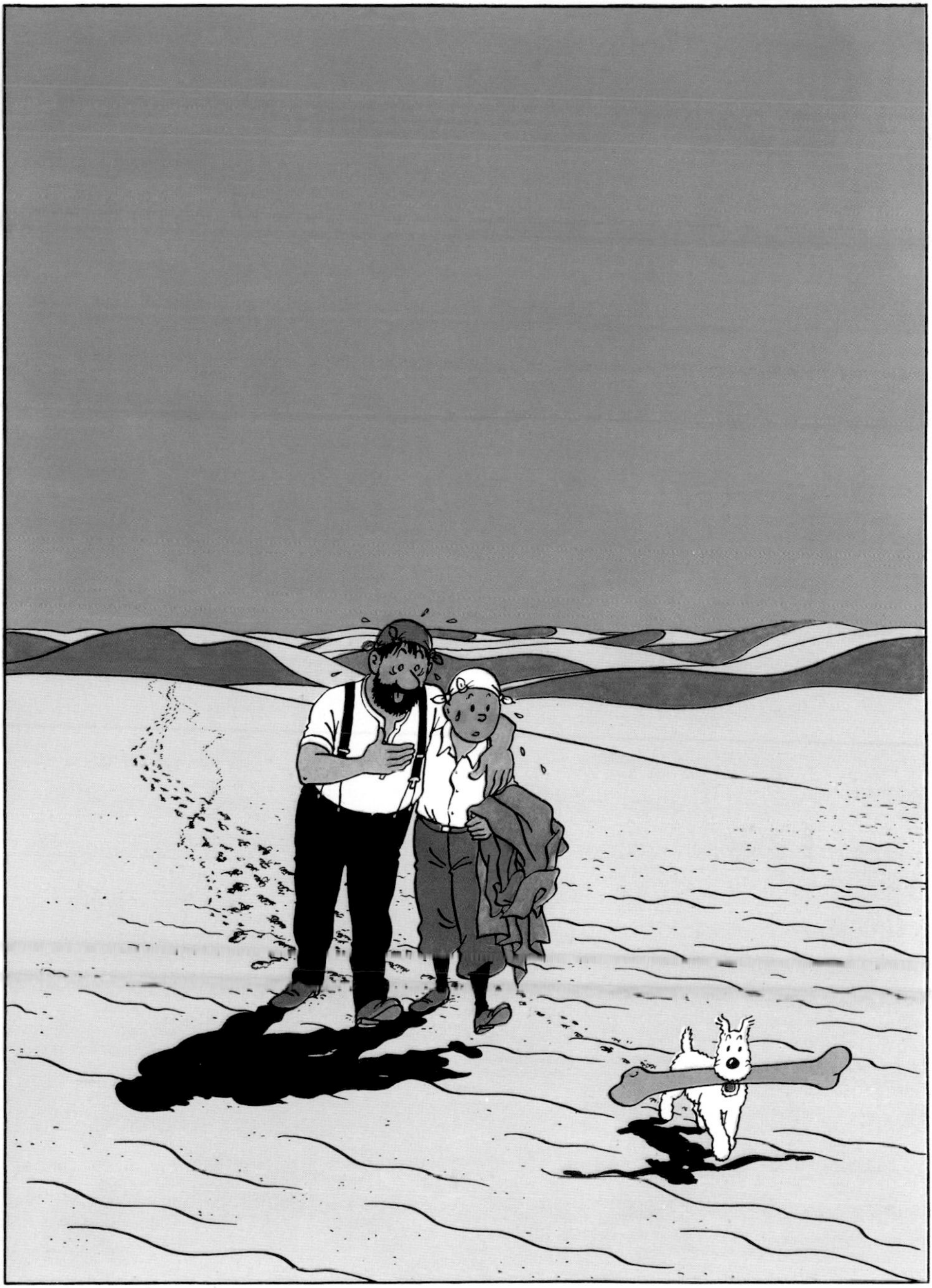

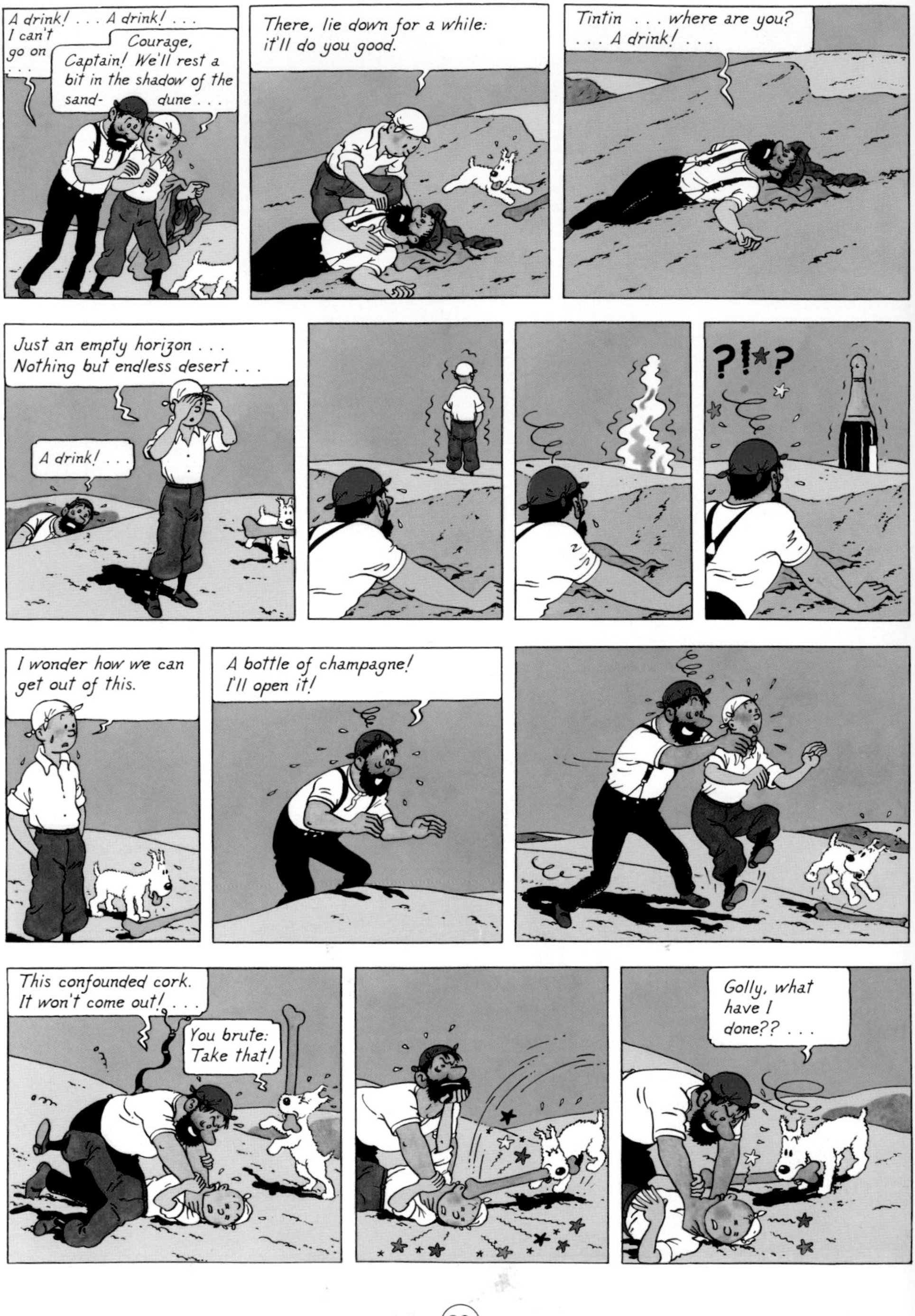
A drink! . . . A drink! . . . I can't go on . . .
Courage, Captain! We'll rest a bit in the shadow of the sand- dune . . .
There, lie down for a while: it'll do you good.
Tintin . . . where are you? . . . A drink! . . .
Just an empty horizon . . . Nothing but endless desert . . .
A drink! . . .
?!*?
I wonder how we can get out of this.
A bottle of champagne! I'll open it!
This confounded cork. It won't come out! . . .
You brute: Take that!
Golly, what have I done?? . . .

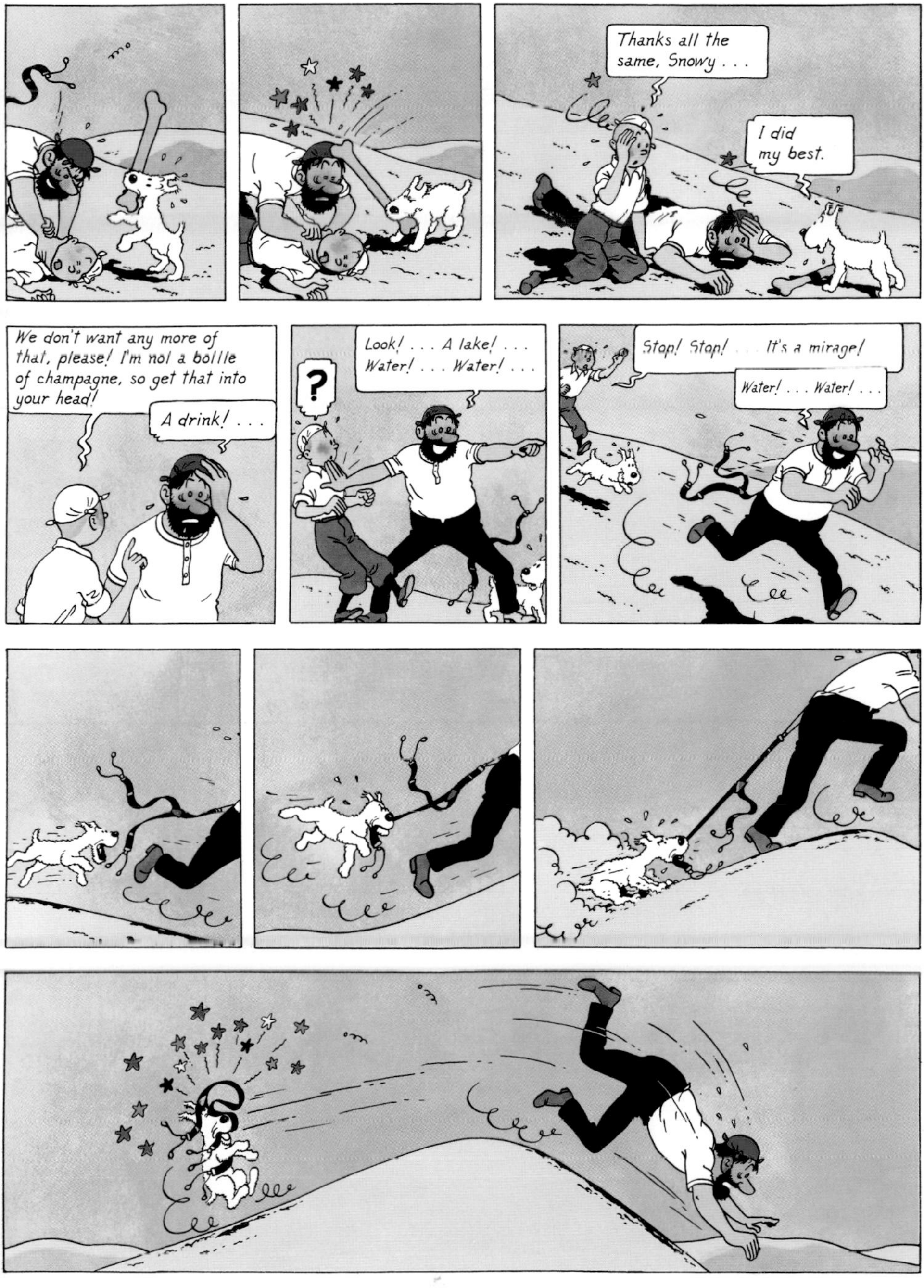
Thanks all the same, Snowy . . .
I did my best.
We don't want any more of that, please! I'm not a bottle of champagne, so get that into your head!
A drink! . . .
?
Look! . . . A lake! . . . Water! . . . Water! . . .
Stop! Stop! . . . It's a mirage!
Water! . . . Water! . . .

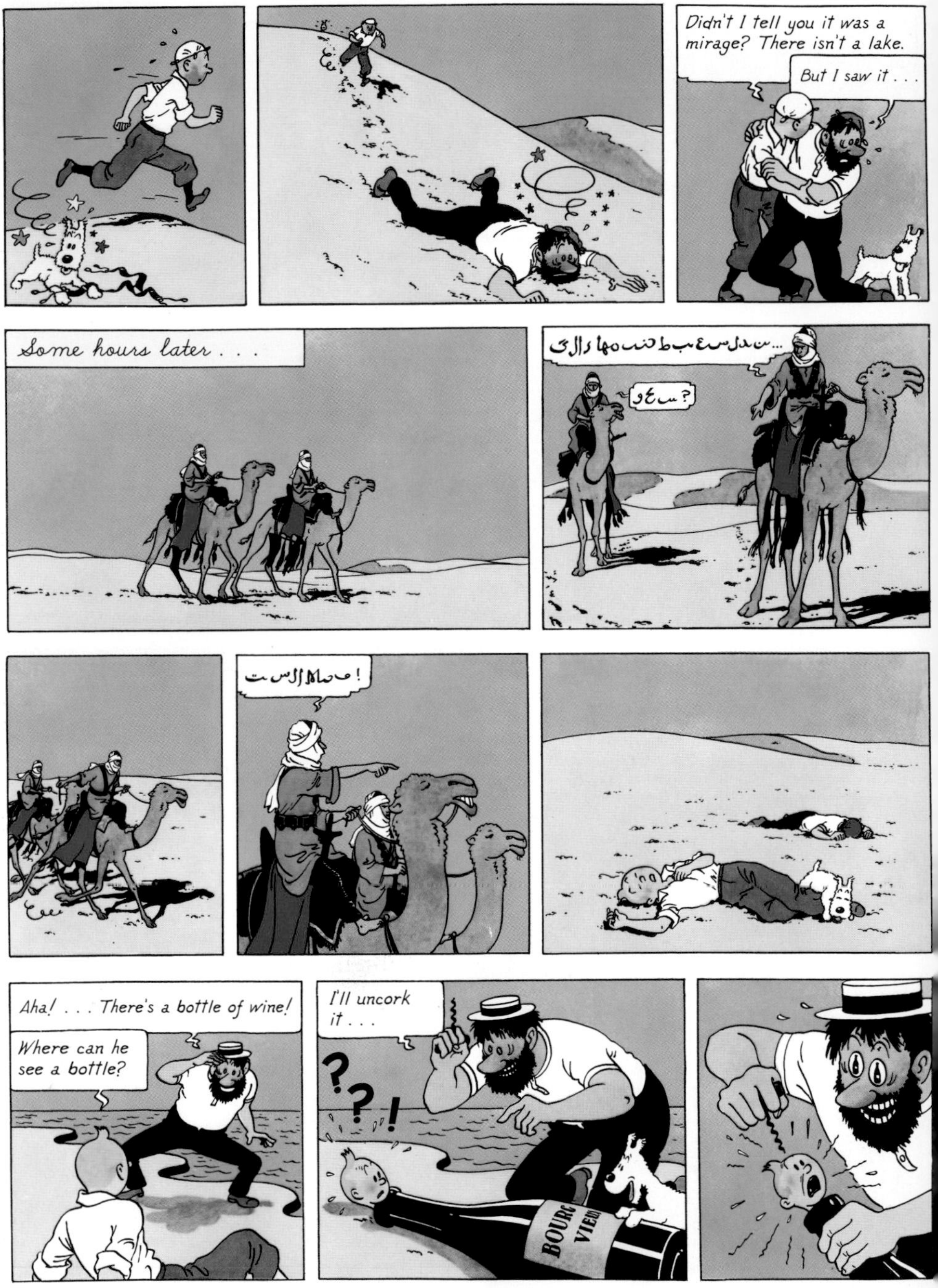
Didn't I tell you it was a mirage? There isn't a lake.
But I saw it . . .
Some hours later . . .
Aha! . . . There's a bottle of wine!
Where can he see a bottle?
I'll uncork it . . .
? ? !

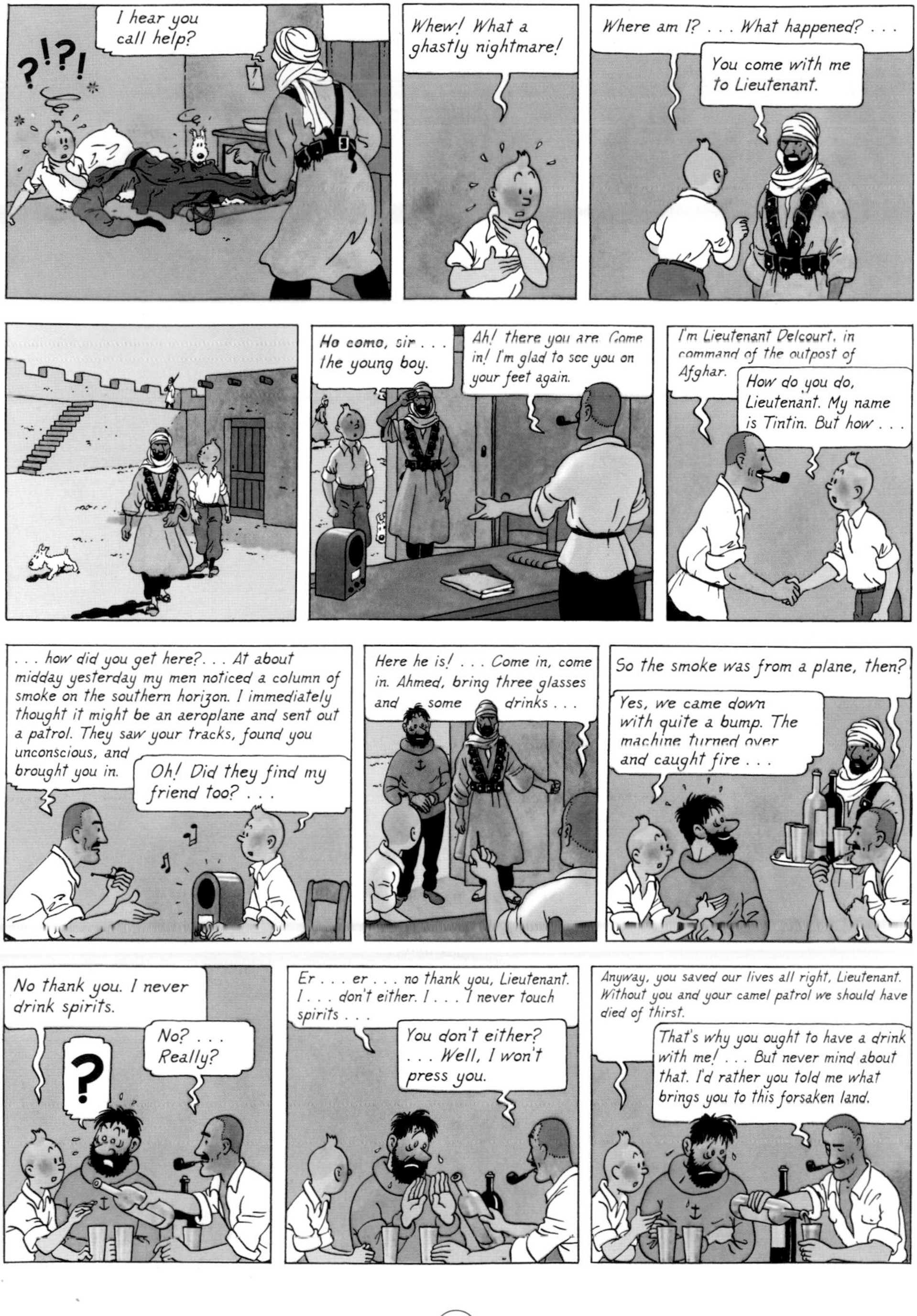
I hear you call help?
?!?!
Whew! What a ghastly nightmare!
Where am I? . . . What happened? . . .
You come with me to Lieutenant.
He come, sir . . . the young boy.
Ah! there you are. Come in! I'm glad to see you on your feet again.
I'm Lieutenant Delcourt, in command of the outpost of Afghar.
How do you do, Lieutenant. My name is Tintin. But how . . .
. . . how did you get here? . . . At about midday yesterday my men noticed a column of smoke on the southern horizon. I immediately thought it might be an aeroplane and sent out a patrol. They saw your tracks, found you unconscious, and brought you in.
Oh! Did they find my friend too? . . .
Here he is! . . . Come in, come in. Ahmed, bring three glasses and some drinks . . .
So the smoke was from a plane, then?
Yes, we came down with quite a bump. The machine turned over and caught fire . . .
No thank you. I never drink spirits.
?
No? . . . Really?
Er . . . er . . . no thank you, Lieutenant. I . . . don't either. I . . . I never touch spirits . . .
You don't either? . . . Well, I won't press you.
Anyway, you saved our lives all right, Lieutenant. Without you and your camel patrol we should have died of thirst.
That's why you ought to have a drink with me! . . . But never mind about that. I'd rather you told me what brings you to this forsaken land.

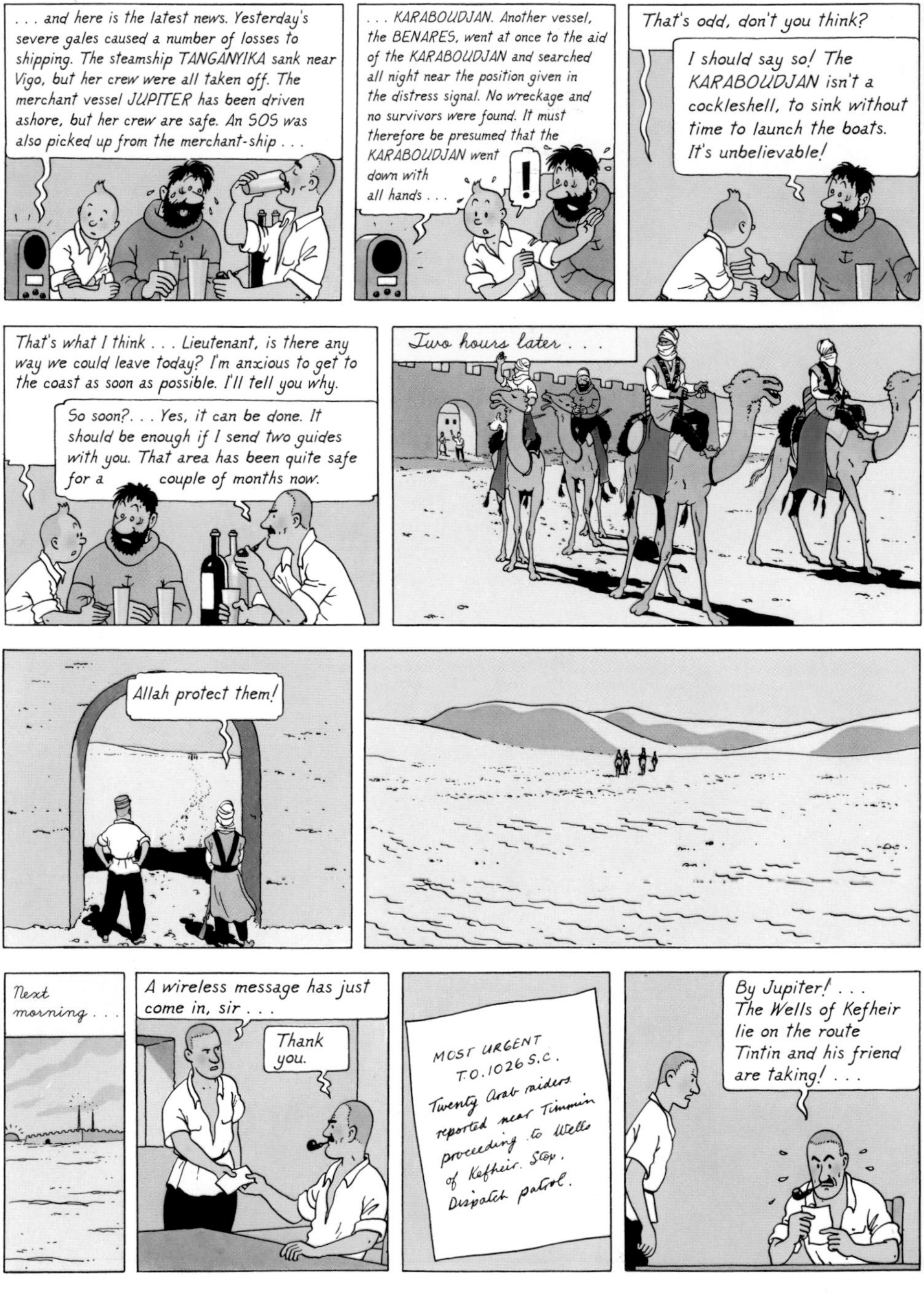
. . . and here is the latest news. Yesterday's severe gales caused a number of losses to shipping. The steamship TANGANYIKA sank near Vigo, but her crew were all taken off. The merchant vessel JUPITER has been driven ashore, but her crew are safe. An SOS was also picked up from the merchant-ship . . .
. . . KARABOUDJAN. Another vessel, the BENARES, went at once to the aid of the KARABOUDJAN and searched all night near the position given in the distress signal. No wreckage and no survivors were found. It must therefore be presumed that the KARABOUDJAN went down with all hands . . .
!
That's odd, don't you think?
I should say so! The KARABOUDJAN isn't a cockleshell, to sink without time to launch the boats. It's unbelievable!
That's what I think . . . Lieutenant, is there any way we could leave today? I'm anxious to get to the coast as soon as possible. I'll tell you why.
So soon?. . . Yes, it can be done. It should be enough if I send two guides with you. That area has been quite safe for a couple of months now.
Two hours later . . .
Allah protect them!
Next morning . . .
A wireless message has just come in, sir . . .
Thank you.
MOST URGENT
T.O. 1026 S.C.
Twenty Arab raiders reported near Timmin proceeding to Wells of Kefheir. Stop. Dispatch patrol.
By Jupiter! . . . The Wells of Kefheir lie on the route Tintin and his friend are taking! . . .

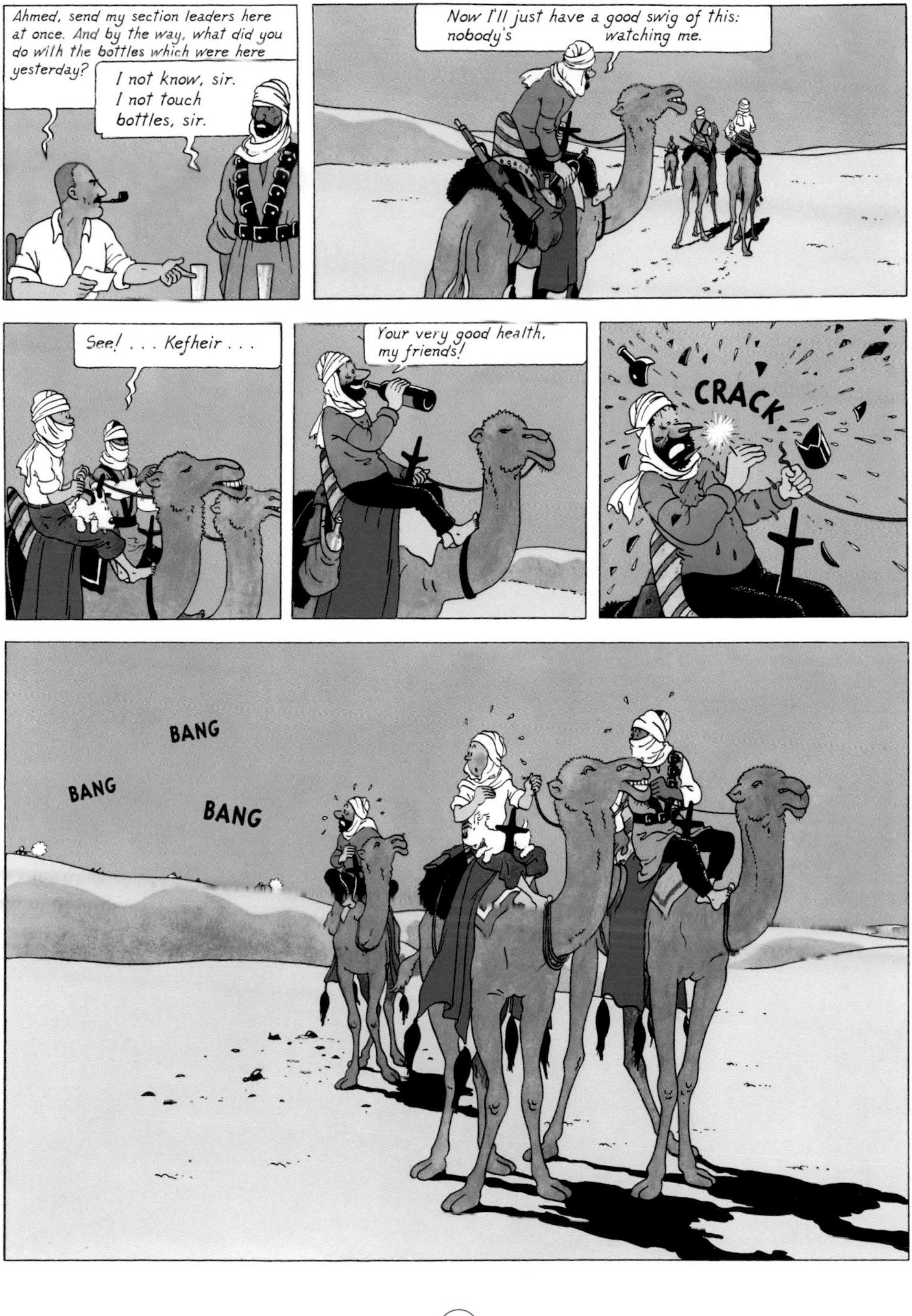

Ahmed, send my section leaders here at once. And by the way, what did you do with the bottles which were here yesterday?
I not know, sir. I not touch bottles, sir.
Now I'll just have a good swig of this: nobody's watching me.
See! . . . Kefheir . . .
Your very good health, my friends!
CRACK
BANG
BANG
BANG

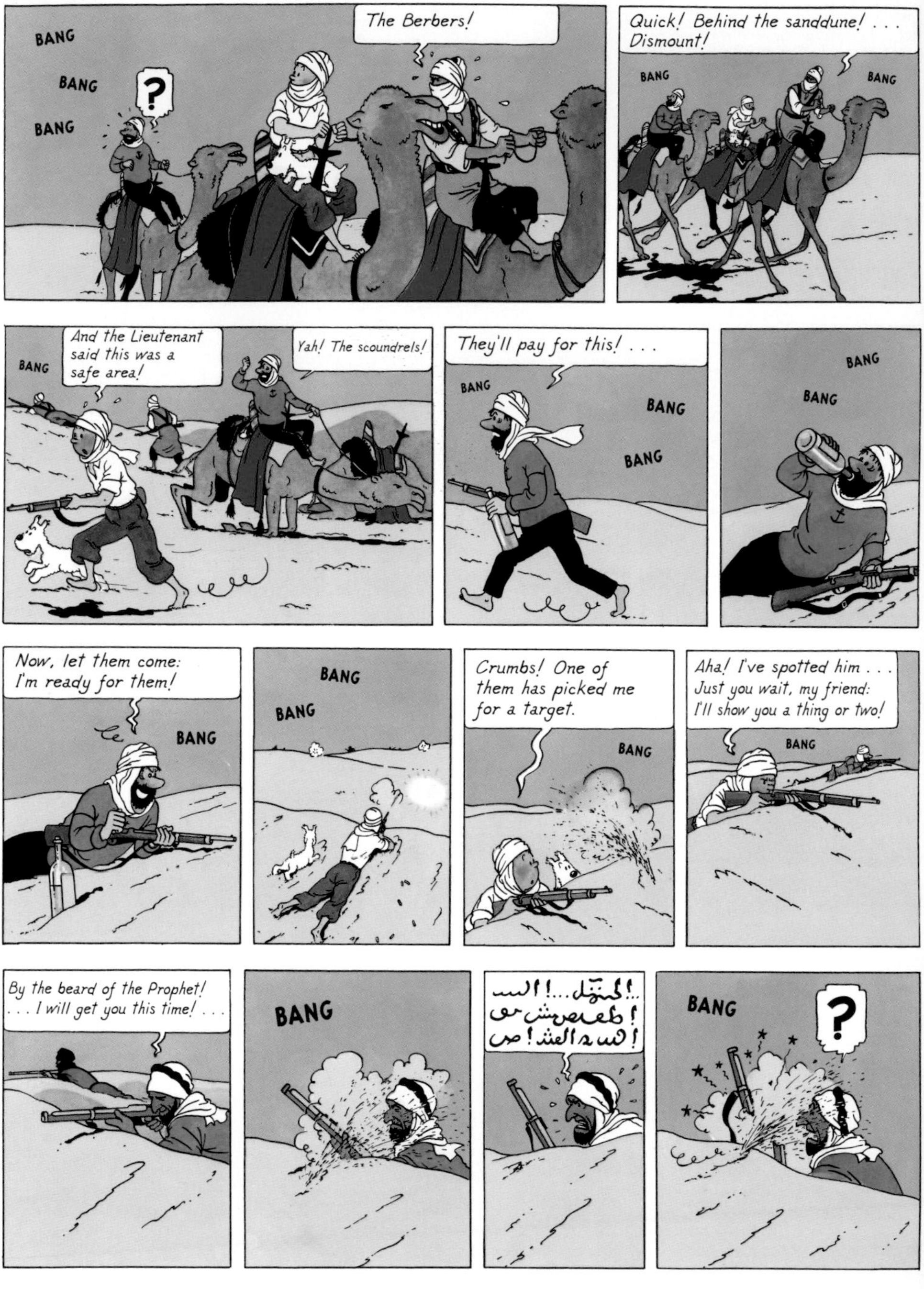
BANG
BANG
BANG
?
The Berbers!
Quick! Behind the sanddune! . . . Dismount!
BANG
BANG
BANG
And the Lieutenant said this was a safe area!
Yah! The scoundrels!
They'll pay for this! . . .
BANG
BANG
BANG
BANG
BANG
Now, let them come: I'm ready for them!
BANG
BANG
BANG
Crumbs! One of them has picked me for a target.
BANG
Aha! I've spotted him . . . Just you wait, my friend: I'll show you a thing or two!
BANG
By the beard of the Prophet! . . . I will get you this time! . . .
BANG
BANG
?

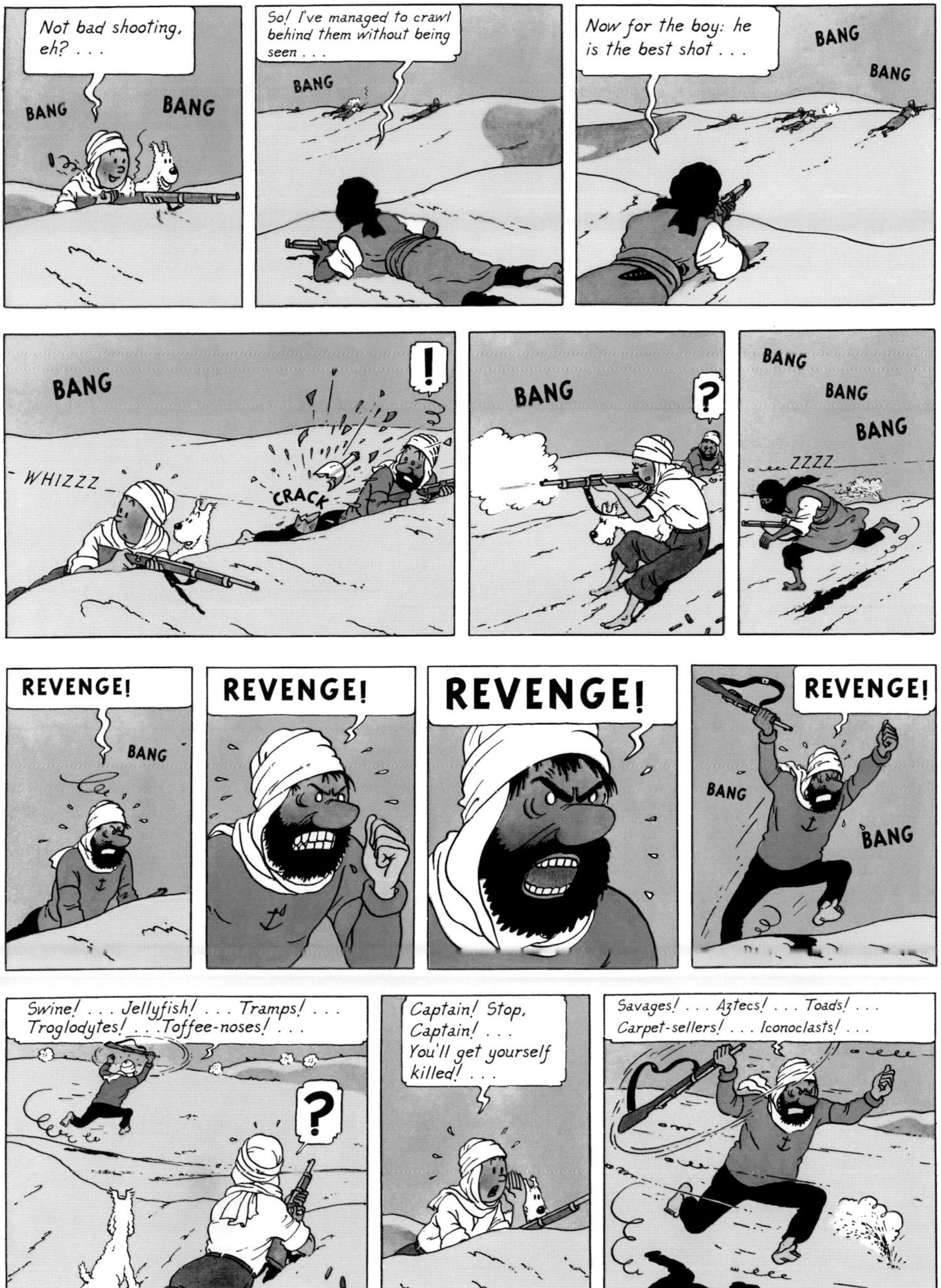
Not bad shooting, eh? . . .
BANG
BANG
So! I've managed to crawl behind them without being seen . . .
BANG
Now for the boy: he is the best shot . . .
BANG
BANG
BANG
!
WHIZZZ
CRACK
BANG
?
BANG
BANG
BANG
ZZZZ
REVENGE!
BANG
REVENGE!
REVENGE!
REVENGE!
BANG
BANG
Swine! . . . Jellyfish! . . . Tramps! . . . Troglodytes! . . . Toffee-noses! . . .
?
Captain! Stop, Captain! . . . You'll get yourself killed! . . .
Savages! . . . Aztecs! . . . Toads! . . . Carpet-sellers! . . . Iconoclasts! . . .

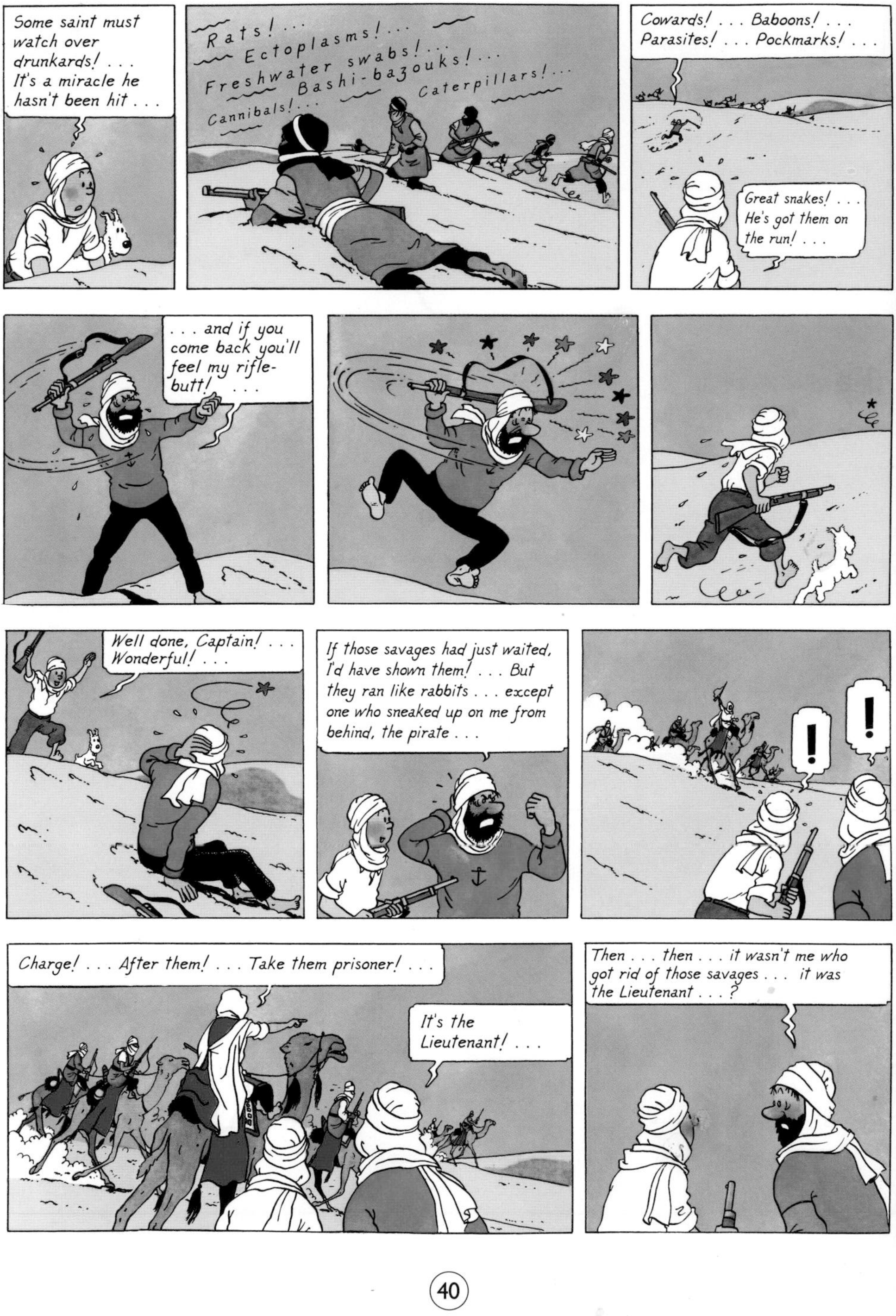

Some saint must watch over drunkards! . . . It's a miracle he hasn't been hit . . .
Rats! . . . Ectoplasms! . . . Freshwater swabs! . . . Bashi-bazouks! . . . Caterpillars! . . . Cannibals! . . .
Cowards! . . . Baboons! . . . Parasites! . . . Pockmarks! . . .
Great snakes! . . . He's got them on the run! . . .
. . . and if you come back you'll feel my rifle-butt! . . .
Well done, Captain! . . . Wonderful! . . .
If those savages had just waited, I'd have shown them! . . . But they ran like rabbits . . . except one who sneaked up on me from behind, the pirate . . .
!
!
Charge! . . . After them! . . . Take them prisoner! . . .
It's the Lieutenant! . . .
Then . . . then . . . it wasn't me who got rid of those savages . . . it was the Lieutenant . . . ?

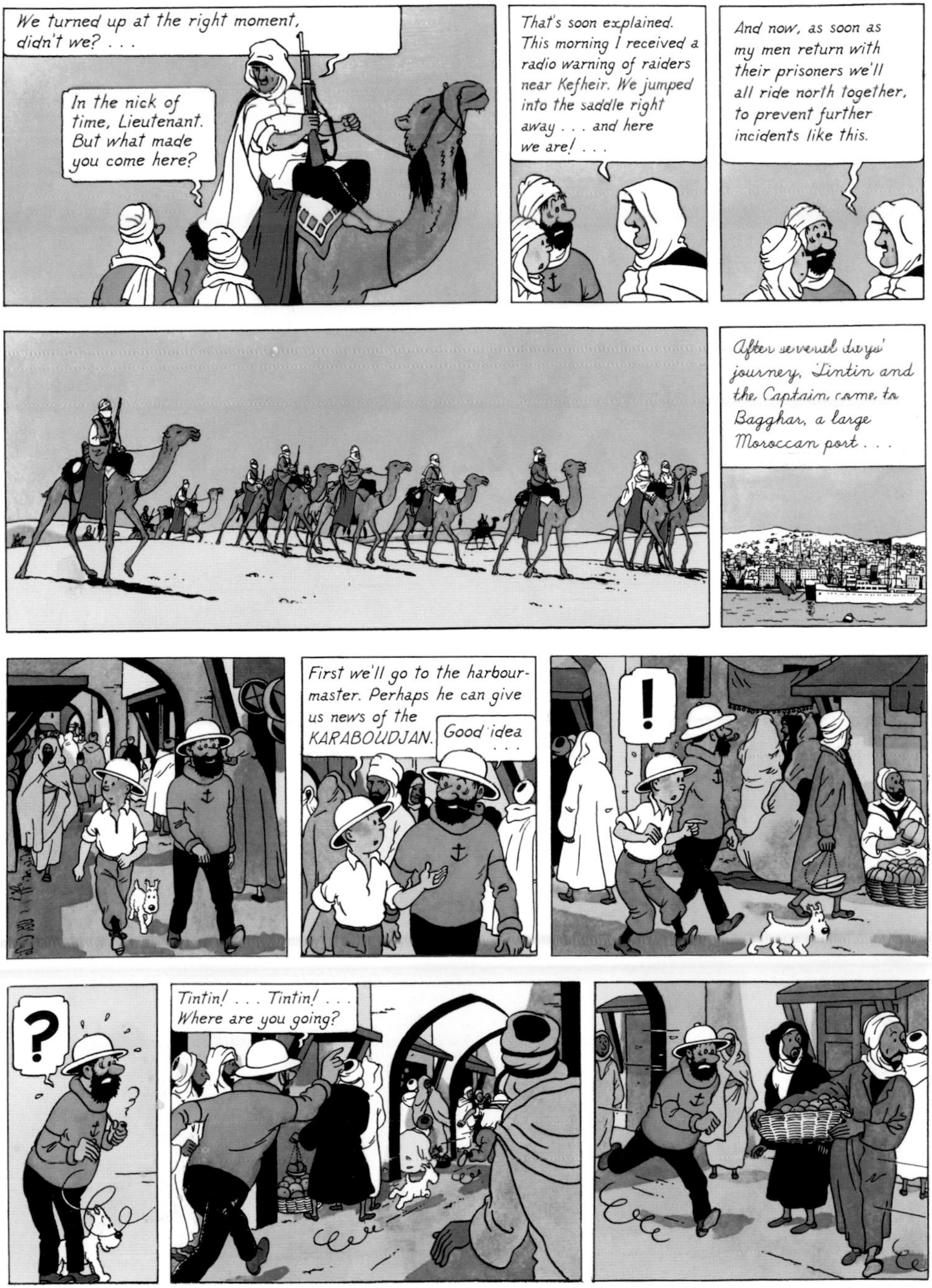
We turned up at the right moment, didn't we? . . .
In the nick of time, Lieutenant. But what made you come here?
That's soon explained. This morning I received a radio warning of raiders near Kefheir. We jumped into the saddle right away . . . and here we are! . . .
And now, as soon as my men return with their prisoners we'll all ride north together, to prevent further incidents like this.
After several days' journey, Tintin and the Captain come to Bagghar, a large Moroccan port . . .
First we'll go to the harbour-master. Perhaps he can give us news of the KARABOUDJAN.
Good idea . . .
!
?
Tintin! . . . Tintin! . . . Where are you going?

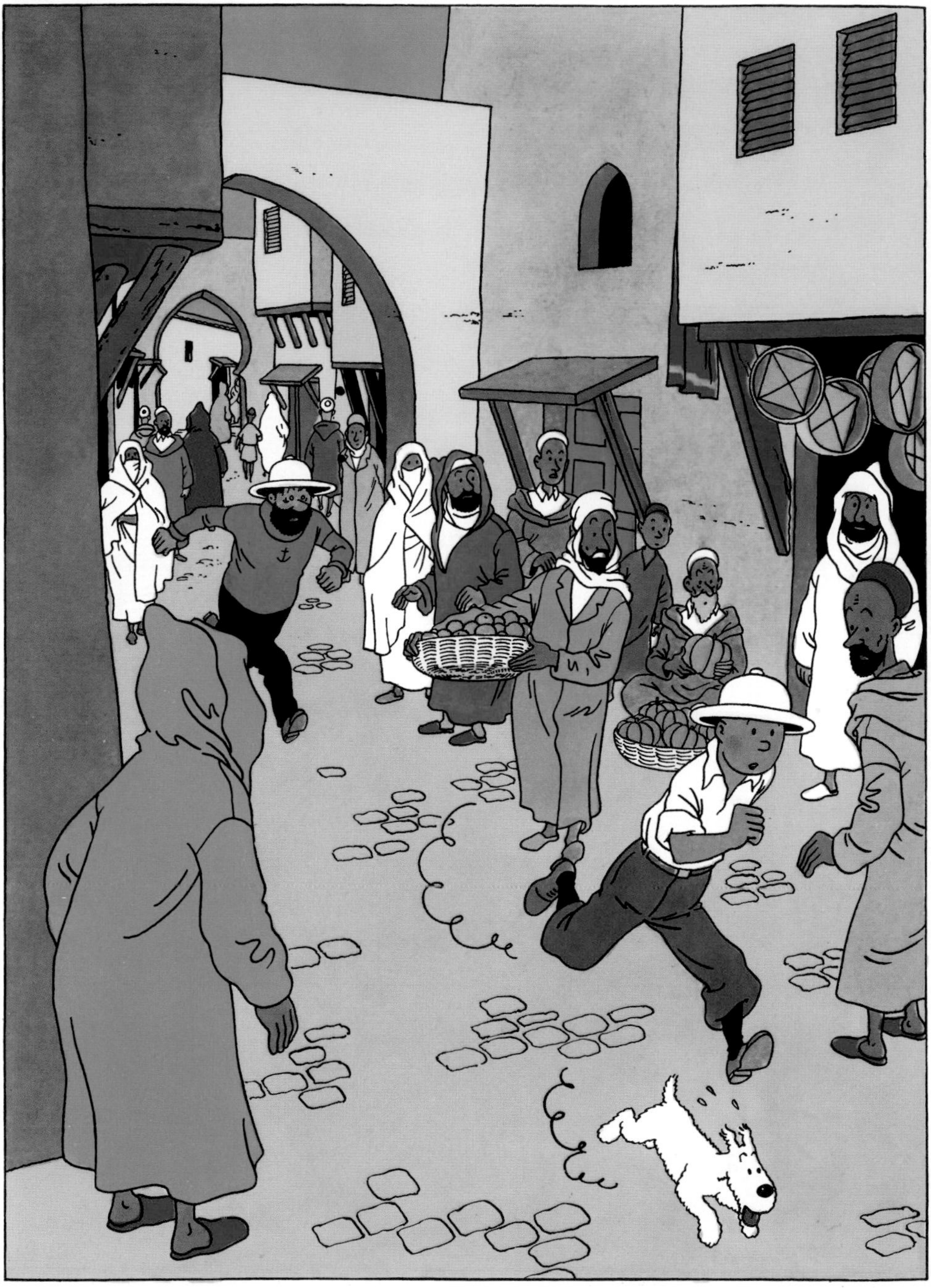

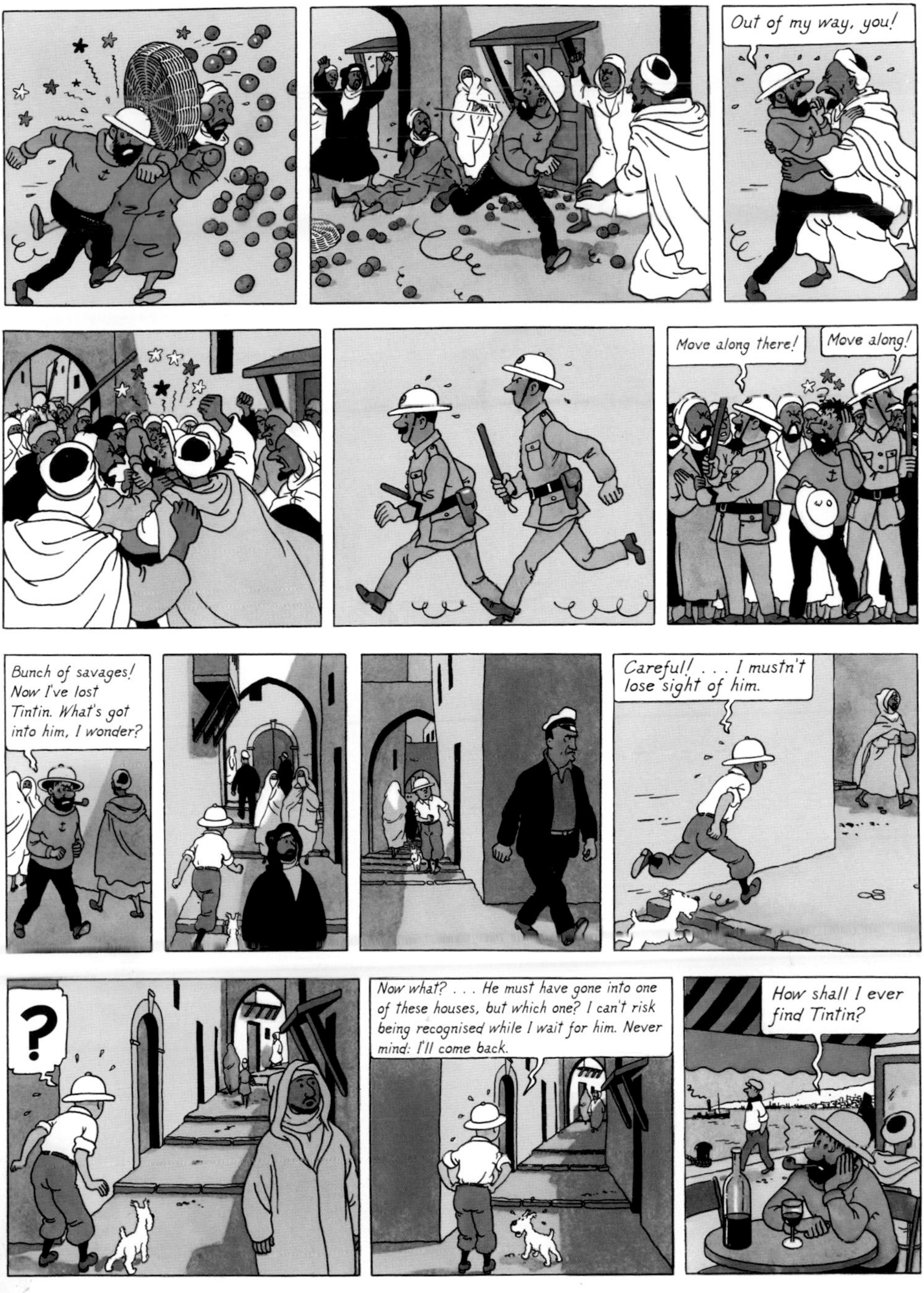
Out of my way, you!
Move along there!
Move along!
Bunch of savages! Now I've lost Tintin. What's got into him, I wonder?
Careful! . . . I mustn't lose sight of him.
?
Now what? . . . He must have gone into one of these houses, but which one? I can't risk being recognised while I wait for him. Never mind: I'll come back.
How shall I ever find Tintin?

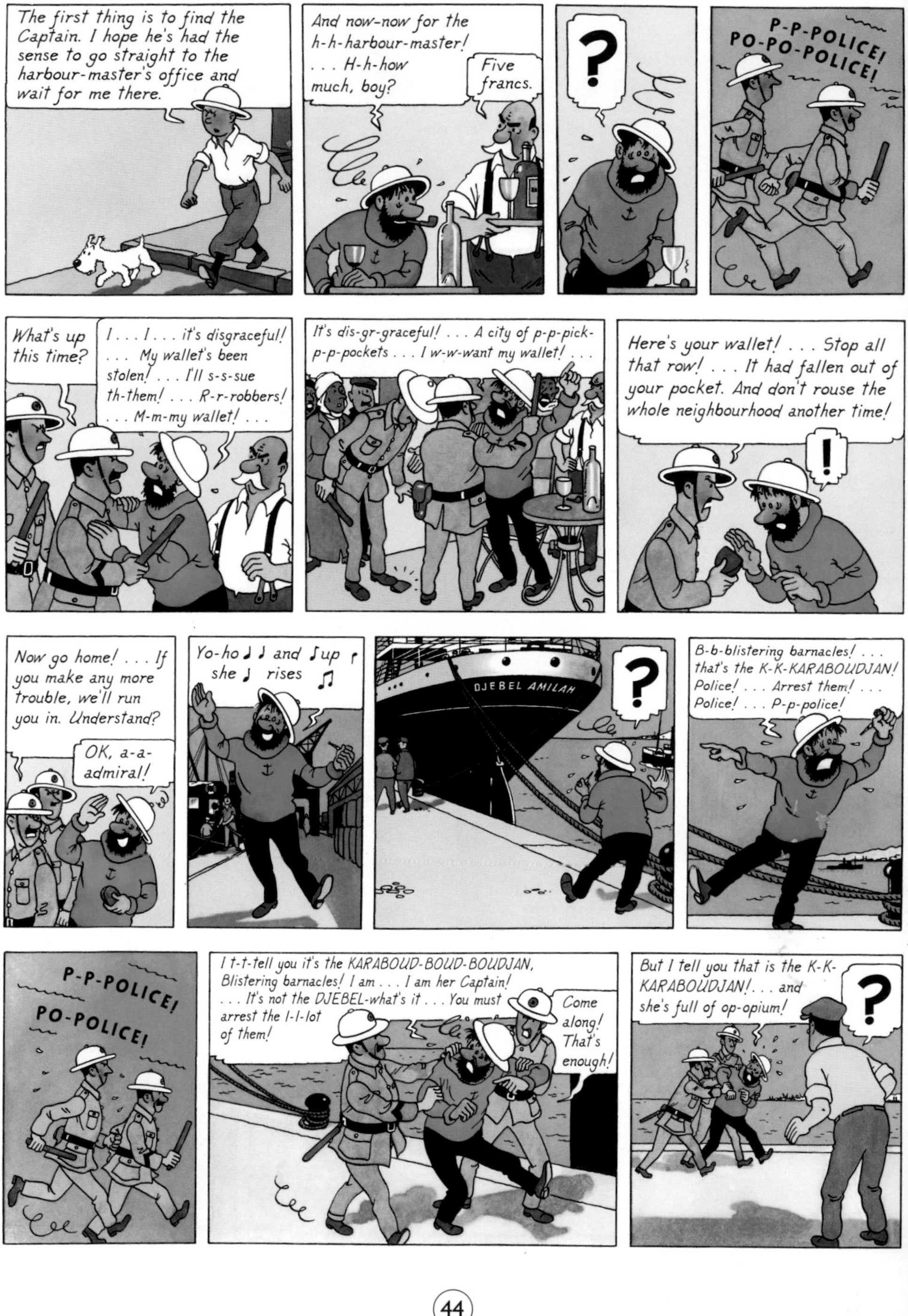
The first thing is to find the Captain. I hope he's had the sense to go straight to the harbour-master's office and wait for me there.
And now-now for the h-h-harbour-master! . . . H-h-how much, boy?
Five francs.
?
P-P-POLICE! PO-PO-POLICE!
What's up this time?
I . . . I . . . it's disgraceful! . . . My wallet's been stolen! . . . I'll s-s-sue th-them! . . . R-r-robbers! . . . M-m-my wallet! . . .
It's dis-gr-graceful! . . . A city of p-p-pick-p-p-pockets . . . I w-w-want my wallet! . . .
Here's your wallet! . . . Stop all that row! . . . It had fallen out of your pocket. And don't rouse the whole neighbourhood another time!
!
Now go home! . . . If you make any more trouble, we'll run you in. Understand?
OK, a-a-admiral!
Yo-ho and up she rises
DJEBEL AMILAH
?
B-b-blistering barnacles! . . . that's the K-K-KARABOUDJAN! Police! . . . Arrest them! . . . Police! . . . P-p-police!
P-P-POLICE! PO-POLICE!
I t-t-tell you it's the KARABOUD-BOUD-BOUDJAN, Blistering barnacles! I am . . . I am her Captain! . . . It's not the DJEBEL-what's it . . . You must arrest the l-l-lot of them!
Come along! That's enough!
But I tell you that is the K-K-KARABOUDJAN! . . . and she's full of op-opium!
?

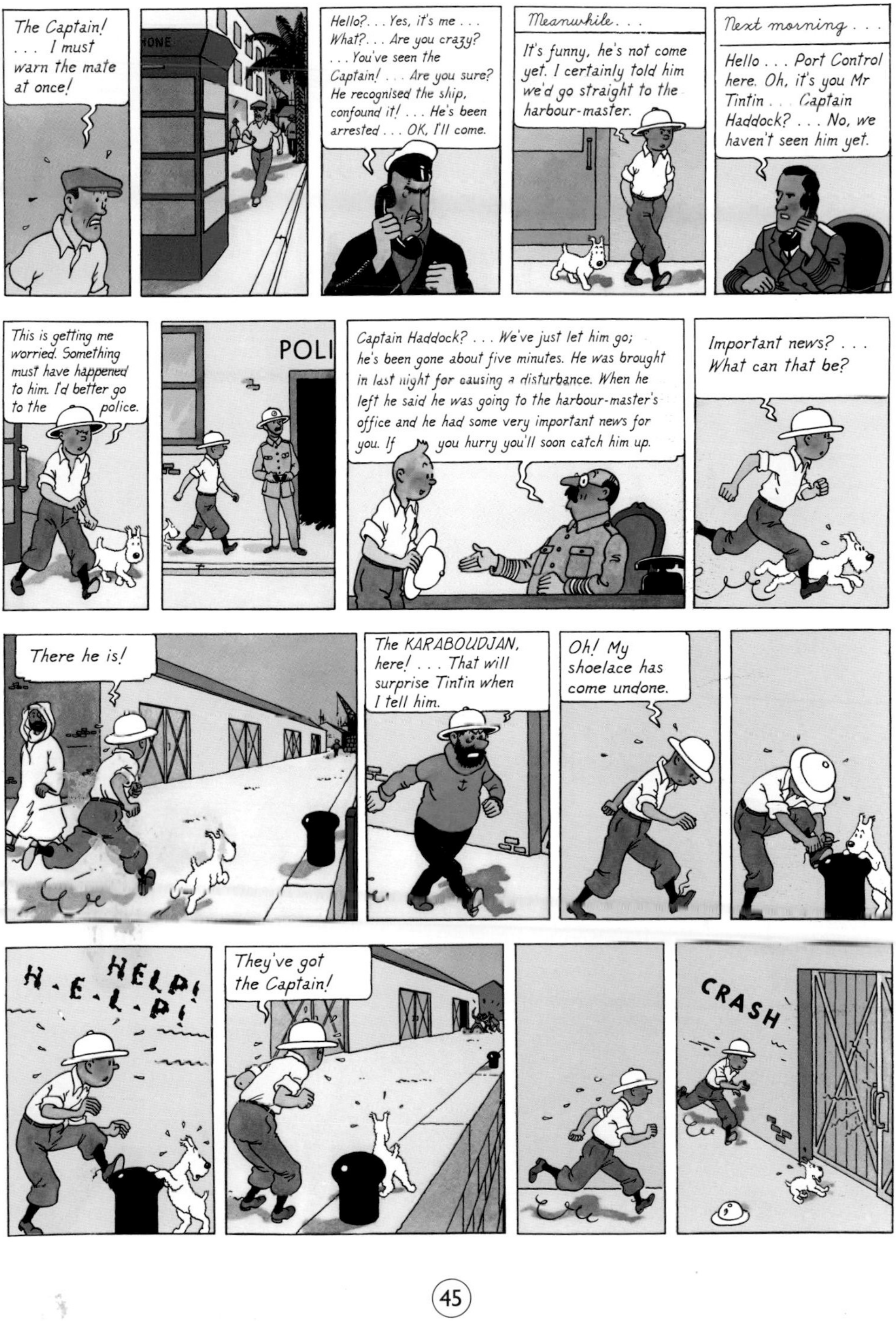
The Captain! . . . I must warn the mate at once!
HONE
Hello?. . . Yes, it's me . . . What?. . . Are you crazy? . . . You've seen the Captain! . . . Are you sure? He recognised the ship, confound it! . . . He's been arrested . . . OK, I'll come.
Meanwhile. . .
It's funny, he's not come yet. I certainly told him we'd go straight to the harbour-master.
Next morning . . .
Hello . . . Port Control here. Oh, it's you Mr Tintin . . . Captain Haddock? . . . No, we haven't seen him yet.
This is getting me worried. Something must have happened to him. I'd better go to the police.
POLI
Captain Haddock? . . . We've just let him go; he's been gone about five minutes. He was brought in last night for causing a disturbance. When he left he said he was going to the harbour-master's office and he had some very important news for you. If you hurry you'll soon catch him up.
Important news? . . . What can that be?
There he is!
The KARABOUDJAN, here! . . . That will surprise Tintin when I tell him.
Oh! My shoelace has come undone.
HELP!
H.E.L.P!
They've got the Captain!
CRASH

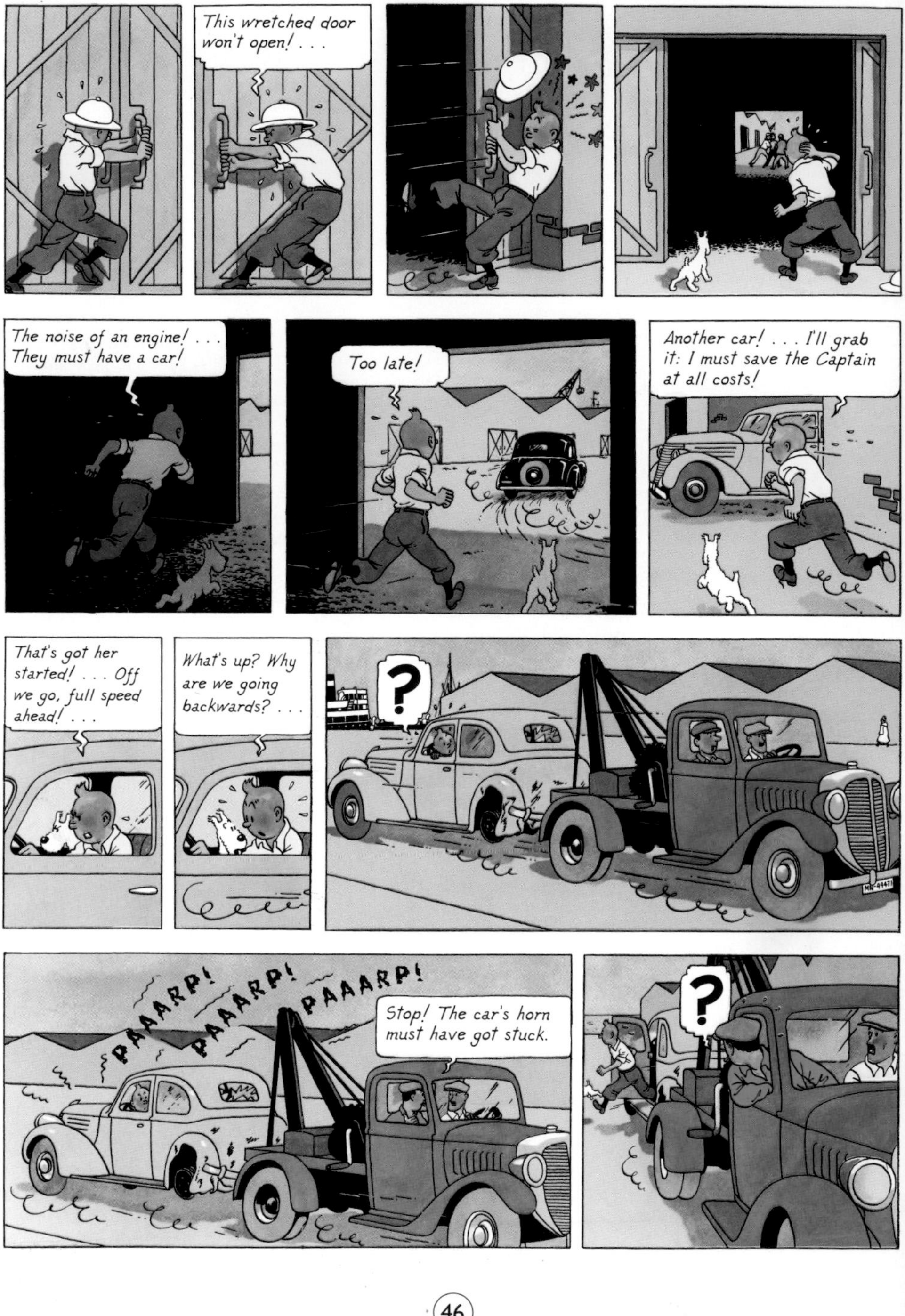
This wretched door won't open! . . .
The noise of an engine! . . . They must have a car!
Too late!
Another car! . . . I'll grab it: I must save the Captain at all costs!
That's got her started! . . . Off we go, full speed ahead! . . .
What's up? Why are we going backwards? . . .
?
PAAARP! PAAARP! PAAARP!
Stop! The car's horn must have got stuck.
?

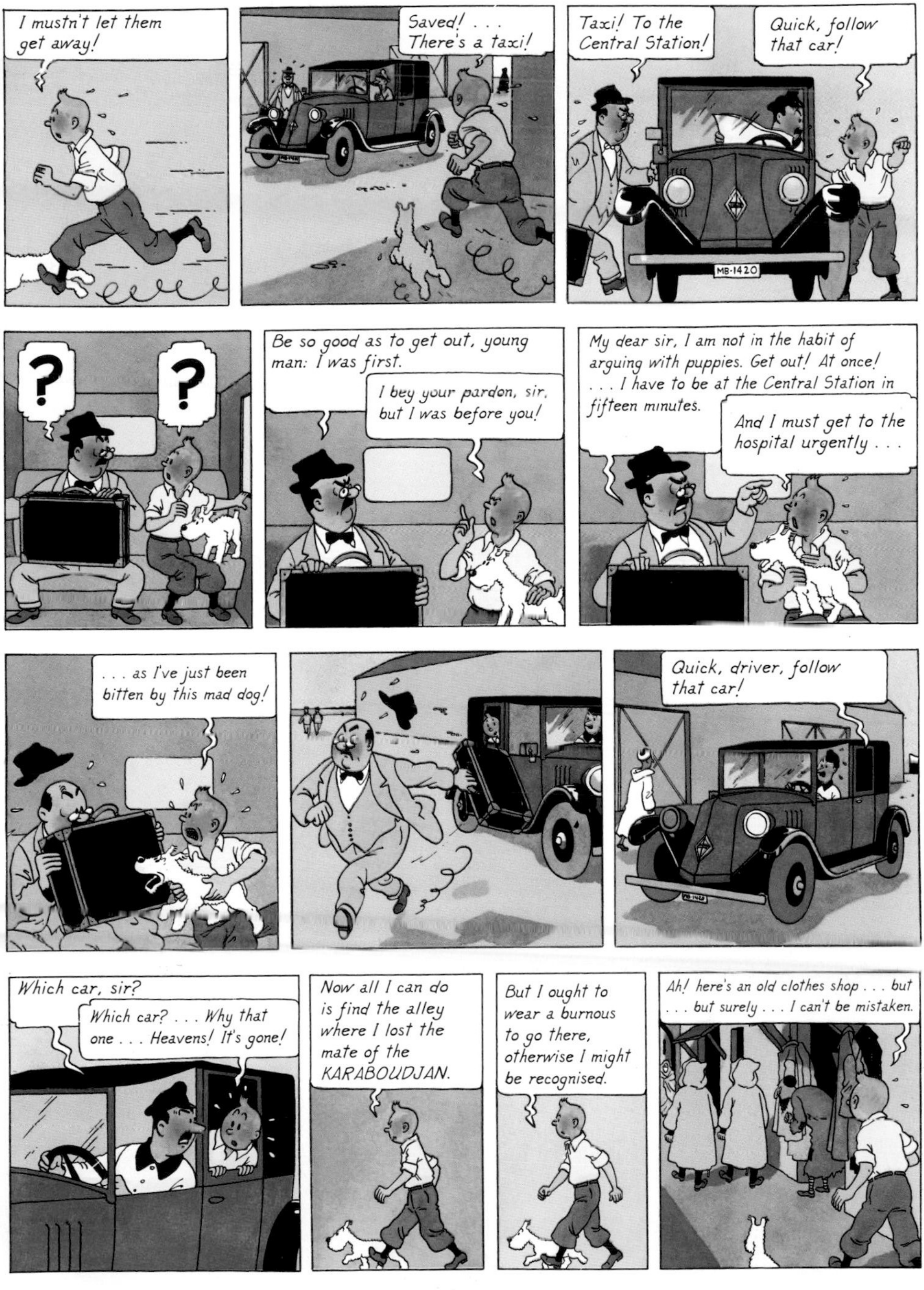
I mustn't let them get away!
Saved! . . . There's a taxi!
Taxi! To the Central Station!
Quick, follow that car!
?
?
Be so good as to get out, young man: I was first.
I beg your pardon, sir, but I was before you!
My dear sir, I am not in the habit of arguing with puppies. Get out! At once! . . . I have to be at the Central Station in fifteen minutes.
And I must get to the hospital urgently . . .
. . . as I've just been bitten by this mad dog!
Quick, driver, follow that car!
Which car, sir?
Which car? . . . Why that one . . . Heavens! It's gone!
Now all I can do is find the alley where I lost the mate of the KARABOUDJAN.
But I ought to wear a burnous to go there, otherwise I might be recognised.
Ah! here's an old clothes shop . . . but . . . but surely . . . I can't be mistaken.

My old friends Thomson and Thompson.

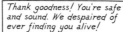

Thank goodness! You're safe and sound. We despaired of ever finding you alive!

I think it's extraordinary, he recognised us at once, in spite of our disguise!

Now tell us: what happened on the KARABOUDJAN? We were amazed when they handed us your wireless signal: 'Have been imprisoned aboard KARABOUDJAN. Am leaving vessel. Cargo includes opium. TINTIN.' We took the first plane for Bagghar . . .

. . . the KARABOUDJAN's next port of call. Then we heard about the shipwreck. Are you certain she was carrying opium?

Quite certain: the drug was hidden in tins bearing a label with a red crab on it, and the words 'EXTRA FINE CRAB'.

Tins of crab? . . . That reminds me . . .

I saw one in the shop where we bought our burnouses just now.

Did you? Quick let's go and see.

It's gone!

What have you done with the tin of crab that was on the table?

!

It's here, sidi. I put tin here in the cupboard.

That's the one! I recognise the label: it's the same.

Open that tin!

!?

There, sidi . . .

Look!

It's crab!

Of course, sidi, there is crab. Good crab, sidi, best quality . . .

Yes, it's crab all right . . . And yet I saw the same tins aboard the KARABOUDJAN, and they contained opium.

Hmm! . . . Very odd.

To be precise: very odd; in fact, very queer . . .

Tell me: where did you buy this tin?

From Mohammed Ben Ali, sidi; the shop on the corner . . .

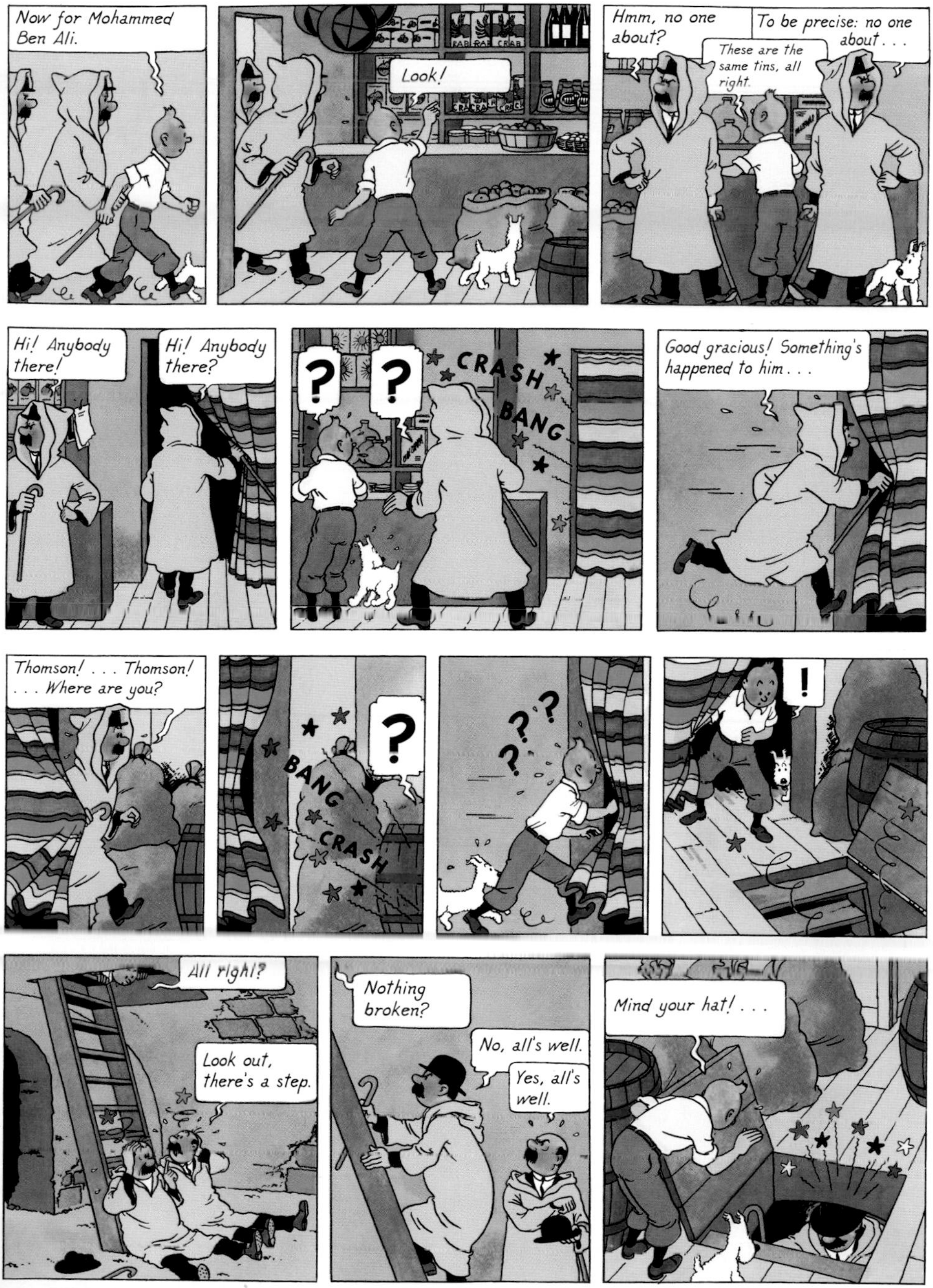

Now for Mohammed Ben Ali.
Look!
Hmm, no one about?
These are the same tins, all right.
To be precise: no one about . . .
Hi! Anybody there!
Hi! Anybody there?
?
?
CRASH
BANG
Good gracious! Something's happened to him . . .
Thomson! . . . Thomson! . . . Where are you?
BANG
CRASH
?
? ? ?
!
All right?
Look out, there's a step.
Nothing broken?
No, all's well.
Yes, all's well.
Mind your hat! . . .

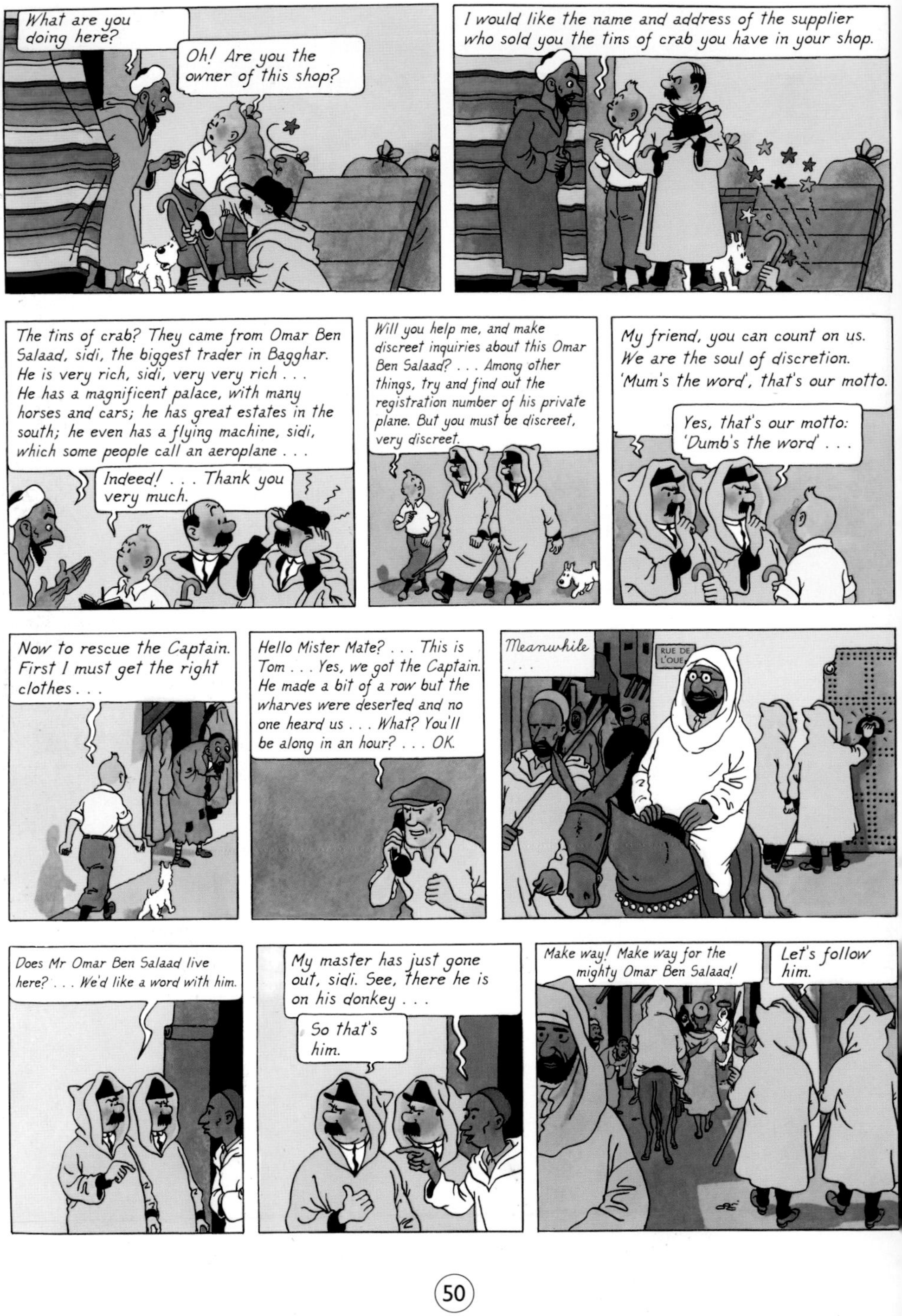
What are you doing here?
Oh! Are you the owner of this shop?
I would like the name and address of the supplier who sold you the tins of crab you have in your shop.
The tins of crab? They came from Omar Ben Salaad, sidi, the biggest trader in Bagghar. He is very rich, sidi, very very rich . . . He has a magnificent palace, with many horses and cars; he has great estates in the south; he even has a flying machine, sidi, which some people call an aeroplane . . .
Indeed! . . . Thank you very much.
Will you help me, and make discreet inquiries about this Omar Ben Salaad? . . . Among other things, try and find out the registration number of his private plane. But you must be discreet, very discreet.
My friend, you can count on us. We are the soul of discretion. 'Mum's the word', that's our motto.
Yes, that's our motto: 'Dumb's the word' . . .
Now to rescue the Captain. First I must get the right clothes . . .
Hello Mister Mate? . . . This is Tom . . . Yes, we got the Captain. He made a bit of a row but the wharves were deserted and no one heard us . . . What? You'll be along in an hour? . . . OK.
Meanwhile . . .
RUE DE L'OUE
Does Mr Omar Ben Salaad live here? . . . We'd like a word with him.
My master has just gone out, sidi. See, there he is on his donkey . . .
So that's him.
Make way! Make way for the mighty Omar Ben Salaad!
Let's follow him.

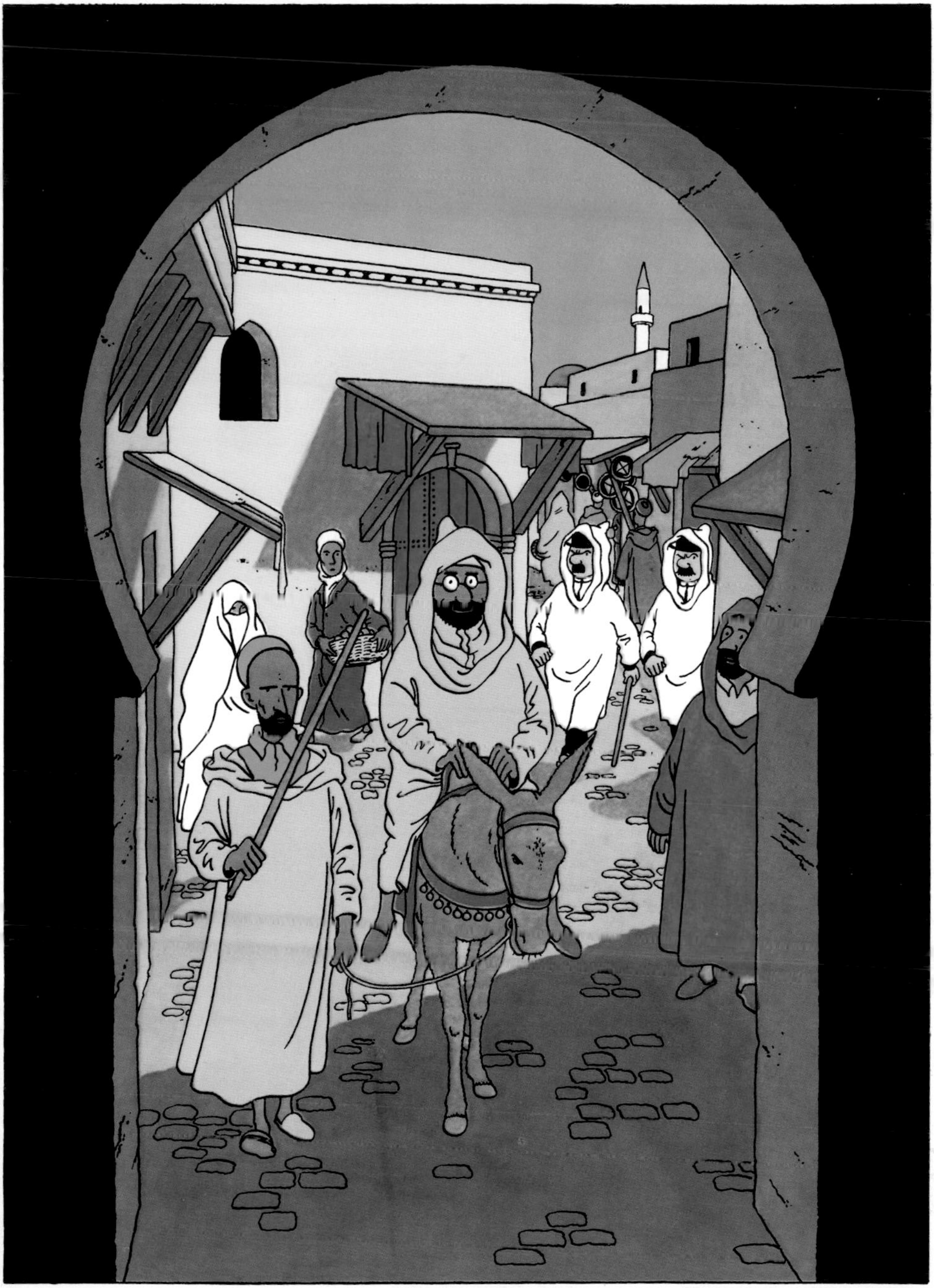

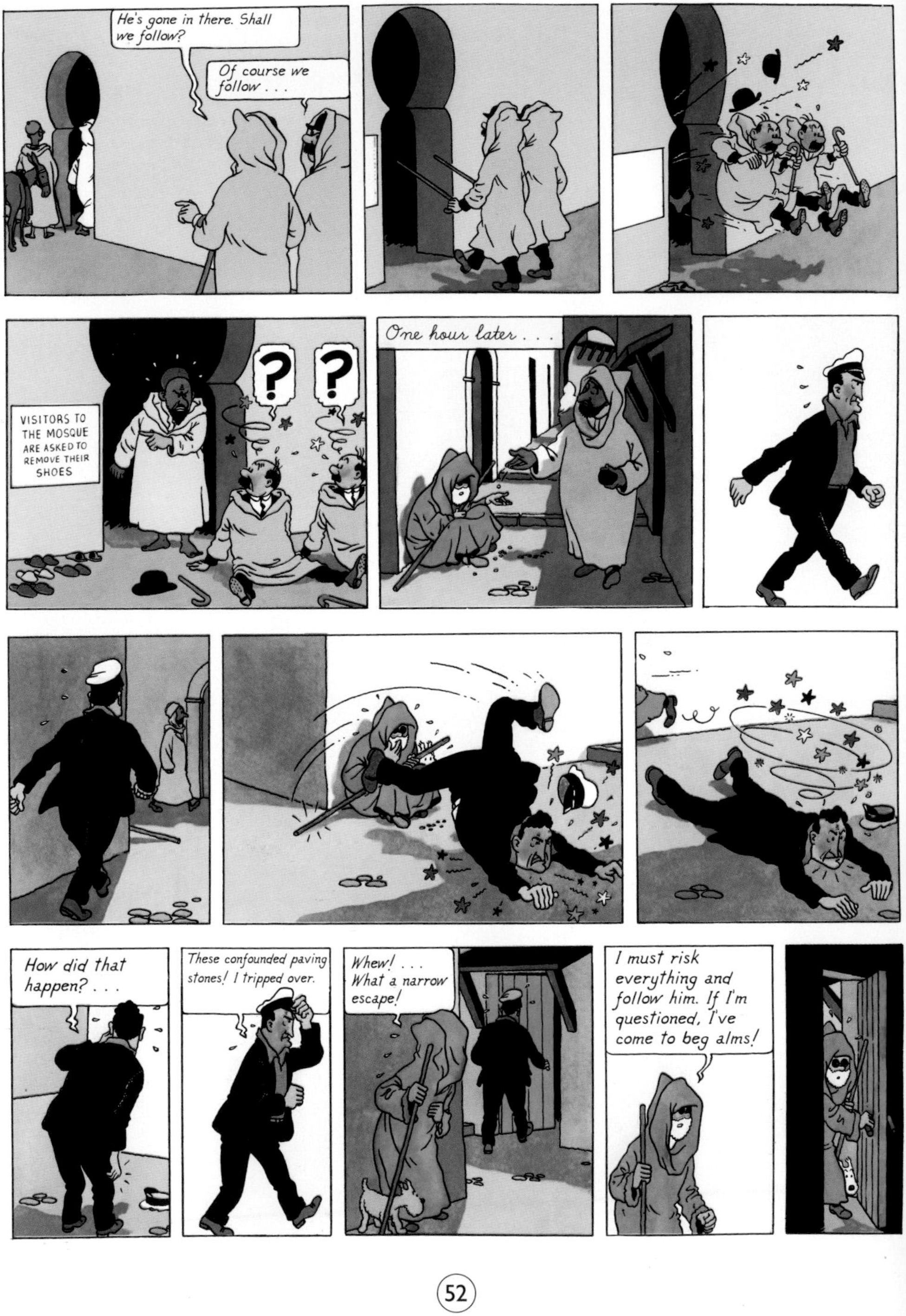

He's gone in there. Shall we follow?
Of course we follow . . .
VISITORS TO THE MOSQUE ARE ASKED TO REMOVE THEIR SHOES
One hour later . . .
How did that happen? . . .
These confounded paving stones! I tripped over.
Whew! . . . What a narrow escape!
I must risk everything and follow him. If I'm questioned, I've come to beg alms!

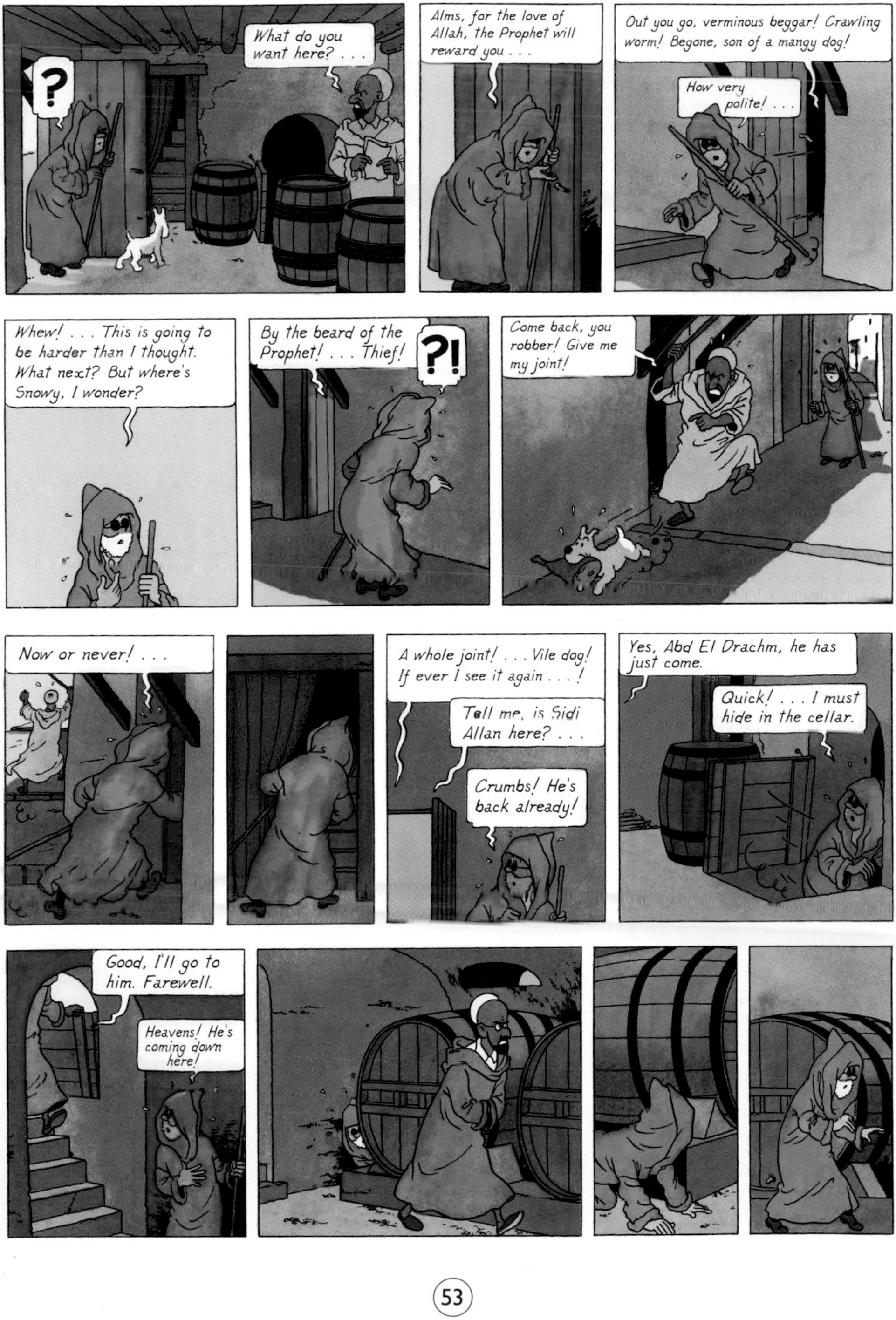
?
What do you want here? . . .
Alms, for the love of Allah, the Prophet will reward you . . .
Out you go, verminous beggar! Crawling worm! Begone, son of a mangy dog!
How very polite! . . .
Whew! . . . This is going to be harder than I thought. What next? But where's Snowy, I wonder?
By the beard of the Prophet! . . . Thief!
?!
Come back, you robber! Give me my joint!
Now or never! . . .
A whole joint! . . . Vile dog! If ever I see it again . . . !
Tell me, is Sidi Allan here? . . .
Crumbs! He's back already!
Yes, Abd El Drachm, he has just come.
Quick! . . . I must hide in the cellar.
Good, I'll go to him. Farewell.
Heavens! He's coming down here!

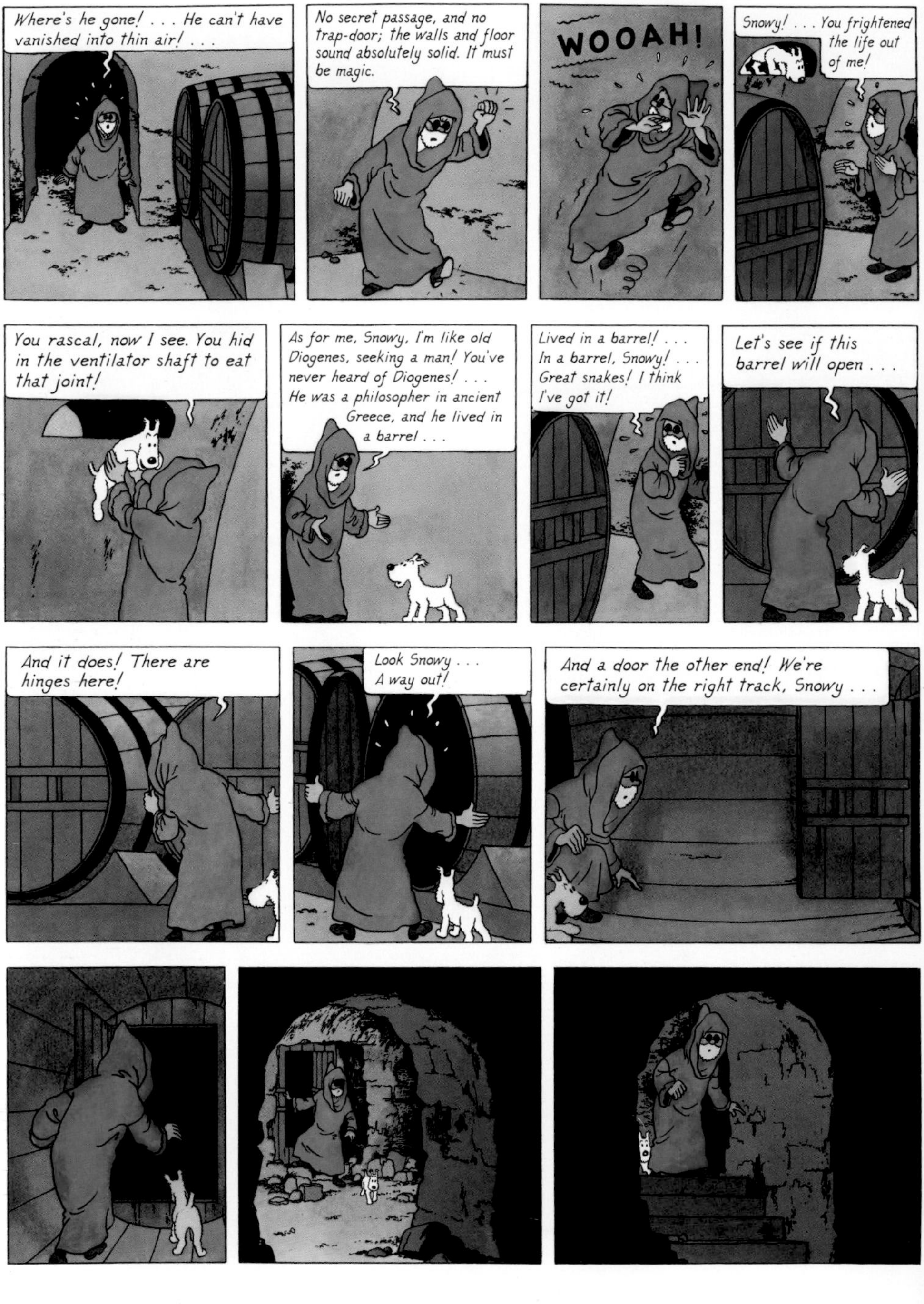
Where's he gone! . . . He can't have vanished into thin air! . . .
No secret passage, and no trap-door; the walls and floor sound absolutely solid. It must be magic.
WOOAH!
Snowy! . . . You frightened the life out of me!
You rascal, now I see. You hid in the ventilator shaft to eat that joint!
As for me, Snowy, I'm like old Diogenes, seeking a man! You've never heard of Diogenes! . . . He was a philosopher in ancient Greece, and he lived in a barrel . . .
Lived in a barrel! . . . In a barrel, Snowy! . . . Great snakes! I think I've got it!
Let's see if this barrel will open . . .
And it does! There are hinges here!
Look Snowy . . . A way out!
And a door the other end! We're certainly on the right track, Snowy . . .

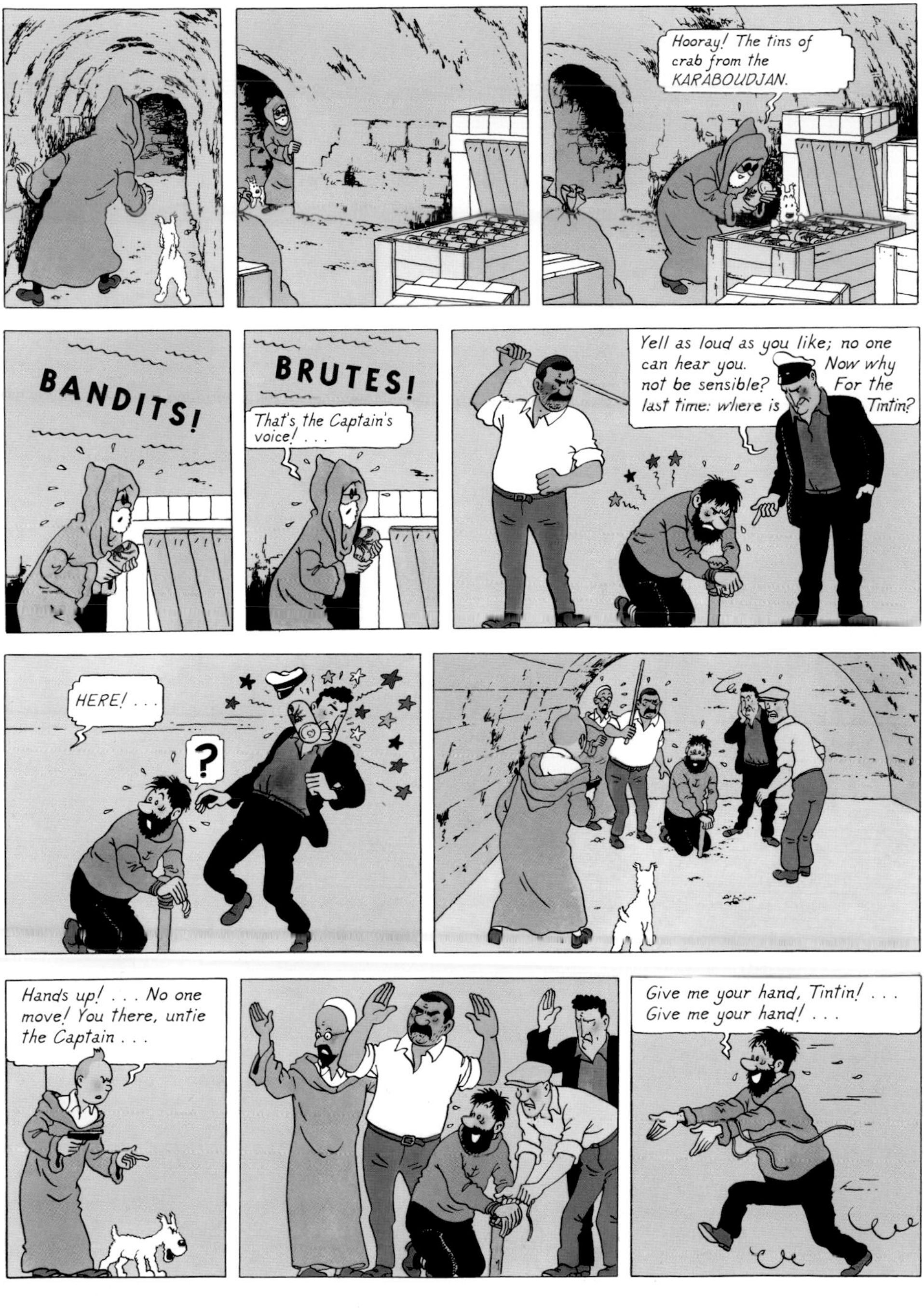

Hooray! The tins of crab from the KARABOUDJAN.
BANDITS!
BRUTES!
That's the Captain's voice! . . .
Yell as loud as you like; no one can hear you. Now why not be sensible? For the last time: where is Tintin?
HERE! . . .
?
Hands up! . . . No one move! You there, untie the Captain . . .
Give me your hand, Tintin! . . . Give me your hand! . . .

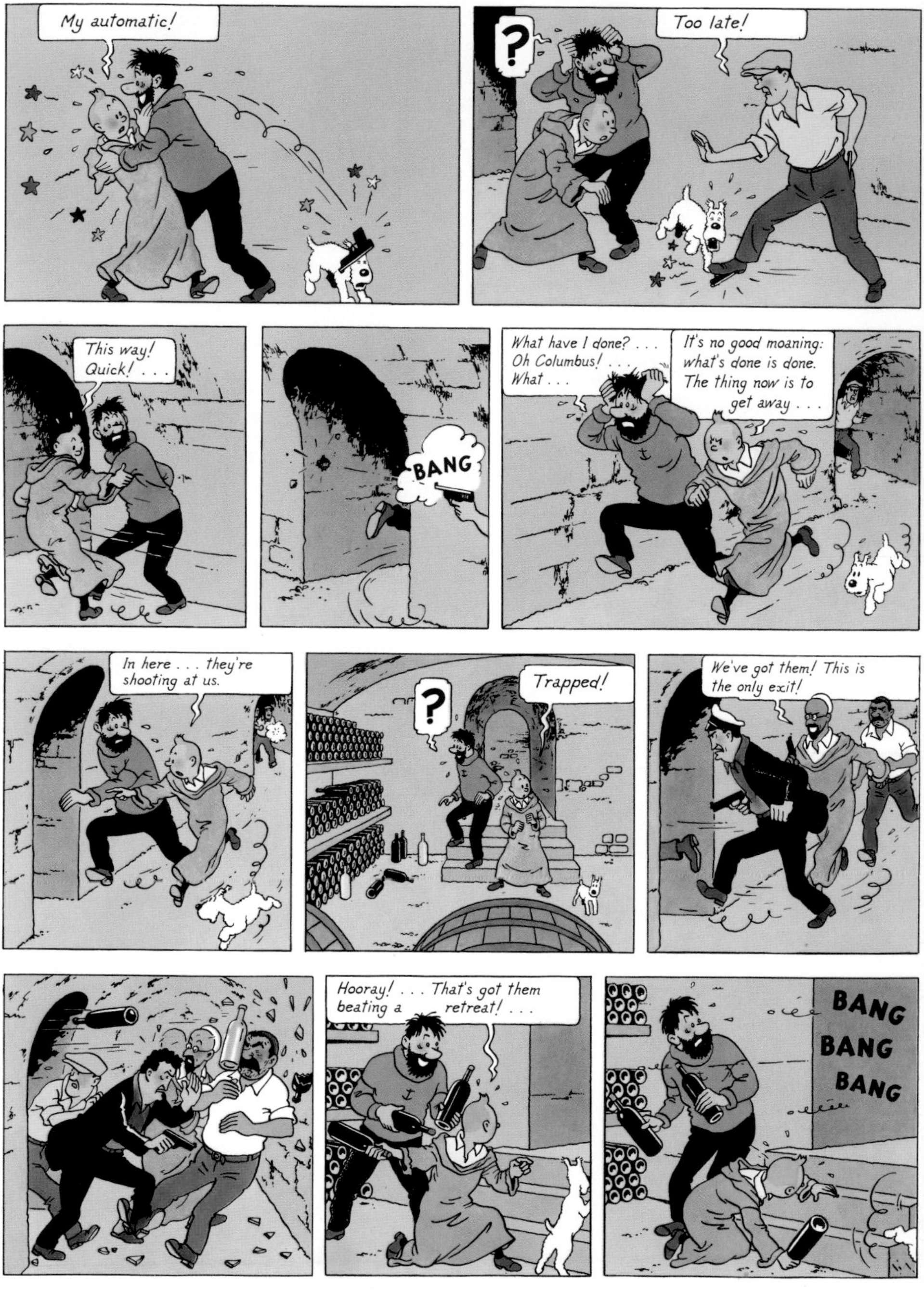

My automatic!
?
Too late!
This way! Quick! . . .
BANG
What have I done? . . . Oh Columbus! . . . What . . .
It's no good moaning: what's done is done. The thing now is to get away . . .
In here . . . they're shooting at us.
?
Trapped!
We've got them! This is the only exit!
Hooray! . . . That's got them beating a retreat! . . .
BANG
BANG
BANG

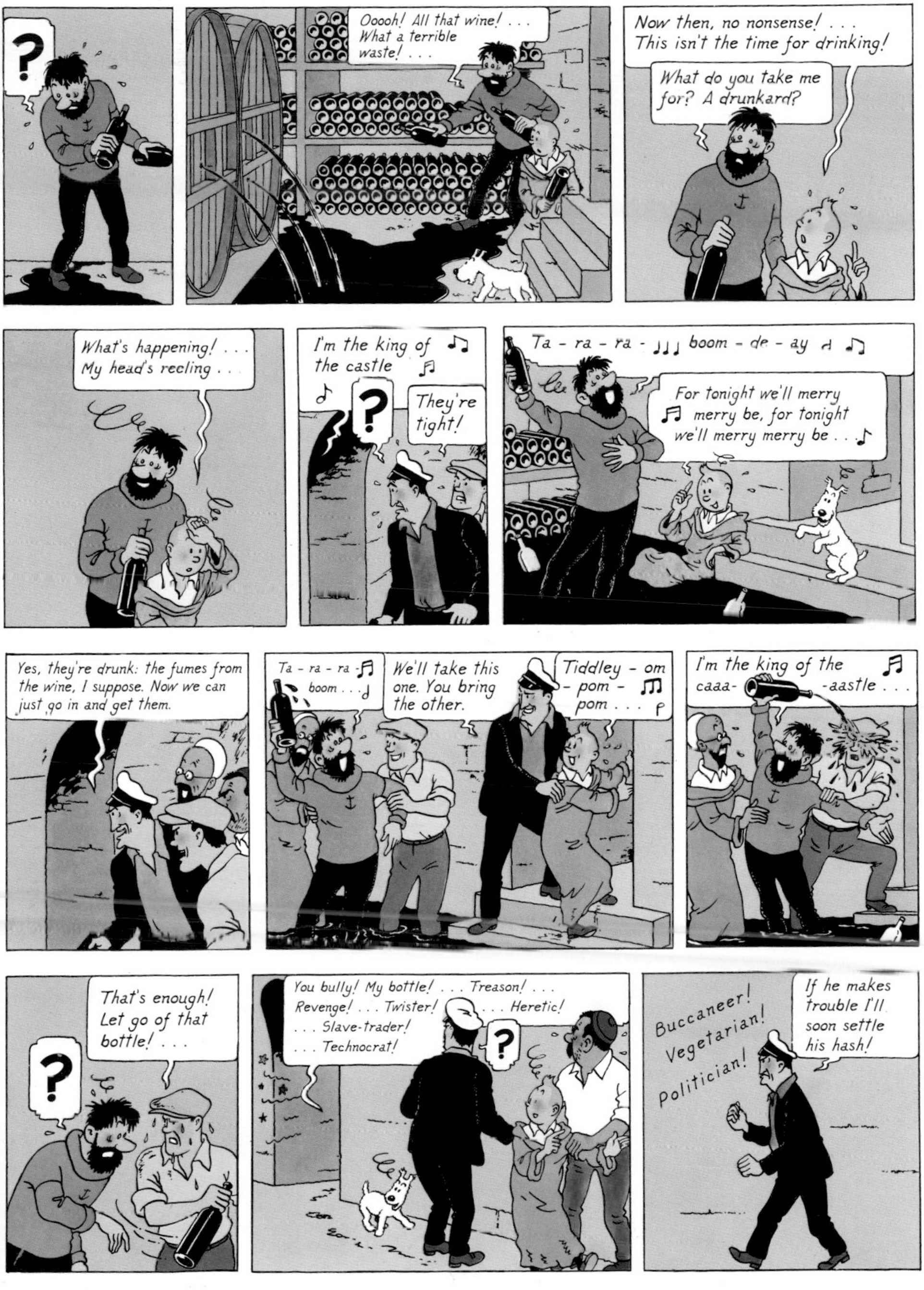
?
Ooooh! All that wine! . . . What a terrible waste! . . .
Now then, no nonsense! . . . This isn't the time for drinking!
What do you take me for? A drunkard?
What's happening! . . . My head's reeling . . .
I'm the king of the castle
?
They're tight!
Ta - ra - ra - boom - de - ay
For tonight we'll merry merry be, for tonight we'll merry merry be . . .
Yes, they're drunk: the fumes from the wine, I suppose. Now we can just go in and get them.
Ta - ra - ra - boom . . .
We'll take this one. You bring the other.
Tiddley - om - pom - pom . . .
I'm the king of the caaa- -aastle . . .
?
That's enough! Let go of that bottle! . . .
You bully! My bottle! . . . Treason! . . . Revenge! . . . Twister! . . . Heretic! . . . Slave-trader! . . . Technocrat!
?
Buccaneer! Vegetarian! Politician!
If he makes trouble I'll soon settle his hash!

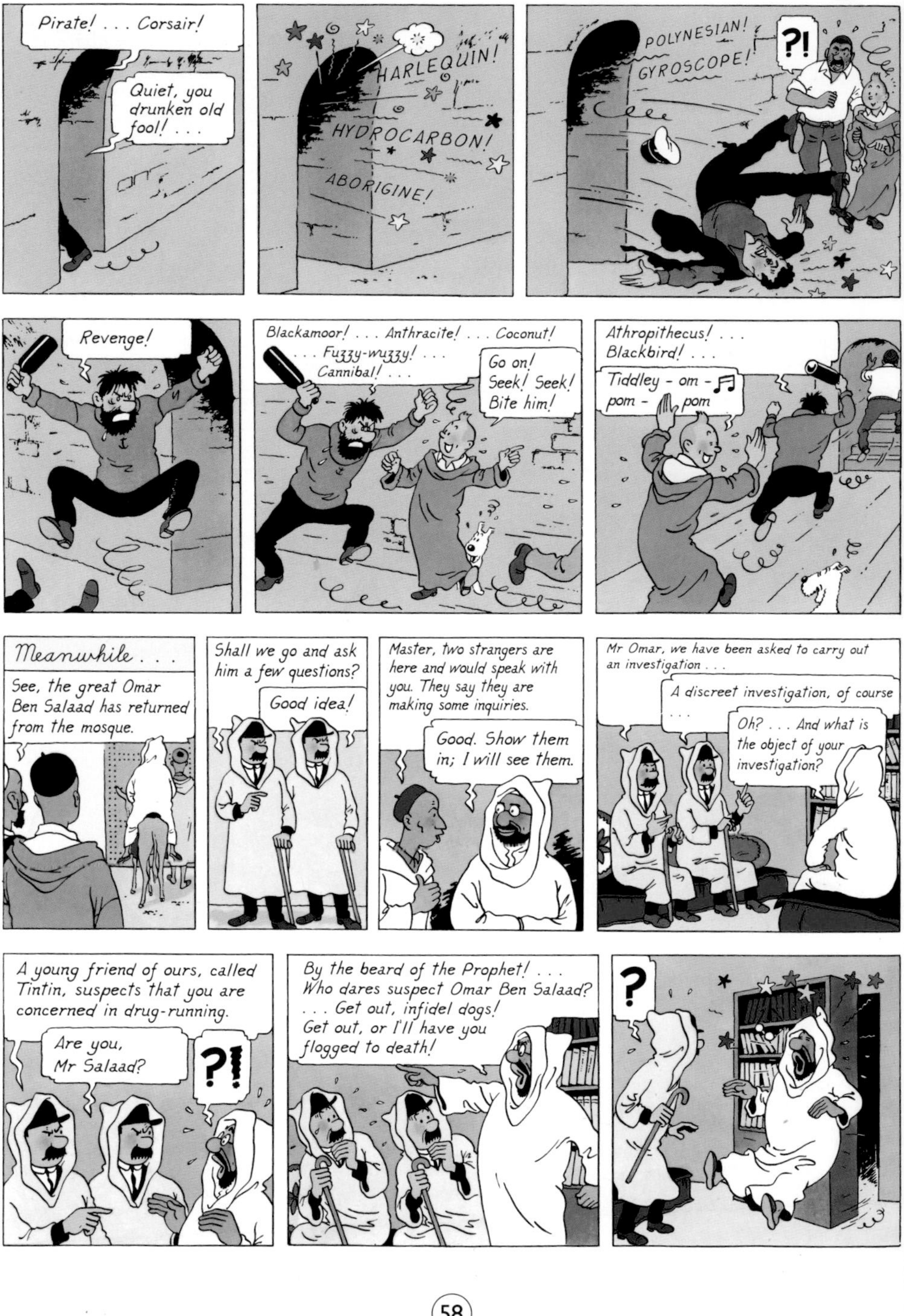
Pirate! . . . Corsair!
Quiet, you drunken old fool! . . .
HARLEQUIN!
HYDROCARBON!
ABORIGINE!
POLYNESIAN!
GYROSCOPE!
?!
Revenge!
Blackamoor! . . . Anthracite! . . . Coconut! . . . Fuzzy-wuzzy! . . . Cannibal! . . .
Go on! Seek! Seek! Bite him!
Athropithecus! . . . Blackbird! . . .
Tiddley - om - pom - pom
Meanwhile . . .
See, the great Omar Ben Salaad has returned from the mosque.
Shall we go and ask him a few questions?
Good idea!
Master, two strangers are here and would speak with you. They say they are making some inquiries.
Good. Show them in; I will see them.
Mr Omar, we have been asked to carry out an investigation . . .
A discreet investigation, of course . . .
Oh? . . . And what is the object of your investigation?
A young friend of ours, called Tintin, suspects that you are concerned in drug-running.
Are you, Mr Salaad?
?!
By the beard of the Prophet! . . . Who dares suspect Omar Ben Salaad? . . . Get out, infidel dogs! Get out, or I'll have you flogged to death!
?

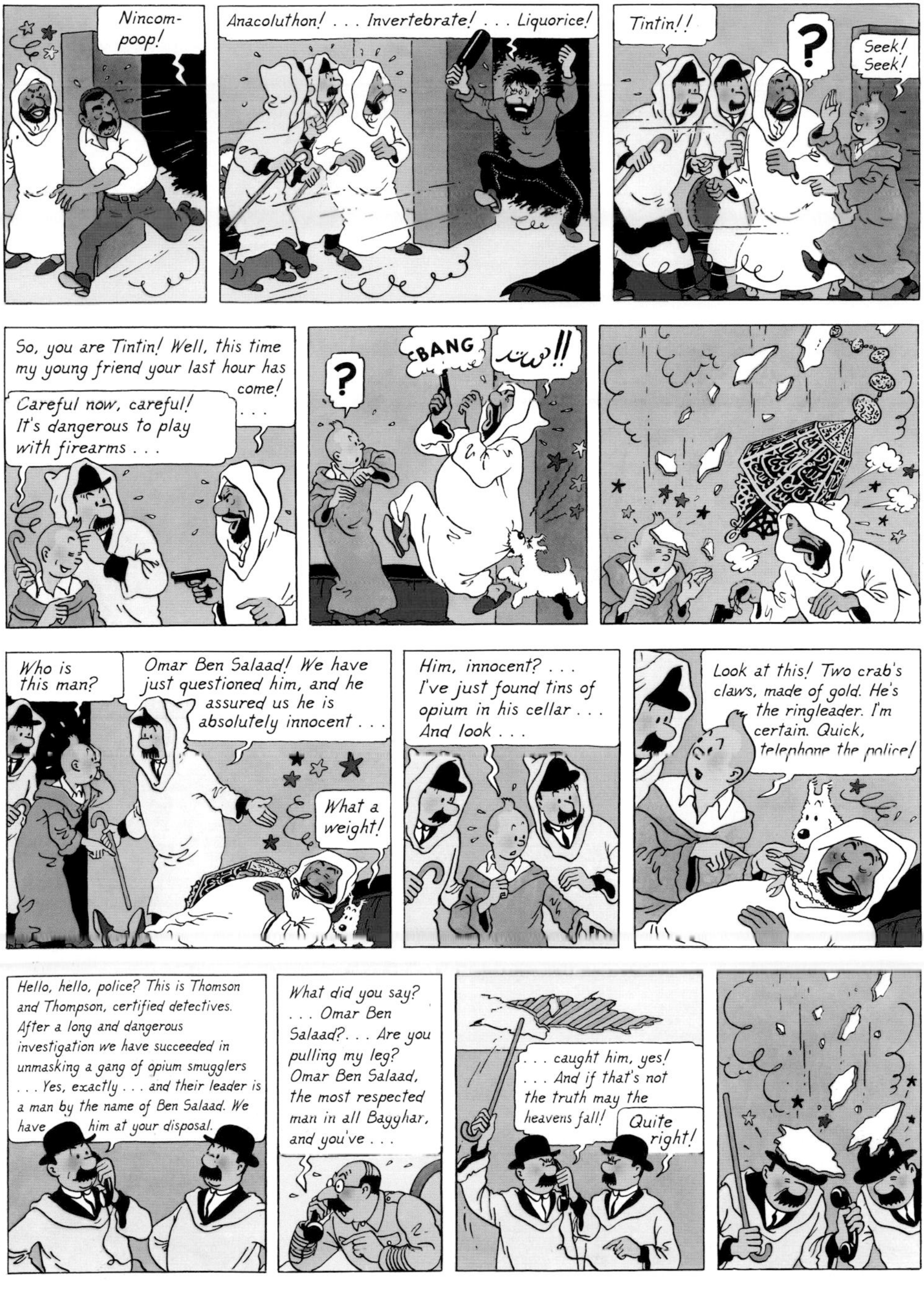
Nincom-poop!
Anacoluthon! . . . Invertebrate! . . . Liquorice!
Tintin!!
?
Seek! Seek!
So, you are Tintin! Well, this time my young friend your last hour has come! . . .
Careful now, careful! It's dangerous to play with firearms . . .
?
BANG
!!
Who is this man?
Omar Ben Salaad! We have just questioned him, and he assured us he is absolutely innocent . . .
What a weight!
Him, innocent? . . . I've just found tins of opium in his cellar . . . And look . . .
Look at this! Two crab's claws, made of gold. He's the ringleader. I'm certain. Quick, telephone the police!
Hello, hello, police? This is Thomson and Thompson, certified detectives. After a long and dangerous investigation we have succeeded in unmasking a gang of opium smugglers . . . Yes, exactly . . . and their leader is a man by the name of Ben Salaad. We have him at your disposal.
What did you say? . . . Omar Ben Salaad? . . . Are you pulling my leg? Omar Ben Salaad, the most respected man in all Bagghar, and you've . . .
. . . caught him, yes! . . . And if that's not the truth may the heavens fall!
Quite right!

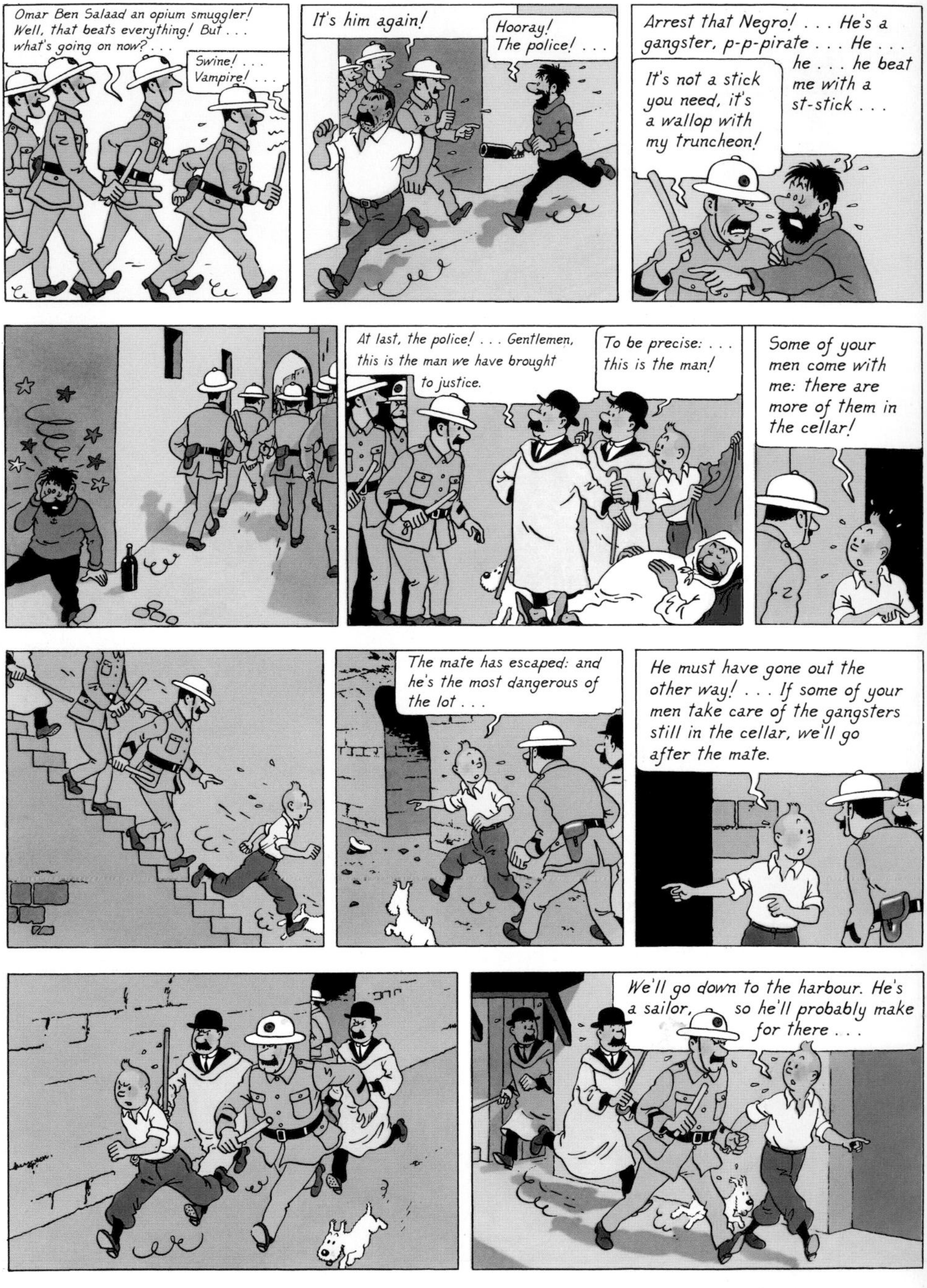
Omar Ben Salaad an opium smuggler! Well, that beats everything! But . . . what's going on now? . . .
Swine! . . . Vampire! . . .
It's him again!
Hooray! The police! . . .
Arrest that Negro! . . . He's a gangster, p-p-pirate . . . He . . . he . . . he beat me with a st-stick . . .
It's not a stick you need, it's a wallop with my truncheon!
At last, the police! . . . Gentlemen, this is the man we have brought to justice.
To be precise: . . . this is the man!
Some of your men come with me: there are more of them in the cellar!
The mate has escaped: and he's the most dangerous of the lot . . .
He must have gone out the other way! . . . If some of your men take care of the gangsters still in the cellar, we'll go after the mate.
We'll go down to the harbour. He's a sailor, so he'll probably make for there . . .

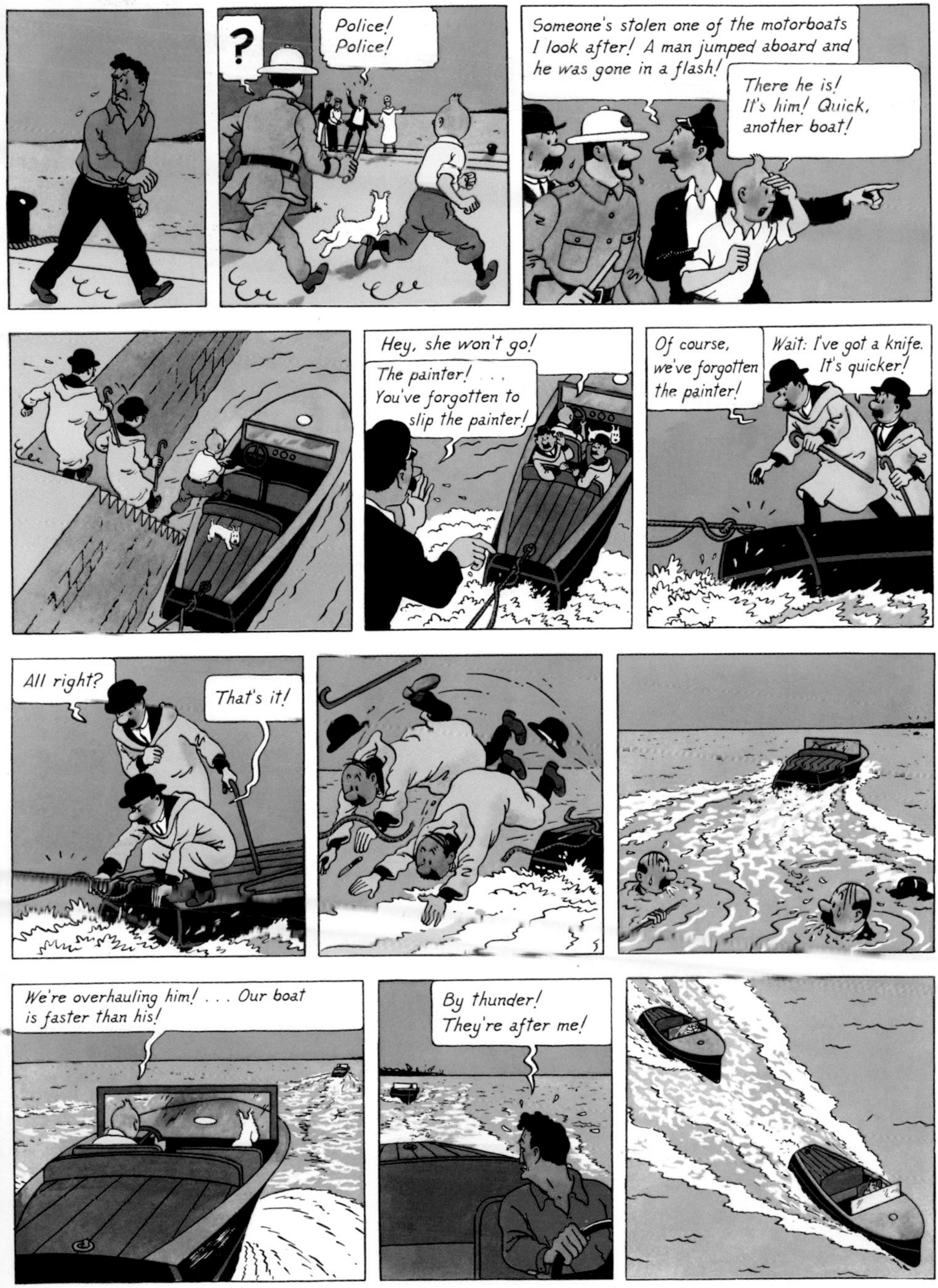
Police!
Police!
Someone's stolen one of the motorboats I look after! A man jumped aboard and he was gone in a flash!
There he is! It's him! Quick, another boat!
Hey, she won't go!
The painter! . . . You've forgotten to slip the painter!
Of course, we've forgotten the painter!
Wait: I've got a knife. It's quicker!
All right?
That's it!
We're overhauling him! . . . Our boat is faster than his!
By thunder! They're after me!

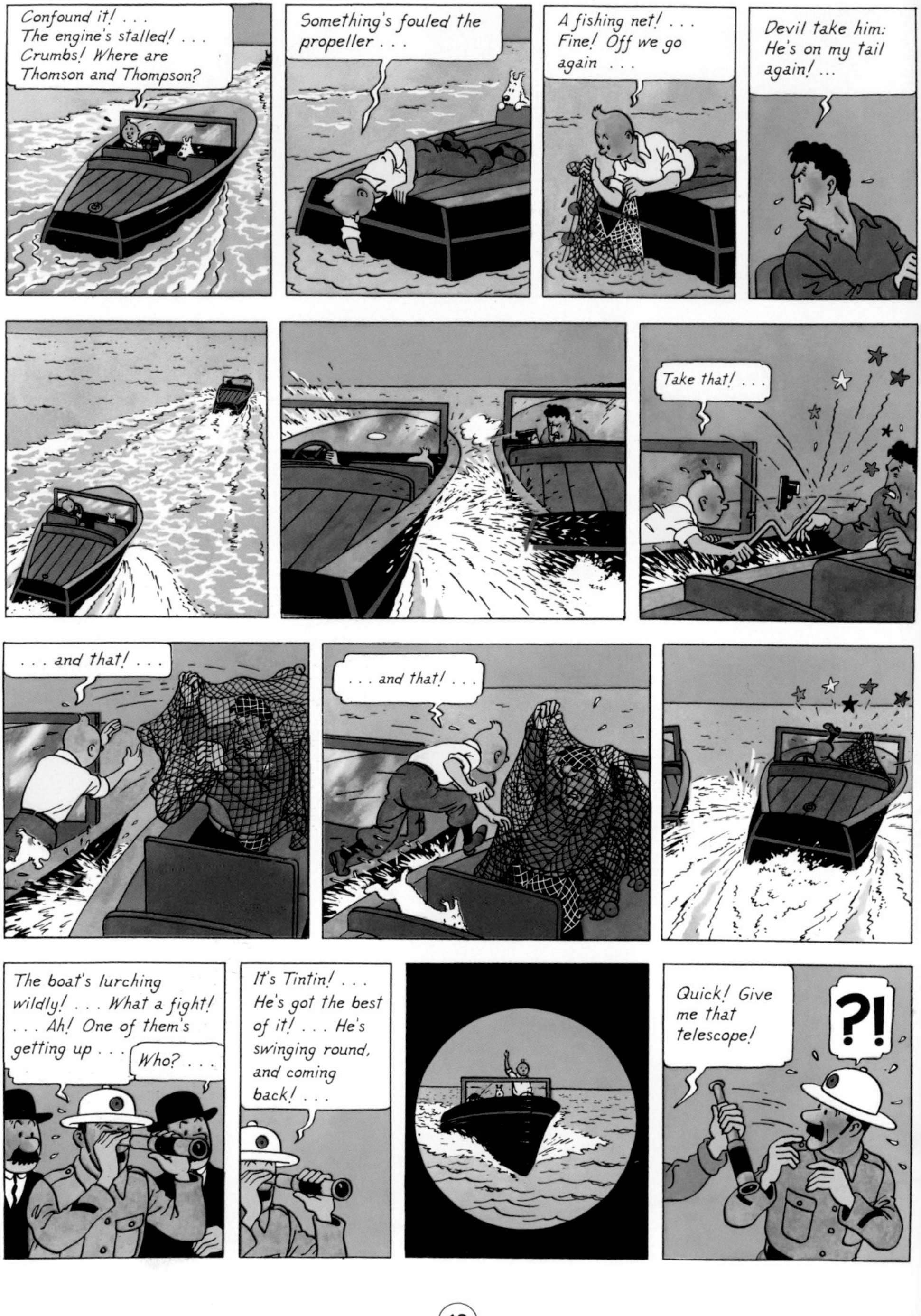
Confound it! . . . The engine's stalled! . . . Crumbs! Where are Thomson and Thompson?
Something's fouled the propeller . . .
A fishing net! . . . Fine! Off we go again . . .
Devil take him: He's on my tail again! ...
Take that! . . .
. . . and that! . . .
. . . and that! . . .
The boat's lurching wildly! . . . What a fight! . . . Ah! One of them's getting up . . .
Who? . . .
It's Tintin! . . . He's got the best of it! . . . He's swinging round, and coming back! . . .
Quick! Give me that telescope!
?!

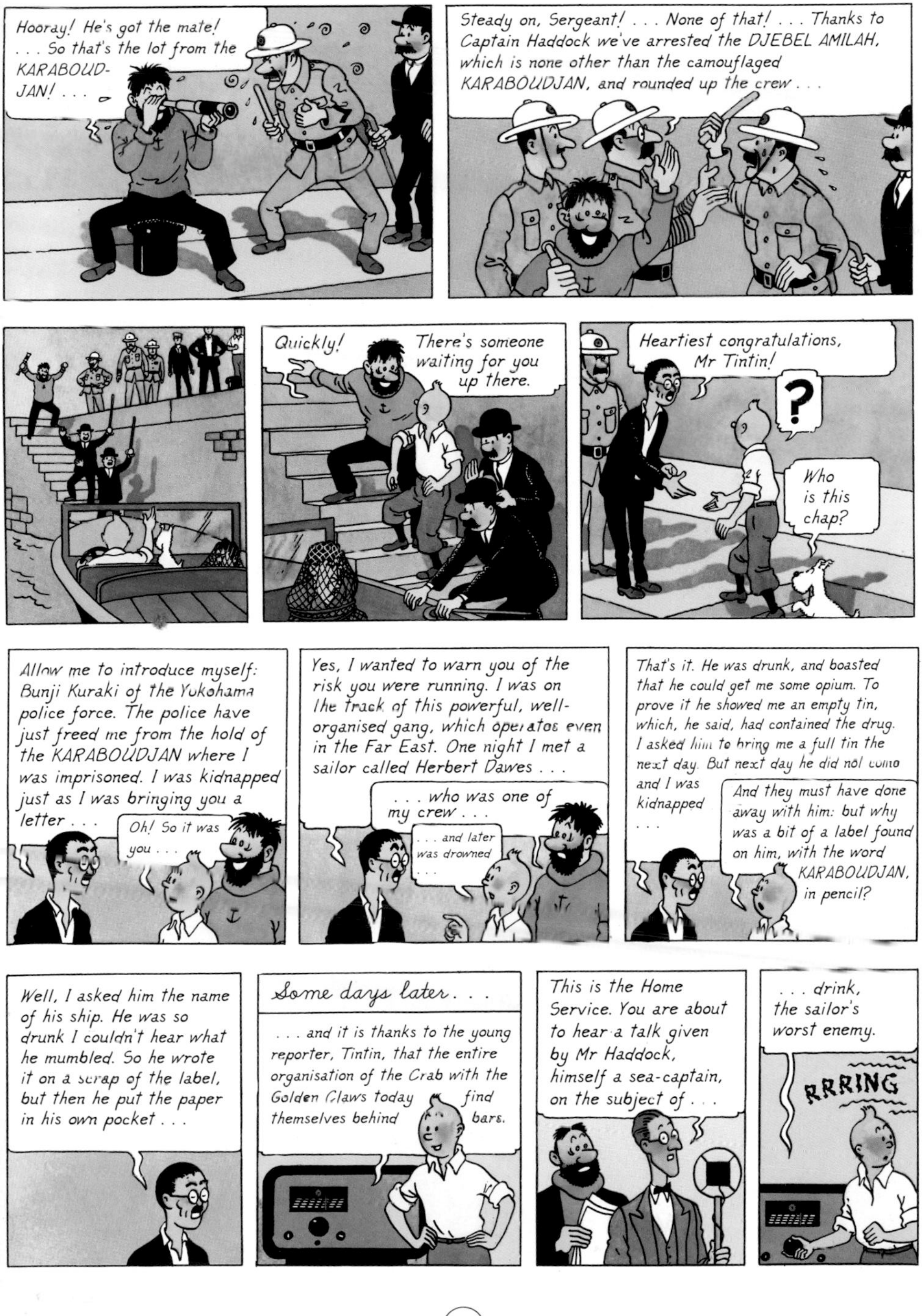
Hooray! He's got the mate! . . . So that's the lot from the KARABOUDJAN! . . .
Steady on, Sergeant! . . . None of that! . . . Thanks to Captain Haddock we've arrested the DJEBEL AMILAH, which is none other than the camouflaged KARABOUDJAN, and rounded up the crew . . .
Quickly!
There's someone waiting for you up there.
Heartiest congratulations, Mr Tintin!
?
Who is this chap?
Allow me to introduce myself: Bunji Kuraki of the Yokohama police force. The police have just freed me from the hold of the KARABOUDJAN where I was imprisoned. I was kidnapped just as I was bringing you a letter . . .
Oh! So it was you . . .
Yes, I wanted to warn you of the risk you were running. I was on the track of this powerful, well-organised gang, which operates even in the Far East. One night I met a sailor called Herbert Dawes . . .
. . . who was one of my crew . . .
. . . and later was drowned . . .
That's it. He was drunk, and boasted that he could get me some opium. To prove it he showed me an empty tin, which, he said, had contained the drug. I asked him to bring me a full tin the next day. But next day he did not come and I was kidnapped . . .
And they must have done away with him: but why was a bit of a label found on him, with the word KARABOUDJAN, in pencil?
Well, I asked him the name of his ship. He was so drunk I couldn't hear what he mumbled. So he wrote it on a scrap of the label, but then he put the paper in his own pocket . . .
Some days later . . .
. . . and it is thanks to the young reporter, Tintin, that the entire organisation of the Crab with the Golden Claws today find themselves behind bars.
This is the Home Service. You are about to hear a talk given by Mr Haddock, himself a sea-captain, on the subject of . . .
. . . drink, the sailor's worst enemy.
RRRING

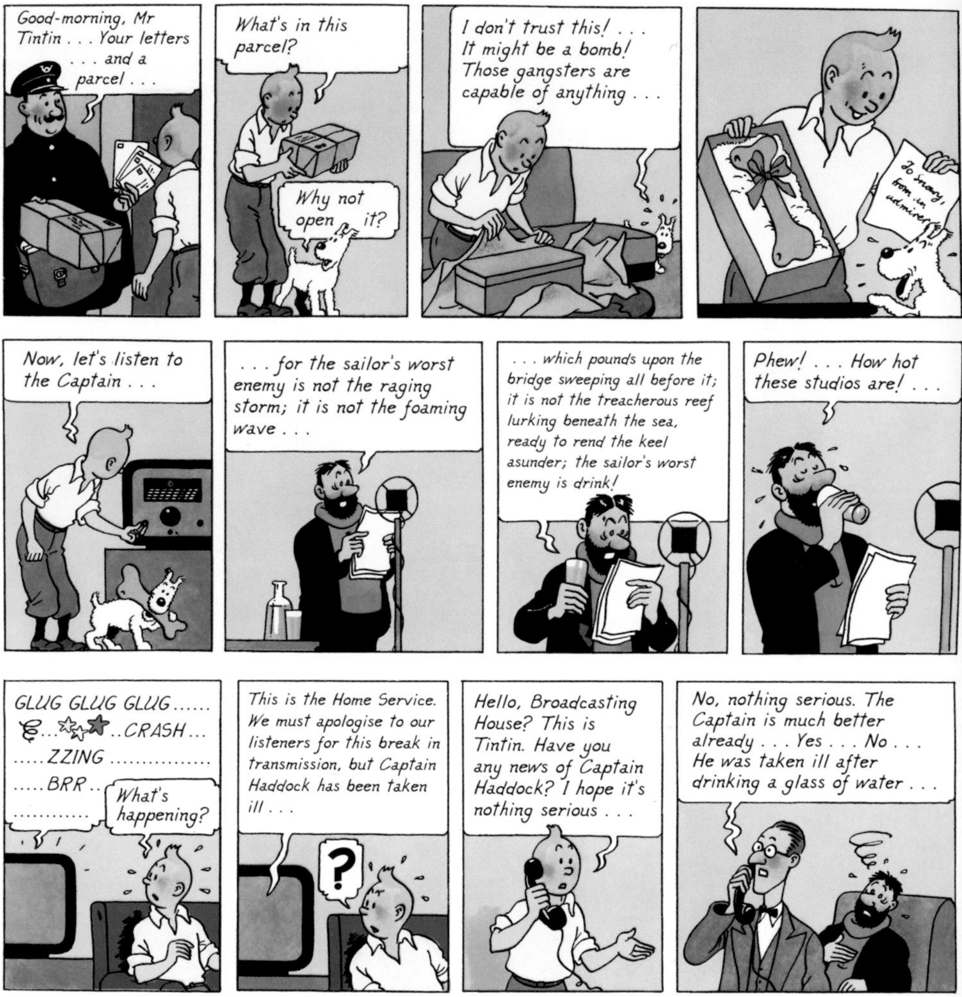
Good-morning, Mr Tintin . . . Your letters . . . and a parcel . . .
What's in this parcel?
Why not open it?
I don't trust this! . . . It might be a bomb! Those gangsters are capable of anything . . .
Now, let's listen to the Captain . . .
. . . for the sailor's worst enemy is not the raging storm; it is not the foaming wave . . .
. . . which pounds upon the bridge sweeping all before it; it is not the treacherous reef lurking beneath the sea, ready to rend the keel asunder; the sailor's worst enemy is drink!
Phew! . . . How hot these studios are! . . .
GLUG GLUG GLUG ....CRASH ... . ZZING .... BRR .. ..
What's happening?
This is the Home Service. We must apologise to our listeners for this break in transmission, but Captain Haddock has been taken ill . . .
?
Hello, Broadcasting House? This is Tintin. Have you any news of Captain Haddock? I hope it's nothing serious . . .
No, nothing serious. The Captain is much better already . . . Yes . . . No . . . He was taken ill after drinking a glass of water . . .

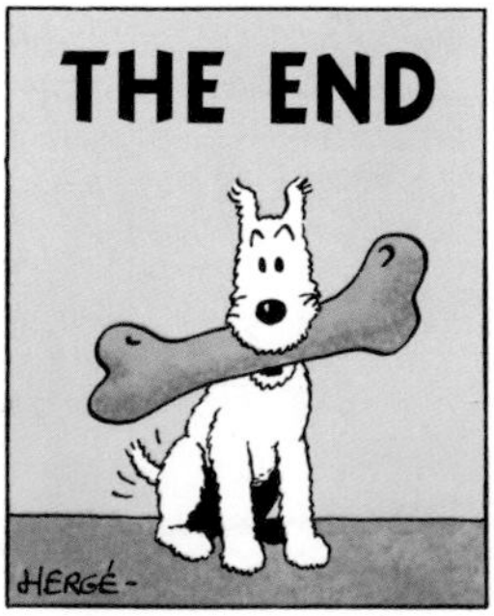
THE END
HERGÉ

HERGÉ

★

THE ADVENTURES OF

TINTIN

★

THE SHOOTING STAR

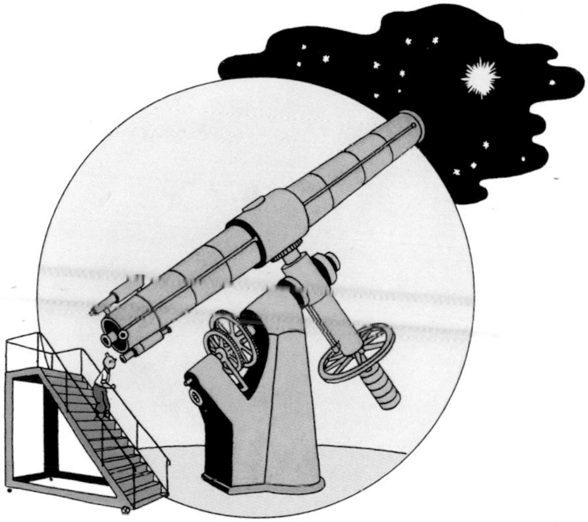

LB

LITTLE, BROWN AND COMPANY

New York Boston

THE SHOOTING STAR

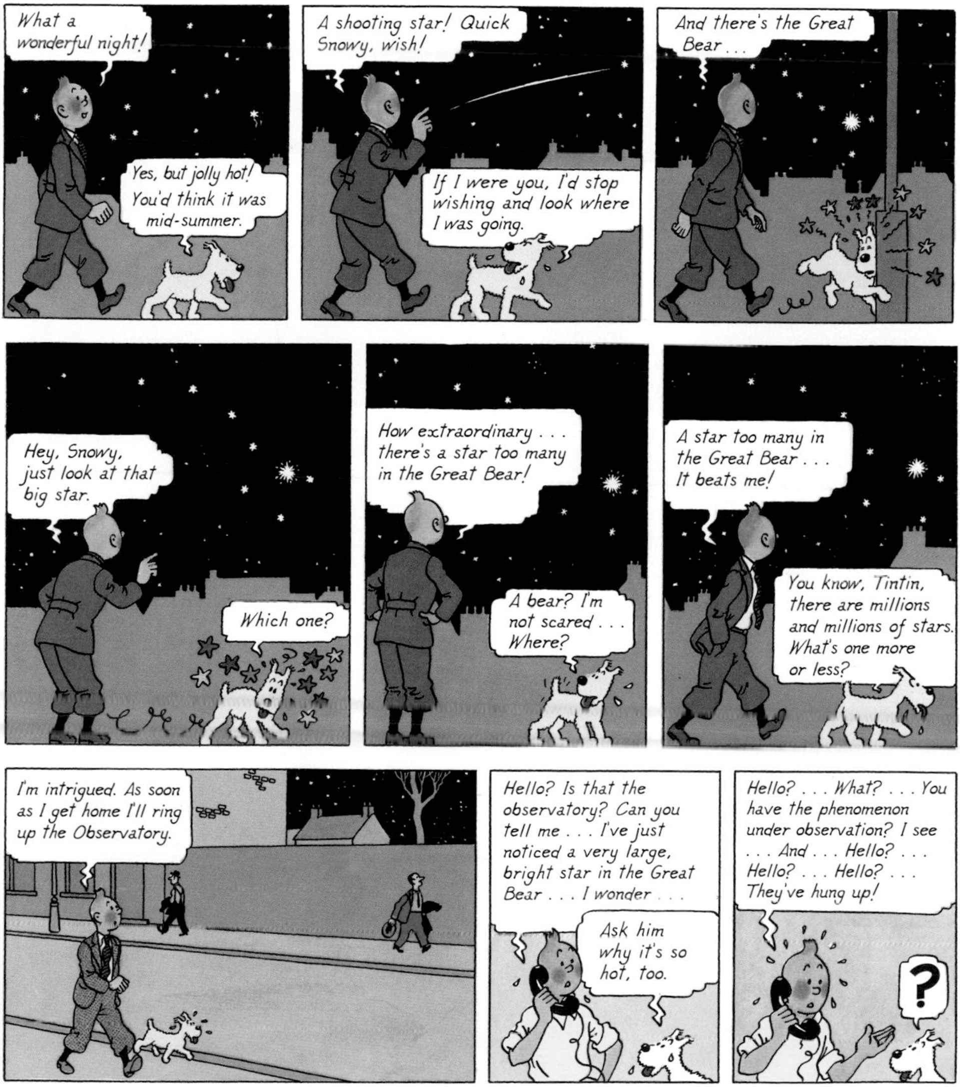

What a wonderful night!
Yes, but jolly hot! You'd think it was mid-summer.
A shooting star! Quick Snowy, wish!
If I were you, I'd stop wishing and look where I was going.
And there's the Great Bear . . .
Hey, Snowy, just look at that big star.
Which one?
How extraordinary . . . there's a star too many in the Great Bear!
A bear? I'm not scared . . . Where?
A star too many in the Great Bear . . . It beats me!
You know, Tintin, there are millions and millions of stars. What's one more or less?
I'm intrigued. As soon as I get home I'll ring up the Observatory.
Hello? Is that the observatory? Can you tell me . . . I've just noticed a very large, bright star in the Great Bear . . . I wonder . . .
Ask him why it's so hot, too.
Hello? . . . What? . . . You have the phenomenon under observation? I see . . . And . . . Hello? . . . Hello? . . . Hello? . . . They've hung up!
?

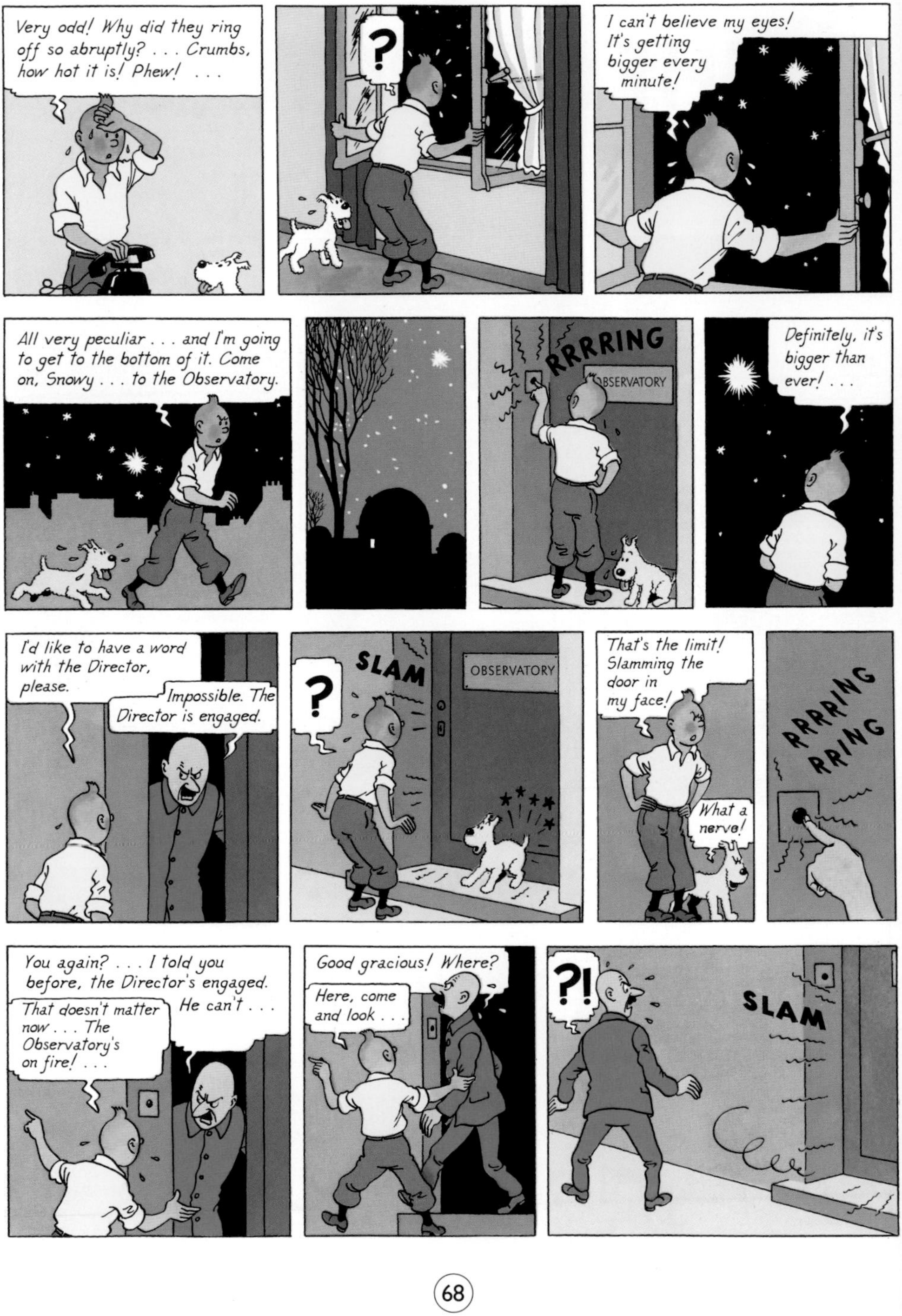
Very odd! Why did they ring off so abruptly? . . . Crumbs, how hot it is! Phew! . . .
?
I can't believe my eyes! It's getting bigger every minute!
All very peculiar . . . and I'm going to get to the bottom of it. Come on, Snowy . . . to the Observatory.
RRRRING
OBSERVATORY
Definitely, it's bigger than ever! . . .
I'd like to have a word with the Director, please.
Impossible. The Director is engaged.
SLAM
?
OBSERVATORY
That's the limit! Slamming the door in my face!
What a nerve!
RRRRING
RRING
You again? . . . I told you before, the Director's engaged. He can't . . .
That doesn't matter now . . . The Observatory's on fire! . . .
Good gracious! Where?
Here, come and look . . .
?!
SLAM

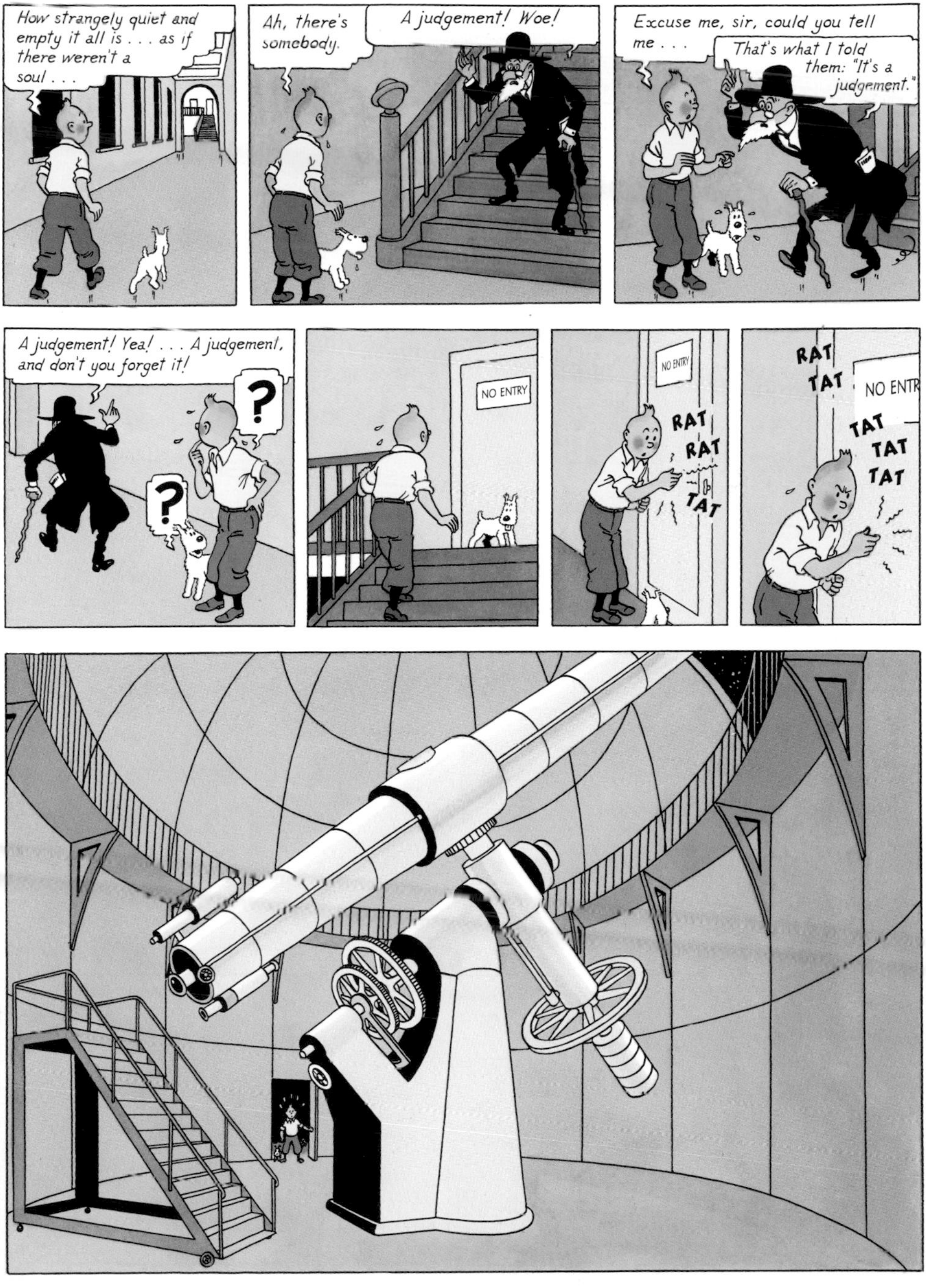
How strangely quiet and empty it all is . . . as if there weren't a soul . . .
Ah, there's somebody.
A judgement! Woe!
Excuse me, sir, could you tell me . . .
That's what I told them: "It's a judgement."
A judgement! Yea! . . . A judgement, and don't you forget it!
?
?
NO ENTRY
NO ENTRY
RAT RAT TAT
RAT TAT
NO ENTR
TAT TAT TAT

Excuse me, I'm looking for the Director of the Observatory.

Ssh! It's me!

It's me, but ssh! . . . Silence! Don't disturb my colleague; he's deep in some very complicated mathematics. While he's finishing, have a look through the telescope, if you like; it's a sight worth seeing.

Let's have a look.

OH!

?

Good heavens, sir! It's horrible . . . horrible!

Yes, in one sense it's horrible . . .

It's enormous! Simply enormous!

Enormous, yes!

And its hairy legs! . . . It makes me shiver to think of them!

Its legs? . . . What legs?

What legs? . . . Why, belonging to that gigantic spider . . .

Spider? . . . Is this your idea of a joke young man?

Come and see for yourself!

By the rings of Saturn! . . . You're right . . . It is, quite definitely, a spider! . . .

You see now!

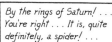

How extraordinary! Extraordinary! . . . It has characteristics of Meta segmentata . . . At least . . . No! It's an Araneus diadematus! An enormous Araneus diadematus!

Anyway, it's a spider! Ugh! What a monster! . . . And it's travelling through space . . . Supposing it . . . ??

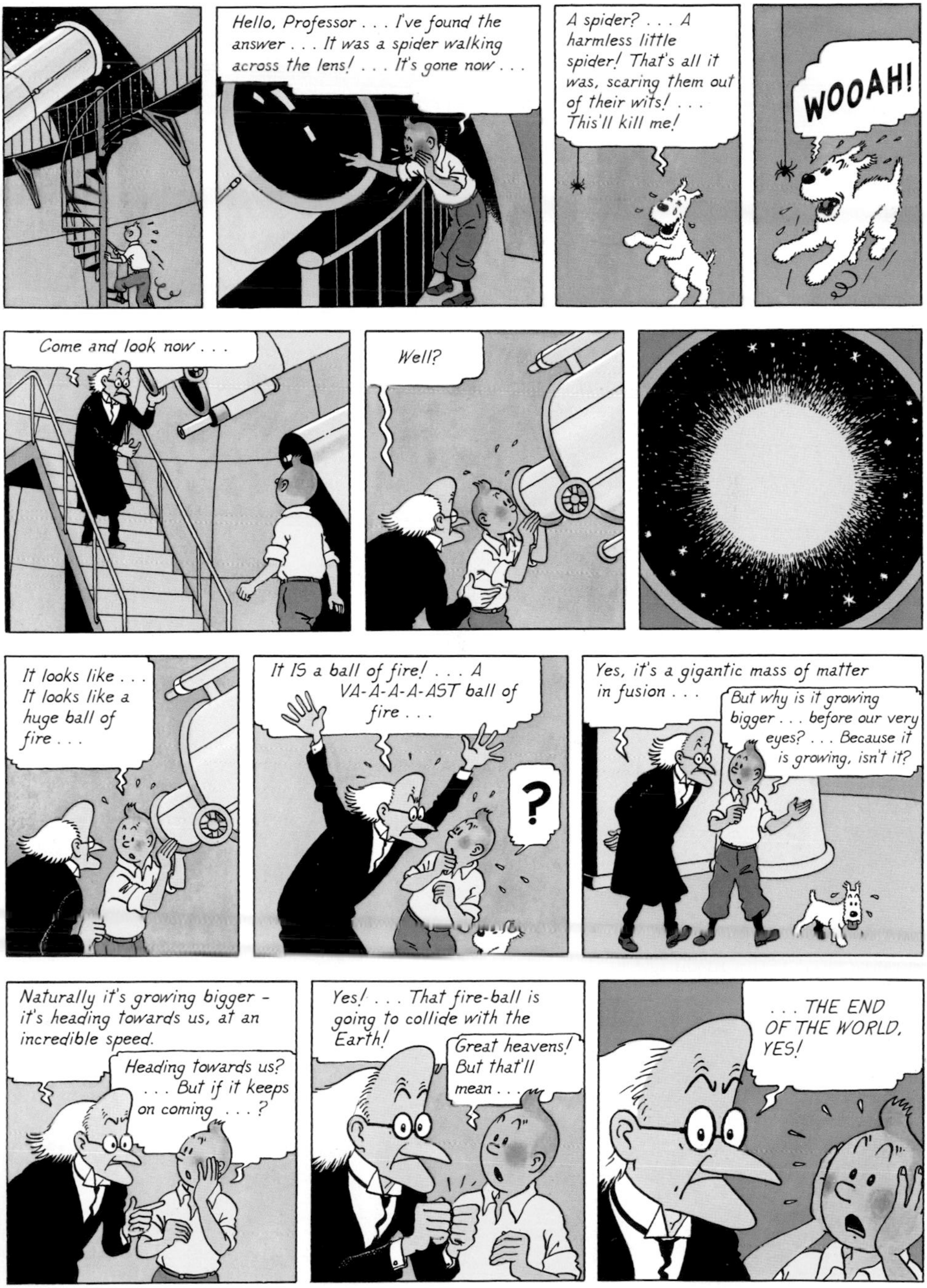
Hello, Professor . . . I've found the answer . . . It was a spider walking across the lens! . . . It's gone now . . .
A spider? . . . A harmless little spider! That's all it was, scaring them out of their wits! . . . This'll kill me!
WOOAH!
Come and look now . . .
Well?
It looks like . . . It looks like a huge ball of fire . . .
It IS a ball of fire! . . . A VA-A-A-AST ball of fire . . .
?
Yes, it's a gigantic mass of matter in fusion . . .
But why is it growing bigger . . . before our very eyes? . . . Because it is growing, isn't it?
Naturally it's growing bigger - it's heading towards us, at an incredible speed.
Heading towards us? . . . But if it keeps on coming . . . ?
Yes! . . . That fire-ball is going to collide with the Earth!
Great heavens! But that'll mean . . .
. . . THE END OF THE WORLD, YES!

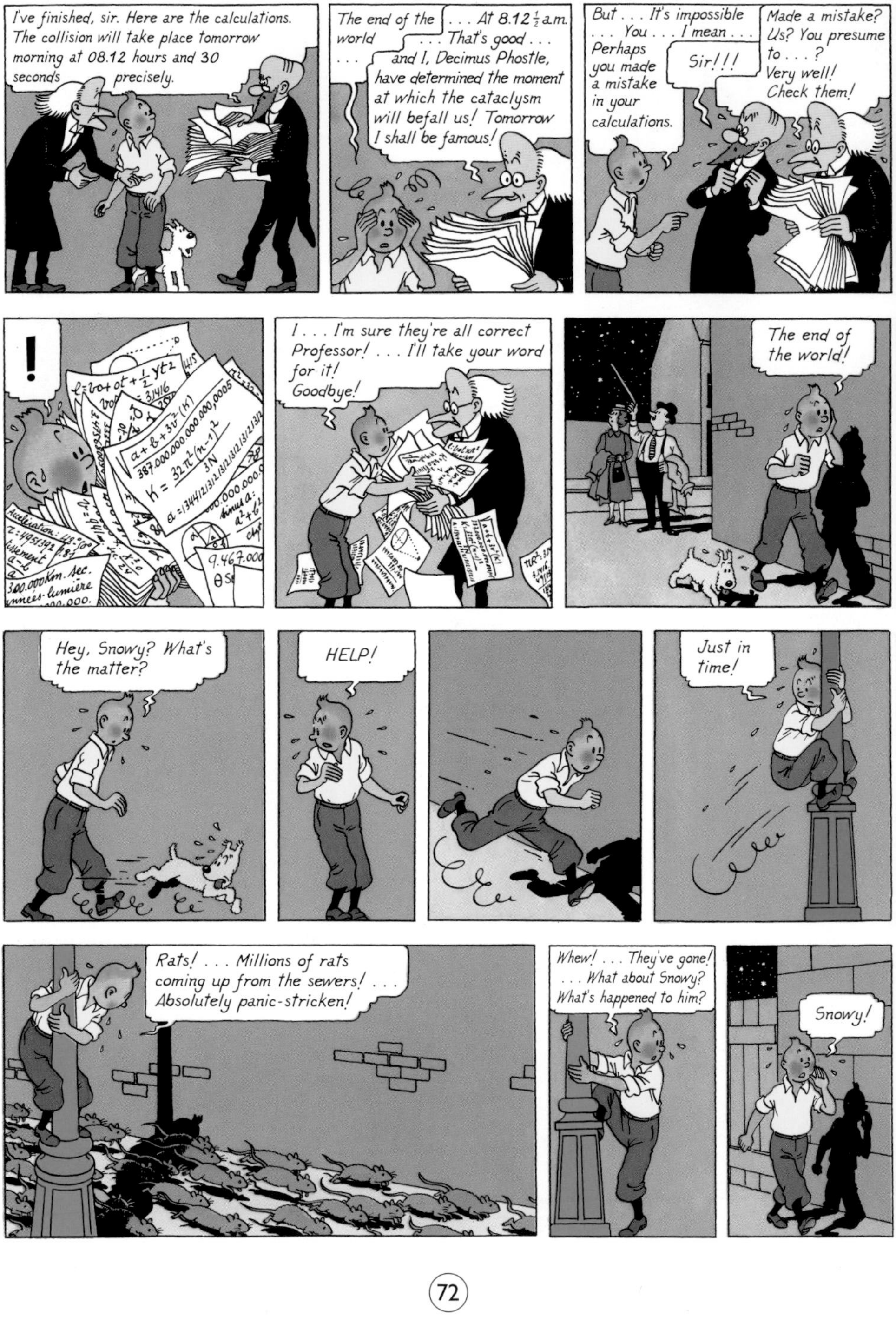

I've finished, sir. Here are the calculations. The collision will take place tomorrow morning at 08.12 hours and 30 seconds precisely.
The end of the world . . .
. . . At 8.12 ½ a.m. . . . That's good . . . and I, Decimus Phostle, have determined the moment at which the cataclysm will befall us! Tomorrow I shall be famous!
But . . . It's impossible . . . You . . . I mean . . . Perhaps you made a mistake in your calculations.
Sir!!!
Made a mistake? Us? You presume to . . . ? Very well! Check them!
!
I . . . I'm sure they're all correct Professor! . . . I'll take your word for it! Goodbye!
The end of the world!
Hey, Snowy? What's the matter?
HELP!
Just in time!
Rats! . . . Millions of rats coming up from the sewers! . . . Absolutely panic-stricken!
Whew! . . . They've gone! . . . What about Snowy? What's happened to him?
Snowy!

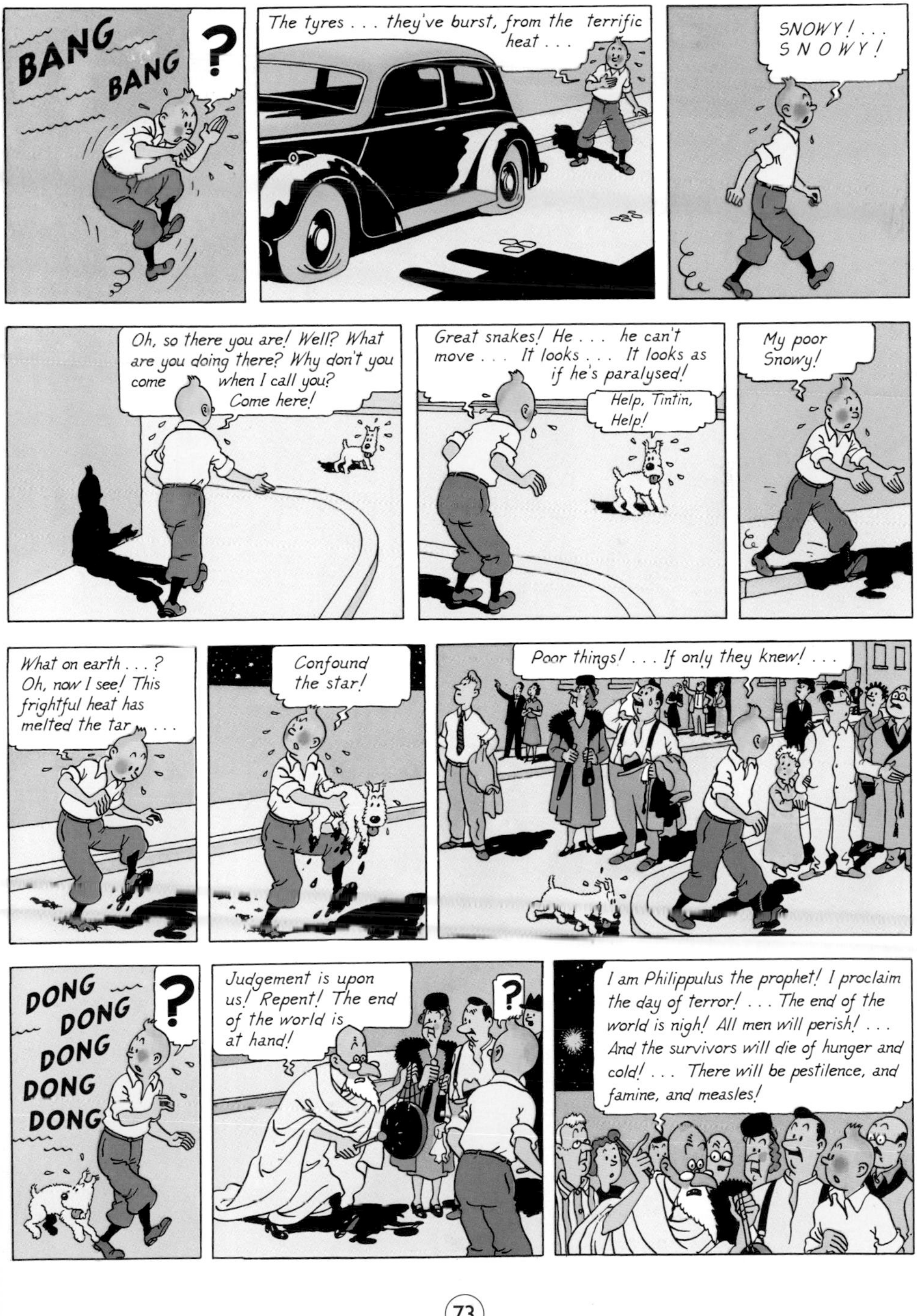

BANG
BANG
?
The tyres . . . they've burst, from the terrific heat . . .
SNOWY! . . . SNOWY!
Oh, so there you are! Well? What are you doing there? Why don't you come when I call you? Come here!
Great snakes! He . . . he can't move . . . It looks . . . It looks as if he's paralysed!
Help, Tintin, Help!
My poor Snowy!
What on earth . . . ? Oh, now I see! This frightful heat has melted the tar . . .
Confound the star!
Poor things! . . . If only they knew! . . .
DONG
DONG
DONG
DONG
DONG
?
Judgement is upon us! Repent! The end of the world is at hand!
?
I am Philippulus the prophet! I proclaim the day of terror! . . . The end of the world is nigh! All men will perish! . . . And the survivors will die of hunger and cold! . . . There will be pestilence, and famine, and measles!

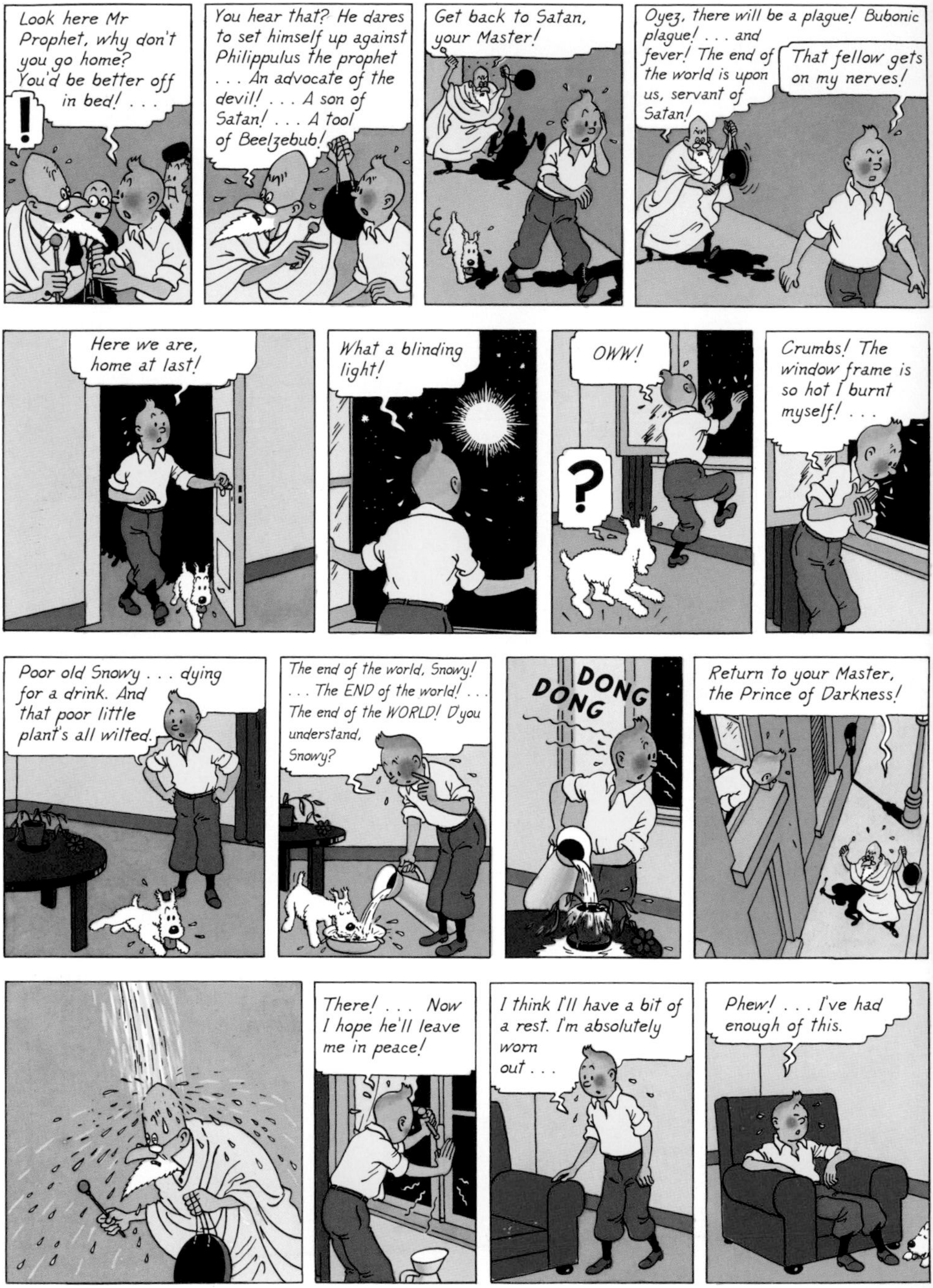
Look here Mr Prophet, why don't you go home? You'd be better off in bed! . . .
!
You hear that? He dares to set himself up against Philippulus the prophet . . . An advocate of the devil! . . . A son of Satan! . . . A tool of Beelzebub!
Get back to Satan, your Master!
Oyez, there will be a plague! Bubonic plague! . . . and fever! The end of the world is upon us, servant of Satan!
That fellow gets on my nerves!
Here we are, home at last!
What a blinding light!
OWW!
?
Crumbs! The window frame is so hot I burnt myself! . . .
Poor old Snowy . . . dying for a drink. And that poor little plant's all wilted.
The end of the world, Snowy! . . . The END of the world! . . . The end of the WORLD! D'you understand, Snowy?
DONG
DONG
Return to your Master, the Prince of Darkness!
There! . . . Now I hope he'll leave me in peace!
I think I'll have a bit of a rest. I'm absolutely worn out . . .
Phew! . . . I've had enough of this.

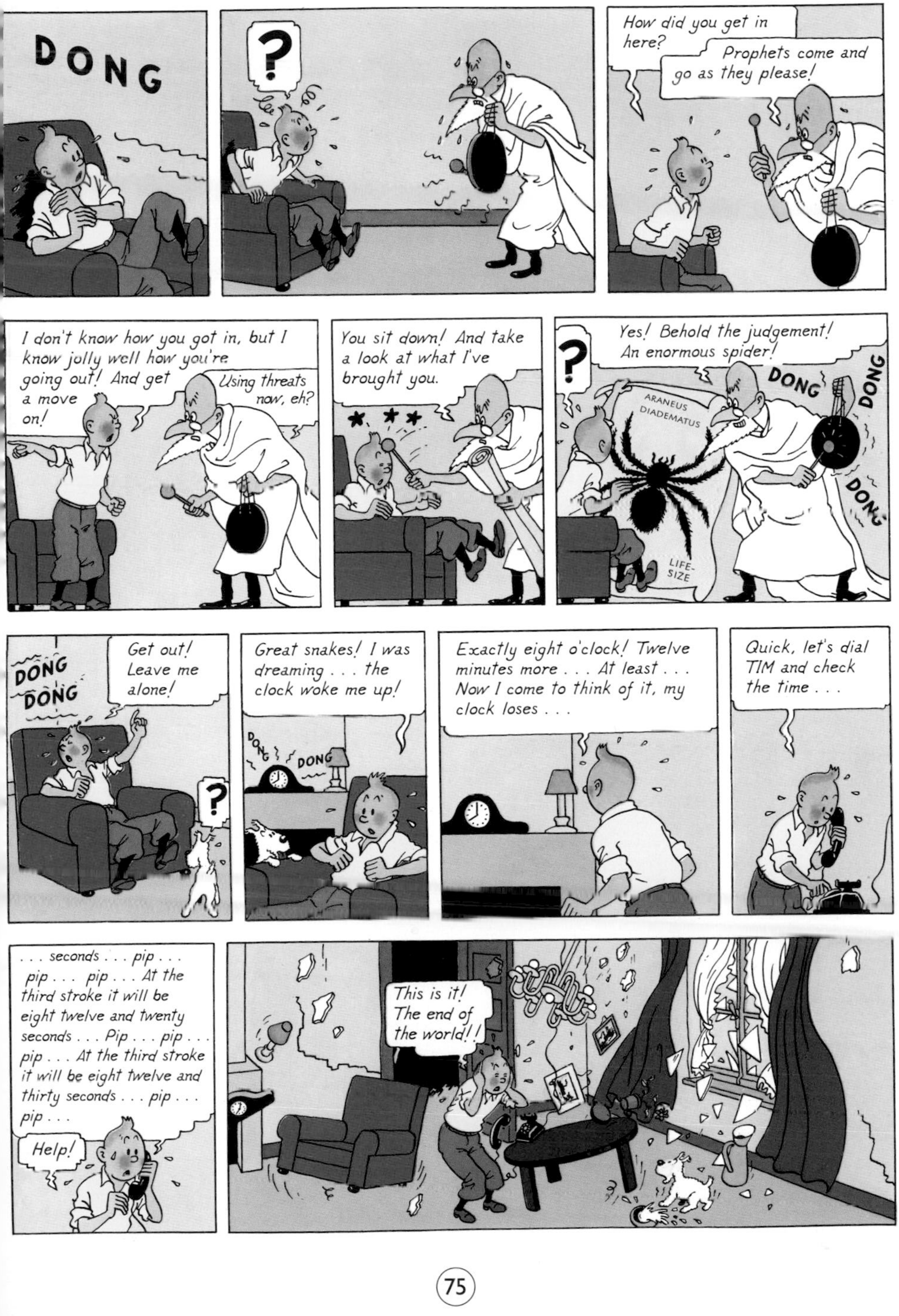
DONG
?
How did you get in here?
Prophets come and go as they please!
I don't know how you got in, but I know jolly well how you're going out! And get a move on!
Using threats now, eh?
You sit down! And take a look at what I've brought you.
?
Yes! Behold the judgement! An enormous spider!
ARANEUS DIADEMATUS
LIFE-SIZE
DONG
DONG
DONG
DONG
DONG
Get out! Leave me alone!
?
Great snakes! I was dreaming . . . the clock woke me up!
DONG
DONG
Exactly eight o'clock! Twelve minutes more . . . At least . . . Now I come to think of it, my clock loses . . .
Quick, let's dial TIM and check the time . . .
. . . seconds . . . pip . . . pip . . . pip . . . At the third stroke it will be eight twelve and twenty seconds . . . Pip . . . pip . . . pip . . . At the third stroke it will be eight twelve and thirty seconds . . . pip . . . pip . . .
Help!
This is it! The end of the world!!

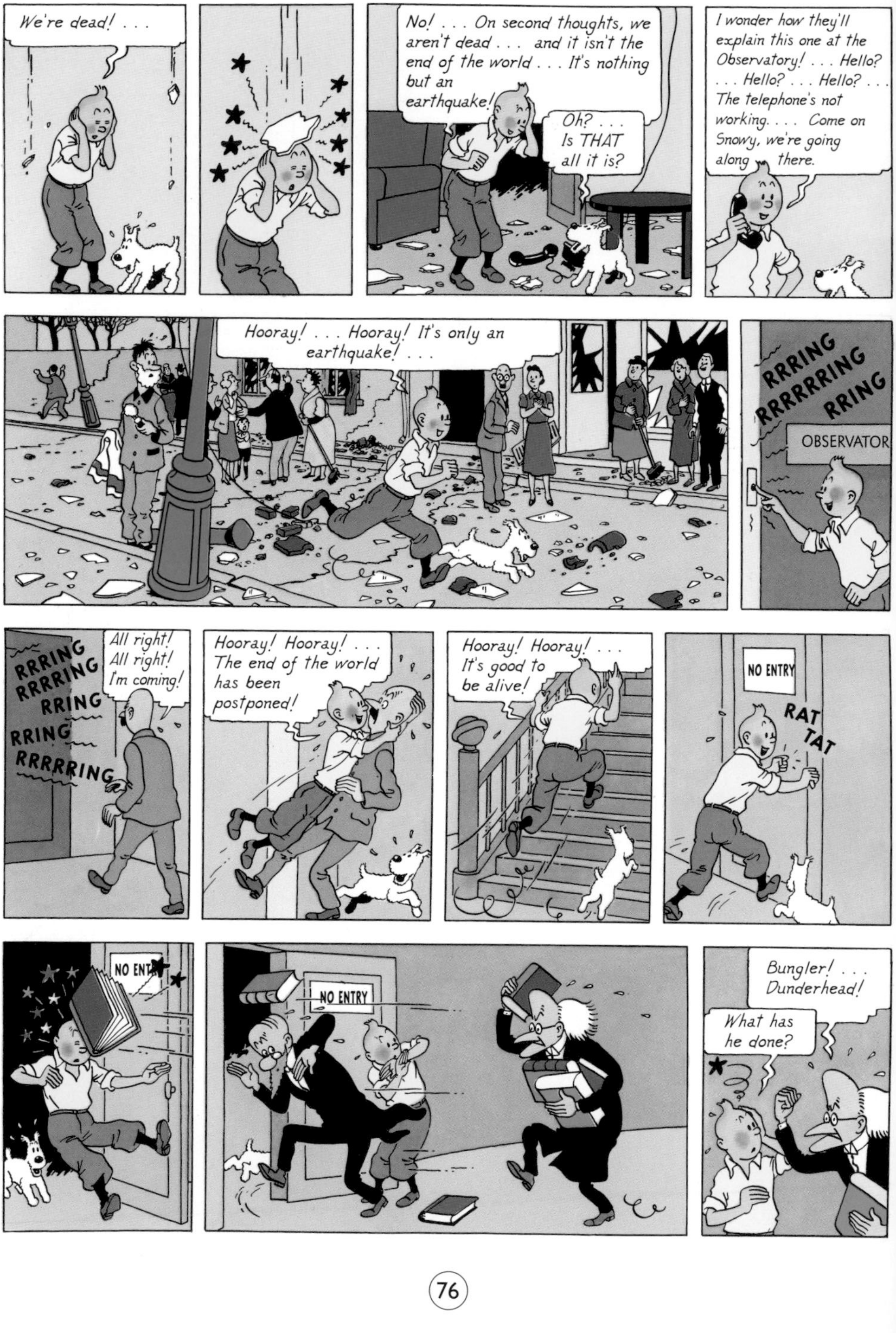

We're dead! . . .
No! . . . On second thoughts, we aren't dead . . . and it isn't the end of the world . . . It's nothing but an earthquake!
Oh? . . . Is THAT all it is?
I wonder how they'll explain this one at the Observatory! . . . Hello? . . . Hello? . . . Hello? . . . The telephone's not working. . . . Come on Snowy, we're going along there.
Hooray! . . . Hooray! It's only an earthquake! . . .
RRRING RRRRRRING RRING
OBSERVATOR
RRRING RRRRING RRING RRING RRRRRING
All right! All right! I'm coming!
Hooray! Hooray! . . . The end of the world has been postponed!
Hooray! Hooray! . . . It's good to be alive!
NO ENTRY
RAT TAT
NO ENT
NO ENTRY
Bungler! . . . Dunderhead!
What has he done?

The idiot! He made a mistake in his calculations! The meteor passed 48,000 km away from the earth, instead of colliding with it and causing the magnificent cataclysm I'd hoped for.

Never mind, Professor; you've still got it in store . . . But tell me: what about the earthquake?

Professor! . . . Professor! . . .

It has just been developed, sir. It is indeed remarkable, don't you agree, sir?

Excellent! . . . Excellent! . . . But, look there. How very extraordinary!

That group of lines, in the centre? Uranium, I presume.

Uranium? Not on your life! . . .

?

By the rings of Saturn! It's prodigious!

Tralala ♪ ♪ - la ♪

It may be prodigious, but it's all Greek to me!

It's prodigious! . . . Incredible! . . . Fantastic! . . . Stupefying!

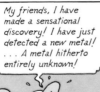

My friends, I have made a sensational discovery! I have just detected a new metal! . . . A metal hitherto entirely unknown!

You've heard of the spectroscope. It's the instrument that enables us to discover elements in stars, elements not yet isolated here on the earth. This is a spectroscopic photograph of the meteor which brushed past us today. Each of these lines, or each group of lines is characteristic of a metal. Those lines in the centre represent an unknown metal, which exists in the meteor. You follow me?

Er . . . more or less . . .

I, Decimus Phostle, have discovered a new metal! I shall give my name to it: phostlite.

My heartiest congratulations!

But Professor, to get back to the meteor . . . It didn't collide with the earth, so why was there an earthquake?

Tell me, young man, do you like bull's-eyes?

?

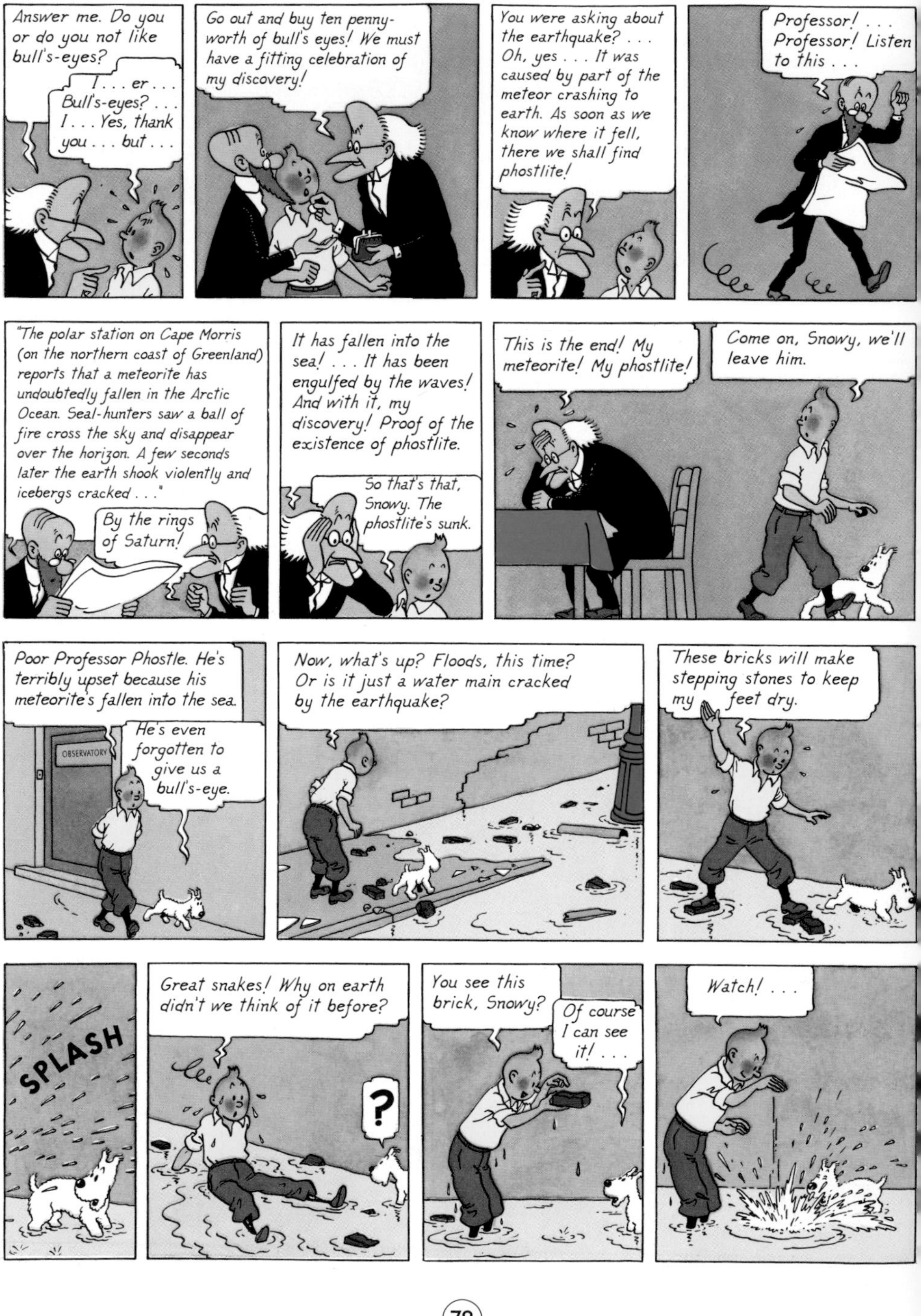

Answer me. Do you or do you not like bull's-eyes?
I . . . er . . . Bull's-eyes? . . . I . . . Yes, thank you . . . but . . .
Go out and buy ten penny-worth of bull's eyes! We must have a fitting celebration of my discovery!
You were asking about the earthquake? . . . Oh, yes . . . It was caused by part of the meteor crashing to earth. As soon as we know where it fell, there we shall find phostlite!
Professor! . . . Professor! Listen to this . . .
"The polar station on Cape Morris (on the northern coast of Greenland) reports that a meteorite has undoubtedly fallen in the Arctic Ocean. Seal-hunters saw a ball of fire cross the sky and disappear over the horizon. A few seconds later the earth shook violently and icebergs cracked . . ."
By the rings of Saturn!
It has fallen into the sea! . . . It has been engulfed by the waves! And with it, my discovery! Proof of the existence of phostlite.
So that's that, Snowy. The phostlite's sunk.
This is the end! My meteorite! My phostlite!
Come on, Snowy, we'll leave him.
Poor Professor Phostle. He's terribly upset because his meteorite's fallen into the sea.
OBSERVATORY
He's even forgotten to give us a bull's-eye.
Now, what's up? Floods, this time? Or is it just a water main cracked by the earthquake?
These bricks will make stepping stones to keep my feet dry.
SPLASH
Great snakes! Why on earth didn't we think of it before?
?
You see this brick, Snowy?
Of course I can see it! . . .
Watch! . . .

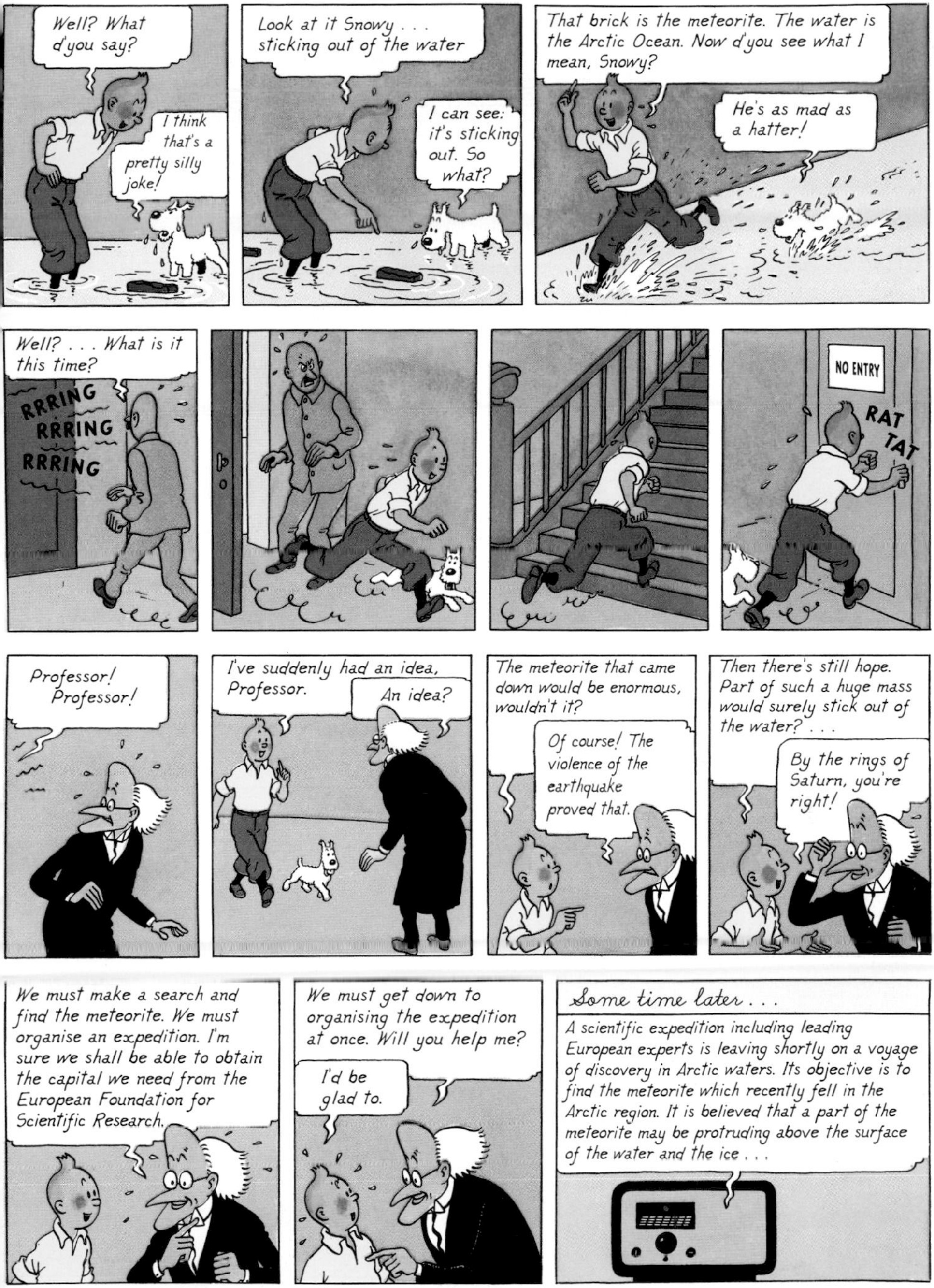

Well? What d'you say?
I think that's a pretty silly joke!
Look at it Snowy . . . sticking out of the water
I can see: it's sticking out. So what?
That brick is the meteorite. The water is the Arctic Ocean. Now d'you see what I mean, Snowy?
He's as mad as a hatter!
Well? . . . What is it this time?
RRRING
RRRING
RRRING
NO ENTRY
RAT
TAT
Professor! Professor!
I've suddenly had an idea, Professor.
An idea?
The meteorite that came down would be enormous, wouldn't it?
Of course! The violence of the earthquake proved that.
Then there's still hope. Part of such a huge mass would surely stick out of the water? . . .
By the rings of Saturn, you're right!
We must make a search and find the meteorite. We must organise an expedition. I'm sure we shall be able to obtain the capital we need from the European Foundation for Scientific Research.
We must get down to organising the expedition at once. Will you help me?
I'd be glad to.
Some time later . . .
A scientific expedition including leading European experts is leaving shortly on a voyage of discovery in Arctic waters. Its objective is to find the meteorite which recently fell in the Arctic region. It is believed that a part of the meteorite may be protruding above the surface of the water and the ice . . .

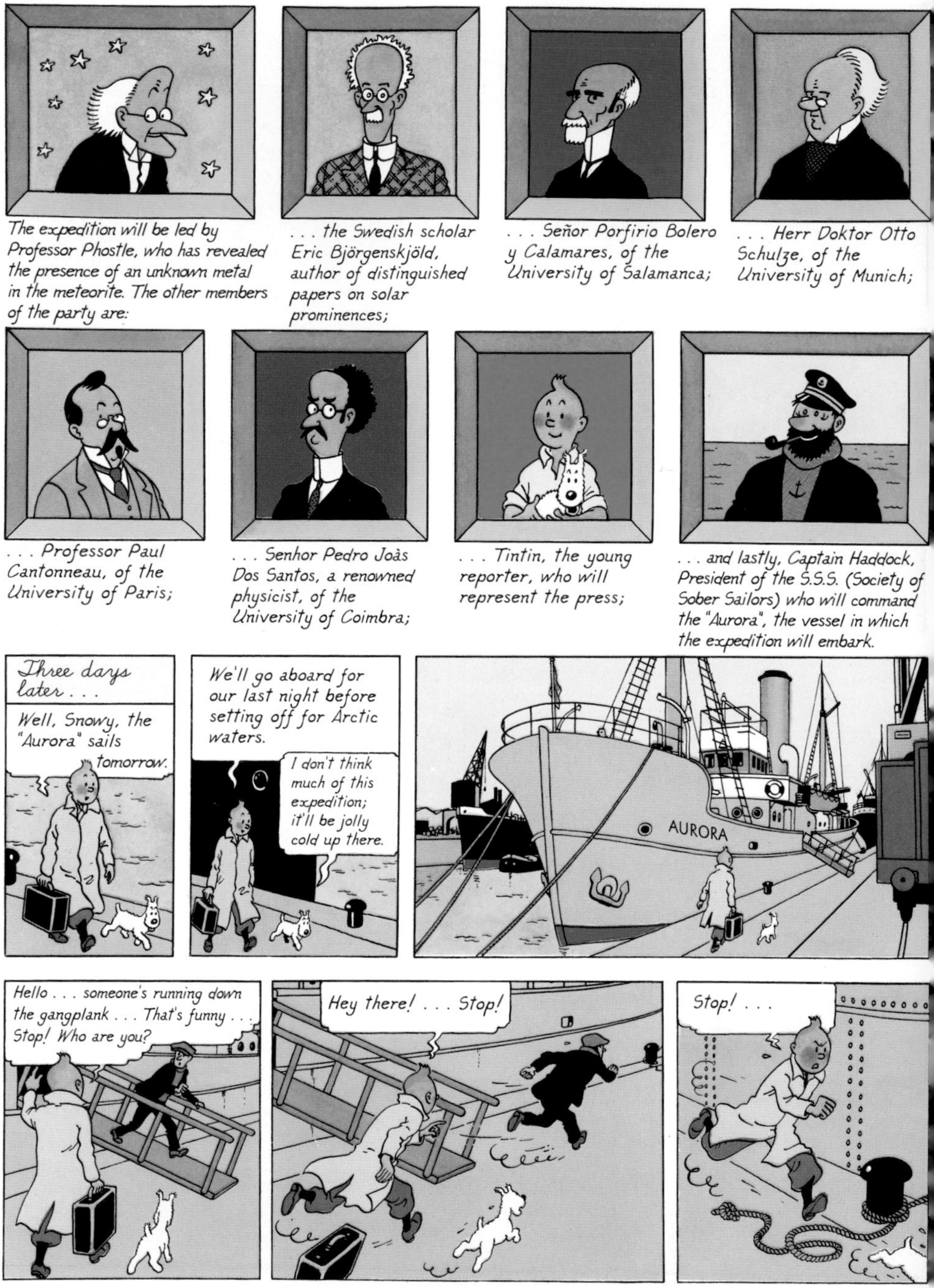
The expedition will be led by Professor Phostle, who has revealed the presence of an unknown metal in the meteorite. The other members of the party are:
. . . the Swedish scholar Eric Björgenskjöld, author of distinguished papers on solar prominences;
. . . Señor Porfirio Bolero y Calamares, of the University of Salamanca;
. . . Herr Doktor Otto Schulze, of the University of Munich;
. . . Professor Paul Cantonneau, of the University of Paris;
. . . Senhor Pedro Joàs Dos Santos, a renowned physicist, of the University of Coimbra;
. . . Tintin, the young reporter, who will represent the press;
. . . and lastly, Captain Haddock, President of the S.S.S. (Society of Sober Sailors) who will command the "Aurora", the vessel in which the expedition will embark.
Three days later . . .
Well, Snowy, the "Aurora" sails tomorrow.
We'll go aboard for our last night before setting off for Arctic waters.
I don't think much of this expedition; it'll be jolly cold up there.
AURORA
Hello . . . someone's running down the gangplank . . . That's funny . . . Stop! Who are you?
Hey there! . . . Stop!
Stop! . . .

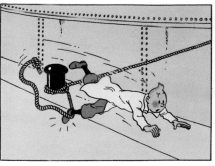

Confound that rope! . . . He's vanished . . . Now, I wonder what that fellow was doing aboard ship.

Are you on watch?

Yes.

You haven't seen anyone prowling around the deck?

No.

Oh! . . . Good! . . . Er . . . Is Captain Haddock in his cabin?

Yes.

Yes . . . No . . . Not very communicative!

Hello, where's Snowy got to? . . . Snowy . . . Snowy! SNOWY!

!

RAT TAT TAT TAT

Come in.

Hello, Captain. I've just seen a man bolting off the ship. He made off when I challenged him! . . .

?

Wooah! . . . Wooah! . . . Wooah! . . .

Ah, there you are Snowy! Hey, what are you doing?

I'd say he wants us to follow him . . .

Wooah! Wooah!

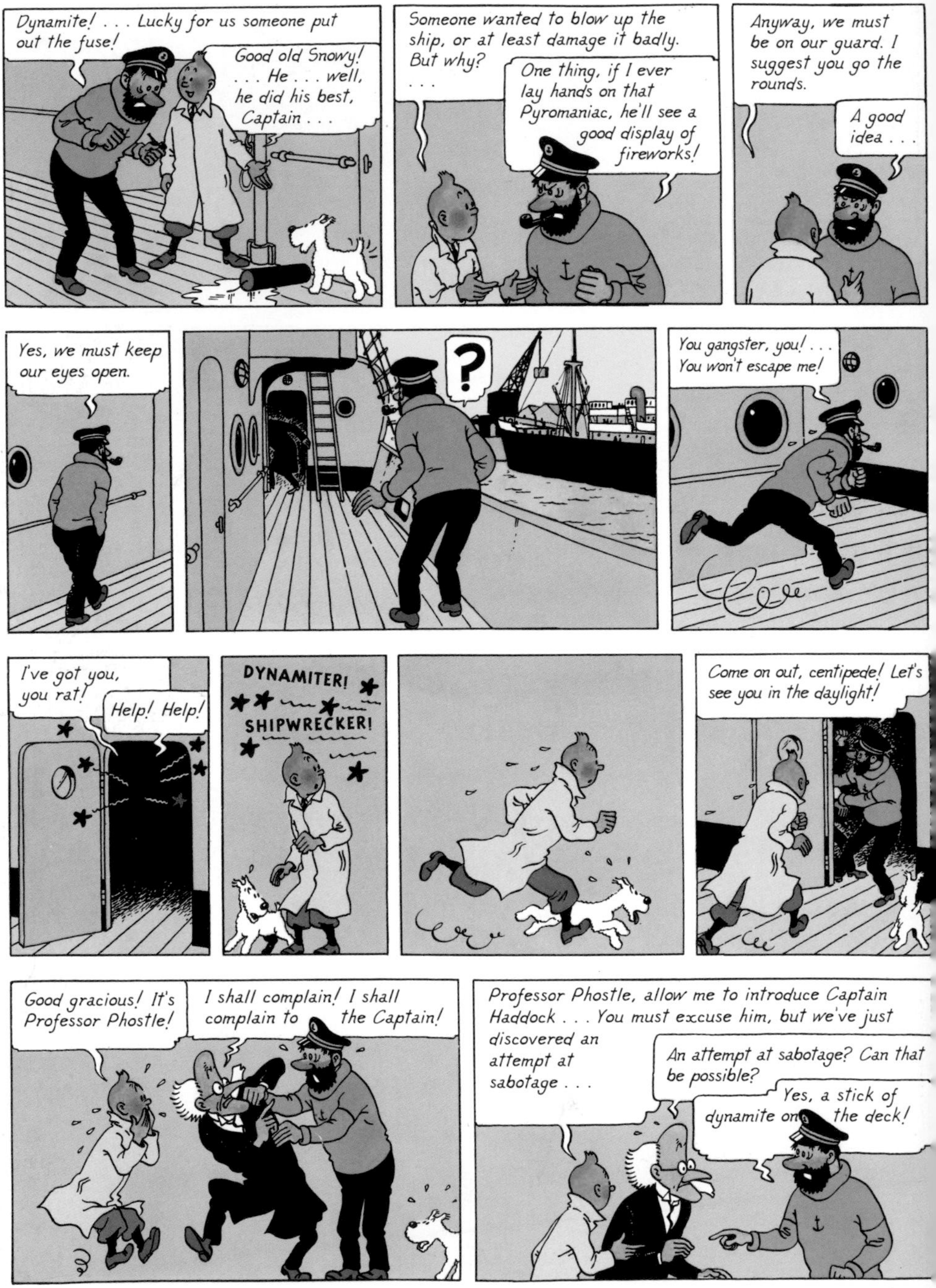

Dynamite! . . . Lucky for us someone put out the fuse!
Good old Snowy! . . . He . . . well, he did his best, Captain . . .
Someone wanted to blow up the ship, or at least damage it badly. But why? . . .
One thing, if I ever lay hands on that Pyromaniac, he'll see a good display of fireworks!
Anyway, we must be on our guard. I suggest you go the rounds.
A good idea . . .
Yes, we must keep our eyes open.
?
You gangster, you! . . . You won't escape me!
I've got you, you rat!
Help! Help!
DYNAMITER!
SHIPWRECKER!
Come on out, centipede! Let's see you in the daylight!
Good gracious! It's Professor Phostle!
I shall complain! I shall complain to the Captain!
Professor Phostle, allow me to introduce Captain Haddock . . . You must excuse him, but we've just discovered an attempt at sabotage . . .
An attempt at sabotage? Can that be possible?
Yes, a stick of dynamite on the deck!

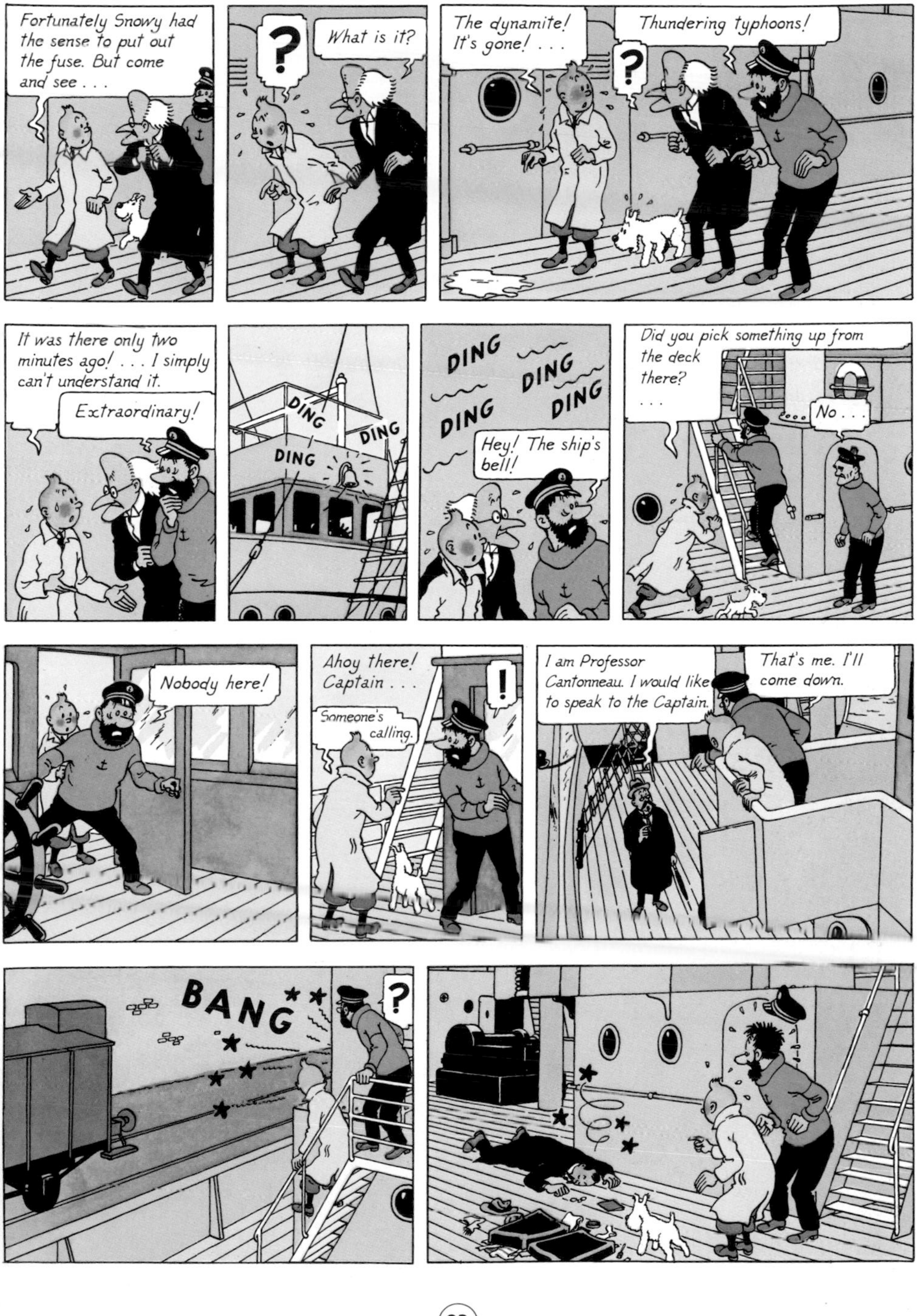

Fortunately Snowy had the sense to put out the fuse. But come and see . . .
?
What is it?
The dynamite! It's gone! . . .
?
Thundering typhoons!
It was there only two minutes ago! . . . I simply can't understand it.
Extraordinary!
DING
DING
DING
DING
DING
DING
DING
Hey! The ship's bell!
Did you pick something up from the deck there? . . .
No . . .
Nobody here!
Ahoy there! Captain . . .
!
Someone's calling.
I am Professor Cantonneau. I would like to speak to the Captain.
That's me. I'll come down.
BANG
?

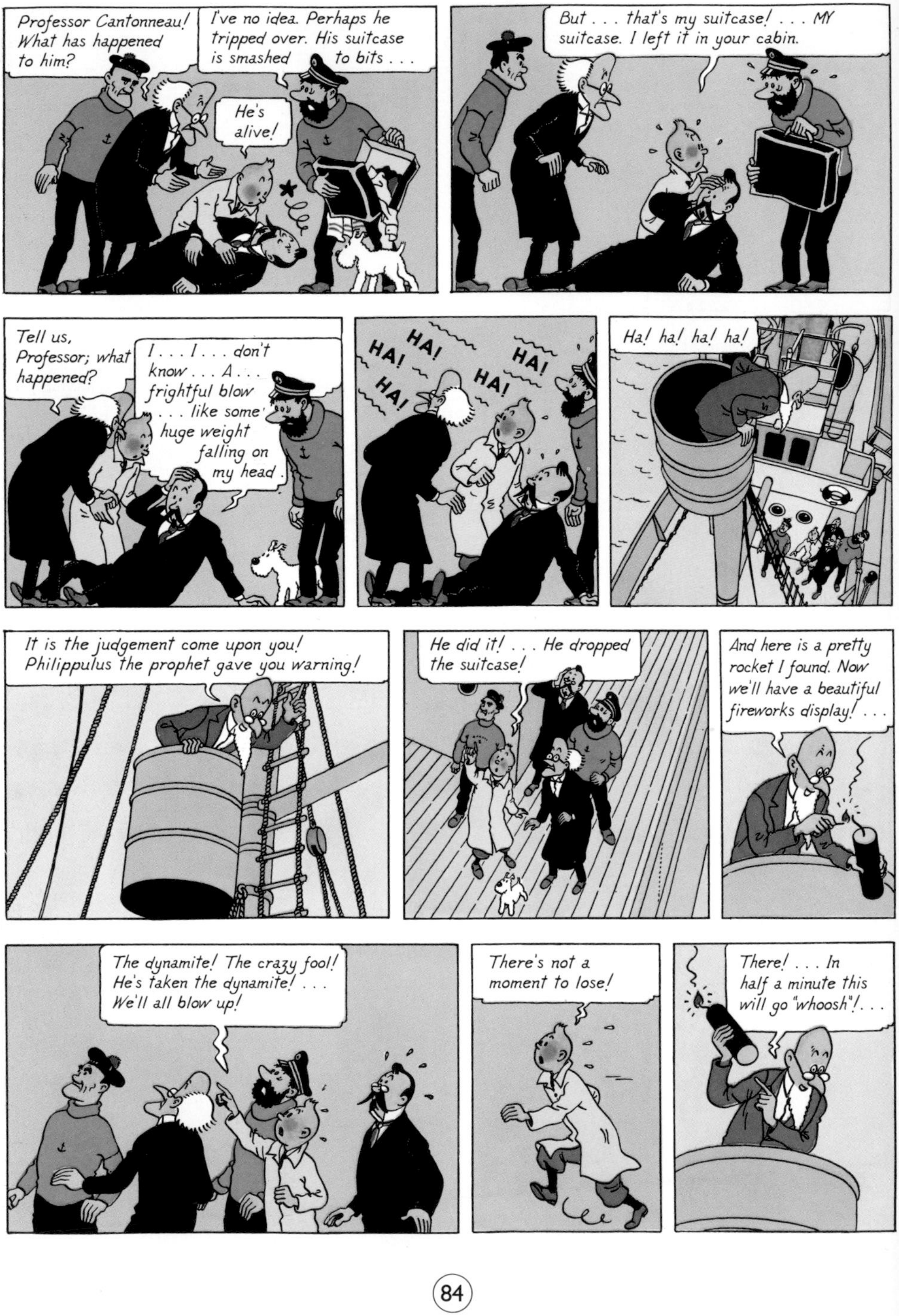

Professor Cantonneau! What has happened to him?
I've no idea. Perhaps he tripped over. His suitcase is smashed to bits . . .
He's alive!
But . . . that's my suitcase! . . . MY suitcase. I left it in your cabin.
Tell us, Professor; what happened?
I . . . I . . . don't know . . . A . . . frightful blow . . . like some huge weight falling on my head . . .
HA! HA! HA! HA! HA! HA!
Ha! ha! ha! ha!
It is the judgement come upon you! Philippulus the prophet gave you warning!
He did it! . . . He dropped the suitcase!
And here is a pretty rocket I found. Now we'll have a beautiful fireworks display! . . .
The dynamite! The crazy fool! He's taken the dynamite! . . . We'll all blow up!
There's not a moment to lose!
There! . . . In half a minute this will go "whoosh"! . . .

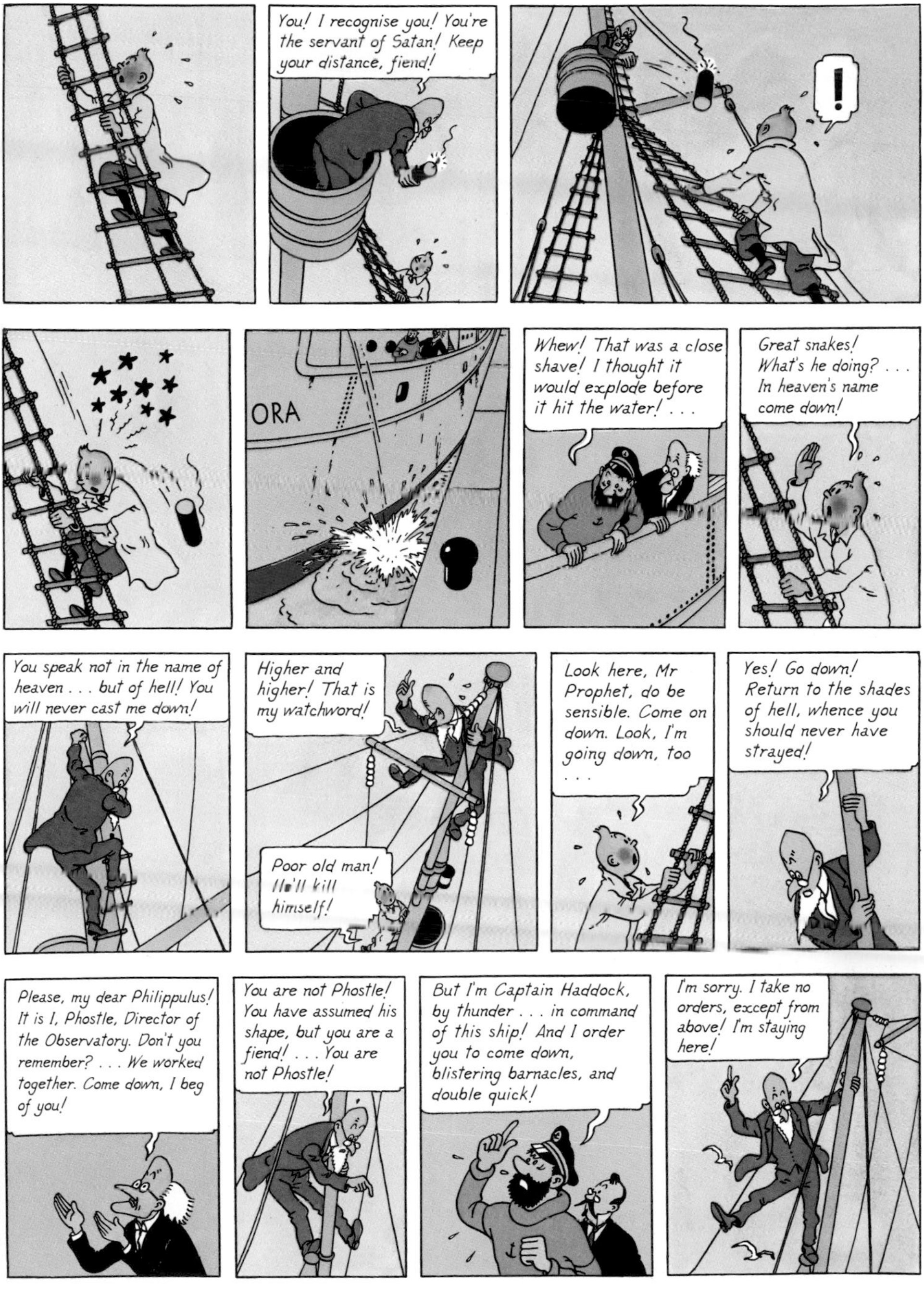
You! I recognise you! You're the servant of Satan! Keep your distance, fiend!
!
Whew! That was a close shave! I thought it would explode before it hit the water! . . .
Great snakes! What's he doing? . . . In heaven's name come down!
You speak not in the name of heaven . . . but of hell! You will never cast me down!
Higher and higher! That is my watchword!
Poor old man! He'll kill himself!
Look here, Mr Prophet, do be sensible. Come on down. Look, I'm going down, too . . .
Yes! Go down! Return to the shades of hell, whence you should never have strayed!
Please, my dear Philippulus! It is I, Phostle, Director of the Observatory. Don't you remember? . . . We worked together. Come down, I beg of you!
You are not Phostle! You have assumed his shape, but you are a fiend! . . . You are not Phostle!
But I'm Captain Haddock, by thunder . . . in command of this ship! And I order you to come down, blistering barnacles, and double quick!
I'm sorry. I take no orders, except from above! I'm staying here!

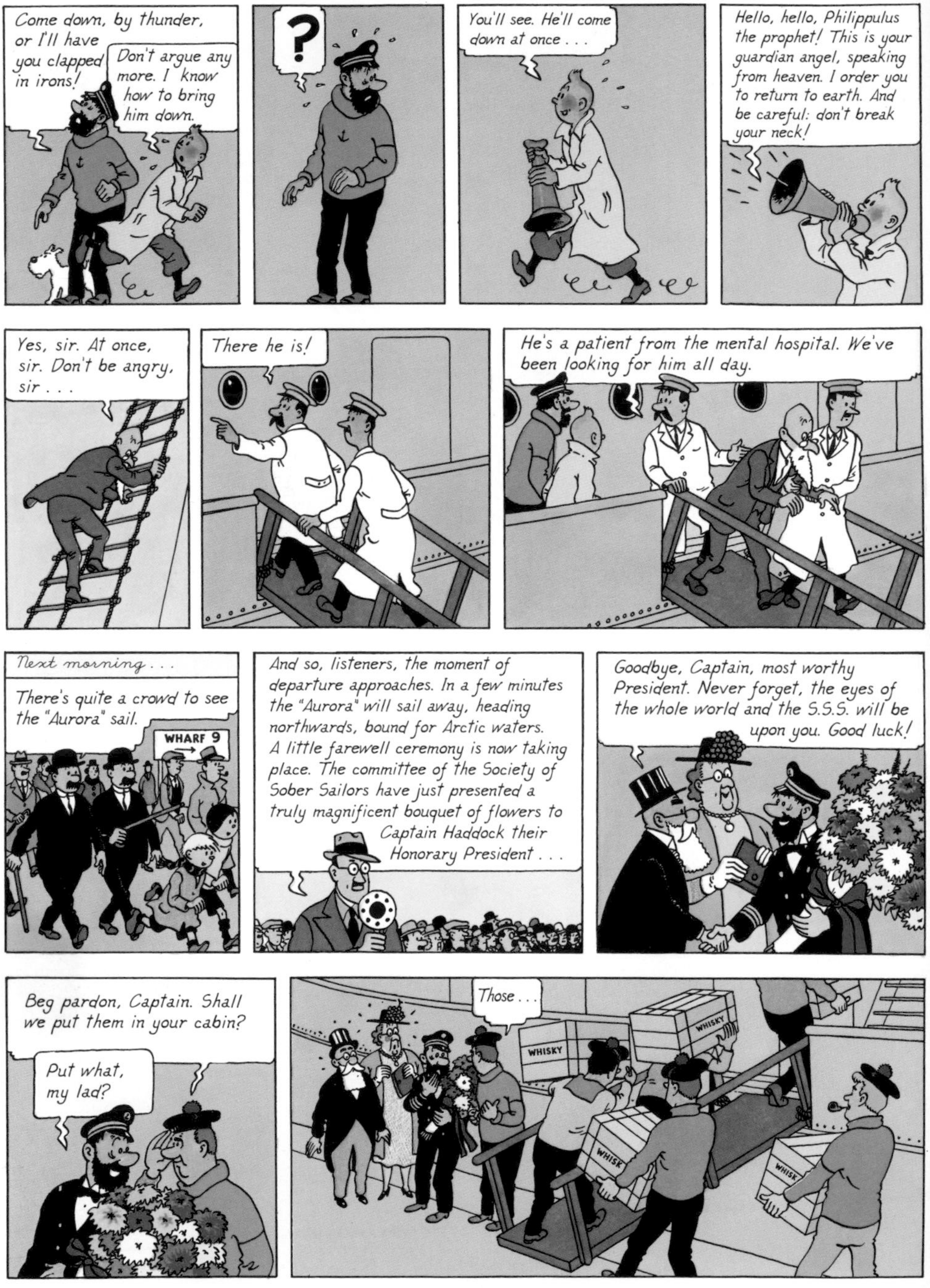
Come down, by thunder, or I'll have you clapped in irons!
Don't argue any more. I know how to bring him down.
?
You'll see. He'll come down at once . . .
Hello, hello, Philippulus the prophet! This is your guardian angel, speaking from heaven. I order you to return to earth. And be careful: don't break your neck!
Yes, sir. At once, sir. Don't be angry, sir . . .
There he is!
He's a patient from the mental hospital. We've been looking for him all day.
Next morning . . .
There's quite a crowd to see the "Aurora" sail.
WHARF 9
And so, listeners, the moment of departure approaches. In a few minutes the "Aurora" will sail away, heading northwards, bound for Arctic waters. A little farewell ceremony is now taking place. The committee of the Society of Sober Sailors have just presented a truly magnificent bouquet of flowers to Captain Haddock their Honorary President . . .
Goodbye, Captain, most worthy President. Never forget, the eyes of the whole world and the S.S.S. will be upon you. Good luck!
Beg pardon, Captain. Shall we put them in your cabin?
Put what, my lad?
Those . . .
WHISKY
WHISKY
WHISK
WHISK

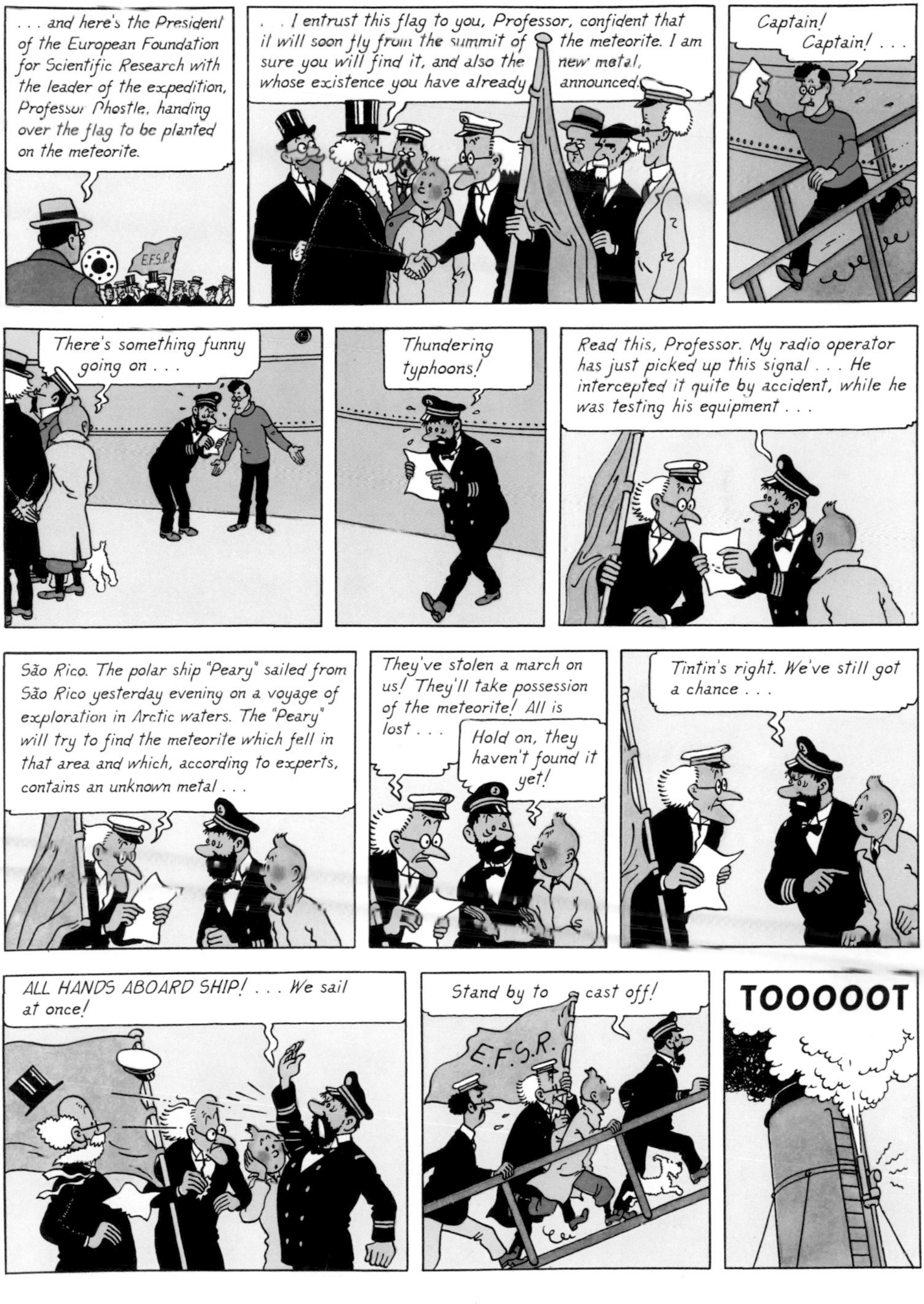

. . . and here's the President of the European Foundation for Scientific Research with the leader of the expedition, Professor Phostle, handing over the flag to be planted on the meteorite.
E.F.S.R.
. . . I entrust this flag to you, Professor, confident that it will soon fly from the summit of the meteorite. I am sure you will find it, and also the new metal, whose existence you have already announced.
Captain! Captain! . . .
There's something funny going on . . .
Thundering typhoons!
Read this, Professor. My radio operator has just picked up this signal . . . He intercepted it quite by accident, while he was testing his equipment . . .
São Rico. The polar ship "Peary" sailed from São Rico yesterday evening on a voyage of exploration in Arctic waters. The "Peary" will try to find the meteorite which fell in that area and which, according to experts, contains an unknown metal . . .
They've stolen a march on us! They'll take possession of the meteorite! All is lost . . .
Hold on, they haven't found it yet!
Tintin's right. We've still got a chance . . .
ALL HANDS ABOARD SHIP! . . . We sail at once!
Stand by to cast off!
E.F.S.R.
TOOOOOT

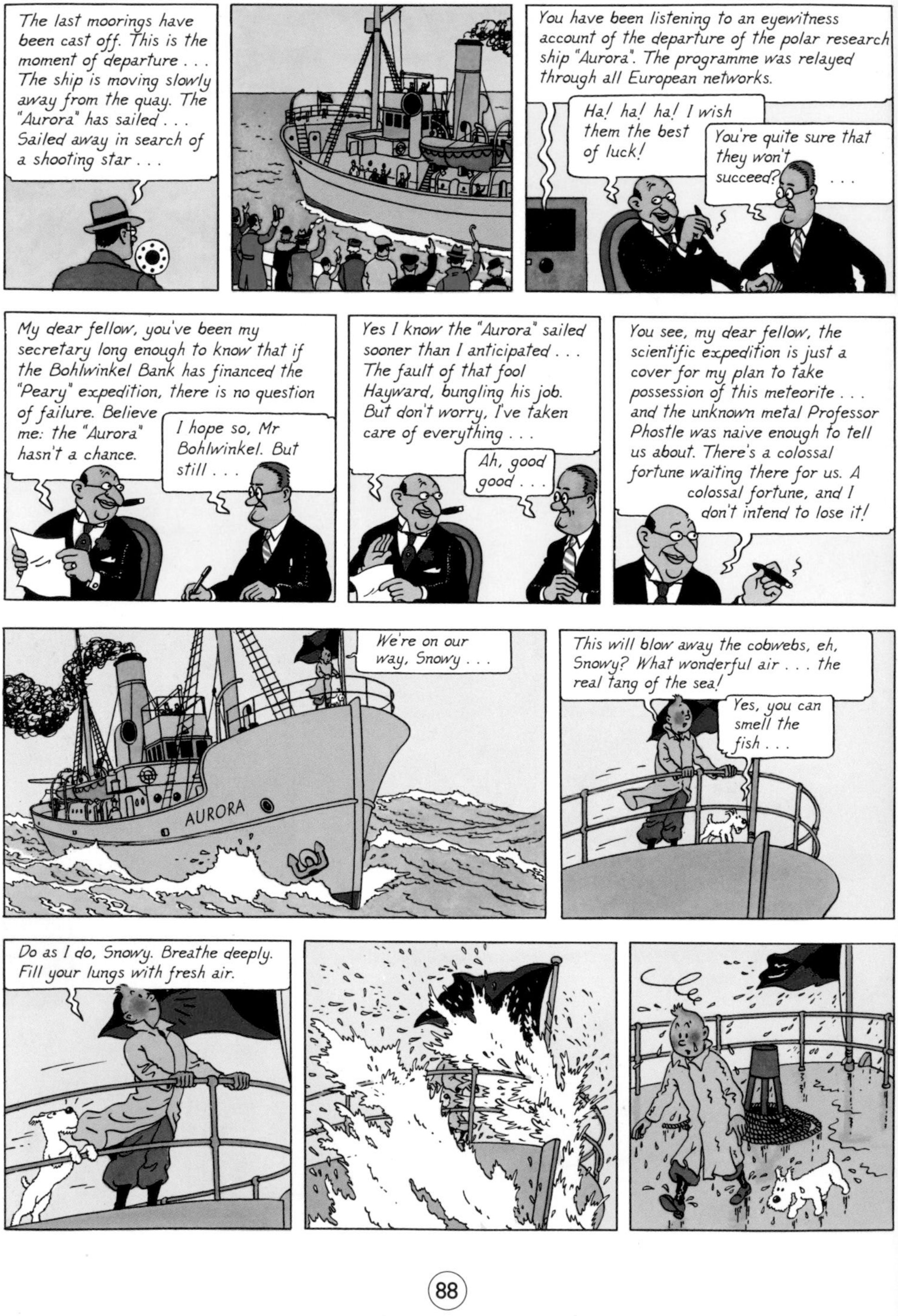
The last moorings have been cast off. This is the moment of departure . . . The ship is moving slowly away from the quay. The "Aurora" has sailed . . . Sailed away in search of a shooting star . . .
You have been listening to an eyewitness account of the departure of the polar research ship "Aurora". The programme was relayed through all European networks.
Ha! ha! ha! I wish them the best of luck!
You're quite sure that they won't succeed? . . .
My dear fellow, you've been my secretary long enough to know that if the Bohlwinkel Bank has financed the "Peary" expedition, there is no question of failure. Believe me: the "Aurora" hasn't a chance.
I hope so, Mr Bohlwinkel. But still . . .
Yes I know the "Aurora" sailed sooner than I anticipated . . . The fault of that fool Hayward, bungling his job. But don't worry, I've taken care of everything . . .
Ah, good good . . .
You see, my dear fellow, the scientific expedition is just a cover for my plan to take possession of this meteorite . . . and the unknown metal Professor Phostle was naive enough to tell us about. There's a colossal fortune waiting there for us. A colossal fortune, and I don't intend to lose it!
AURORA
We're on our way, Snowy . . .
This will blow away the cobwebs, eh, Snowy? What wonderful air . . . the real tang of the sea!
Yes, you can smell the fish . . .
Do as I do, Snowy. Breathe deeply. Fill your lungs with fresh air.

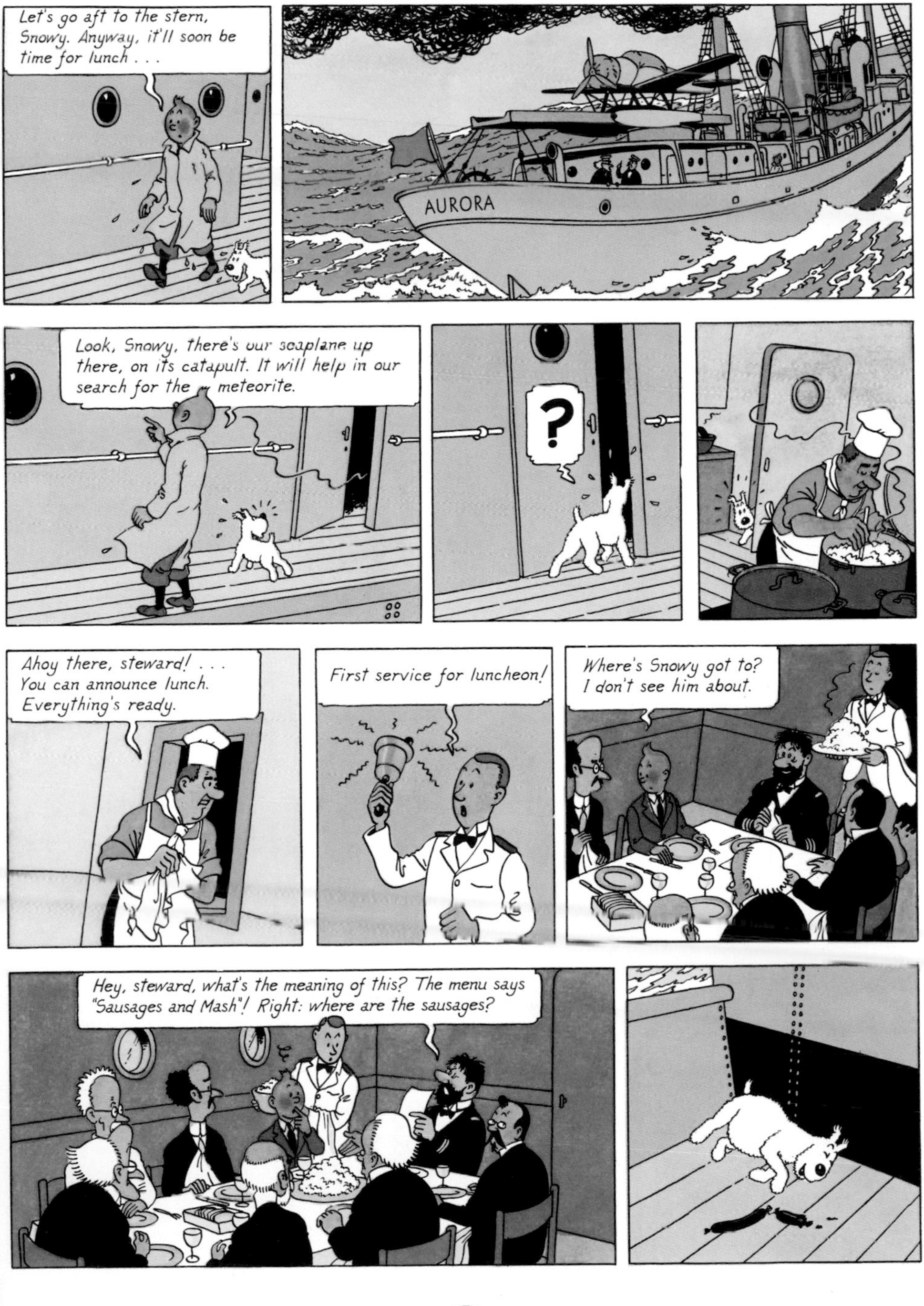

Let's go aft to the stern, Snowy. Anyway, it'll soon be time for lunch . . .
AURORA
Look, Snowy, there's our seaplane up there, on its catapult. It will help in our search for the meteorite.
?
Ahoy there, steward! . . . You can announce lunch. Everything's ready.
First service for luncheon!
Where's Snowy got to? I don't see him about.
Hey, steward, what's the meaning of this? The menu says "Sausages and Mash"! Right: where are the sausages?

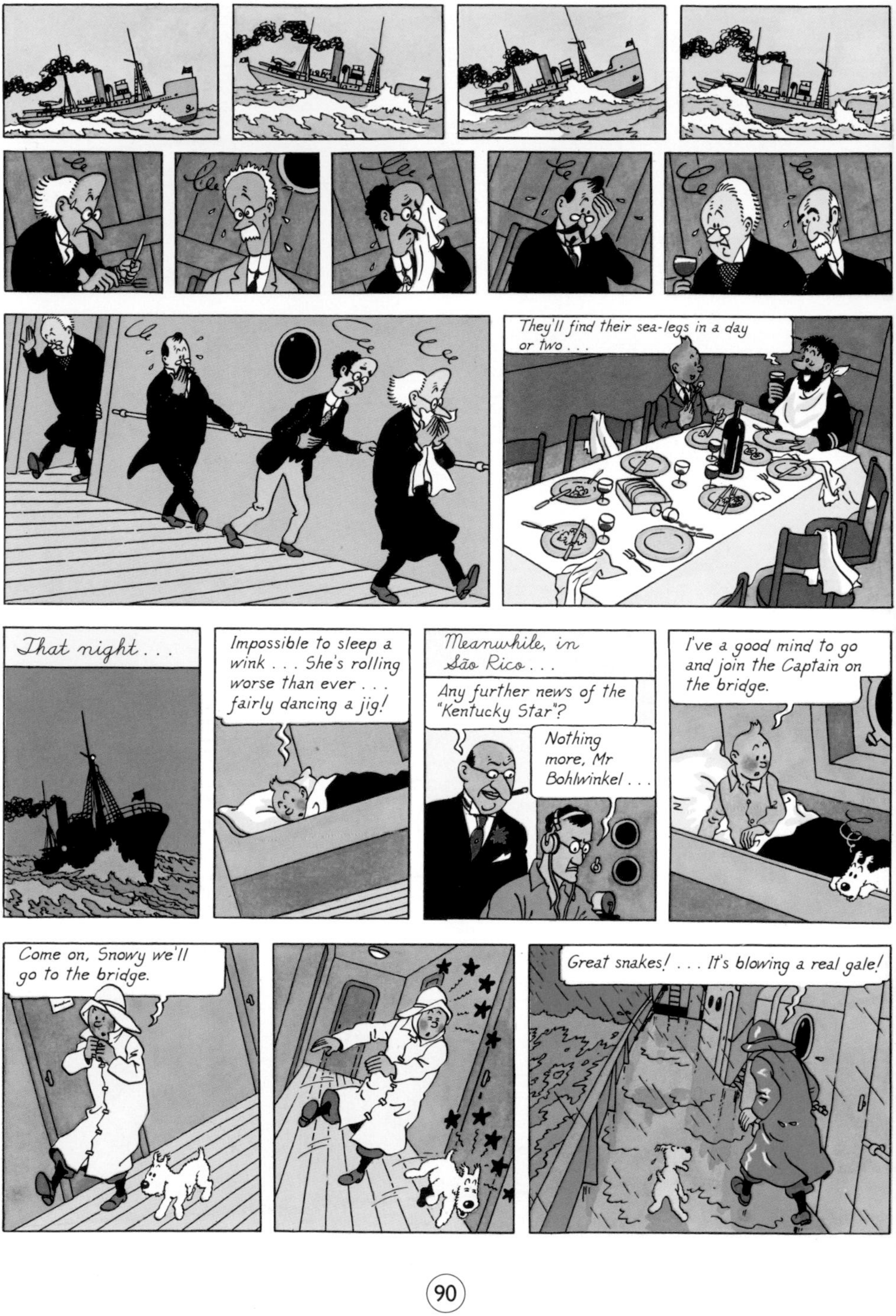
They'll find their sea-legs in a day or two . . .
That night . . .
Impossible to sleep a wink . . . She's rolling worse than ever . . . fairly dancing a jig!
Meanwhile, in São Rico . . .
Any further news of the "Kentucky Star"?
Nothing more, Mr Bohlwinkel . . .
I've a good mind to go and join the Captain on the bridge.
Come on, Snowy we'll go to the bridge.
Great snakes! . . . It's blowing a real gale!

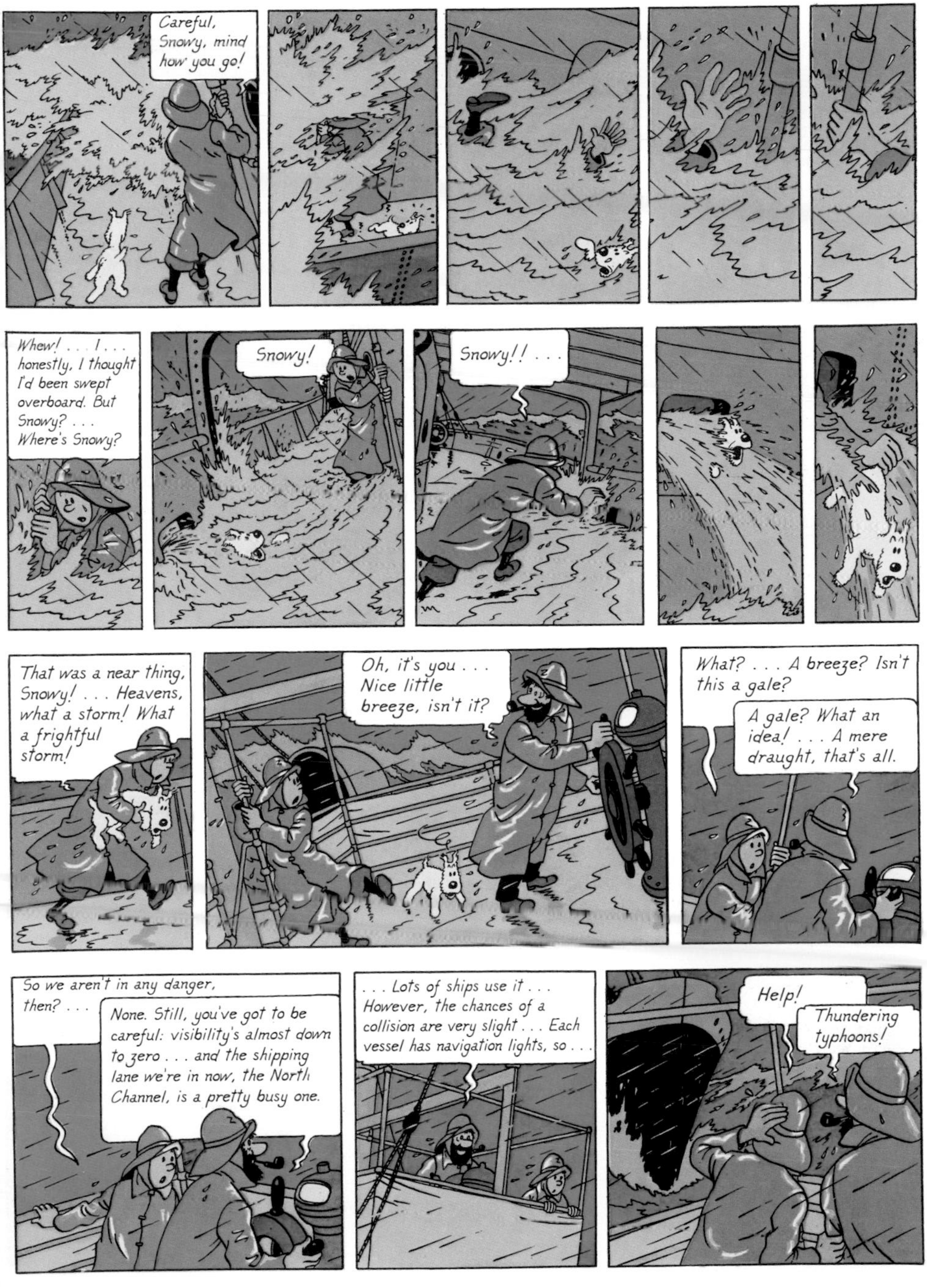
Careful, Snowy, mind how you go!
Whew! . . . I . . . honestly, I thought I'd been swept overboard. But Snowy? . . . Where's Snowy?
Snowy!
Snowy!! . . .
That was a near thing, Snowy! . . . Heavens, what a storm! What a frightful storm!
Oh, it's you . . . Nice little breeze, isn't it?
What? . . . A breeze? Isn't this a gale?
A gale? What an idea! . . . A mere draught, that's all.
So we aren't in any danger, then? . . .
None. Still, you've got to be careful: visibility's almost down to zero . . . and the shipping lane we're in now, the North Channel, is a pretty busy one.
. . . Lots of ships use it . . . However, the chances of a collision are very slight . . . Each vessel has navigation lights, so . . .
Help!
Thundering typhoons!

Hard a starboard! . . .

Pirates! . . . Shipwreckers! . . . Sea-lice! . . . Filibusters! . . . Hoodlums! . . . Road-hogs! . . . Freshwater swabs!

Saved!

The lunatic! A little bit closer and he'd have cut us in two . . . He must be crazy sailing like that, without any lights . . . He couldn't have judged it better if he'd meant to sink us.

And why not? That might be precisely what he intended.

What do you mean? I mean, Captain, that someone's already tried to sabotage the "Aurora" . . . the night before we sailed. The accident we just avoided looks remarkably like another attempt . . .

Thundering typhoons! . . . You're right! . . . But who on earth . . . ?

Who would be anxious to prevent us carrying out our search? Who but the "Peary" expedition, or whoever has financed it? . . .

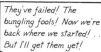
Is that the "Kentucky Star" this time?

Yes, coming in now Mr Bohlwinkel. A radio signal . . .

S.S. Kentucky Star. Obeying orders received, attempted to sink Aurora. Operation miscarried. Awaiting instructions.

They've failed! The bungling fools! Now we're back where we started! . . . But I'll get them yet!

Oh, misery! I feel so ill! I feel horribly ill!

I feel sick . . . Ooooooh . . .

Would you mind if I opened the window a little bit? Some fresh air would do us good.

Do as you please . . . just let me die in peace.

Aaaah! . . . I feel better already.

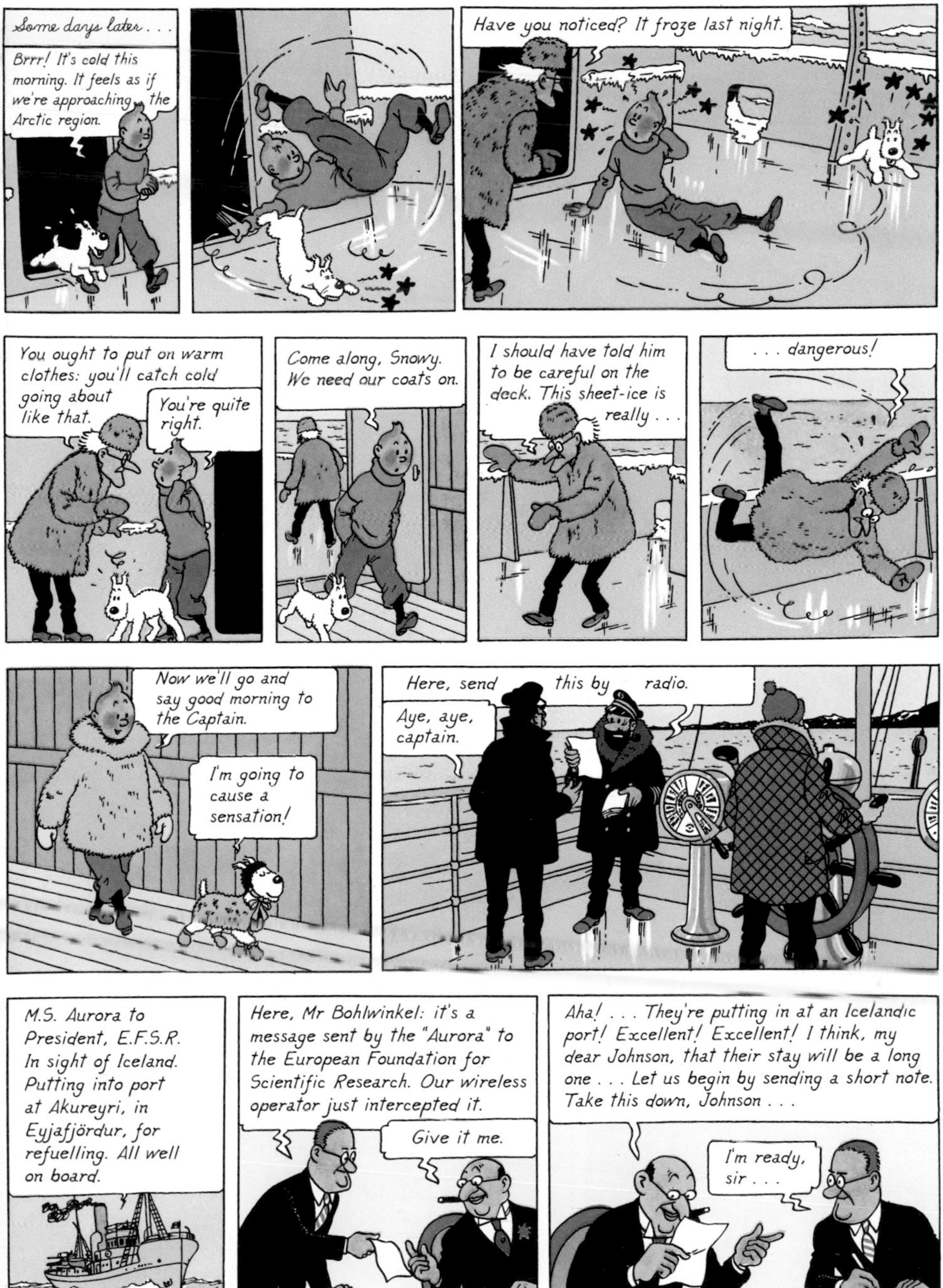

Some days later . . .
Brrr! It's cold this morning. It feels as if we're approaching the Arctic region.
Have you noticed? It froze last night.
You ought to put on warm clothes: you'll catch cold going about like that.
You're quite right.
Come along, Snowy. We need our coats on.
I should have told him to be careful on the deck. This sheet-ice is really . . .
. . . dangerous!
Now we'll go and say good morning to the Captain.
I'm going to cause a sensation!
Here, send this by radio.
Aye, aye, captain.
M.S. Aurora to President, E.F.S.R. In sight of Iceland. Putting into port at Akureyri, in Eyjafjördur, for refuelling. All well on board.
Here, Mr Bohlwinkel: it's a message sent by the "Aurora" to the European Foundation for Scientific Research. Our wireless operator just intercepted it.
Give it me.
Aha! . . . They're putting in at an Icelandic port! Excellent! Excellent! I think, my dear Johnson, that their stay will be a long one . . . Let us begin by sending a short note. Take this down, Johnson . . .
I'm ready, sir . . .

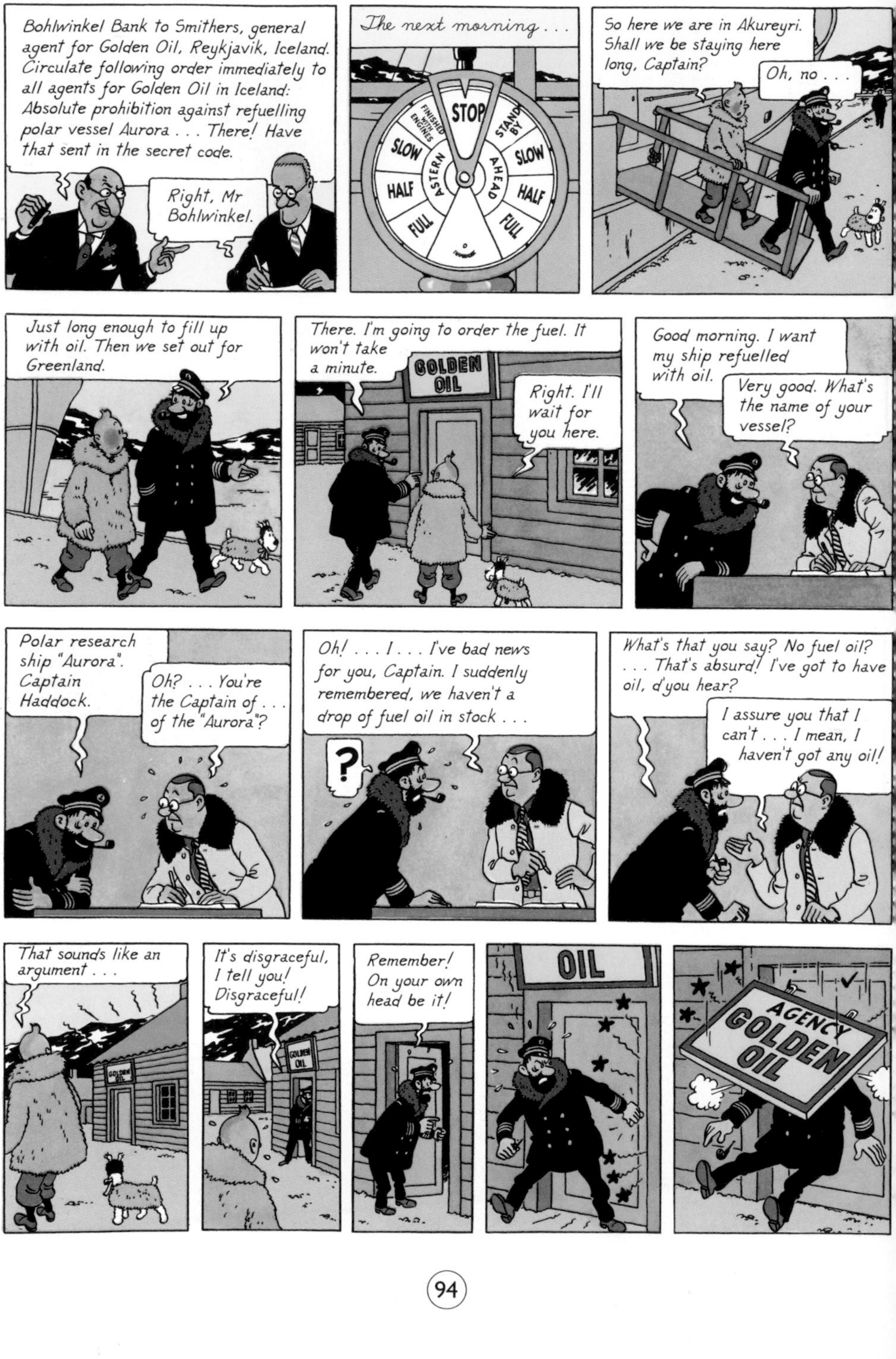
Bohlwinkel Bank to Smithers, general agent for Golden Oil, Reykjavik, Iceland. Circulate following order immediately to all agents for Golden Oil in Iceland: Absolute prohibition against refuelling polar vessel Aurora . . . There! Have that sent in the secret code.
Right, Mr Bohlwinkel.
The next morning . . .
FINISHED WITH ENGINES
STOP
STAND BY
SLOW
HALF
FULL
ASTERN
AHEAD
So here we are in Akureyri. Shall we be staying here long, Captain?
Oh, no . . .
Just long enough to fill up with oil. Then we set out for Greenland.
There. I'm going to order the fuel. It won't take a minute.
GOLDEN OIL
Right. I'll wait for you here.
Good morning. I want my ship refuelled with oil.
Very good. What's the name of your vessel?
Polar research ship "Aurora". Captain Haddock.
Oh? . . . You're the Captain of . . . of the "Aurora"?
Oh! . . . I . . . I've bad news for you, Captain. I suddenly remembered, we haven't a drop of fuel oil in stock . . .
?
What's that you say? No fuel oil? . . . That's absurd! I've got to have oil, d'you hear?
I assure you that I can't . . . I mean, I haven't got any oil!
That sounds like an argument . . .
It's disgraceful, I tell you! Disgraceful!
Remember! On your own head be it!
OIL
AGENCY GOLDEN OIL

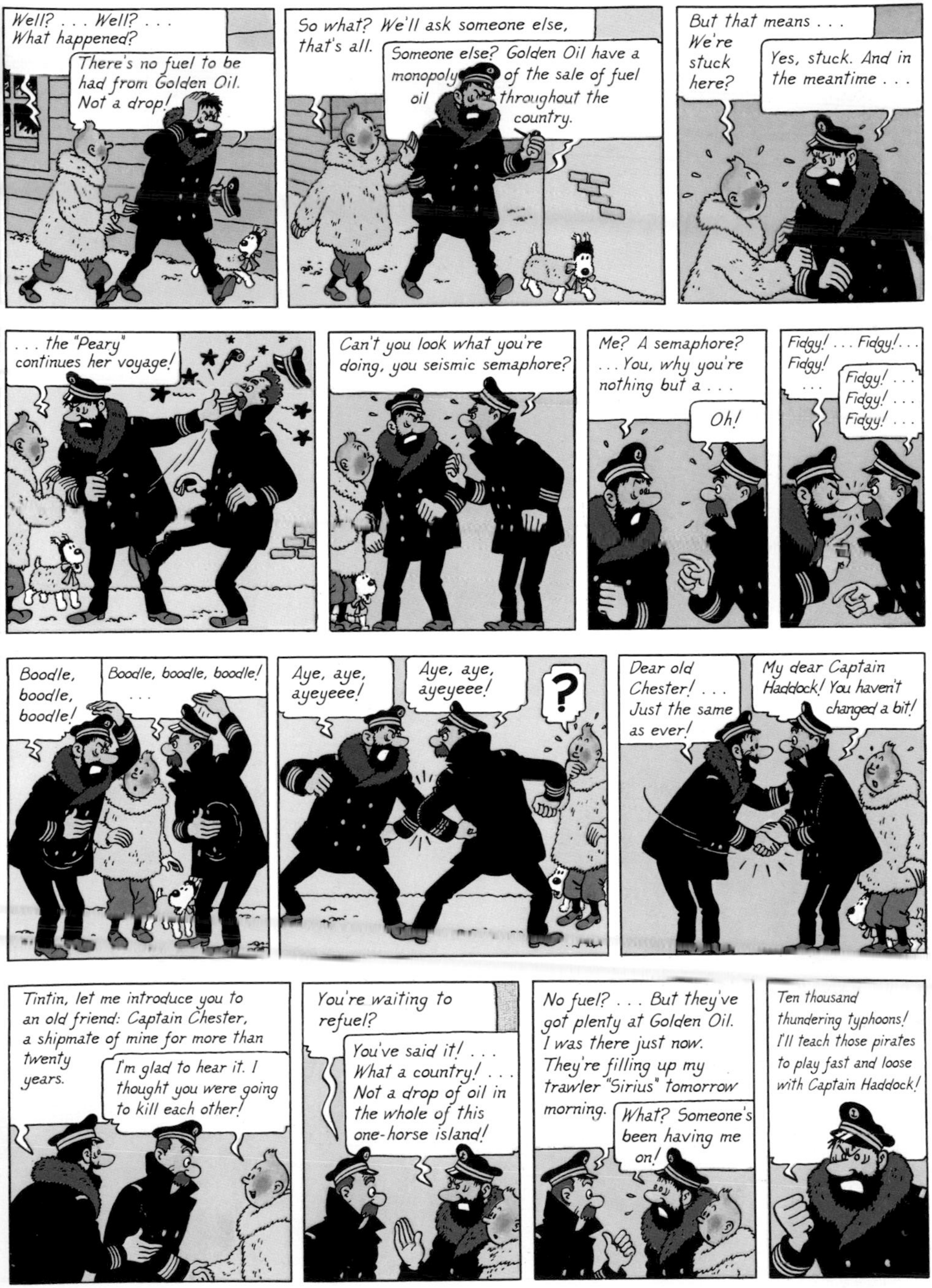

Well? . . . Well? . . . What happened?
There's no fuel to be had from Golden Oil. Not a drop!
So what? We'll ask someone else, that's all.
Someone else? Golden Oil have a monopoly of the sale of fuel oil throughout the country.
But that means . . . We're stuck here?
Yes, stuck. And in the meantime . . .
. . . the "Peary" continues her voyage!
Can't you look what you're doing, you seismic semaphore?
Me? A semaphore? . . . You, why you're nothing but a . . .
Oh!
Fidgy! . . . Fidgy! . . . Fidgy! . . .
Fidgy! . . . Fidgy! . . . Fidgy! . . .
Boodle, boodle, boodle!
Boodle, boodle, boodle! . . .
Aye, aye, ayeyeee!
Aye, aye, ayeyeee!
?
Dear old Chester! . . . Just the same as ever!
My dear Captain Haddock! You haven't changed a bit!
Tintin, let me introduce you to an old friend: Captain Chester, a shipmate of mine for more than twenty years.
I'm glad to hear it. I thought you were going to kill each other!
You're waiting to refuel?
You've said it! . . . What a country! . . . Not a drop of oil in the whole of this one-horse island!
No fuel? . . . But they've got plenty at Golden Oil. I was there just now. They're filling up my trawler "Sirius" tomorrow morning.
What? Someone's been having me on!
Ten thousand thundering typhoons! I'll teach those pirates to play fast and loose with Captain Haddock!

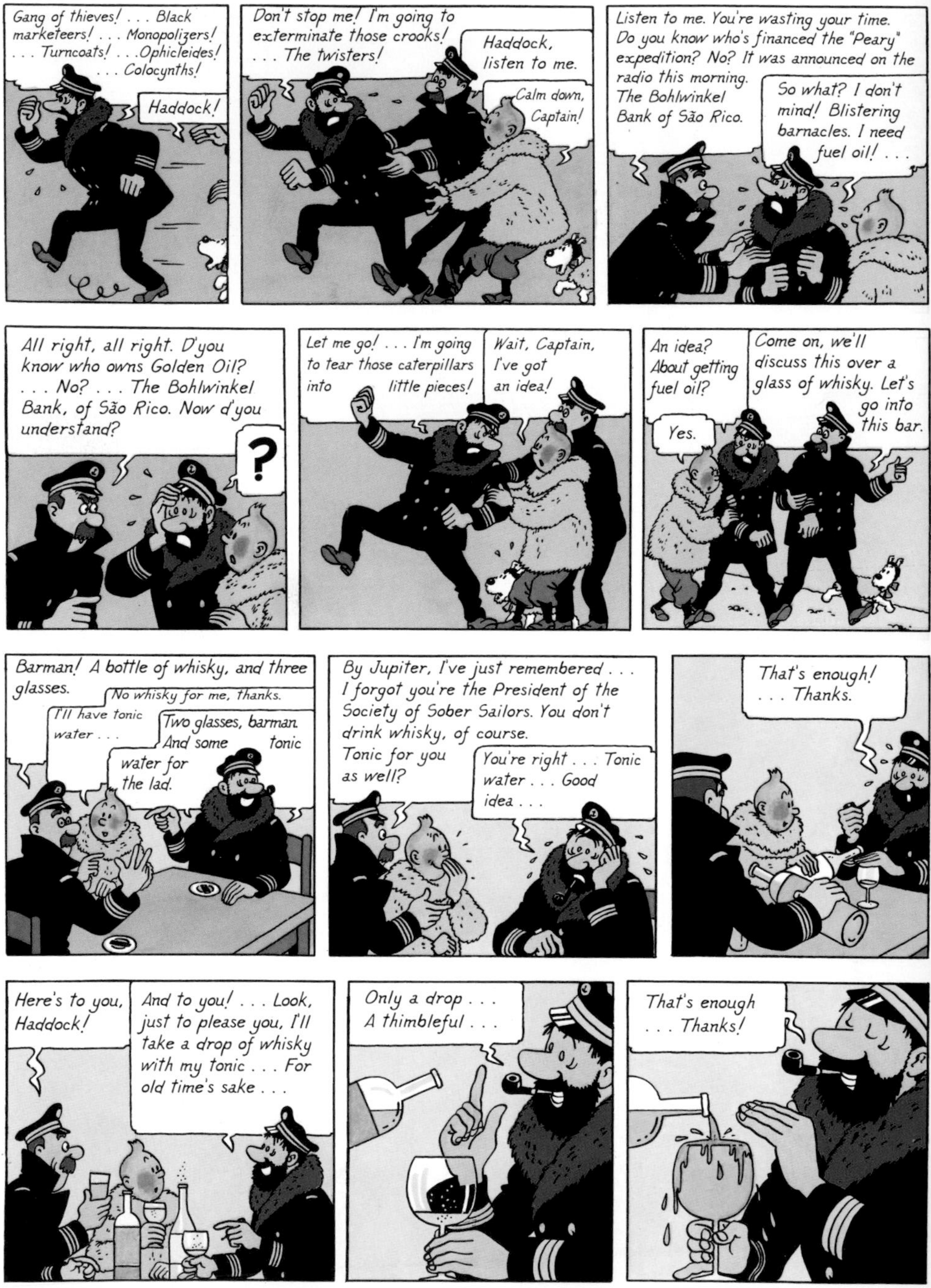

Gang of thieves! . . . Black marketeers! . . . Monopolizers! . . . Turncoats! . . . Ophicleides! . . . Colocynths!
Haddock!
Don't stop me! I'm going to exterminate those crooks! . . . The twisters!
Haddock, listen to me.
Calm down, Captain!
Listen to me. You're wasting your time. Do you know who's financed the "Peary" expedition? No? It was announced on the radio this morning. The Bohlwinkel Bank of São Rico.
So what? I don't mind! Blistering barnacles. I need fuel oil! . . .
All right, all right. D'you know who owns Golden Oil? . . . No? . . . The Bohlwinkel Bank, of São Rico. Now d'you understand?
?
Let me go! . . . I'm going to tear those caterpillars into little pieces!
Wait, Captain, I've got an idea!
An idea? About getting fuel oil?
Yes.
Come on, we'll discuss this over a glass of whisky. Let's go into this bar.
Barman! A bottle of whisky, and three glasses.
No whisky for me, thanks.
I'll have tonic water . . .
Two glasses, barman. And some tonic water for the lad.
By Jupiter, I've just remembered . . . I forgot you're the President of the Society of Sober Sailors. You don't drink whisky, of course. Tonic for you as well?
You're right . . . Tonic water . . . Good idea . . .
That's enough! . . . Thanks.
Here's to you, Haddock!
And to you! . . . Look, just to please you, I'll take a drop of whisky with my tonic . . . For old time's sake . . .
Only a drop . . . A thimbleful . . .
That's enough . . . Thanks!

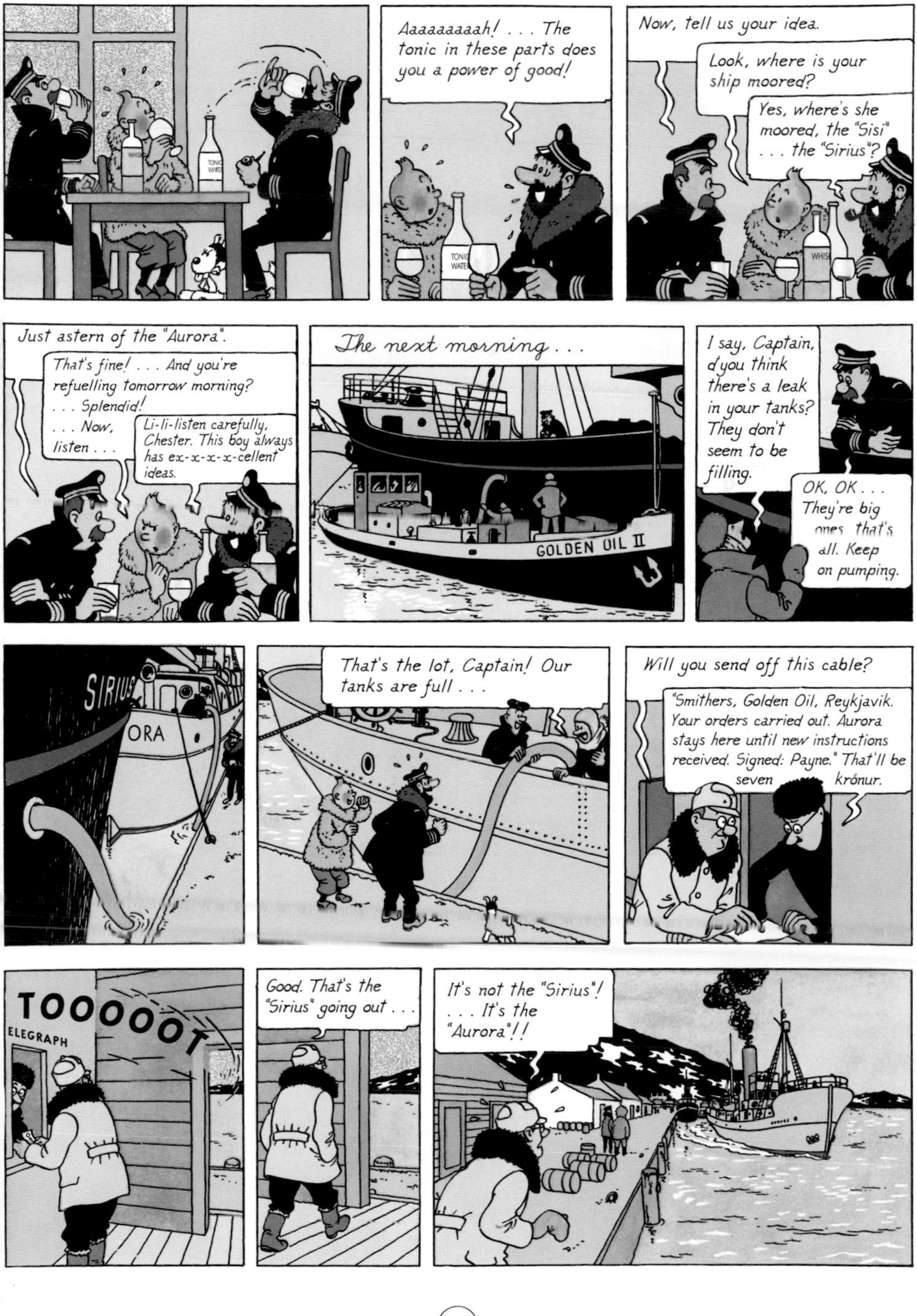

Aaaaaaaaah! . . . The tonic in these parts does you a power of good!
Now, tell us your idea.
Look, where is your ship moored?
Yes, where's she moored, the "Sisi" . . . the "Sirius"?
Just astern of the "Aurora".
That's fine! . . . And you're refuelling tomorrow morning? . . . Splendid! . . . Now, listen . . .
Li-li-listen carefully, Chester. This boy always has ex-x-x-x-cellent ideas.
The next morning . . .
GOLDEN OIL II
I say, Captain, d'you think there's a leak in your tanks? They don't seem to be filling.
OK, OK . . . They're big ones that's all. Keep on pumping.
SIRIUS
ORA
That's the lot, Captain! Our tanks are full . . .
Will you send off this cable?
"Smithers, Golden Oil, Reykjavik. Your orders carried out. Aurora stays here until new instructions received. Signed: Payne." That'll be seven krónur.
TOOOOOT
ELEGRAPH
Good. That's the "Sirius" going out . . .
It's not the "Sirius"! . . . It's the "Aurora"!!

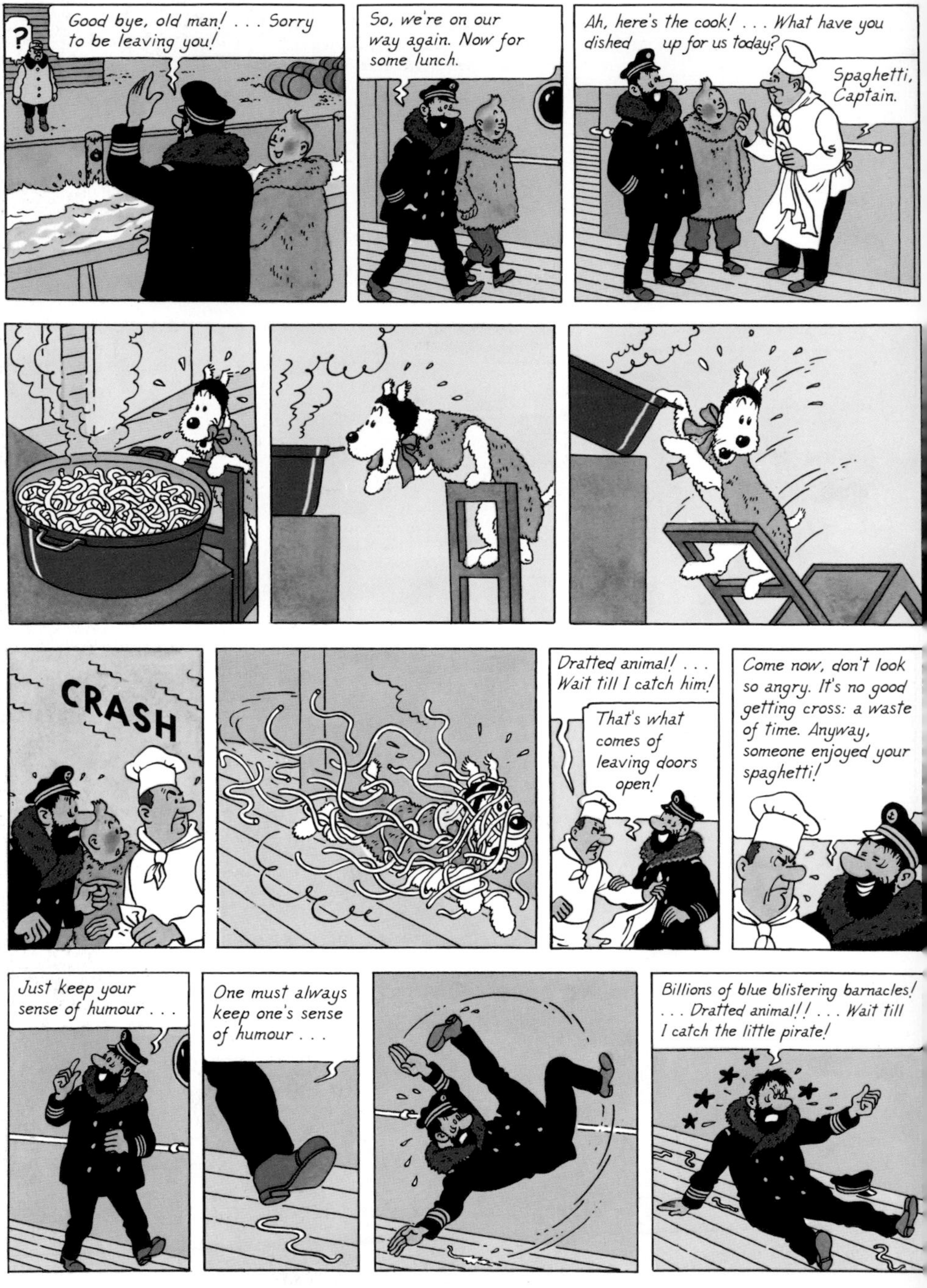
?
Good bye, old man! . . . Sorry to be leaving you!
So, we're on our way again. Now for some lunch.
Ah, here's the cook! . . . What have you dished up for us today?
Spaghetti, Captain.
CRASH
Dratted animal! . . . Wait till I catch him!
That's what comes of leaving doors open!
Come now, don't look so angry. It's no good getting cross: a waste of time. Anyway, someone enjoyed your spaghetti!
Just keep your sense of humour . . .
One must always keep one's sense of humour . . .
Billions of blue blistering barnacles! . . . Dratted animal!! . . . Wait till I catch the little pirate!

A week later . . .

This is where we are. We've crossed the 72nd parallel. You will confine your search to an area between 73 and 78 North, and 8 and 13 West . . . You understand?

Right.

Above all, don't take risks: don't go beyond the limits we fixed.

And don't forget to maintain contact by radio. Goodbye, and good luck. Keep your eyes skinned for the meteorite.

There they go . . .

Let's hope they don't run into any trouble.

Hello? . . . Hello? . . .

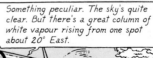
Hello? . . . Receiving you loud and clear . . . What? . . . You've seen something?

The meteorite?

Something peculiar. The sky's quite clear. But there's a great column of white vapour rising from one spot about 20° East.

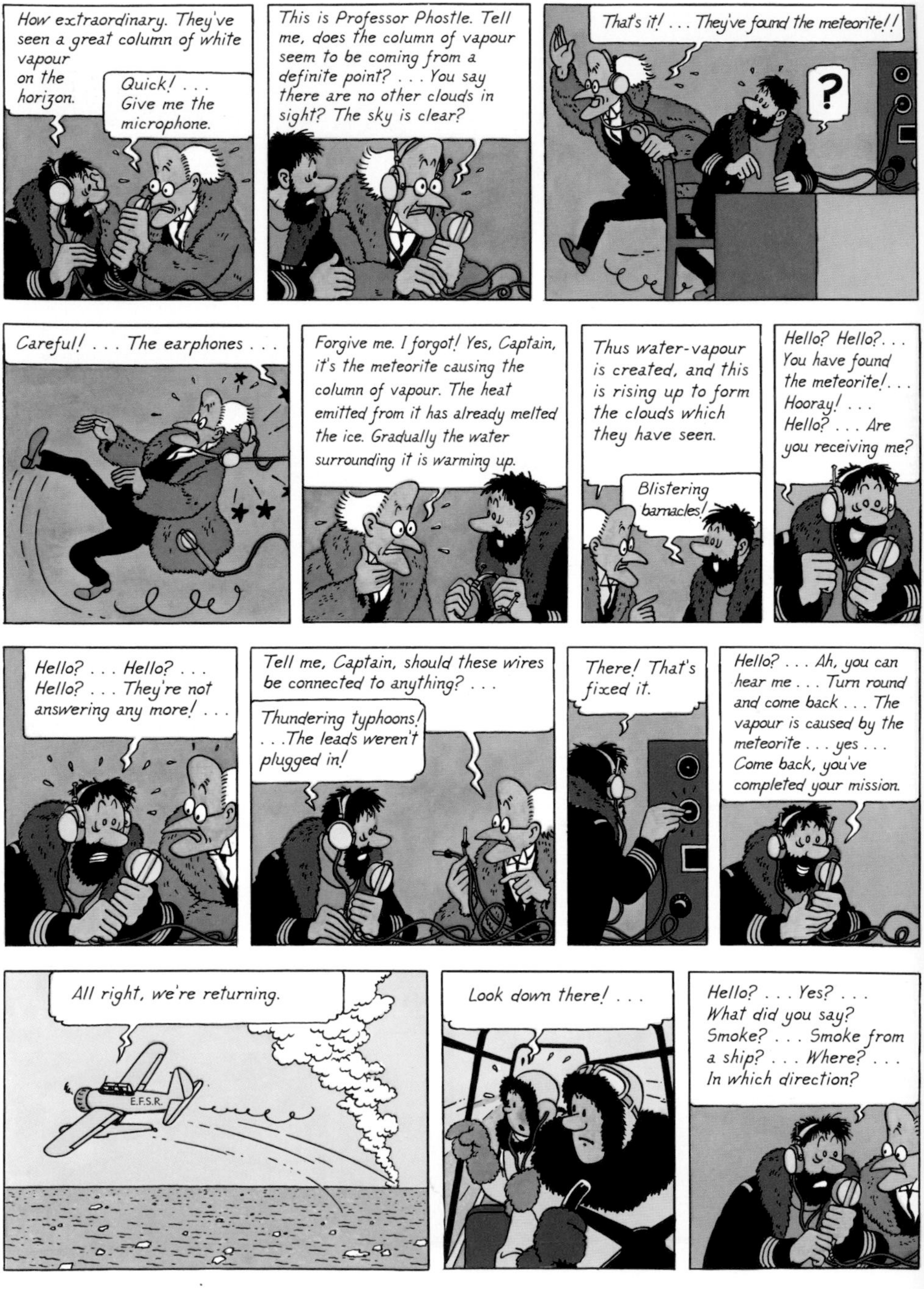
How extraordinary. They've seen a great column of white vapour on the horizon.
Quick! . . . Give me the microphone.
This is Professor Phostle. Tell me, does the column of vapour seem to be coming from a definite point? . . . You say there are no other clouds in sight? The sky is clear?
That's it! . . . They've found the meteorite!!
?
Careful! . . . The earphones . . .
Forgive me. I forgot! Yes, Captain, it's the meteorite causing the column of vapour. The heat emitted from it has already melted the ice. Gradually the water surrounding it is warming up.
Thus water-vapour is created, and this is rising up to form the clouds which they have seen.
Blistering barnacles!
Hello? Hello?. . . You have found the meteorite!. . . Hooray! . . . Hello? . . . Are you receiving me?
Hello? . . . Hello? . . . Hello? . . . They're not answering any more! . . .
Tell me, Captain, should these wires be connected to anything? . . .
Thundering typhoons! . . .The leads weren't plugged in!
There! That's fixed it.
Hello? . . . Ah, you can hear me . . . Turn round and come back . . . The vapour is caused by the meteorite . . . yes . . . Come back, you've completed your mission.
All right, we're returning.
E.F.S.R.
Look down there! . . .
Hello? . . . Yes? . . . What did you say? Smoke? . . . Smoke from a ship? . . . Where? . . . In which direction?

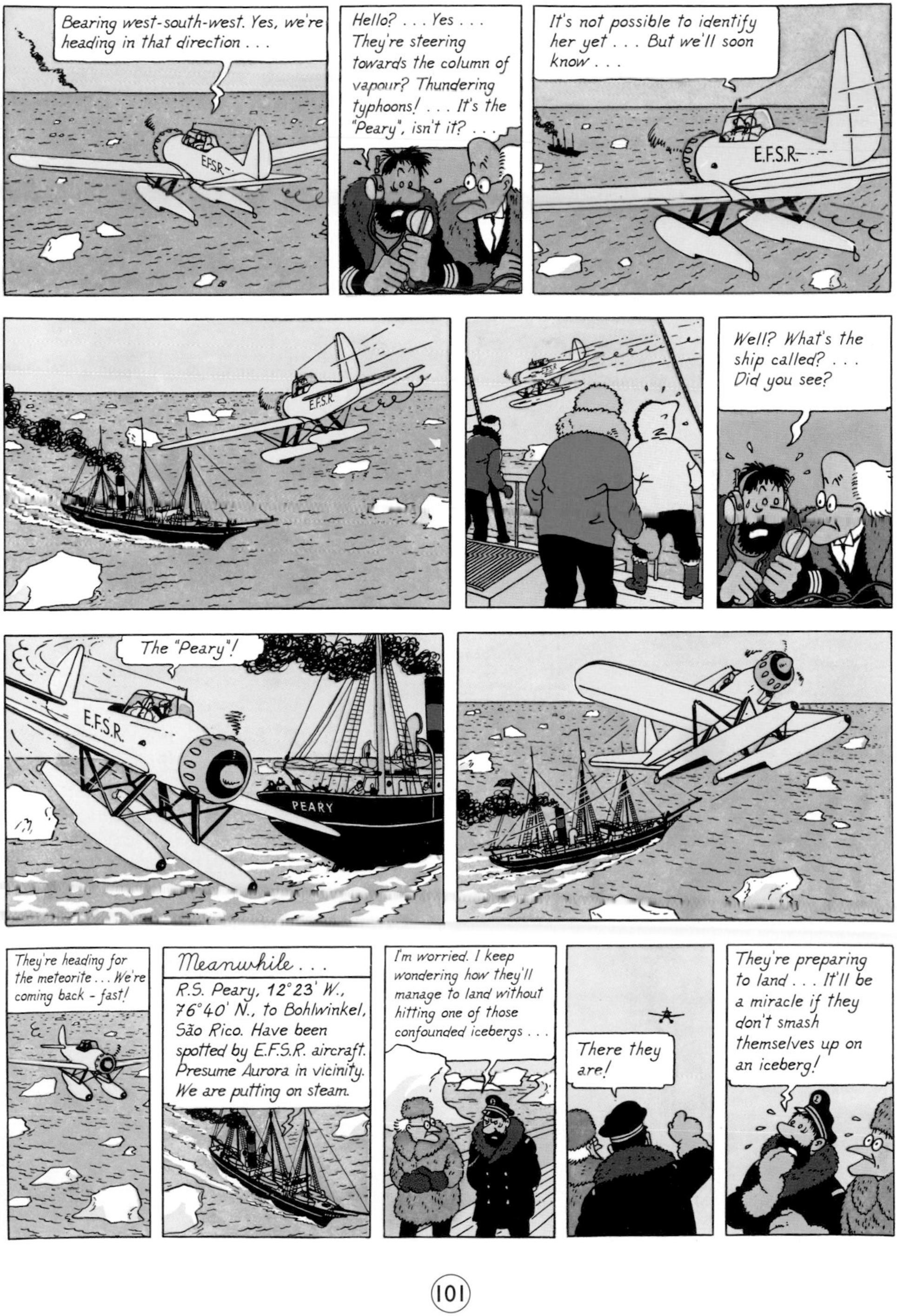
Bearing west-south-west. Yes, we're heading in that direction . . .
Hello? . . . Yes . . . They're steering towards the column of vapour? Thundering typhoons! . . . It's the "Peary", isn't it? . . .
It's not possible to identify her yet . . . But we'll soon know . . .
E.F.S.R.
E.F.S.R.
E.F.S.R.
Well? What's the ship called? . . . Did you see?
The "Peary"!
E.F.S.R.
PEARY
They're heading for the meteorite . . . We're coming back - fast!
Meanwhile . . .
R.S. Peary, 12°23' W., 76°40' N., to Bohlwinkel, São Rico. Have been spotted by E.F.S.R. aircraft. Presume Aurora in vicinity. We are putting on steam.
I'm worried. I keep wondering how they'll manage to land without hitting one of those confounded icebergs . . .
There they are!
They're preparing to land . . . It'll be a miracle if they don't smash themselves up on an iceberg!

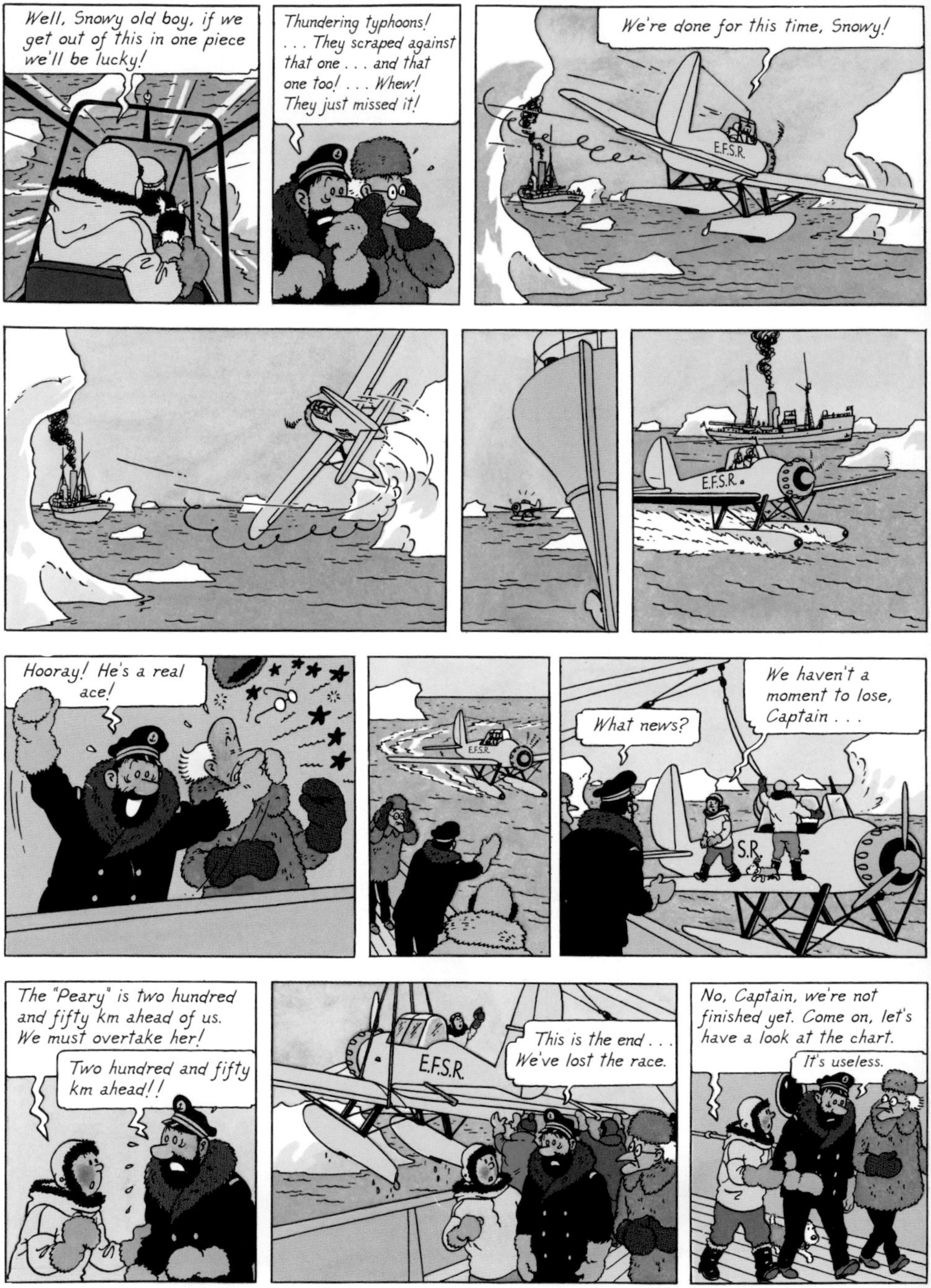
Well, Snowy old boy, if we get out of this in one piece we'll be lucky!
Thundering typhoons! . . . They scraped against that one . . . and that one too! . . . Whew! They just missed it!
We're done for this time, Snowy!
E.F.S.R.
E.F.S.R.
Hooray! He's a real ace!
E.F.S.R.
What news?
We haven't a moment to lose, Captain . . .
S.R.
The "Peary" is two hundred and fifty km ahead of us. We must overtake her!
Two hundred and fifty km ahead!!
E.F.S.R.
This is the end . . . We've lost the race.
No, Captain, we're not finished yet. Come on, let's have a look at the chart.
It's useless.

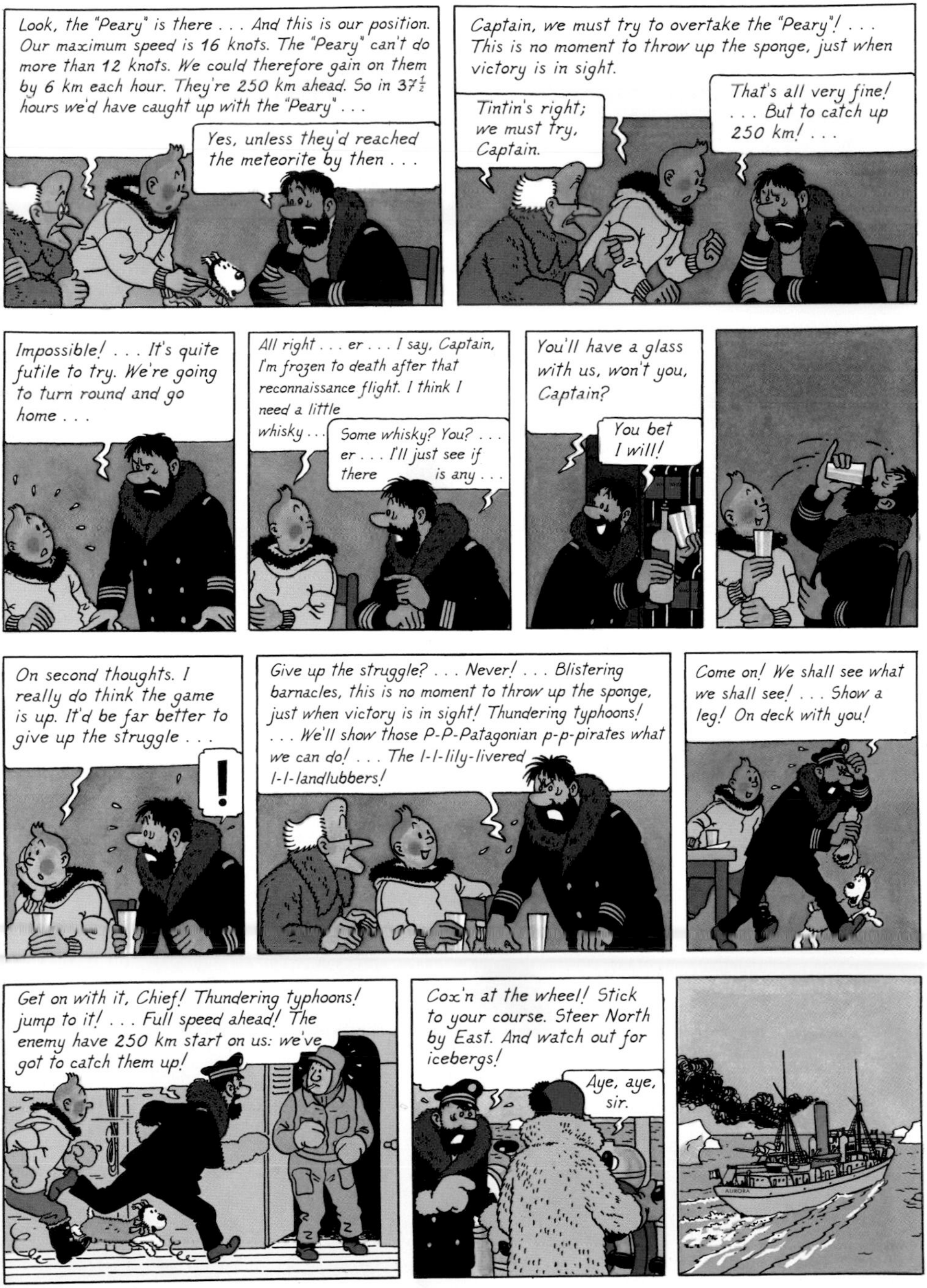
Look, the "Peary" is there . . . And this is our position. Our maximum speed is 16 knots. The "Peary" can't do more than 12 knots. We could therefore gain on them by 6 km each hour. They're 250 km ahead. So in 37½ hours we'd have caught up with the "Peary" . . .
Yes, unless they'd reached the meteorite by then . . .
Captain, we must try to overtake the "Peary"! . . . This is no moment to throw up the sponge, just when victory is in sight.
Tintin's right; we must try, Captain.
That's all very fine! . . . But to catch up 250 km! . . .
Impossible! . . . It's quite futile to try. We're going to turn round and go home . . .
All right . . . er . . . I say, Captain, I'm frozen to death after that reconnaissance flight. I think I need a little whisky . . .
Some whisky? You? . . . er . . . I'll just see if there is any . . .
You'll have a glass with us, won't you, Captain?
You bet I will!
On second thoughts. I really do think the game is up. It'd be far better to give up the struggle . . .
!
Give up the struggle? . . . Never! . . . Blistering barnacles, this is no moment to throw up the sponge, just when victory is in sight! Thundering typhoons! . . . We'll show those P-P-Patagonian p-p-pirates what we can do! . . . The l-l-lily-livered l-l-landlubbers!
Come on! We shall see what we shall see! . . . Show a leg! On deck with you!
Get on with it, Chief! Thundering typhoons! jump to it! . . . Full speed ahead! The enemy have 250 km start on us: we've got to catch them up!
Cox'n at the wheel! Stick to your course. Steer North by East. And watch out for icebergs!
Aye, aye, sir.
AURORA

Noon next day . . .

Hooray! . . . There she is! . . . That's smoke from the "Peary"!

We're steaming faster than she is! . . . We'll overtake them this evening, or during the night.

Captain! . . . A signal!

!

Read it! . . . This is the last straw! . . . What are we going to do? Blistering barnacles, what are we going to do?

!

Ask our scientists to come to the saloon. Tell them I have important news . . .

Gentlemen, I'd like to read you a signal we've just picked up. It's a distress call. The text is disjointed, as if the transmitter was damaged. Even the name of the ship is incomplete.

S.O.S. S.O.S. S.O.S.
CIT . . . 70°45' N.,
19°12' W. IN
COLLISION WITH
ICEB . . . TAKING
WATER IN FORWA . .
. . QUEST
ASSISTANCE
URGE . . .

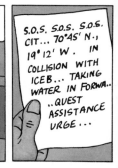

There it is, gentlemen. Either we can go to the aid of this ship, and abandon all hope of reaching the meteorite before the "Peary", or else we can continue on our course, and not answer this call . . . It's up to you to decide.

There's no question about it, Captain. Human lives are in danger. We must go to their aid, even if it does cost us our prize . . .

I was sure of your answer, Professor. We'll go about right away . . .

Bravo!

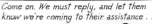

Come on. We must reply, and let them know we're coming to their assistance . . .

I've forgotten to shut that confounded door again . . .

Polar research ship Aurora to Cit . . . in distress. Your message received. We are steaming towards you. Keep in touch with us. Good luck!

Well?

That's the third time I've sent out the message . . . There's no reply.

I suppose their radio has packed up for good . . .

Yes, unless . . .

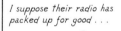

Unless they have . . . gone down? Is that what you mean to say?

No, it's not that . . .

Captain, will you let me send out a message myself?

Naturally, but . . .

?

Is that the text of what you want to send? It's absurd! What does the ship's name matter to us? . . . Anyway, you'll spend all night waiting for replies.

All night. Yes, I know.

You do as you like, but I think it's absolutely crazy. I'm going to turn in. Good night!

Good night, Captain . . . There. Could you send that off?

Right.

Polar research ship Aurora to all shipping companies. Please will all companies owning ships with name commencing "CIT" please advise us immediately of full names of these ships. Also inform us if one is in distress, position 70°45' N., 19°12' W.

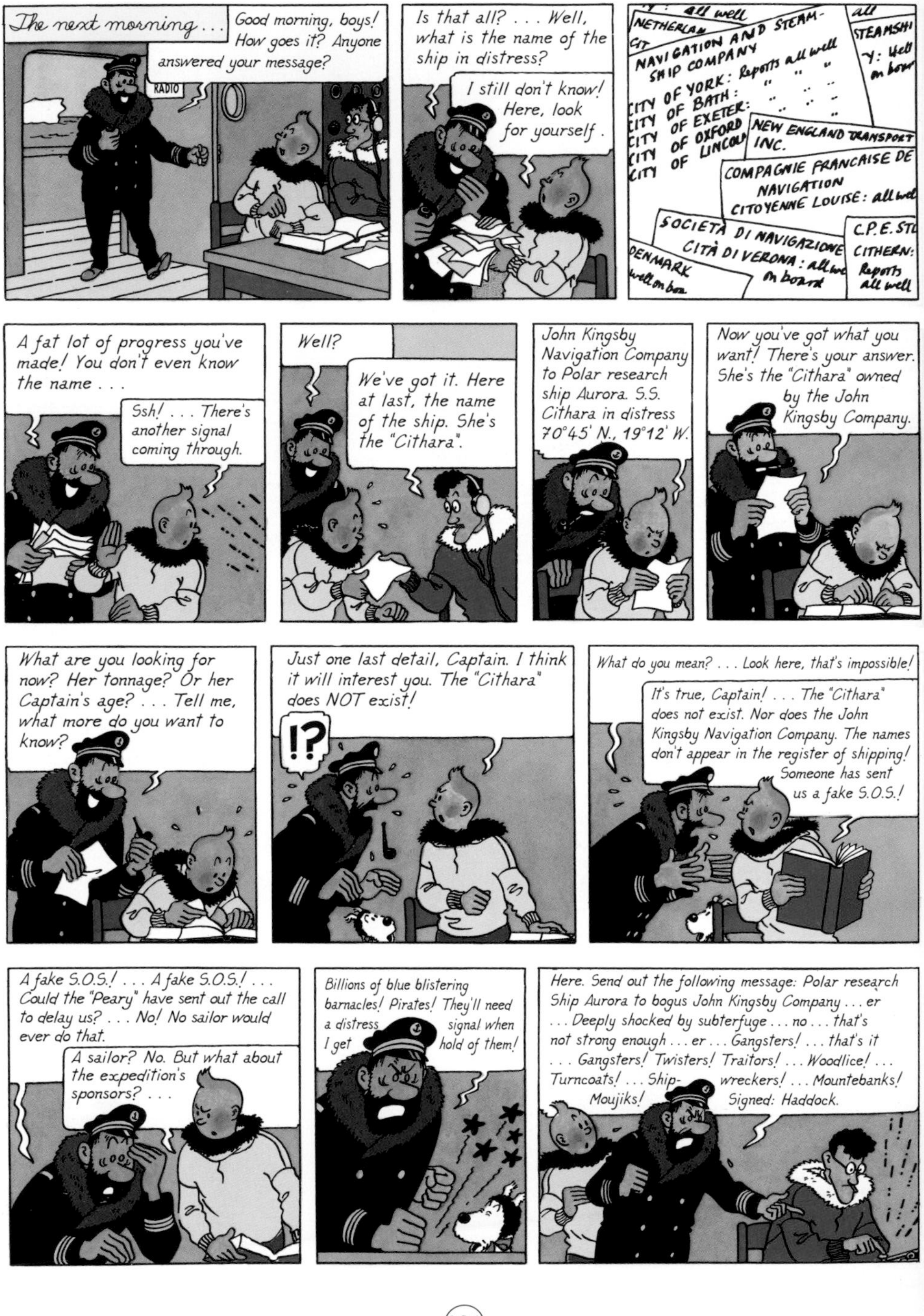

The next morning . . .
Good morning, boys! How goes it? Anyone answered your message?
RADIO
Is that all? . . . Well, what is the name of the ship in distress?
I still don't know! Here, look for yourself .
NETHERLAN
NAVIGATION AND STEAM-SHIP COMPANY
CITY OF YORK: Reports all well
CITY OF BATH:
CITY OF EXETER:
CITY OF OXFORD
CITY OF LINCOL
STEAMSHI
NEW ENGLAND TRANSPORT INC.
COMPAGNIE FRANCAISE DE NAVIGATION
CITOYENNE LOUISE: all well
SOCIETA DI NAVIGAZIONE
CITÀ DI VERONA: all well on board
DENMARK
C.P.E. STE
CITHERN: Reports all well
A fat lot of progress you've made! You don't even know the name . . .
Ssh! . . . There's another signal coming through.
Well?
We've got it. Here at last, the name of the ship. She's the "Cithara".
John Kingsby Navigation Company to Polar research ship Aurora. S.S. Cithara in distress 70°45' N., 19°12' W.
Now you've got what you want! There's your answer. She's the "Cithara" owned by the John Kingsby Company.
What are you looking for now? Her tonnage? Or her Captain's age? . . . Tell me, what more do you want to know?
Just one last detail, Captain. I think it will interest you. The "Cithara" does NOT exist!
!?
What do you mean? . . . Look here, that's impossible!
It's true, Captain! . . . The "Cithara" does not exist. Nor does the John Kingsby Navigation Company. The names don't appear in the register of shipping! Someone has sent us a fake S.O.S.!
A fake S.O.S.! . . . A fake S.O.S.! . . . Could the "Peary" have sent out the call to delay us? . . . No! No sailor would ever do that.
A sailor? No. But what about the expedition's sponsors? . . .
Billions of blue blistering barnacles! Pirates! They'll need a distress signal when I get hold of them!
Here. Send out the following message: Polar research Ship Aurora to bogus John Kingsby Company . . . er . . . Deeply shocked by subterfuge . . . no . . . that's not strong enough . . . er . . . Gangsters! . . . that's it . . . Gangsters! Twisters! Traitors! . . . Woodlice! . . . Turncoats! . . . Ship-wreckers! . . . Mountebanks! Moujiks! Signed: Haddock.

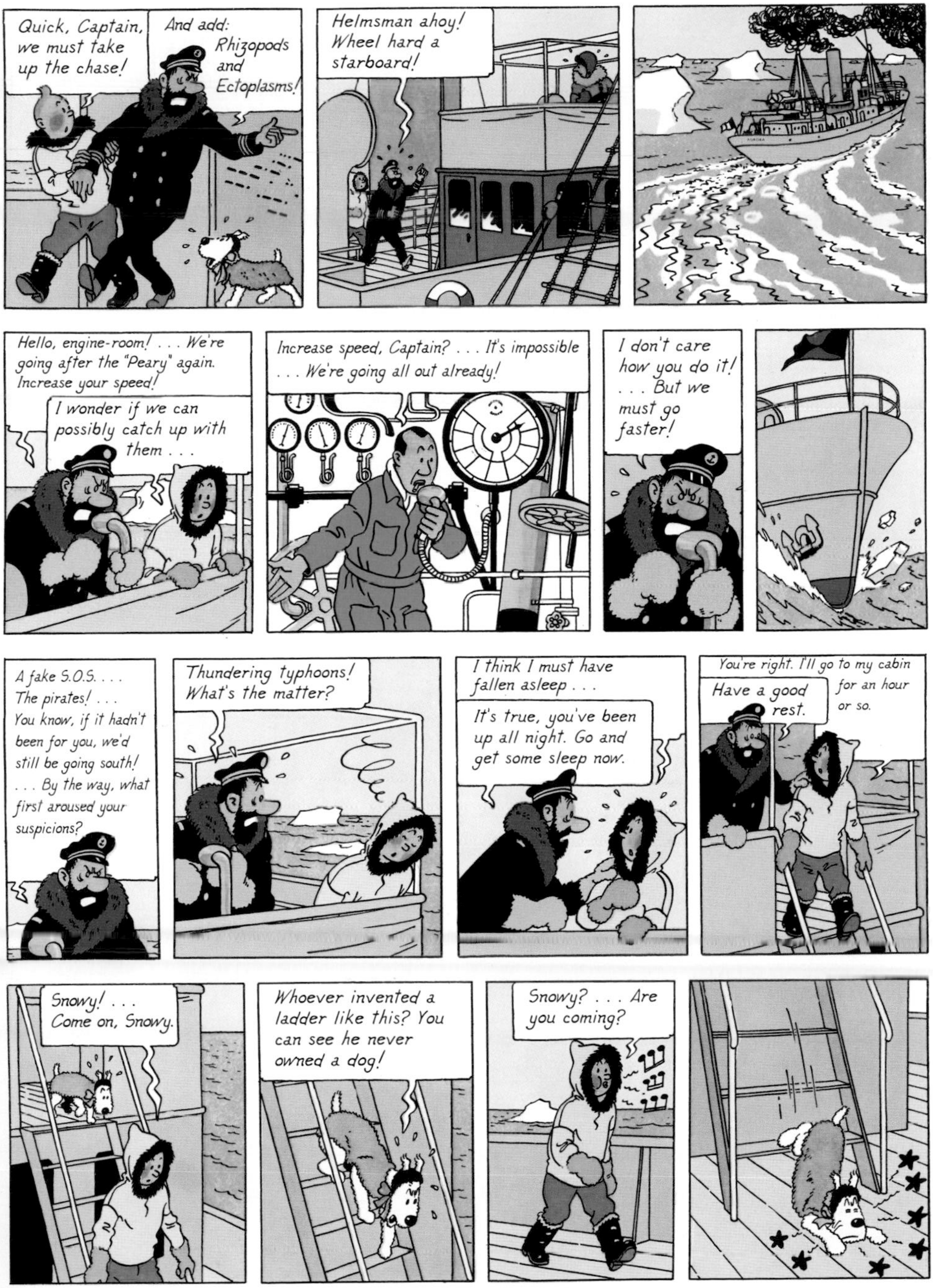
Quick, Captain, we must take up the chase!
And add: Rhizopods and Ectoplasms!
Helmsman ahoy! Wheel hard a starboard!
Hello, engine-room! . . . We're going after the "Peary" again. Increase your speed!
I wonder if we can possibly catch up with them . . .
Increase speed, Captain? . . . It's impossible . . . We're going all out already!
I don't care how you do it! . . . But we must go faster!
A fake S.O.S. . . . The pirates! . . . You know, if it hadn't been for you, we'd still be going south! . . . By the way, what first aroused your suspicions?
Thundering typhoons! What's the matter?
I think I must have fallen asleep . . .
It's true, you've been up all night. Go and get some sleep now.
You're right. I'll go to my cabin for an hour or so.
Have a good rest.
Snowy! . . . Come on, Snowy.
Whoever invented a ladder like this? You can see he never owned a dog!
Snowy? . . . Are you coming?

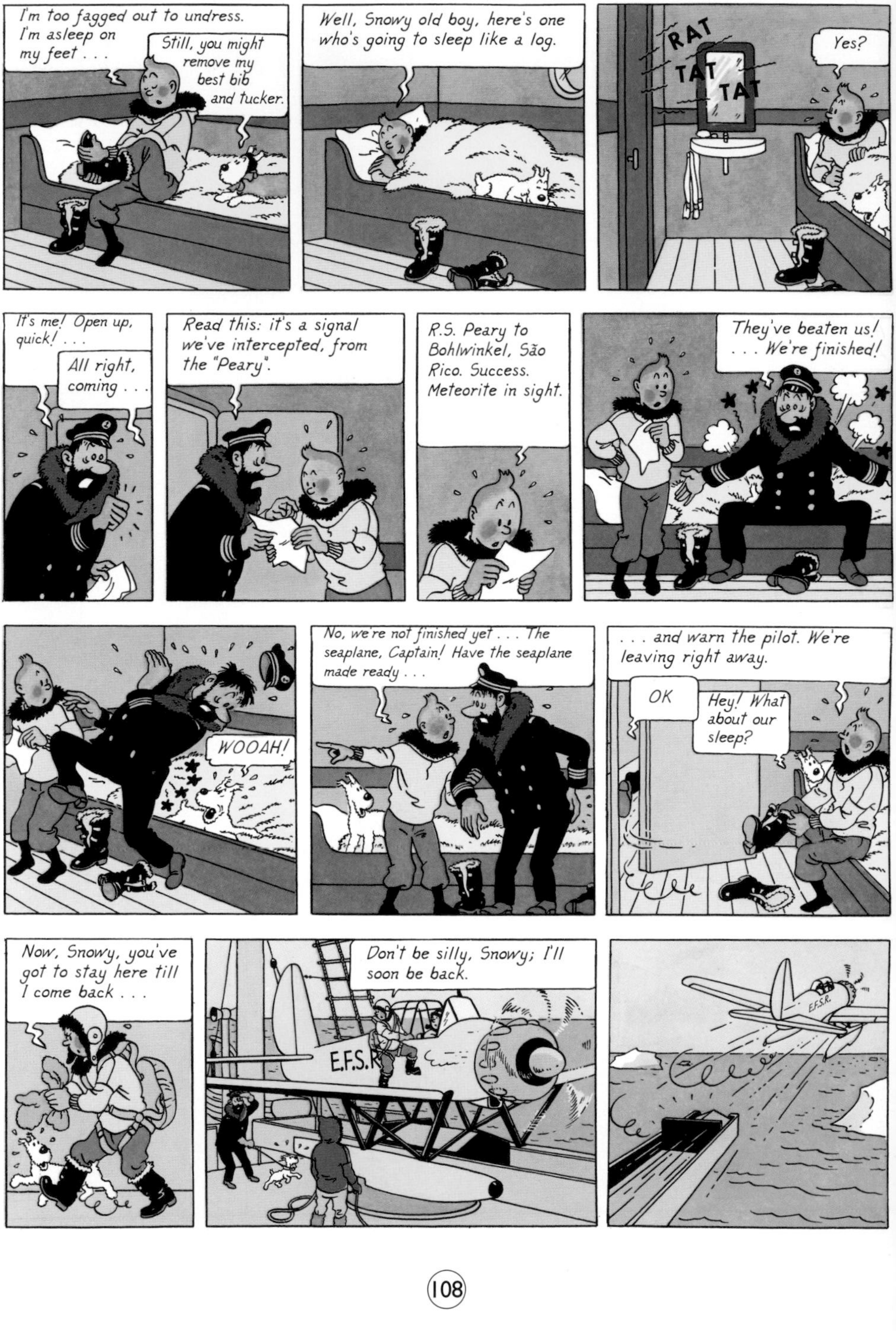
I'm too fagged out to undress. I'm asleep on my feet . . .
Still, you might remove my best bib and tucker.
Well, Snowy old boy, here's one who's going to sleep like a log.
RAT TAT TAT
Yes?
It's me! Open up, quick! . . .
All right, coming . . .
Read this: it's a signal we've intercepted, from the "Peary".
R.S. Peary to Bohlwinkel, São Rico. Success. Meteorite in sight.
They've beaten us! . . . We're finished!
WOOAH!
No, we're not finished yet . . . The seaplane, Captain! Have the seaplane made ready . . .
. . . and warn the pilot. We're leaving right away.
OK
Hey! What about our sleep?
Now, Snowy, you've got to stay here till I come back . . .
Don't be silly, Snowy; I'll soon be back.
E.F.S.R.
E.F.S.R.

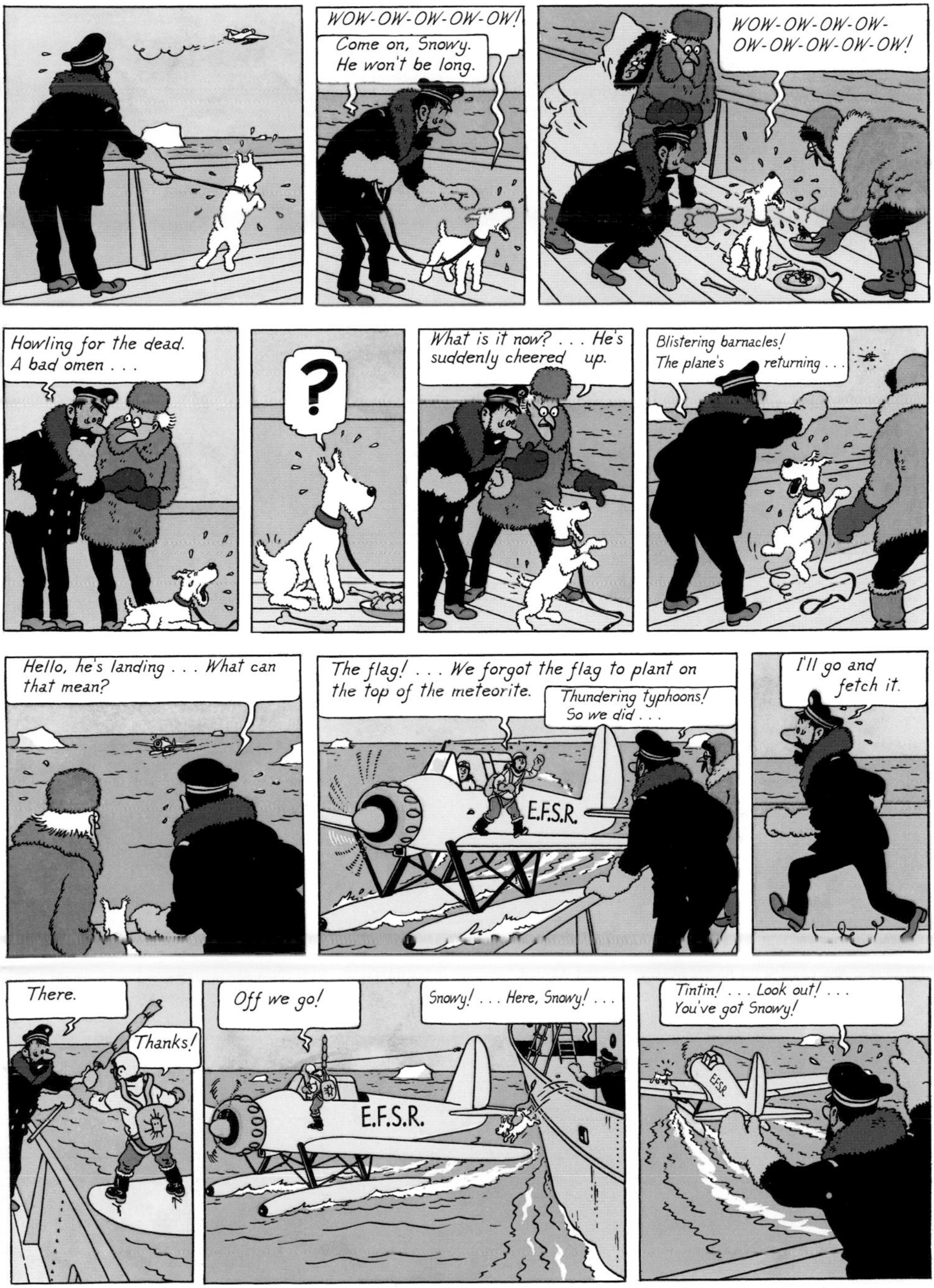
WOW-OW-OW-OW-OW!
Come on, Snowy. He won't be long.
WOW-OW-OW-OW-OW-OW-OW-OW-OW!
Howling for the dead. A bad omen . . .
?
What is it now? . . . He's suddenly cheered up.
Blistering barnacles! The plane's returning . . .
Hello, he's landing . . . What can that mean?
The flag! . . . We forgot the flag to plant on the top of the meteorite.
Thundering typhoons! So we did . . .
E.F.S.R.
I'll go and fetch it.
There.
Thanks!
Off we go!
Snowy! . . . Here, Snowy! . . .
E.F.S.R.
Tintin! . . . Look out! . . . You've got Snowy!
E.F.S.R.

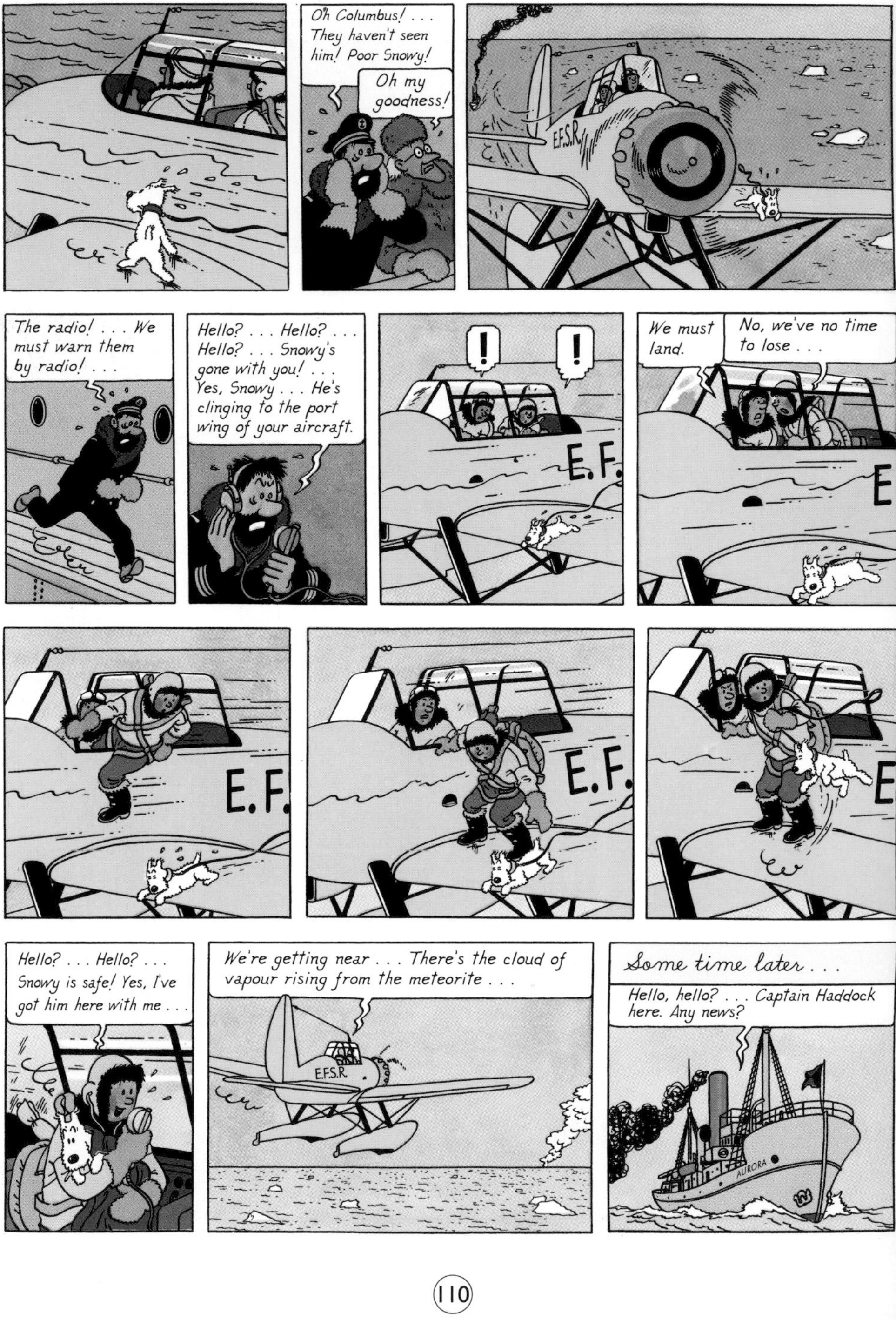
Oh Columbus! . . . They haven't seen him! Poor Snowy!
Oh my goodness!
E.F.S.R.
The radio! . . . We must warn them by radio! . . .
Hello? . . . Hello? . . . Hello? . . . Snowy's gone with you! . . . Yes, Snowy . . . He's clinging to the port wing of your aircraft.
!
!
E.F.
We must land.
No, we've no time to lose . . .
E
E.F.
E.F.
E
Hello? . . . Hello? . . . Snowy is safe! Yes, I've got him here with me . . .
We're getting near . . . There's the cloud of vapour rising from the meteorite . . .
E.F.S.R.
Some time later . . .
Hello, hello? . . . Captain Haddock here. Any news?
AURORA

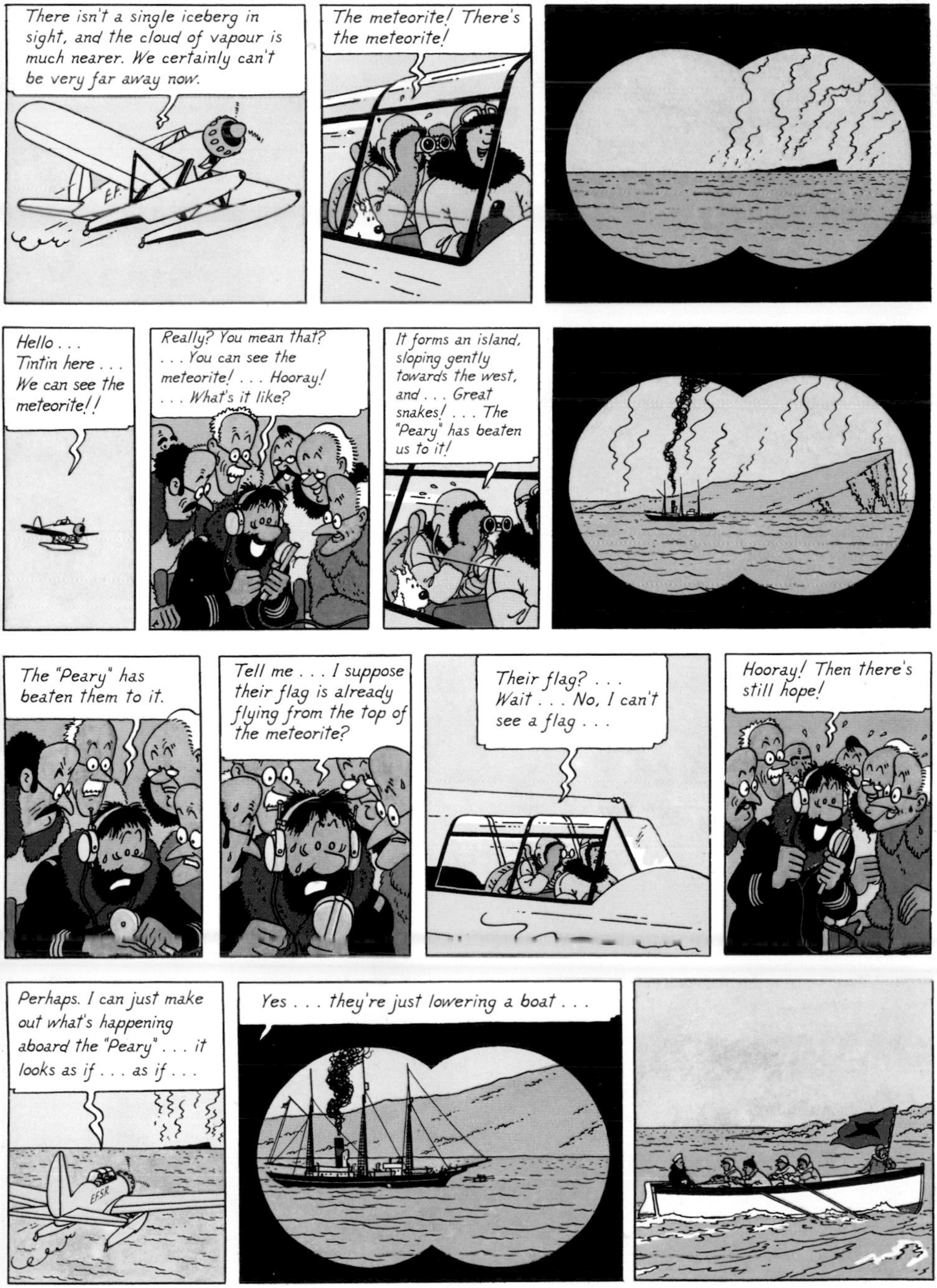
There isn't a single iceberg in sight, and the cloud of vapour is much nearer. We certainly can't be very far away now.
The meteorite! There's the meteorite!
Hello . . . Tintin here . . . We can see the meteorite!!
Really? You mean that? . . . You can see the meteorite! . . . Hooray! . . . What's it like?
It forms an island, sloping gently towards the west, and . . . Great snakes! . . . The "Peary" has beaten us to it!
The "Peary" has beaten them to it.
Tell me . . . I suppose their flag is already flying from the top of the meteorite?
Their flag? . . . Wait . . . No, I can't see a flag . . .
Hooray! Then there's still hope!
Perhaps. I can just make out what's happening aboard the "Peary" . . . it looks as if . . . as if . . .
Yes . . . they're just lowering a boat . . .

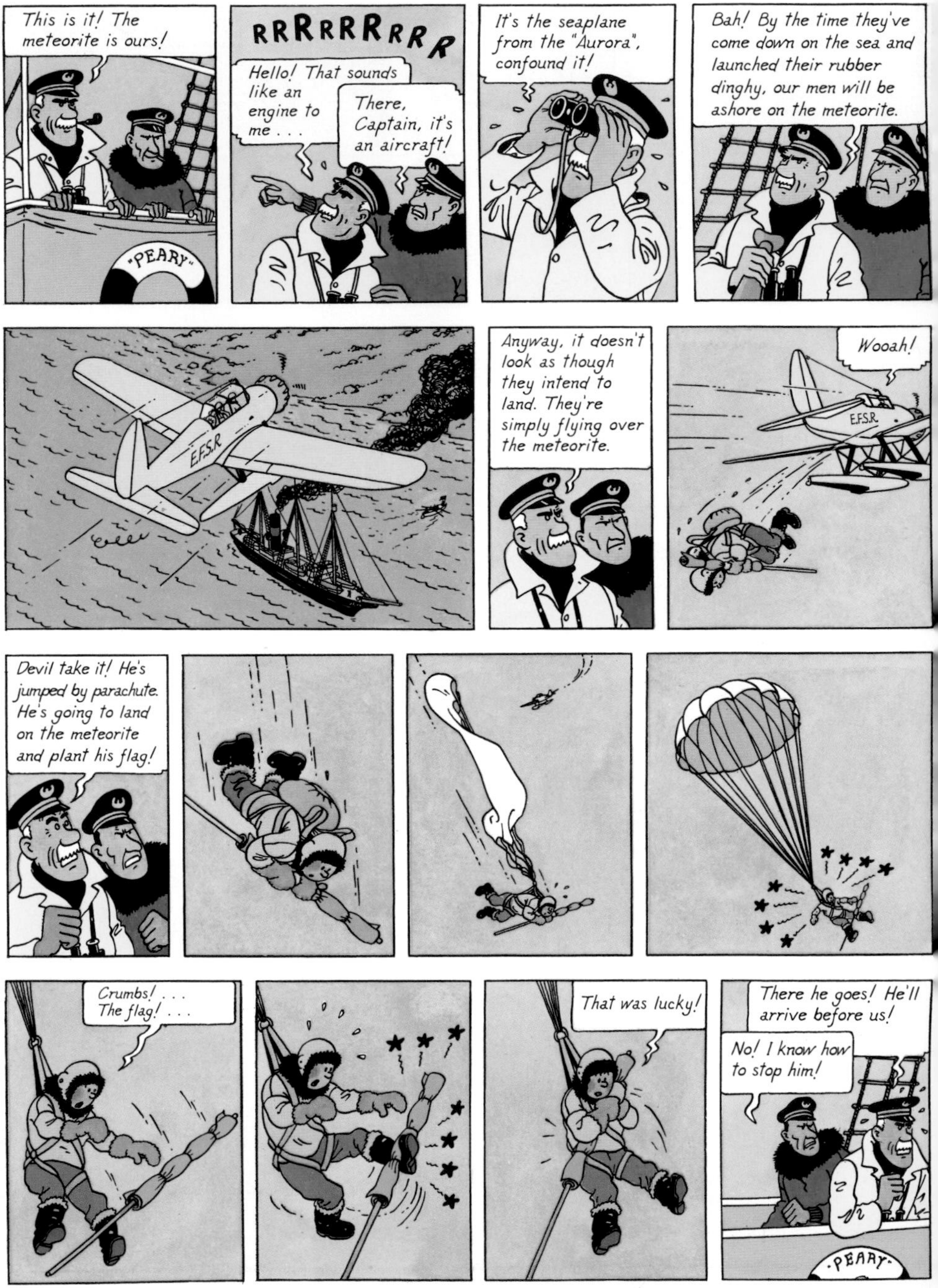
This is it! The meteorite is ours!
RRRRRRRRRR
Hello! That sounds like an engine to me . . .
There, Captain, it's an aircraft!
It's the seaplane from the "Aurora", confound it!
Bah! By the time they've come down on the sea and launched their rubber dinghy, our men will be ashore on the meteorite.
"PEARY"
E.F.S.R.
Anyway, it doesn't look as though they intend to land. They're simply flying over the meteorite.
Wooah!
E.F.S.R.
Devil take it! He's jumped by parachute. He's going to land on the meteorite and plant his flag!
Crumbs! . . . The flag! . . .
That was lucky!
There he goes! He'll arrive before us!
No! I know how to stop him!
PEARY

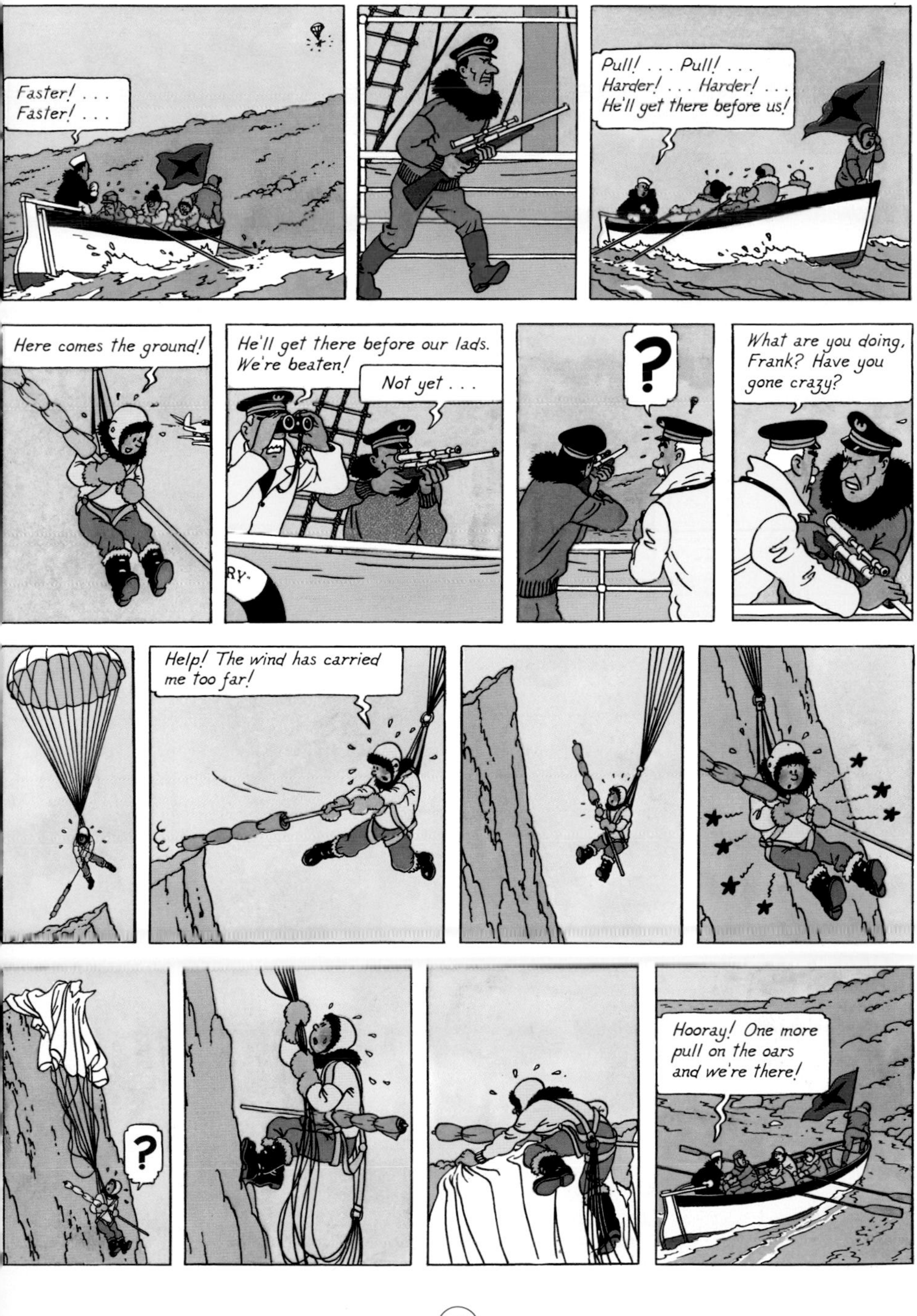
Faster! . . .
Faster! . . .
Pull! . . . Pull! . . .
Harder! . . . Harder! . . .
He'll get there before us!
Here comes the ground!
He'll get there before our lads. We're beaten!
Not yet . . .
?
What are you doing, Frank? Have you gone crazy?
Help! The wind has carried me too far!
?
Hooray! One more pull on the oars and we're there!

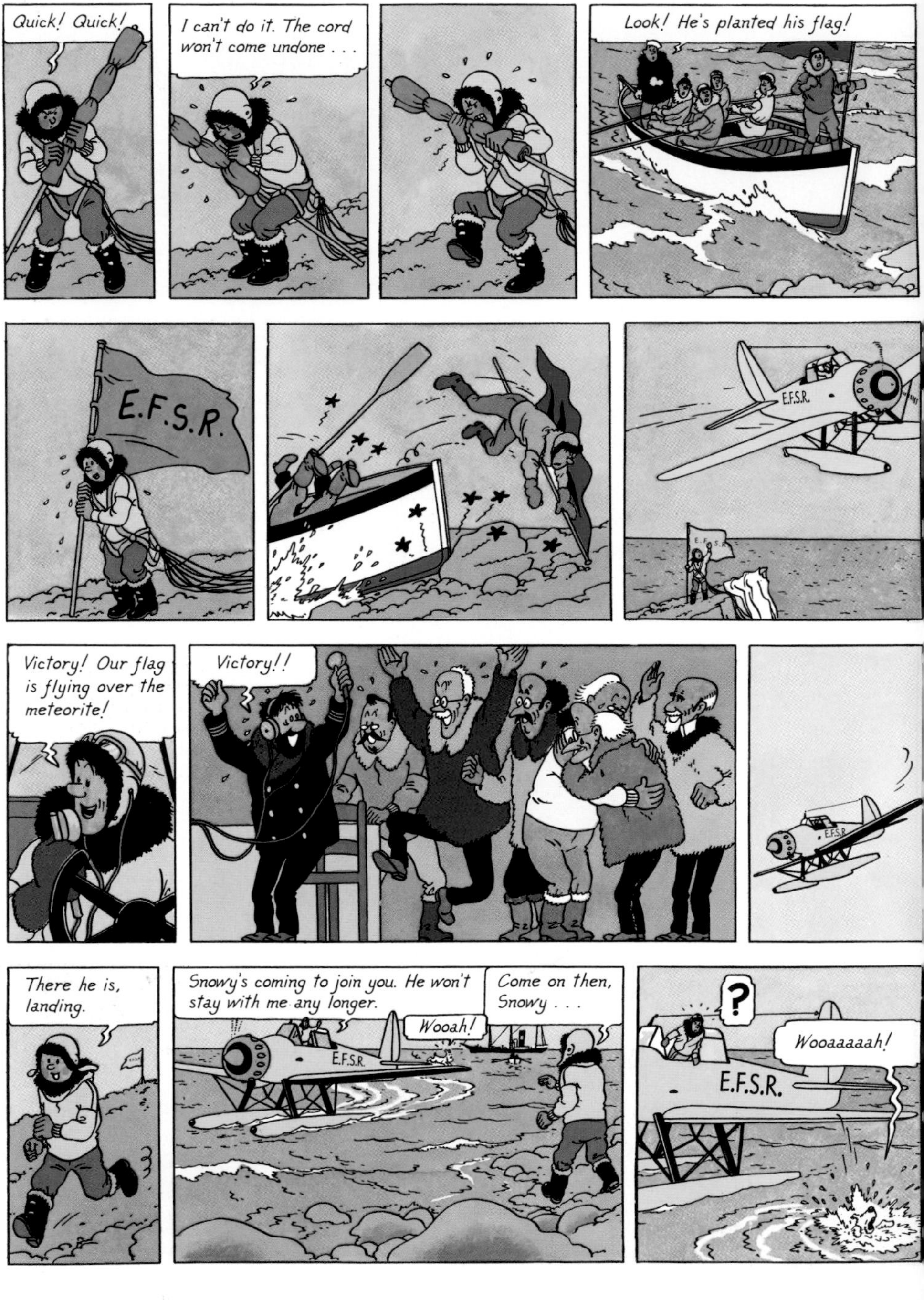
Quick! Quick!
I can't do it. The cord won't come undone . . .
Look! He's planted his flag!
E.F.S.R.
E.F.S.R.
Victory! Our flag is flying over the meteorite!
Victory!!
There he is, landing.
Snowy's coming to join you. He won't stay with me any longer.
Wooah!
E.F.S.R.
Come on then, Snowy . . .
?
Wooaaaaah!
E.F.S.R.

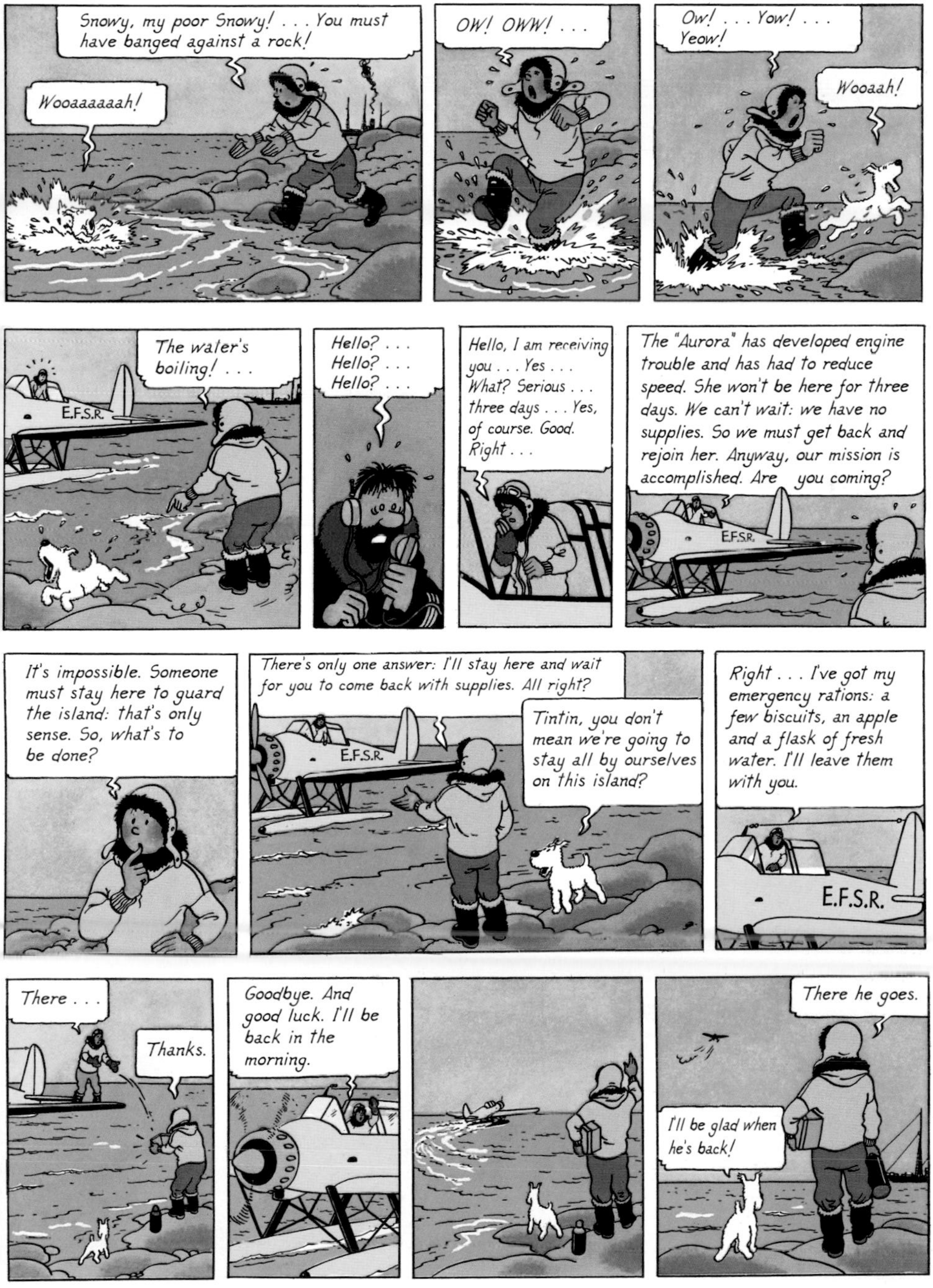
Snowy, my poor Snowy! . . . You must have banged against a rock!
Wooaaaaaah!
OW! OWW! . . .
Ow! . . . Yow! . . . Yeow!
Wooaah!
The water's boiling! . . .
E.F.S.R.
Hello? . . . Hello? . . . Hello? . . .
Hello, I am receiving you . . . Yes . . . What? Serious . . . three days . . . Yes, of course. Good. Right . . .
The "Aurora" has developed engine trouble and has had to reduce speed. She won't be here for three days. We can't wait: we have no supplies. So we must get back and rejoin her. Anyway, our mission is accomplished. Are you coming?
E.F.S.R.
It's impossible. Someone must stay here to guard the island: that's only sense. So, what's to be done?
There's only one answer: I'll stay here and wait for you to come back with supplies. All right?
Tintin, you don't mean we're going to stay all by ourselves on this island?
E.F.S.R.
Right . . . I've got my emergency rations: a few biscuits, an apple and a flask of fresh water. I'll leave them with you.
E.F.S.R.
There . . .
Thanks.
Goodbye. And good luck. I'll be back in the morning.
There he goes.
I'll be glad when he's back!

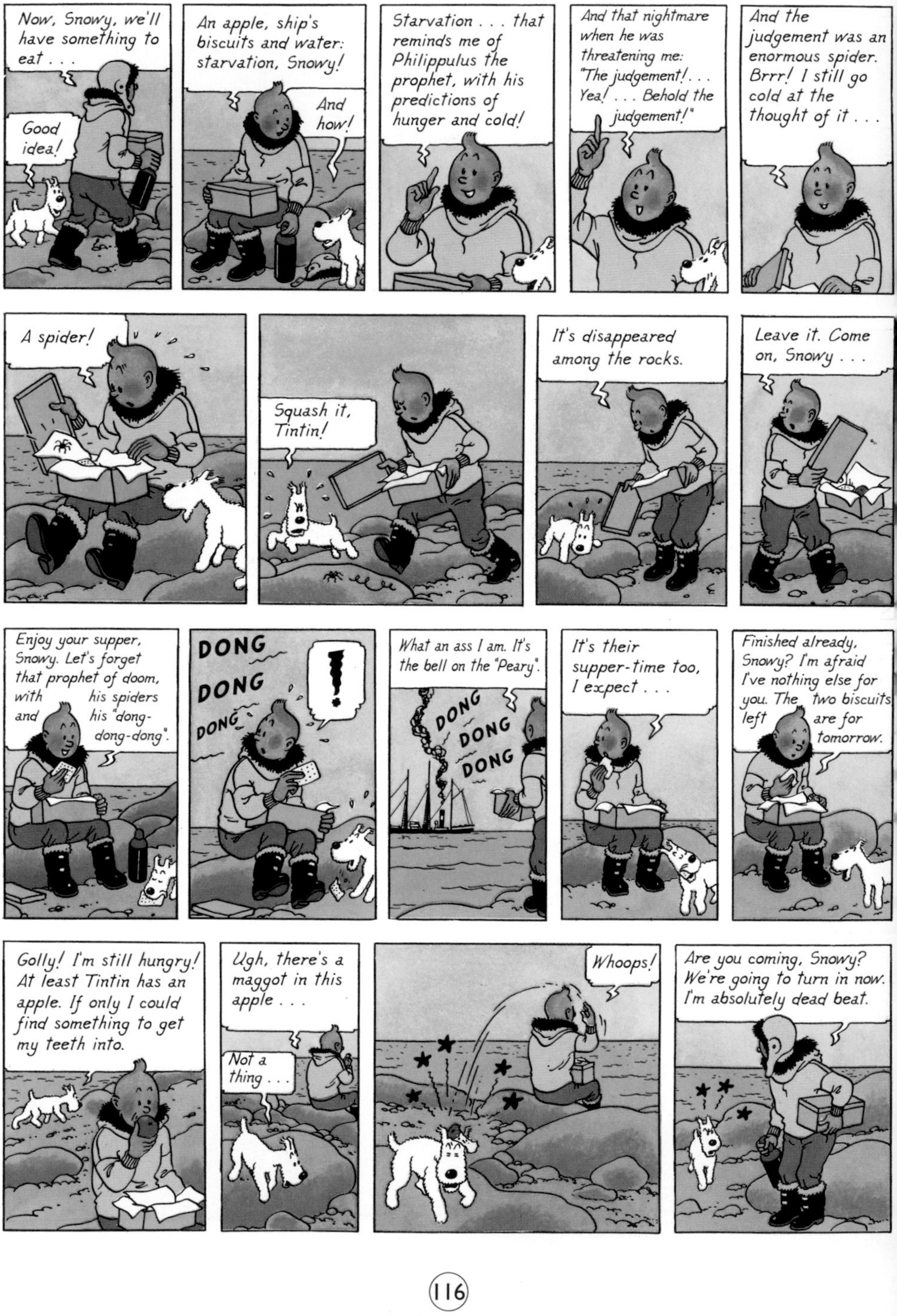
Now, Snowy, we'll have something to eat . . .
Good idea!
An apple, ship's biscuits and water: starvation, Snowy!
And how!
Starvation . . . that reminds me of Philippulus the prophet, with his predictions of hunger and cold!
And that nightmare when he was threatening me: "The judgement! . . . Yea! . . . Behold the judgement!"
And the judgement was an enormous spider. Brrr! I still go cold at the thought of it . . .
A spider!
Squash it, Tintin!
It's disappeared among the rocks.
Leave it. Come on, Snowy . . .
Enjoy your supper, Snowy. Let's forget that prophet of doom, with his spiders and his "dong-dong-dong".
DONG
DONG
DONG
!
What an ass I am. It's the bell on the "Peary".
DONG
DONG
DONG
It's their supper-time too, I expect . . .
Finished already, Snowy? I'm afraid I've nothing else for you. The two biscuits left are for tomorrow.
Golly! I'm still hungry! At least Tintin has an apple. If only I could find something to get my teeth into.
Ugh, there's a maggot in this apple . . .
Not a thing . . .
Whoops!
Are you coming, Snowy? We're going to turn in now. I'm absolutely dead beat.

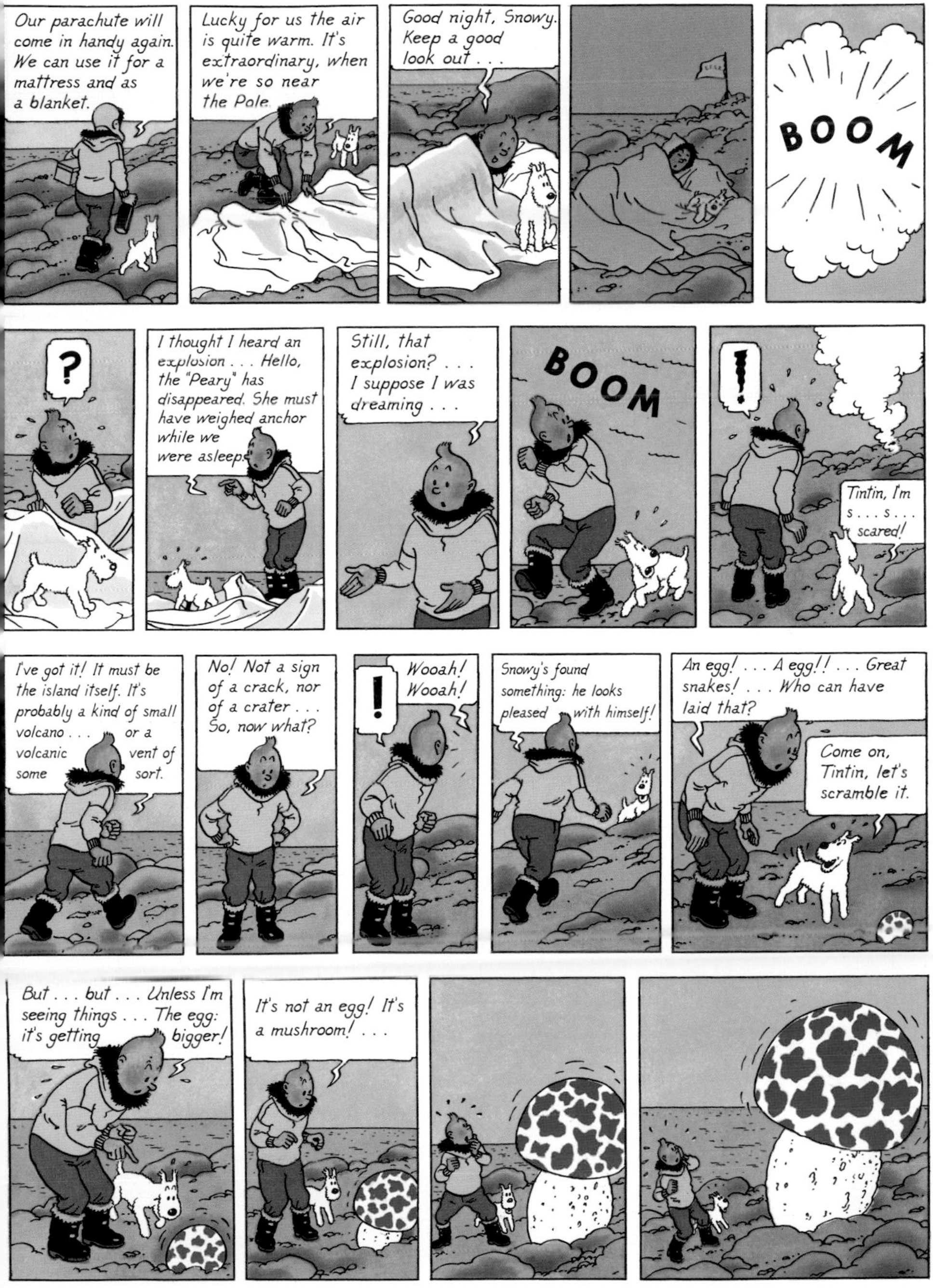

Our parachute will come in handy again. We can use it for a mattress and as a blanket.
Lucky for us the air is quite warm. It's extraordinary, when we're so near the Pole.
Good night, Snowy. Keep a good look out . . .
BOOM
I thought I heard an explosion . . . Hello, the "Peary" has disappeared. She must have weighed anchor while we were asleep.
Still, that explosion? . . . I suppose I was dreaming . . .
BOOM
Tintin, I'm s . . . s . . . scared!
I've got it! It must be the island itself. It's probably a kind of small volcano . . . or a volcanic vent of some sort.
No! Not a sign of a crack, nor of a crater . . . So, now what?
Wooah! Wooah!
Snowy's found something: he looks pleased with himself!
An egg! . . . A egg!! . . . Great snakes! . . . Who can have laid that?
Come on, Tintin, let's scramble it.
But . . . but . . . Unless I'm seeing things . . . The egg: it's getting bigger!
It's not an egg! It's a mushroom! . . .

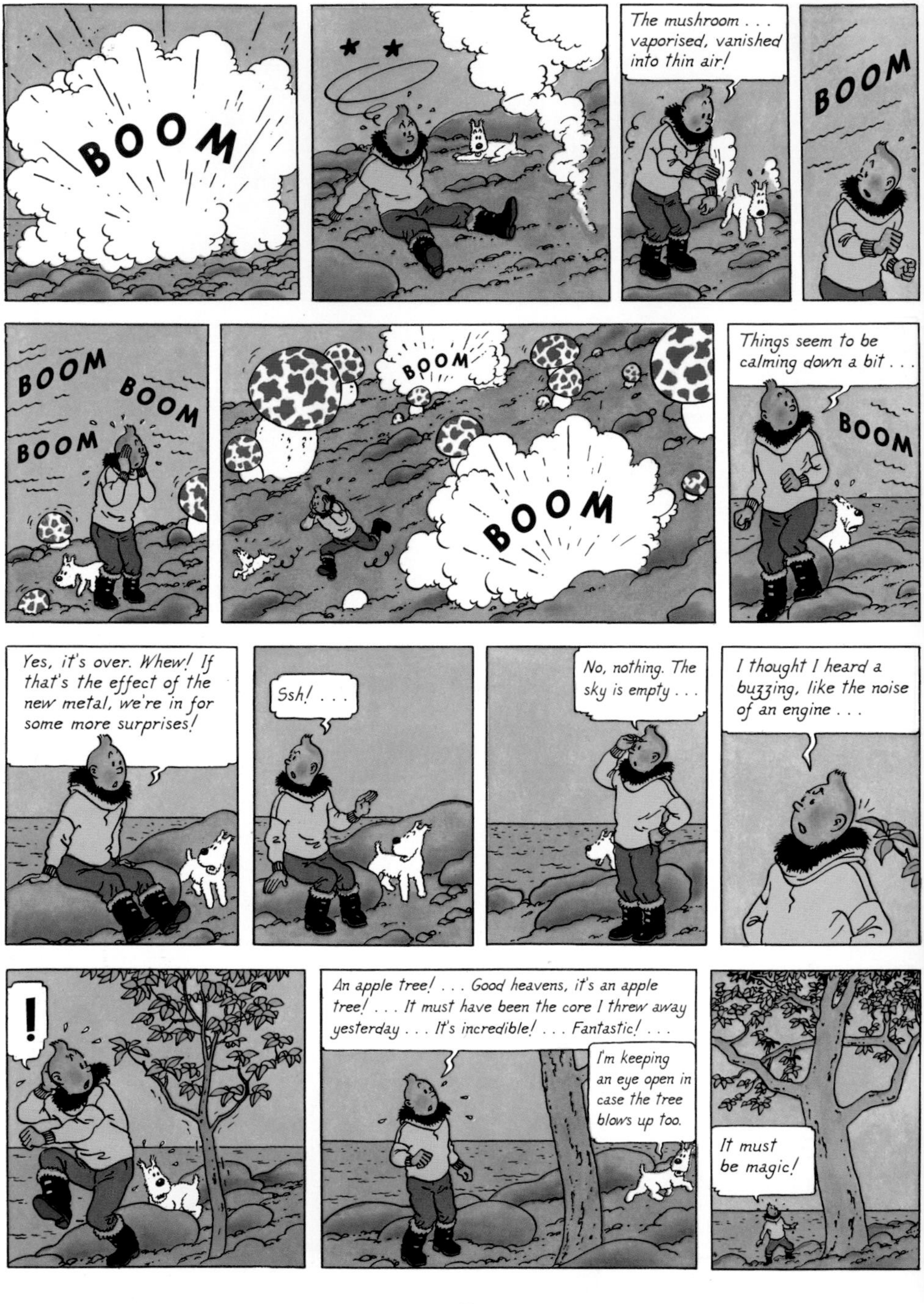
BOOM
The mushroom . . . vaporised, vanished into thin air!
BOOM
BOOM
BOOM
BOOM
BOOM
BOOM
Things seem to be calming down a bit . . .
BOOM
Yes, it's over. Whew! If that's the effect of the new metal, we're in for some more surprises!
Ssh! . . .
No, nothing. The sky is empty . . .
I thought I heard a buzzing, like the noise of an engine . . .
!
An apple tree! . . . Good heavens, it's an apple tree! . . . It must have been the core I threw away yesterday . . . It's incredible! . . . Fantastic! . . .
I'm keeping an eye open in case the tree blows up too.
It must be magic!

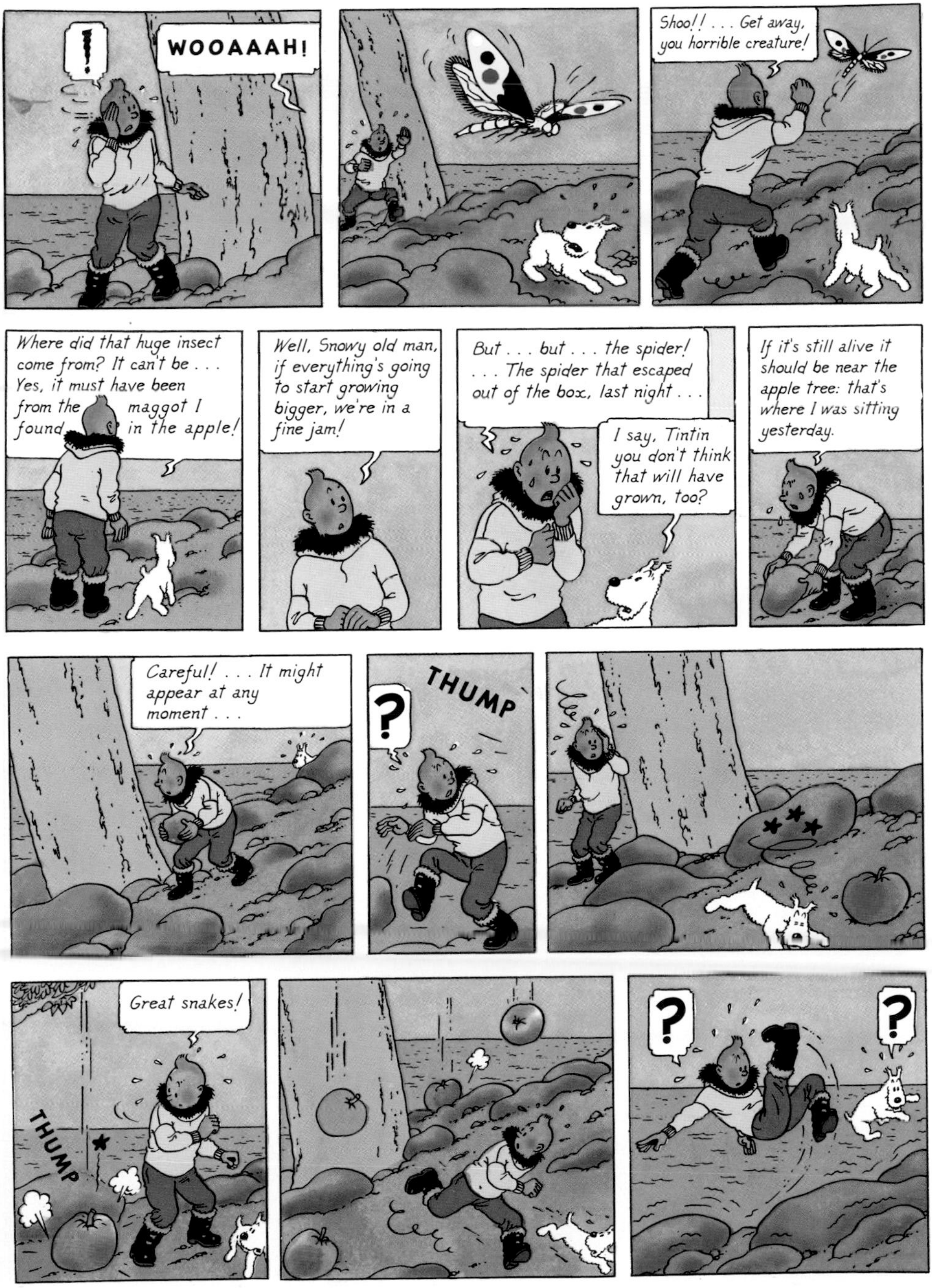

!
WOOAAAH!
Shoo!! . . . Get away, you horrible creature!
Where did that huge insect come from? It can't be . . . Yes, it must have been from the maggot I found in the apple!
Well, Snowy old man, if everything's going to start growing bigger, we're in a fine jam!
But . . . but . . . the spider! . . . The spider that escaped out of the box, last night . . .
I say, Tintin you don't think that will have grown, too?
If it's still alive it should be near the apple tree: that's where I was sitting yesterday.
Careful! . . . It might appear at any moment . . .
?
THUMP
Great snakes!
THUMP
?
?

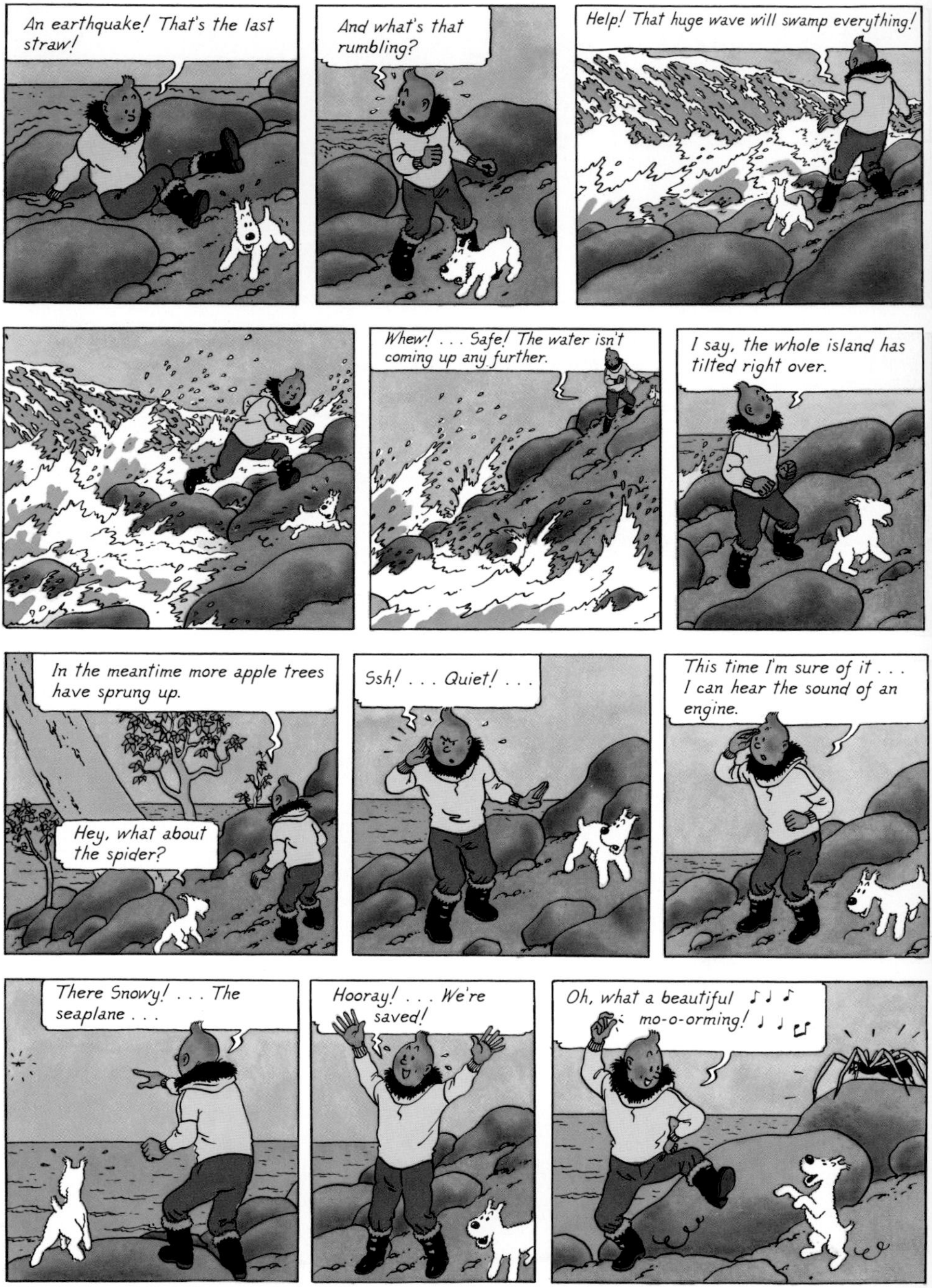

An earthquake! That's the last straw!
And what's that rumbling?
Help! That huge wave will swamp everything!
Whew! . . . Safe! The water isn't coming up any further.
I say, the whole island has tilted right over.
In the meantime more apple trees have sprung up.
Hey, what about the spider?
Ssh! . . . Quiet! . . .
This time I'm sure of it . . . I can hear the sound of an engine.
There Snowy! . . . The seaplane . . .
Hooray! . . . We're saved!
Oh, what a beautiful mo-o-orning!

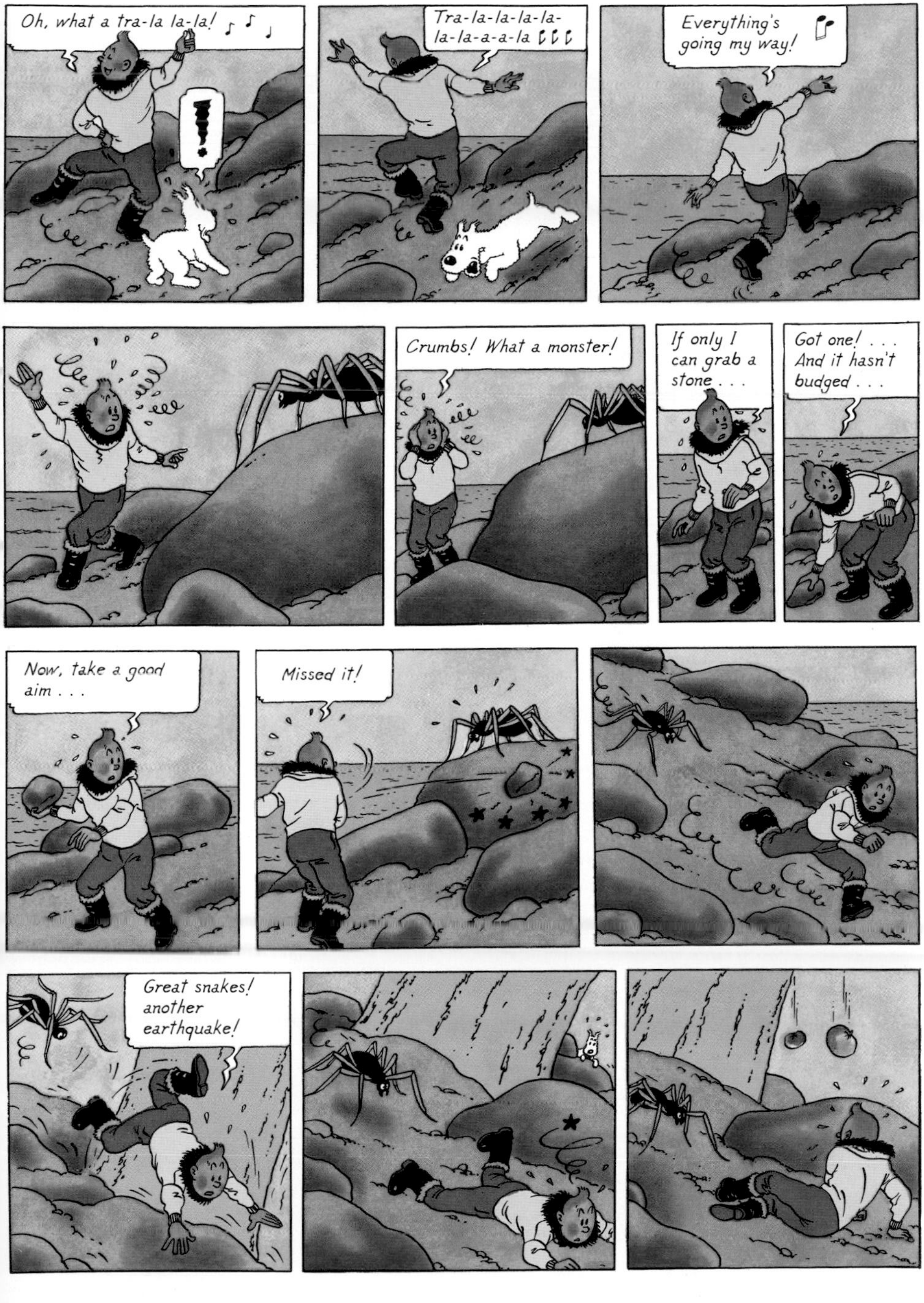

Oh, what a tra-la la-la!
Tra-la-la-la-la-la-la-a-a-la
Everything's going my way!
Crumbs! What a monster!
If only I can grab a stone . . .
Got one! . . . And it hasn't budged . . .
Now, take a good aim . . .
Missed it!
Great snakes! another earthquake!

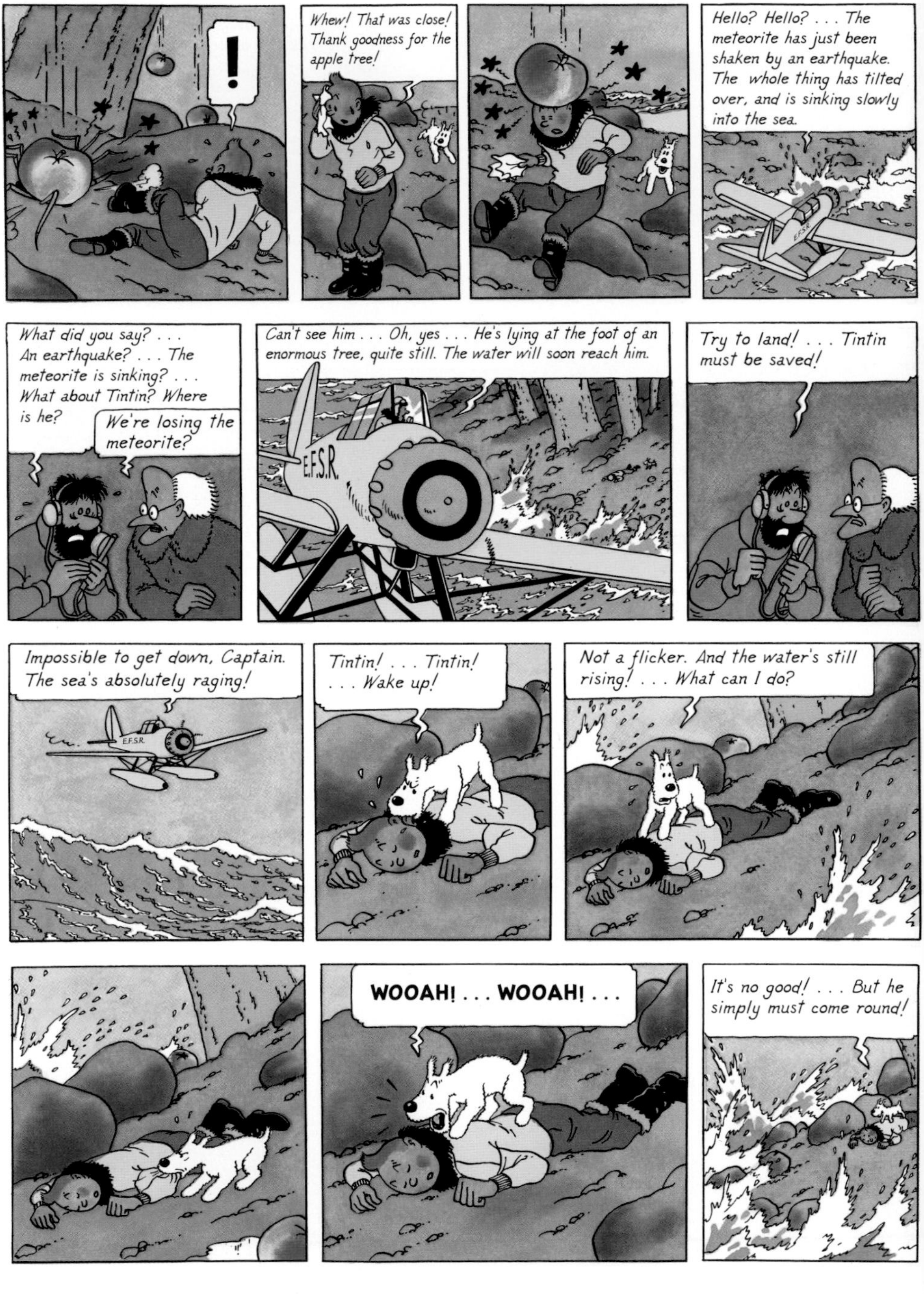
!
Whew! That was close! Thank goodness for the apple tree!
Hello? Hello? . . . The meteorite has just been shaken by an earthquake. The whole thing has tilted over, and is sinking slowly into the sea.
What did you say? . . . An earthquake? . . . The meteorite is sinking? . . . What about Tintin? Where is he?
We're losing the meteorite?
Can't see him . . . Oh, yes . . . He's lying at the foot of an enormous tree, quite still. The water will soon reach him.
E.F.S.R.
Try to land! . . . Tintin must be saved!
Impossible to get down, Captain. The sea's absolutely raging!
E.F.S.R.
Tintin! . . . Tintin! . . . Wake up!
Not a flicker. And the water's still rising! . . . What can I do?
WOOAH! . . . WOOAH! . . .
It's no good! . . . But he simply must come round!

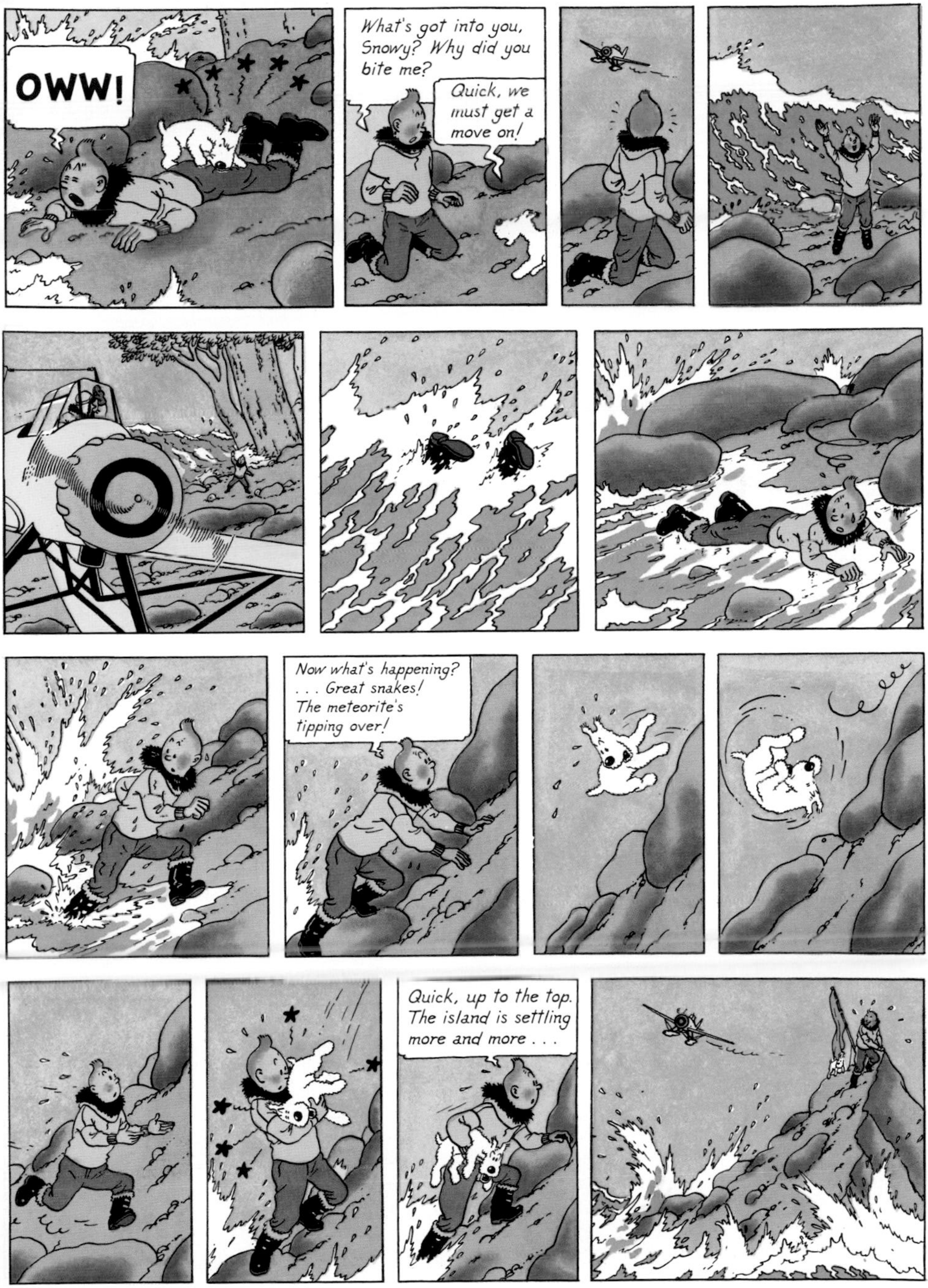
OWW!
What's got into you, Snowy? Why did you bite me?
Quick, we must get a move on!
Now what's happening? . . . Great snakes! The meteorite's tipping over!
Quick, up to the top. The island is settling more and more . . .

Here goes! It's neck or nothing! I simply must save him!

What's he doing? . . . Is he going to land? . . . It's sheer lunacy!

I can't see him any more. I hope to heaven he hasn't crashed . . .

He made it! He managed to get down safely!

Now he's hidden by the waves again . . .

Hooray! He's succeeded in launching the rubber dinghy.

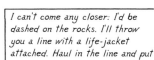
I can't come any closer: I'd be dashed on the rocks. I'll throw you a line with a life-jacket attached. Haul in the line and put the life-jacket on.

Right!

Here quickly, Snowy. We'll try to reach the dinghy . . .

Jump in? . . . Me? Never again!

Snowy! . . . Snowy! . . . Come on, come here at once!

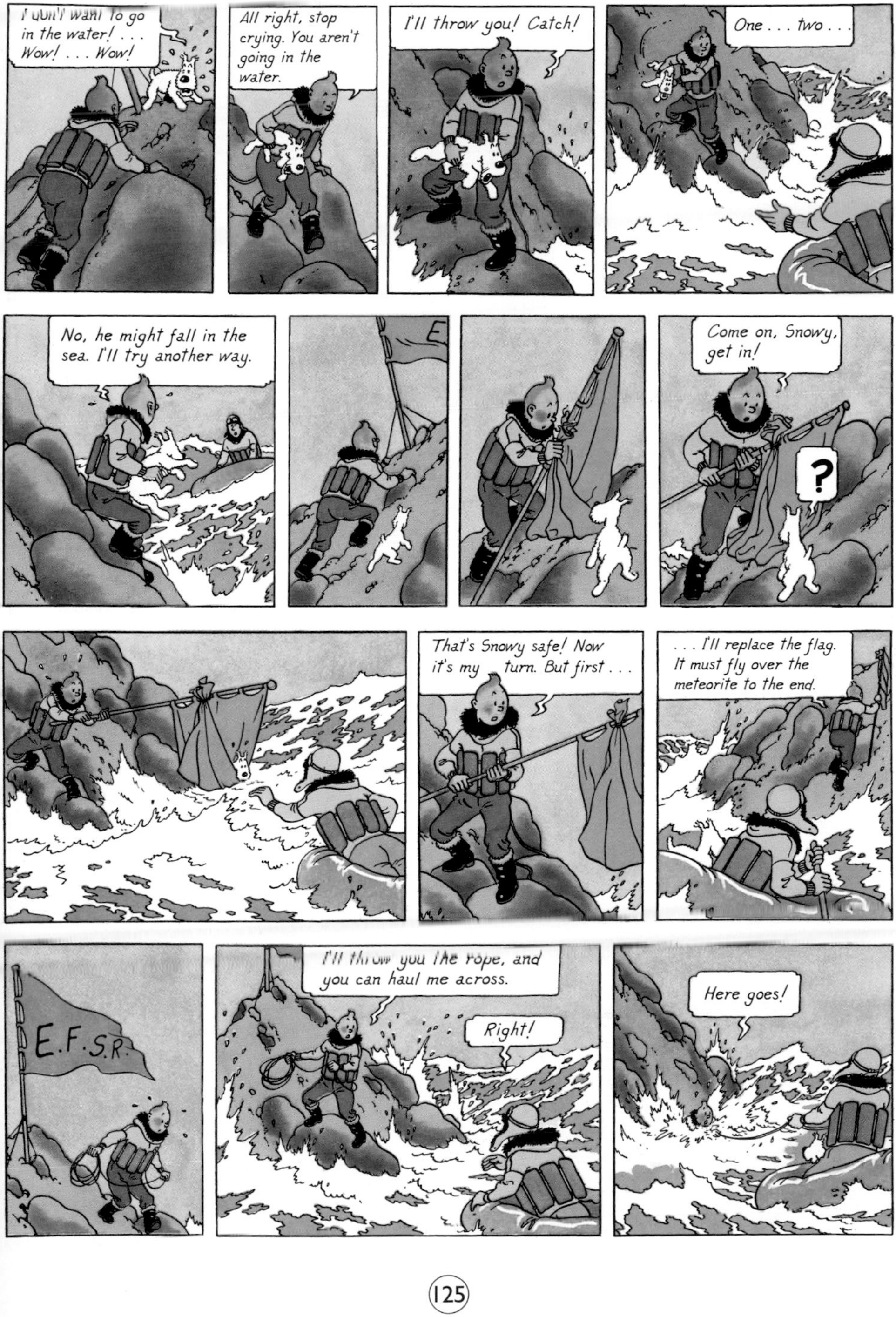
I don't want to go in the water! . . . Wow! . . . Wow!
All right, stop crying. You aren't going in the water.
I'll throw you! Catch!
One . . . two . . .
No, he might fall in the sea. I'll try another way.
Come on, Snowy, get in!
?
That's Snowy safe! Now it's my turn. But first . . .
. . . I'll replace the flag. It must fly over the meteorite to the end.
E.F.S.R.
I'll throw you the rope, and you can haul me across.
Right!
Here goes!

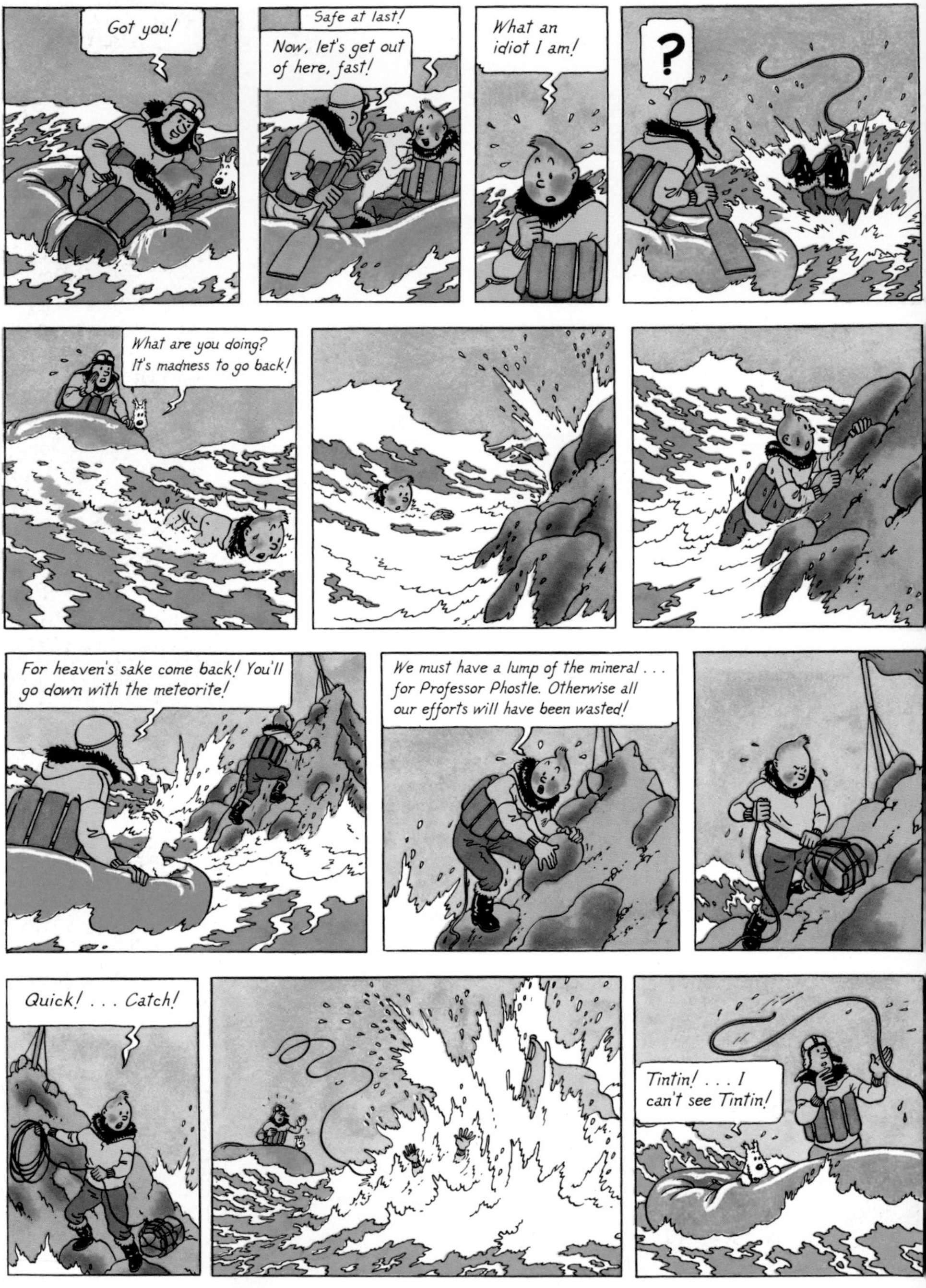
Got you!
Safe at last!
Now, let's get out of here, fast!
What an idiot I am!
?
What are you doing? It's madness to go back!
For heaven's sake come back! You'll go down with the meteorite!
We must have a lump of the mineral . . . for Professor Phostle. Otherwise all our efforts will have been wasted!
Quick! . . . Catch!
Tintin! . . . I can't see Tintin!

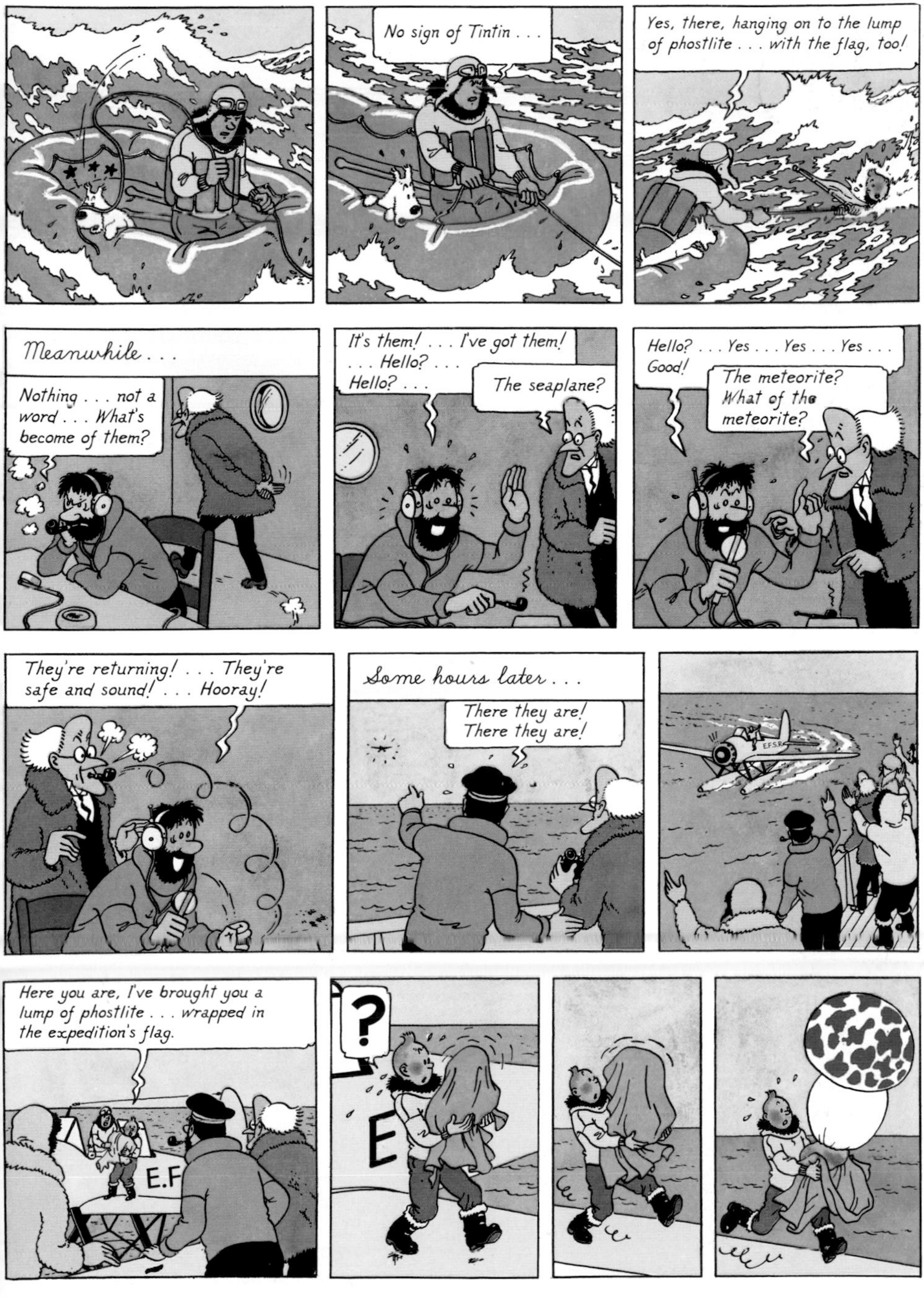
No sign of Tintin . . .
Yes, there, hanging on to the lump of phostlite . . . with the flag, too!
Meanwhile . . .
Nothing . . . not a word . . . What's become of them?
It's them! . . . I've got them! . . . Hello? . . . Hello? . . .
The seaplane?
Hello? . . . Yes . . . Yes . . . Yes . . . Good!
The meteorite? What of the meteorite?
They're returning! . . . They're safe and sound! . . . Hooray!
Some hours later . . .
There they are! There they are!
E.F.S.R.
Here you are, I've brought you a lump of phostlite . . . wrapped in the expedition's flag.
E.F
?
E

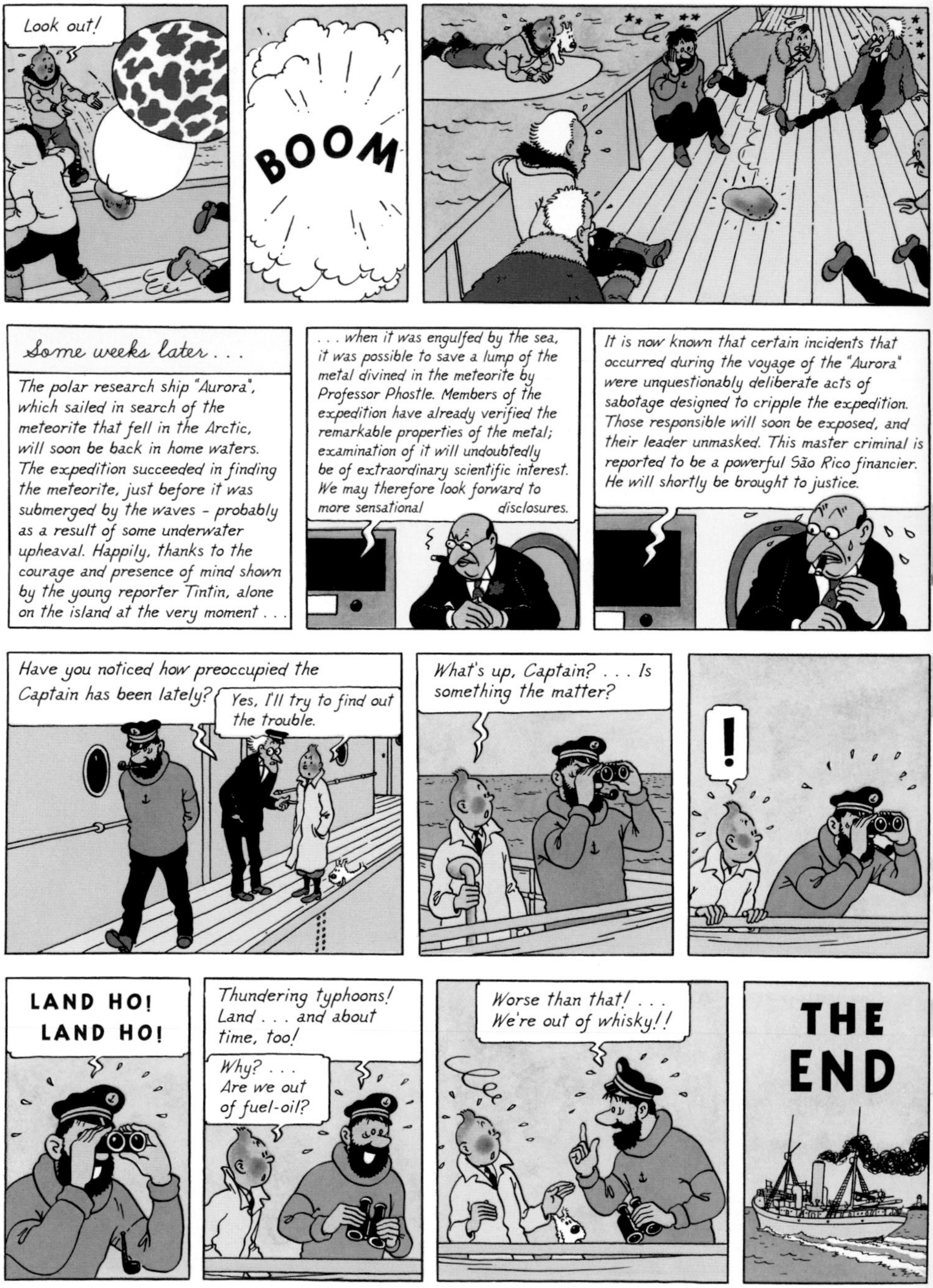
Look out!
BOOM
Some weeks later . . .
The polar research ship "Aurora", which sailed in search of the meteorite that fell in the Arctic, will soon be back in home waters. The expedition succeeded in finding the meteorite, just before it was submerged by the waves - probably as a result of some underwater upheaval. Happily, thanks to the courage and presence of mind shown by the young reporter Tintin, alone on the island at the very moment . . .
. . . when it was engulfed by the sea, it was possible to save a lump of the metal divined in the meteorite by Professor Phostle. Members of the expedition have already verified the remarkable properties of the metal; examination of it will undoubtedly be of extraordinary scientific interest. We may therefore look forward to more sensational disclosures.
It is now known that certain incidents that occurred during the voyage of the "Aurora" were unquestionably deliberate acts of sabotage designed to cripple the expedition. Those responsible will soon be exposed, and their leader unmasked. This master criminal is reported to be a powerful São Rico financier. He will shortly be brought to justice.
Have you noticed how preoccupied the Captain has been lately?
Yes, I'll try to find out the trouble.
What's up, Captain? . . . Is something the matter?
!
LAND HO! LAND HO!
Thundering typhoons! Land . . . and about time, too!
Why? . . . Are we out of fuel-oil?
Worse than that! . . . We're out of whisky!!
THE END

HERGÉ
★
THE ADVENTURES OF
TINTIN
★

THE SECRET
OF
THE UNICORN

LITTLE, BROWN AND COMPANY
New York   Boston

THE SECRET OF *THE UNICORN*

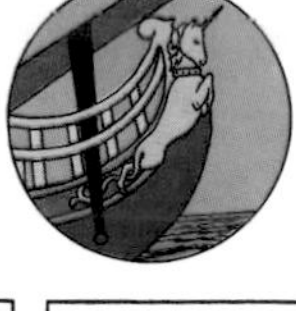

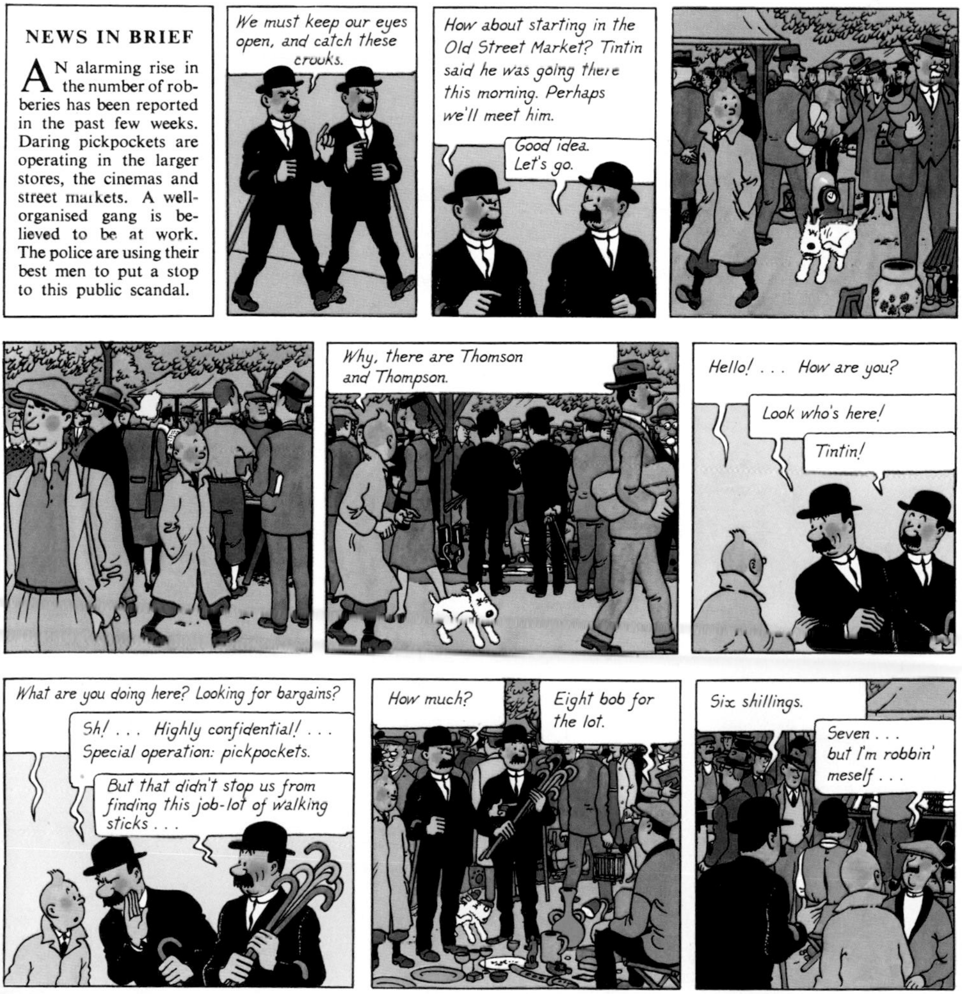
NEWS IN BRIEF
AN alarming rise in the number of robberies has been reported in the past few weeks. Daring pickpockets are operating in the larger stores, the cinemas and street markets. A well-organised gang is believed to be at work. The police are using their best men to put a stop to this public scandal.
We must keep our eyes open, and catch these crooks.
How about starting in the Old Street Market? Tintin said he was going there this morning. Perhaps we'll meet him.
Good idea. Let's go.
Why, there are Thomson and Thompson.
Hello! . . . How are you?
Look who's here!
Tintin!
What are you doing here? Looking for bargains?
Sh! . . . Highly confidential! . . . Special operation: pickpockets.
But that didn't stop us from finding this job-lot of walking sticks . . .
How much?
Eight bob for the lot.
Six shillings.
Seven . . . but I'm robbin' meself . . .

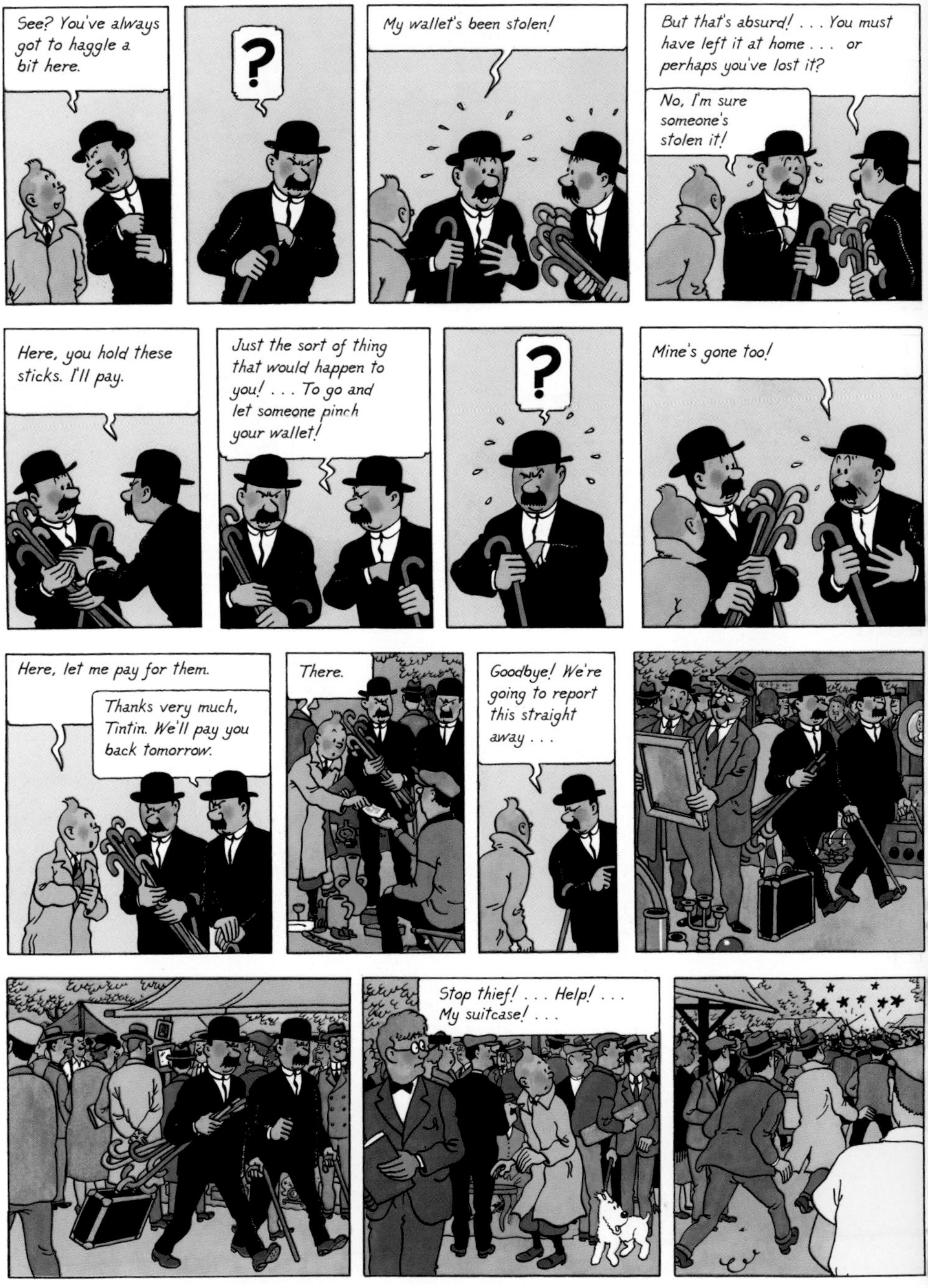
See? You've always got to haggle a bit here.
?
My wallet's been stolen!
But that's absurd! . . . You must have left it at home . . . or perhaps you've lost it?
No, I'm sure someone's stolen it!
Here, you hold these sticks. I'll pay.
Just the sort of thing that would happen to you! . . . To go and let someone pinch your wallet!
?
Mine's gone too!
Here, let me pay for them.
Thanks very much, Tintin. We'll pay you back tomorrow.
There.
Goodbye! We're going to report this straight away . . .
Stop thief! . . . Help! . . . My suitcase! . . .

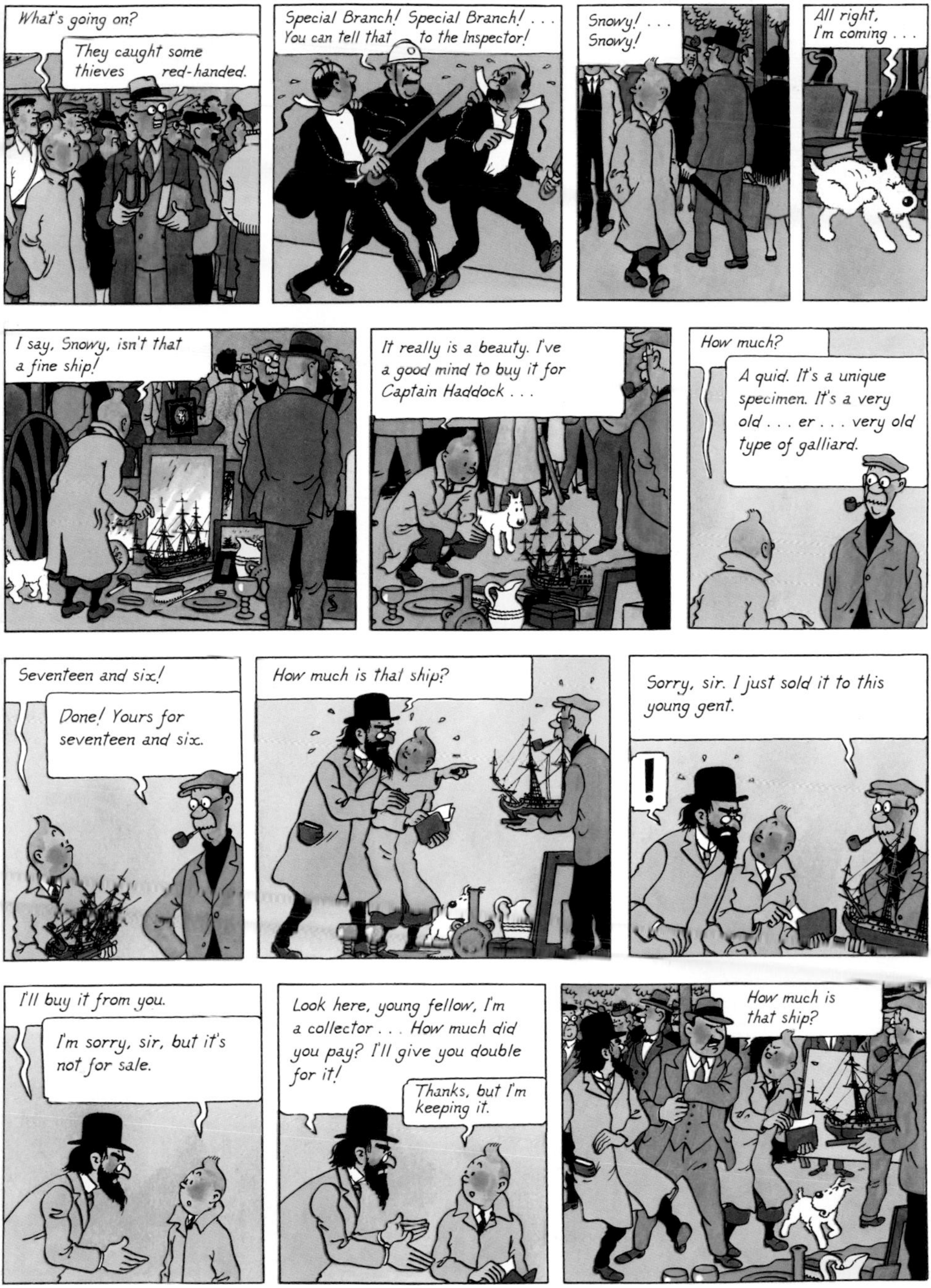

What's going on?
They caught some thieves red-handed.
Special Branch! Special Branch! . . . You can tell that to the Inspector!
Snowy! . . . Snowy!
All right, I'm coming . . .
I say, Snowy, isn't that a fine ship!
It really is a beauty. I've a good mind to buy it for Captain Haddock . . .
How much?
A quid. It's a unique specimen. It's a very old . . . er . . . very old type of galliard.
Seventeen and six!
Done! Yours for seventeen and six.
How much is that ship?
Sorry, sir. I just sold it to this young gent.
!
I'll buy it from you.
I'm sorry, sir, but it's not for sale.
Look here, young fellow, I'm a collector . . . How much did you pay? I'll give you double for it!
Thanks, but I'm keeping it.
How much is that ship?

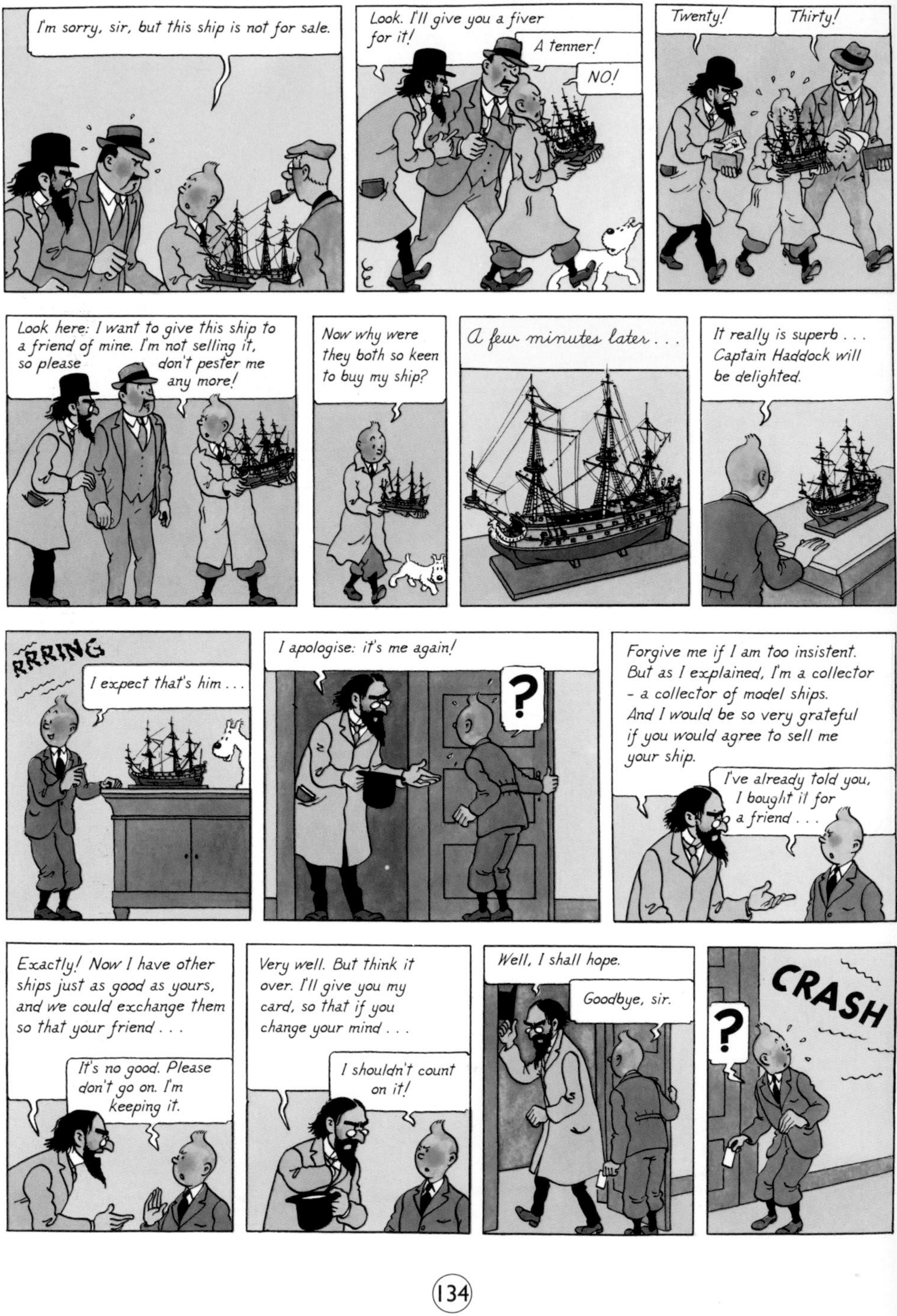
I'm sorry, sir, but this ship is not for sale.
Look. I'll give you a fiver for it!
A tenner!
NO!
Twenty!
Thirty!
Look here: I want to give this ship to a friend of mine. I'm not selling it, so please don't pester me any more!
Now why were they both so keen to buy my ship?
A few minutes later . . .
It really is superb . . . Captain Haddock will be delighted.
RRRING
I expect that's him . . .
I apologise: it's me again!
?
Forgive me if I am too insistent. But as I explained, I'm a collector - a collector of model ships. And I would be so very grateful if you would agree to sell me your ship.
I've already told you, I bought it for a friend . . .
Exactly! Now I have other ships just as good as yours, and we could exchange them so that your friend . . .
It's no good. Please don't go on. I'm keeping it.
Very well. But think it over. I'll give you my card, so that if you change your mind . . .
I shouldn't count on it!
Well, I shall hope.
Goodbye, sir.
?
CRASH

What's happened?

Snowy! . . . What have you done?

Look, now it's broken!

Luckily it's not too bad. I can soon mend it.

RRRRING

This time it must be the Captain.

Hello!

Hello, Captain. Just the person I wanted to see.

Come on in.   I've got a surprise for you.

Tintin, what a magnificent ship!

Thundering typhoons!

Where . . . where did you find this ship?

In the Old Street Market . . . Why?

Ten thousand thundering typhoons! . . . What a remarkable coincidence! . . . Imagine! . . .

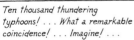

No! Come with me: then you'll see!

Remarkable! . . . It's really remarkable!

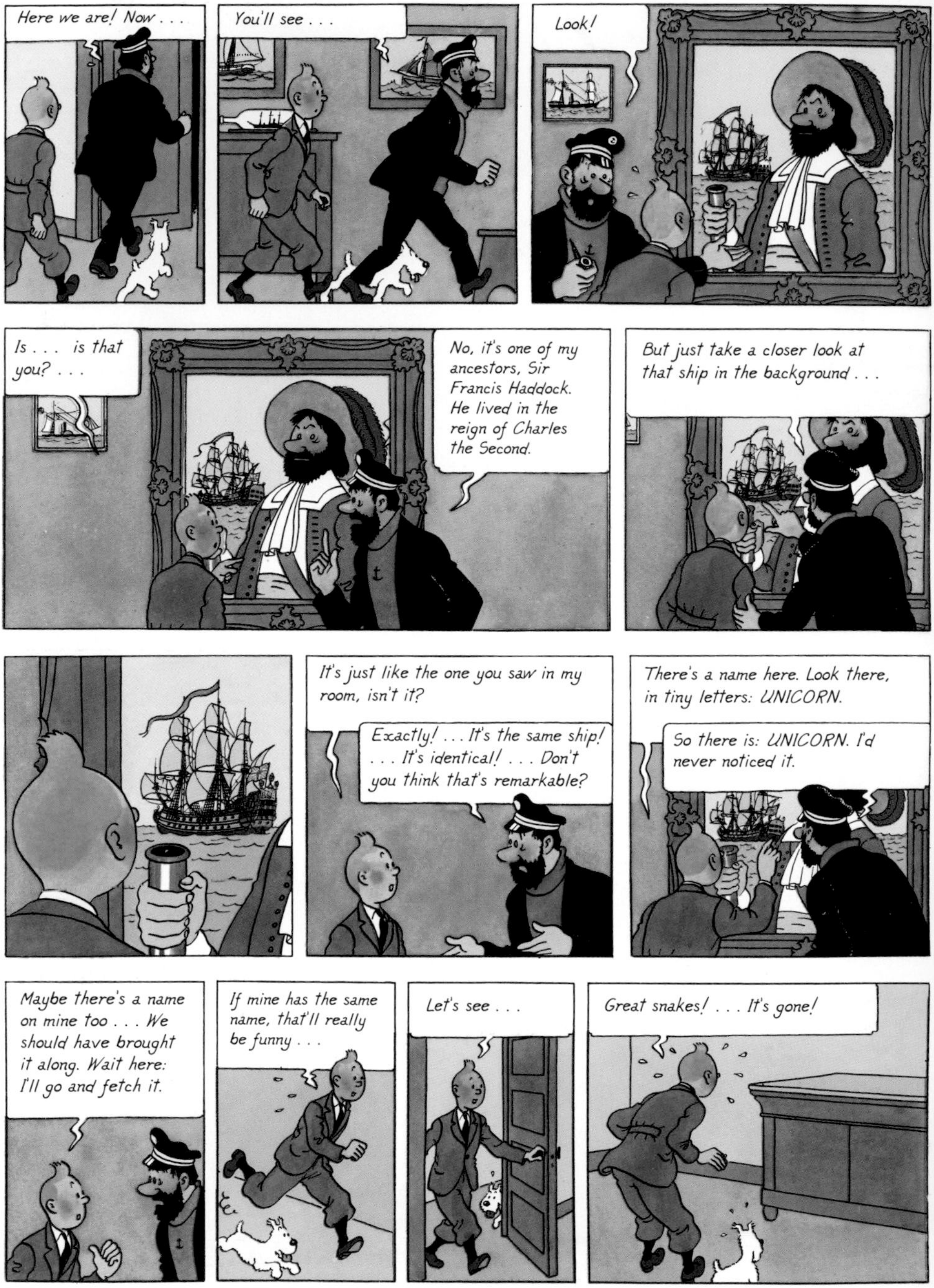
Here we are! Now . . .
You'll see . . .
Look!
Is . . . is that you? . . .
No, it's one of my ancestors, Sir Francis Haddock. He lived in the reign of Charles the Second.
But just take a closer look at that ship in the background . . .
It's just like the one you saw in my room, isn't it?
Exactly! . . . It's the same ship! . . . It's identical! . . . Don't you think that's remarkable?
There's a name here. Look there, in tiny letters: UNICORN.
So there is: UNICORN. I'd never noticed it.
Maybe there's a name on mine too . . . We should have brought it along. Wait here: I'll go and fetch it.
If mine has the same name, that'll really be funny . . .
Let's see . . .
Great snakes! . . . It's gone!

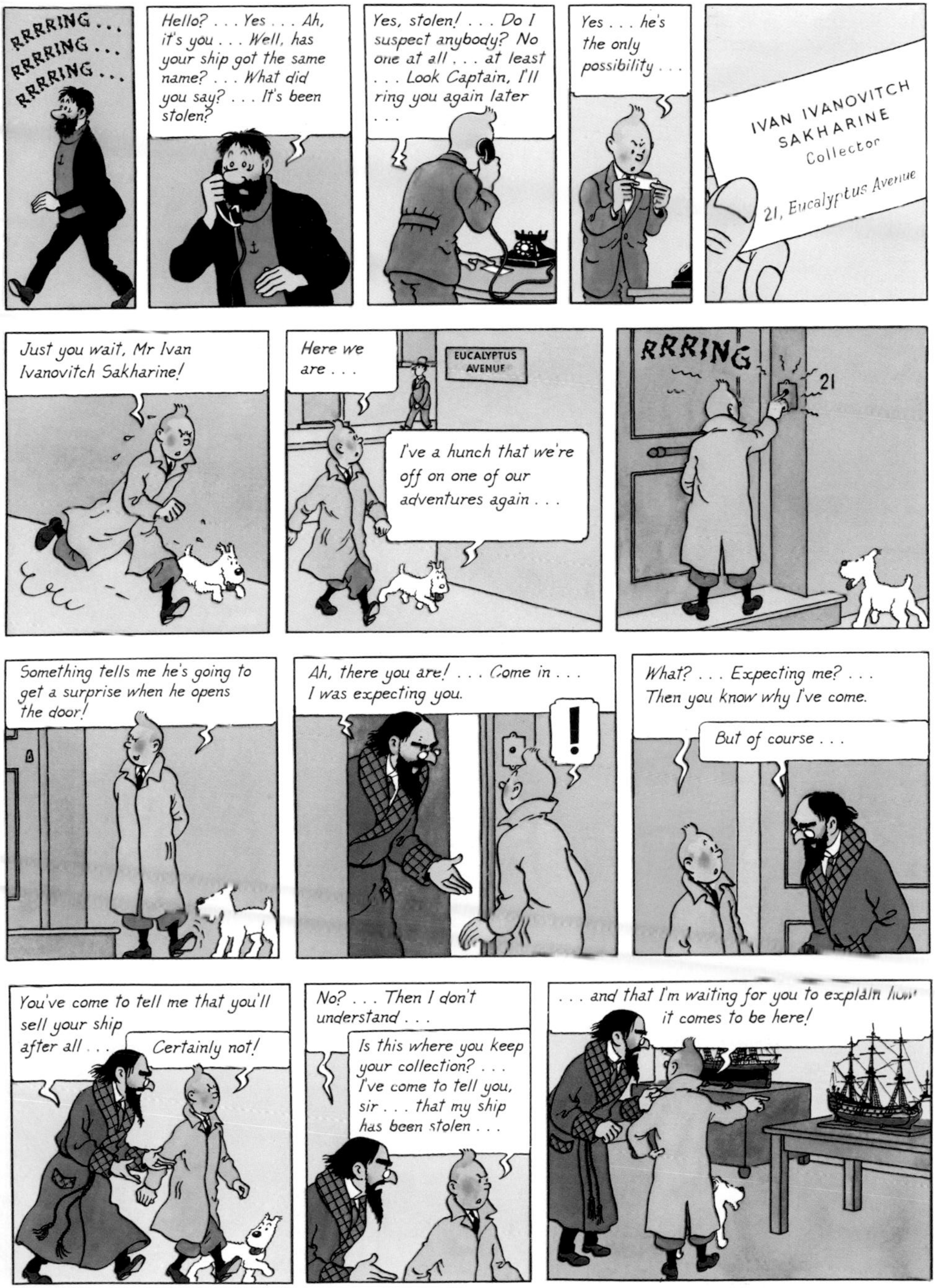
RRRRING . . .
RRRRING . . .
RRRRING . . .
Hello? . . . Yes . . . Ah, it's you . . . Well, has your ship got the same name? . . . What did you say? . . . It's been stolen?
Yes, stolen! . . . Do I suspect anybody? No one at all . . . at least . . . Look Captain, I'll ring you again later . . .
Yes . . . he's the only possibility . . .
IVAN IVANOVITCH SAKHARINE
Collector
21, Eucalyptus Avenue
Just you wait, Mr Ivan Ivanovitch Sakharine!
Here we are . . .
EUCALYPTUS AVENUE
I've a hunch that we're off on one of our adventures again . . .
RRRING
21
Something tells me he's going to get a surprise when he opens the door!
Ah, there you are! . . . Come in . . . I was expecting you.
!
What? . . . Expecting me? . . . Then you know why I've come.
But of course . . .
You've come to tell me that you'll sell your ship after all . . .
Certainly not!
No? . . . Then I don't understand . . .
Is this where you keep your collection? . . . I've come to tell you, sir . . . that my ship has been stolen . . .
. . . and that I'm waiting for you to explain how it comes to be here!

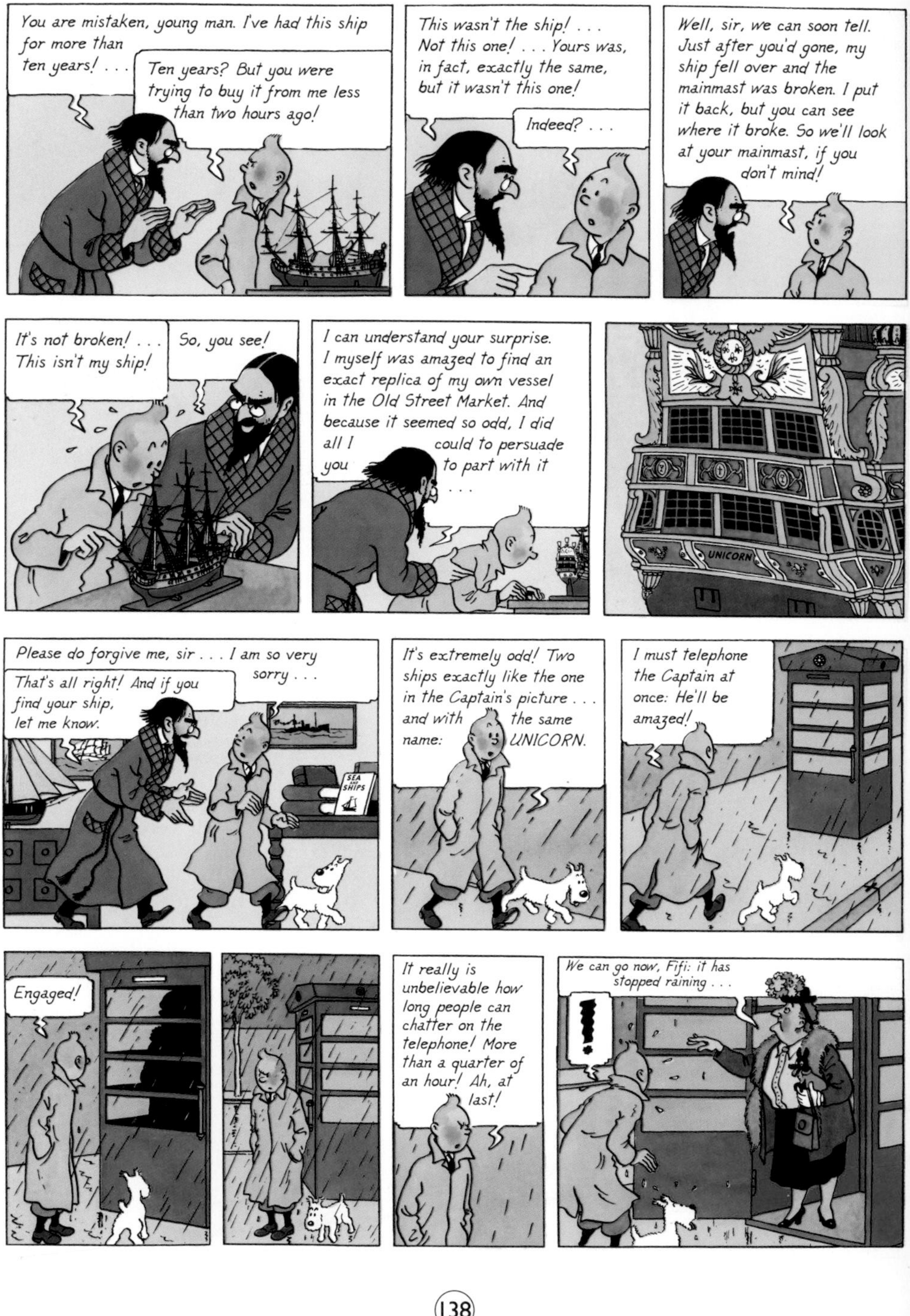

You are mistaken, young man. I've had this ship for more than ten years! . . .
Ten years? But you were trying to buy it from me less than two hours ago!
This wasn't the ship! . . . Not this one! . . . Yours was, in fact, exactly the same, but it wasn't this one!
Indeed? . . .
Well, sir, we can soon tell. Just after you'd gone, my ship fell over and the mainmast was broken. I put it back, but you can see where it broke. So we'll look at your mainmast, if you don't mind!
It's not broken! . . . This isn't my ship!
So, you see!
I can understand your surprise. I myself was amazed to find an exact replica of my own vessel in the Old Street Market. And because it seemed so odd, I did all I could to persuade you to part with it . . .
UNICORN
Please do forgive me, sir . . . I am so very sorry . . .
That's all right! And if you find your ship, let me know.
SEA AND SHIPS
It's extremely odd! Two ships exactly like the one in the Captain's picture . . . and with the same name: UNICORN.
I must telephone the Captain at once: He'll be amazed!
Engaged!
It really is unbelievable how long people can chatter on the telephone! More than a quarter of an hour! Ah, at last!
We can go now, Fifi: it has stopped raining . . .

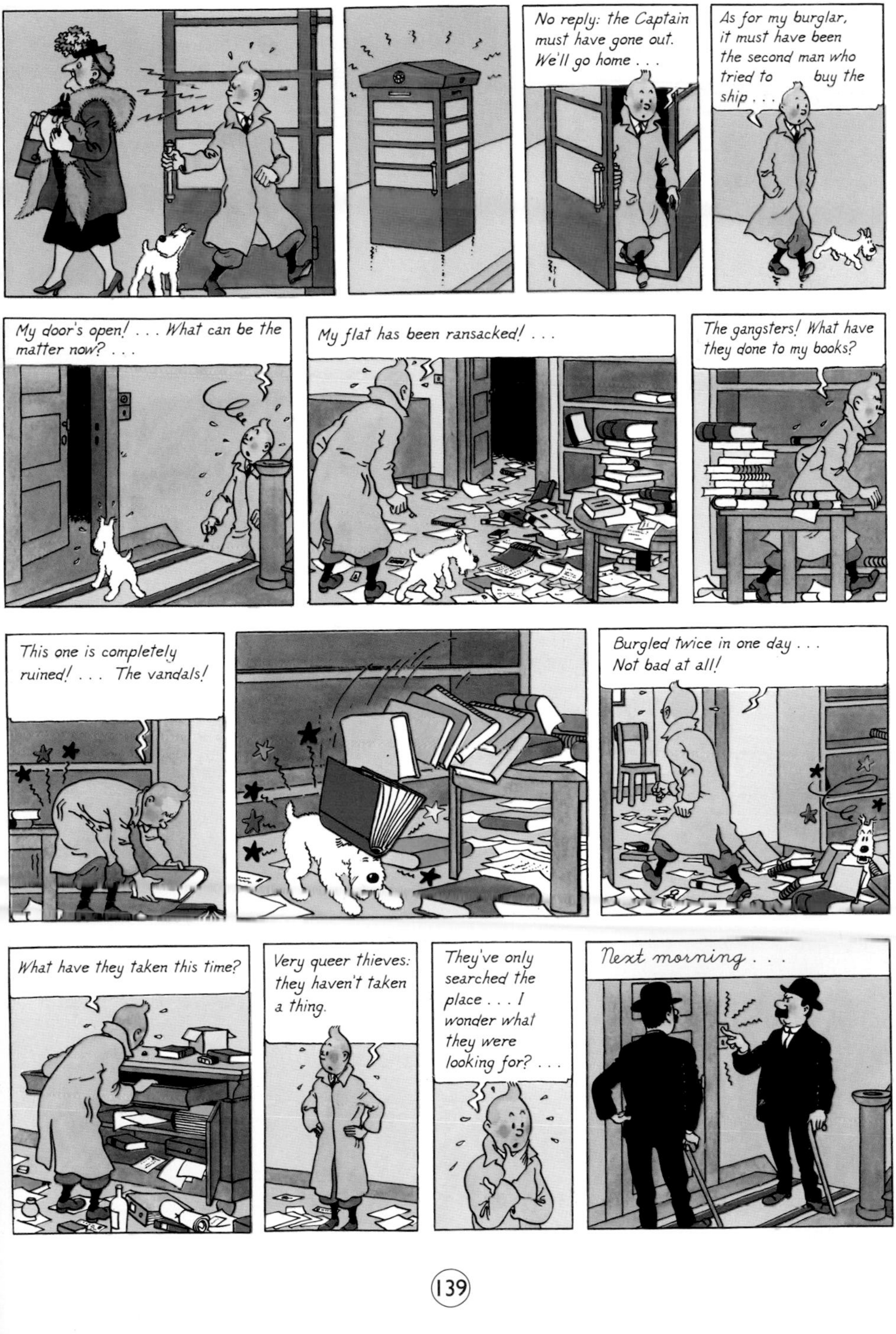
No reply: the Captain must have gone out. We'll go home . . .
As for my burglar, it must have been the second man who tried to buy the ship . . .
My door's open! . . . What can be the matter now? . . .
My flat has been ransacked! . . .
The gangsters! What have they done to my books?
This one is completely ruined! . . . The vandals!
Burgled twice in one day . . . Not bad at all!
What have they taken this time?
Very queer thieves: they haven't taken a thing.
They've only searched the place . . . I wonder what they were looking for? . . .
Next morning . . .

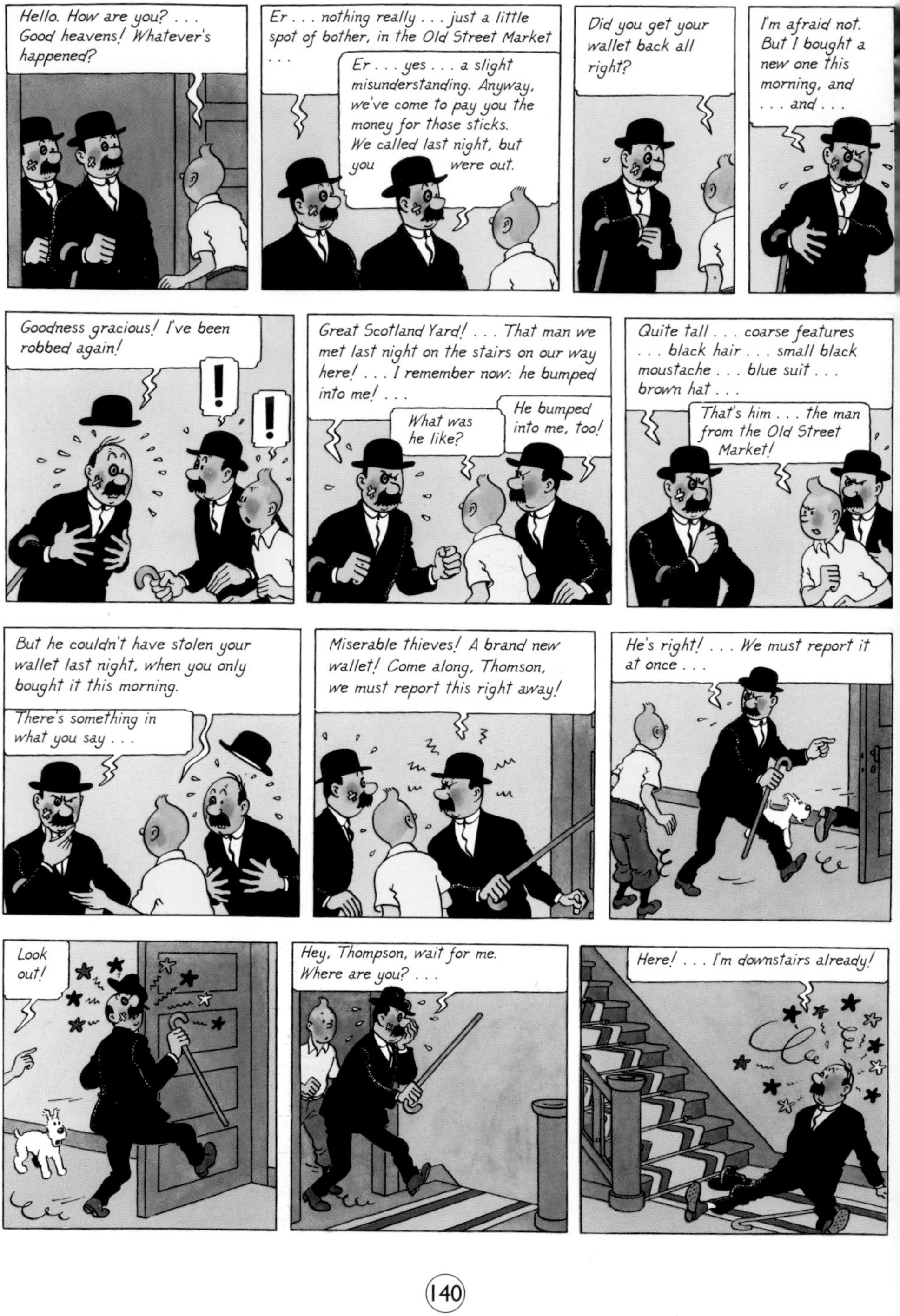
Hello. How are you? . . . Good heavens! Whatever's happened?
Er . . . nothing really . . . just a little spot of bother, in the Old Street Market . . .
Er . . . yes . . . a slight misunderstanding. Anyway, we've come to pay you the money for those sticks. We called last night, but you were out.
Did you get your wallet back all right?
I'm afraid not. But I bought a new one this morning, and . . . and . . .
Goodness gracious! I've been robbed again!
!
!
Great Scotland Yard! . . . That man we met last night on the stairs on our way here! . . . I remember now: he bumped into me! . . .
What was he like?
He bumped into me, too!
Quite tall . . . coarse features . . . black hair . . . small black moustache . . . blue suit . . . brown hat . . .
That's him . . . the man from the Old Street Market!
But he couldn't have stolen your wallet last night, when you only bought it this morning.
There's something in what you say . . .
Miserable thieves! A brand new wallet! Come along, Thomson, we must report this right away!
He's right! . . . We must report it at once . . .
Look out!
Hey, Thompson, wait for me. Where are you? . . .
Here! . . . I'm downstairs already!

Poor old Thomsons, they do have rotten luck! . . . There seems to be quite an epidemic of larceny and house-breaking.

Oh well, let's try and get these papers sorted out . . .

What are you after, Snowy?

A cigarette, under there? That's a funny place . . .

Why, it's not a cigarette . . . it's a little scroll of parchment . . .

But this isn't mine! Where ever did it come from? . . . Let's have a closer look at it . . .

Here's another mystery!

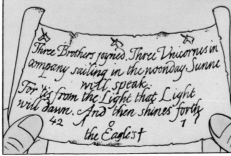

Three Brothers joyned. Three Unicornes in company sailing in the noonday Sunne will speak. For 'tis from the Light that Light will dawn. And then shines forth the Eagle's †
42   1

But it's all gibberish! And where on earth did this parchment come from, anyway?

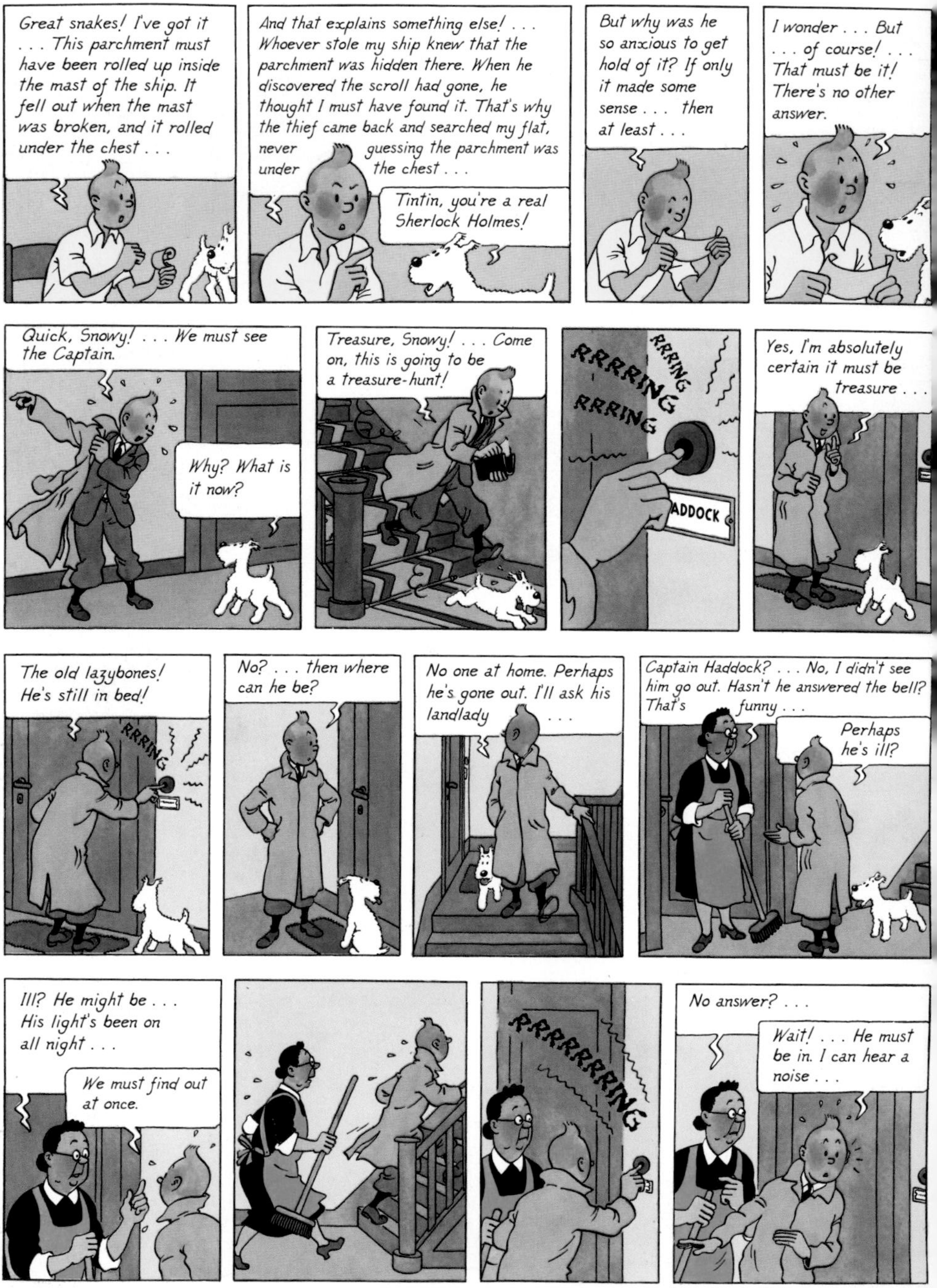
Great snakes! I've got it . . . This parchment must have been rolled up inside the mast of the ship. It fell out when the mast was broken, and it rolled under the chest . . .
And that explains something else! . . . Whoever stole my ship knew that the parchment was hidden there. When he discovered the scroll had gone, he thought I must have found it. That's why the thief came back and searched my flat, never guessing the parchment was under the chest . . .
Tintin, you're a real Sherlock Holmes!
But why was he so anxious to get hold of it? If only it made some sense . . . then at least . . .
I wonder . . . But . . . of course! . . . That must be it! There's no other answer.
Quick, Snowy! . . . We must see the Captain.
Why? What is it now?
Treasure, Snowy! . . . Come on, this is going to be a treasure-hunt!
RRRING
RRRRING
RRRING
ADDOCK
Yes, I'm absolutely certain it must be treasure . . .
The old lazybones! He's still in bed!
RRRING
No? . . . then where can he be?
No one at home. Perhaps he's gone out. I'll ask his landlady . . .
Captain Haddock? . . . No, I didn't see him go out. Hasn't he answered the bell? That's funny . . .
Perhaps he's ill?
Ill? He might be . . . His light's been on all night . . .
We must find out at once.
RRRRRRRRING
No answer? . . .
Wait! . . . He must be in. I can hear a noise . . .

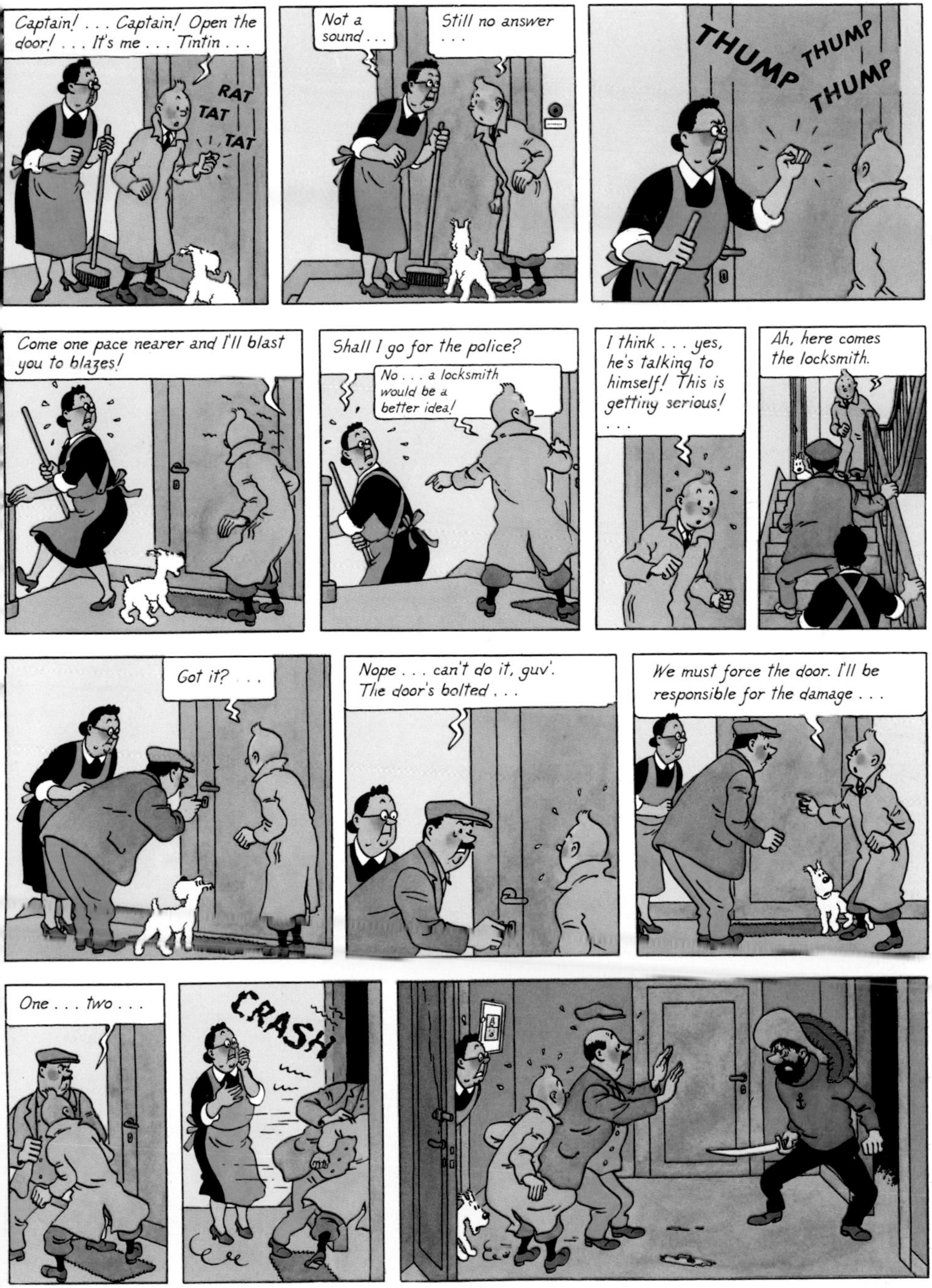
Captain! . . . Captain! Open the door! . . . It's me . . . Tintin . . .
RAT TAT TAT
Not a sound . . .
Still no answer . . .
THUMP THUMP THUMP
Come one pace nearer and I'll blast you to blazes!
Shall I go for the police?
No . . . a locksmith would be a better idea!
I think . . . yes, he's talking to himself! This is getting serious! . . .
Ah, here comes the locksmith.
Got it? . . .
Nope . . . can't do it, guv'. The door's bolted . . .
We must force the door. I'll be responsible for the damage . . .
One . . . two . . .
CRASH

Avast, pirates! Avast there!

Captain! . . .

Avast, you dogs! . . . Sea-gherkins! . . . Baboons!

Buccaneers! . . . Fili-busters! . . . Bagpipers! . . . Gallows-fodder!

We've won! . . . That's got them on the run! . . . With a yo-ho-ho and a bottle of rum!

What's all this play-acting for?

Play-acting? . . . This isn't a play! . . . Come in, and you'll understand . . .

You see that man?

Yes, he's one of your ancestors. What about it?

Well, last night, when I was thinking about this strange business of the ships, I suddenly remembered that up in the attic I had an old sea-chest belonging to my ancestor. This is it . . .

In the chest I found this hat and cutlass, and also . . .

I know! Treasure! . . . Or a treasure-map!

No, not treasure, but something like it! . . . Old manuscripts by Sir Francis Haddock . . . Look, I started reading them yester-day evening, and read all night . . .

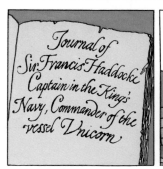

Journal of
Sir Francis Haddock,
Captain in the King's
Navy, Commander of the
vessel Unicorn

I was still reading when you came in. That's why you found me a little . . . over-excited. But what a story! Just listen to it!

It is the year 1676. The UNICORN, a valiant ship of King Charles II's fleet, has left Barbados in the West Indies, and set sail for home. She carries a cargo of . . . well, anyway, there's a good deal of rum aboard . . .

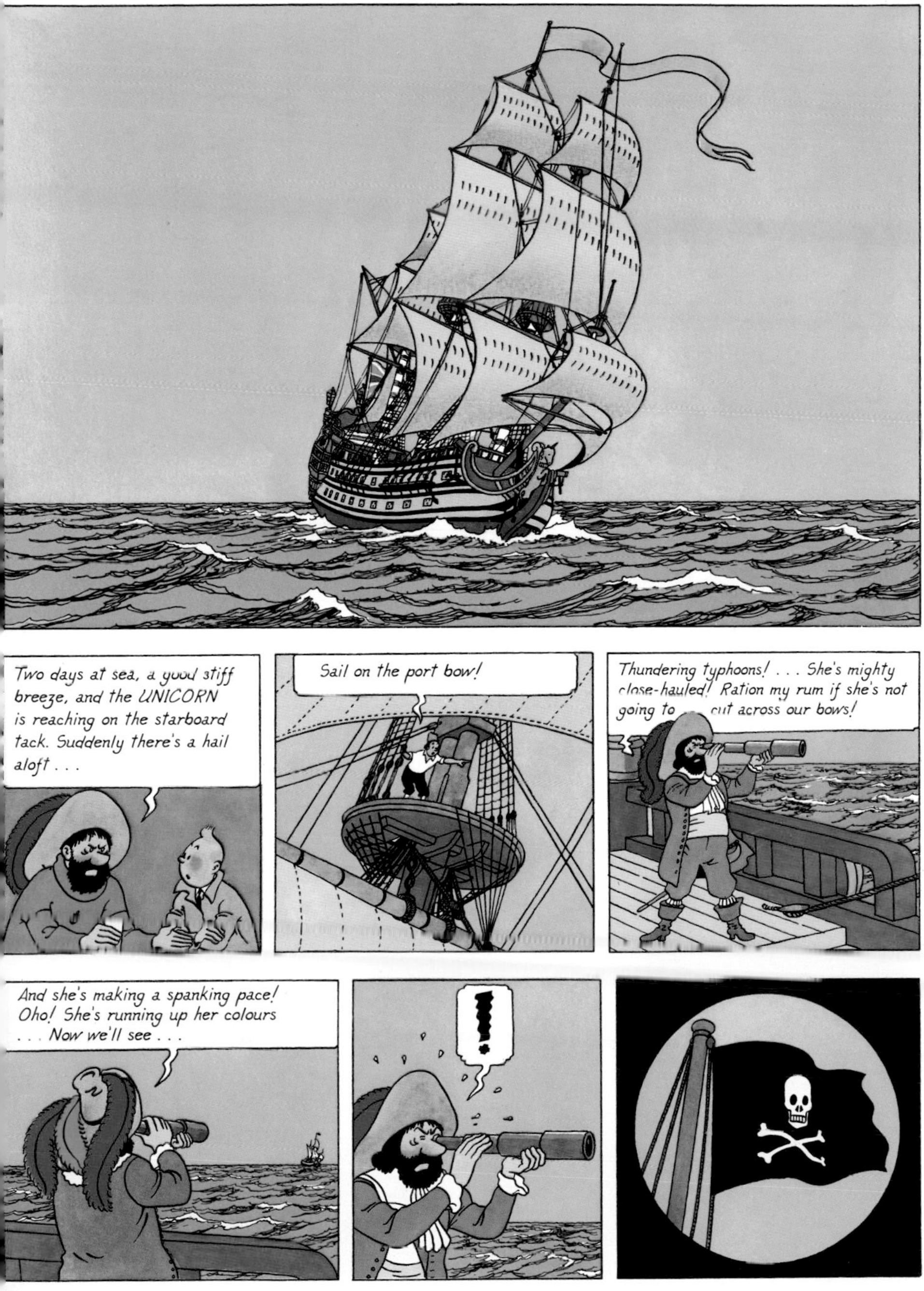

Two days at sea, a good stiff breeze, and the UNICORN is reaching on the starboard tack. Suddenly there's a hail aloft . . .
Sail on the port bow!
Thundering typhoons! . . . She's mighty close-hauled! Ration my rum if she's not going to . . . cut across our bows!
And she's making a spanking pace! Oho! She's running up her colours . . . Now we'll see . . .
!

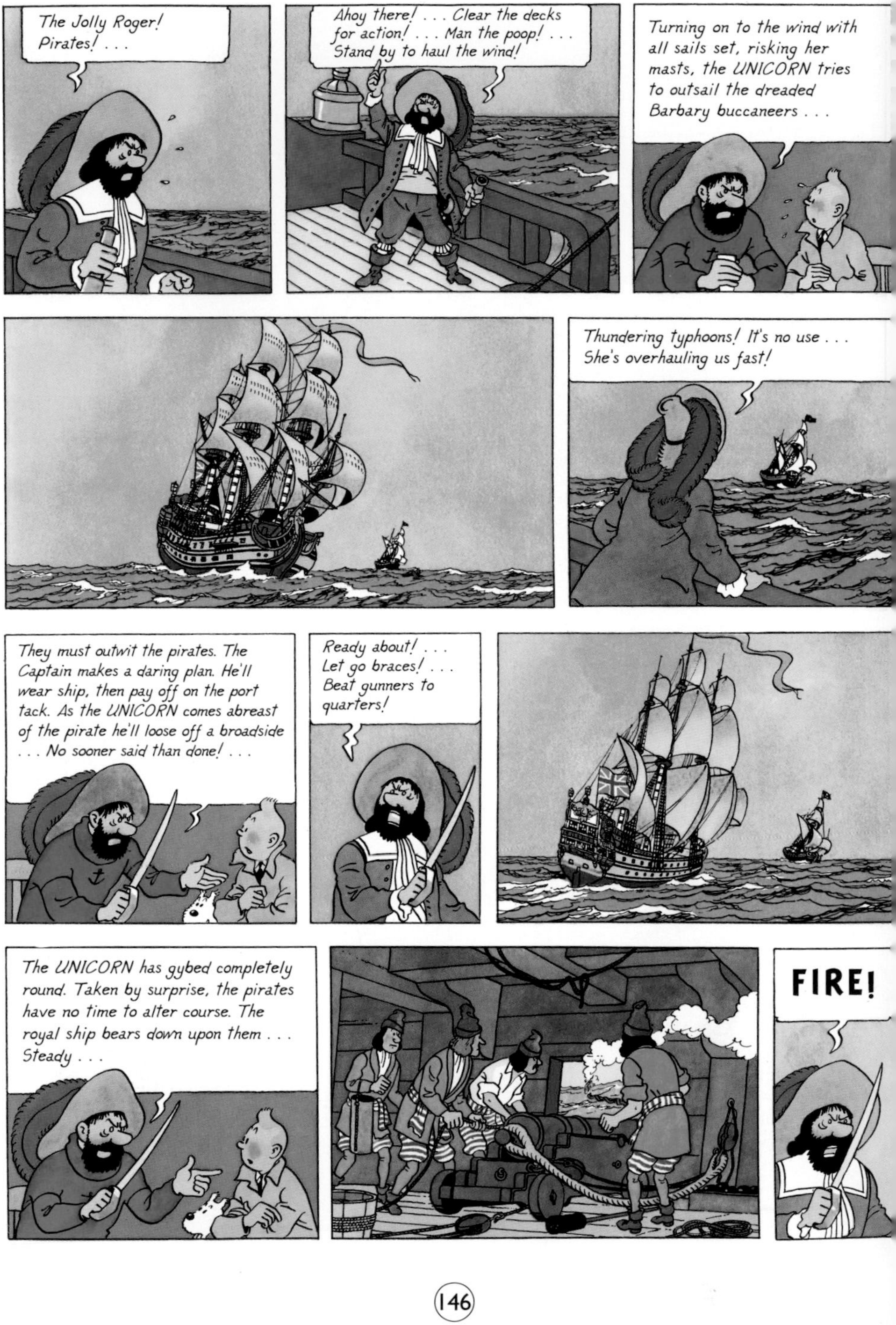

The Jolly Roger! Pirates! . . .
Ahoy there! . . . Clear the decks for action! . . . Man the poop! . . . Stand by to haul the wind!
Turning on to the wind with all sails set, risking her masts, the UNICORN tries to outsail the dreaded Barbary buccaneers . . .
Thundering typhoons! It's no use . . . She's overhauling us fast!
They must outwit the pirates. The Captain makes a daring plan. He'll wear ship, then pay off on the port tack. As the UNICORN comes abreast of the pirate he'll loose off a broadside . . . No sooner said than done! . . .
Ready about! . . . Let go braces! . . . Beat gunners to quarters!
The UNICORN has gybed completely round. Taken by surprise, the pirates have no time to alter course. The royal ship bears down upon them . . . Steady . . .
FIRE!

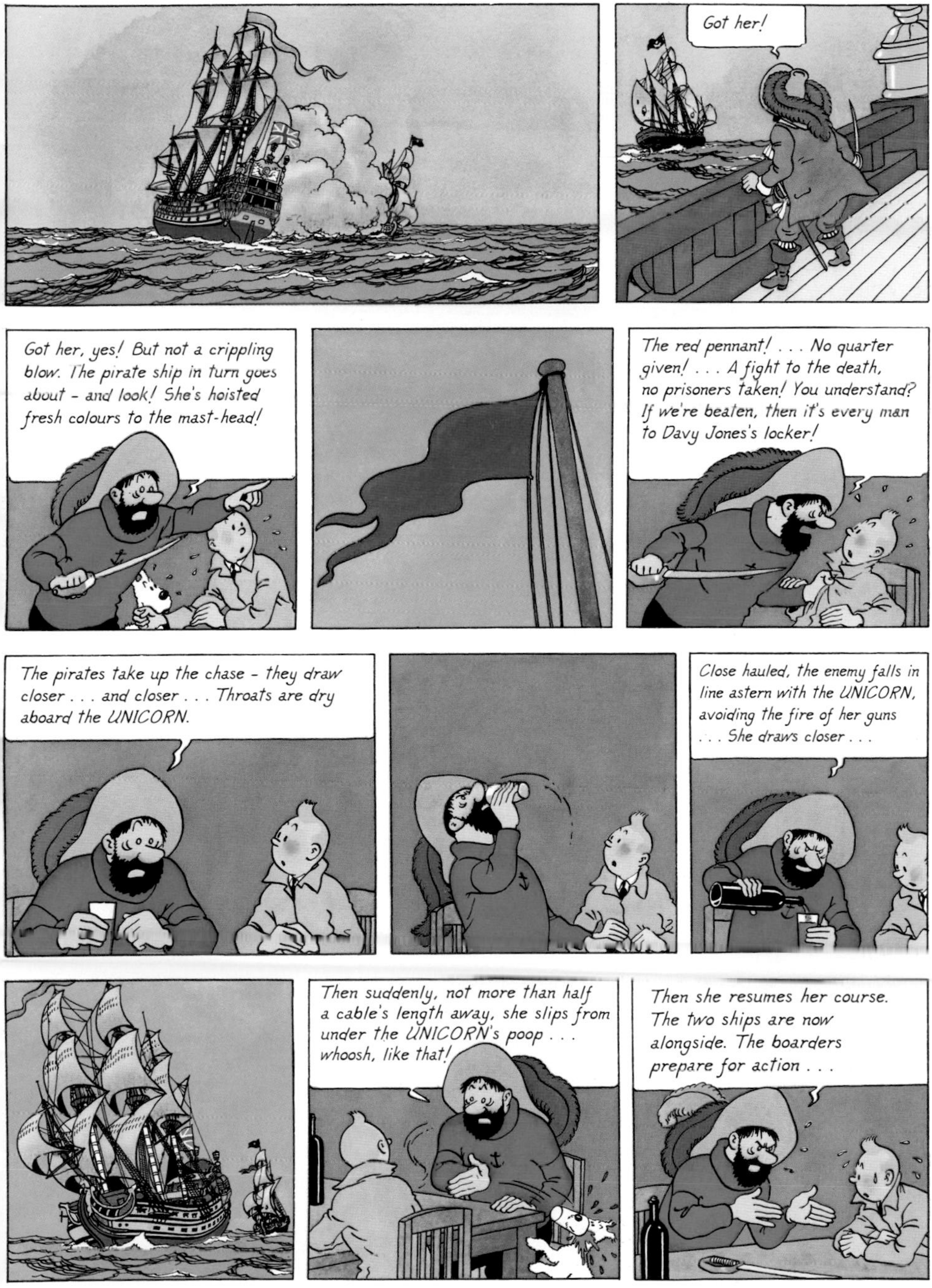
Got her!
Got her, yes! But not a crippling blow. The pirate ship in turn goes about – and look! She's hoisted fresh colours to the mast-head!
The red pennant! . . . No quarter given! . . . A fight to the death, no prisoners taken! You understand? If we're beaten, then it's every man to Davy Jones's locker!
The pirates take up the chase – they draw closer . . . and closer . . . Throats are dry aboard the UNICORN.
Close hauled, the enemy falls in line astern with the UNICORN, avoiding the fire of her guns . . . She draws closer . . .
Then suddenly, not more than half a cable's length away, she slips from under the UNICORN's poop . . . whoosh, like that!
Then she resumes her course. The two ships are now alongside. The boarders prepare for action . . .

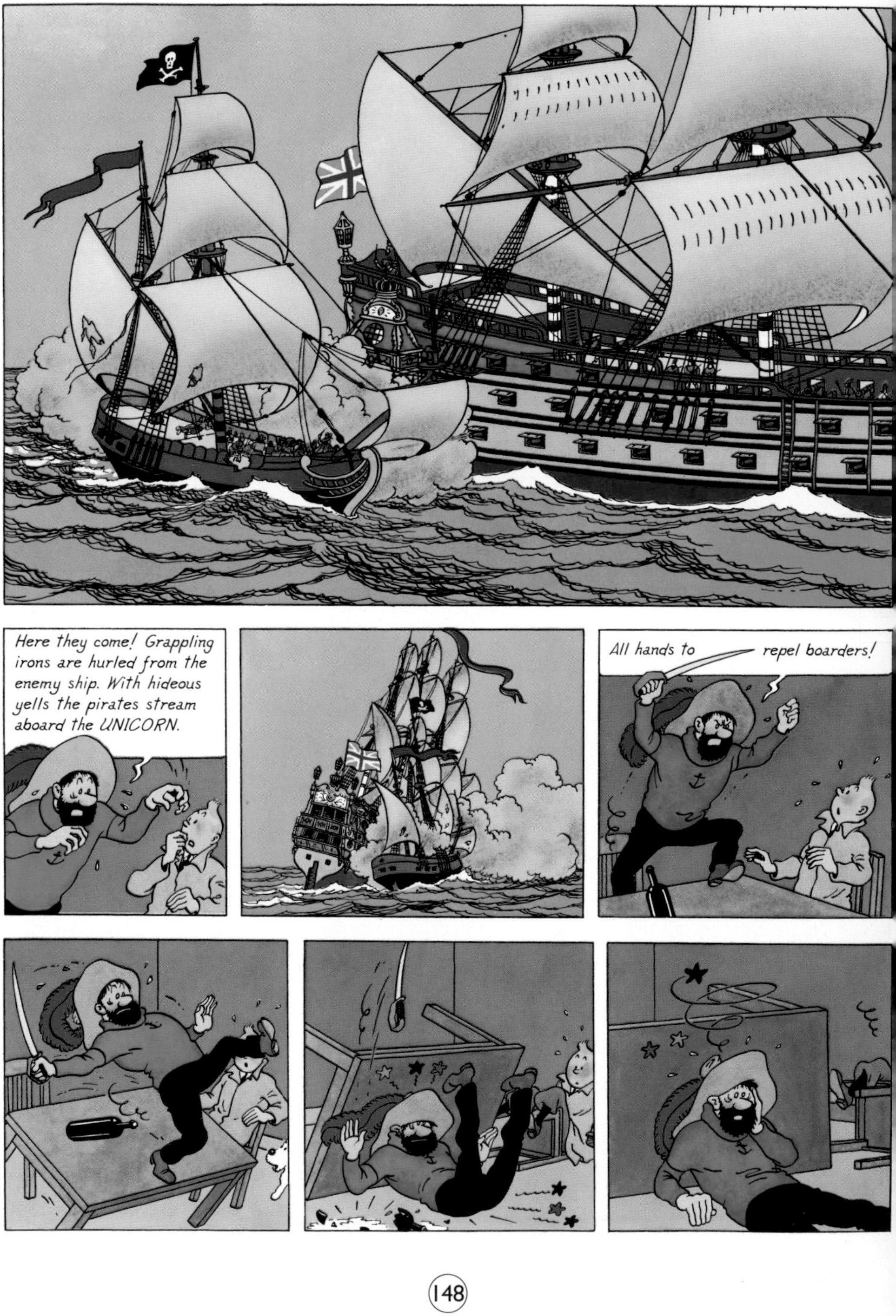
Here they come! Grappling irons are hurled from the enemy ship. With hideous yells the pirates stream aboard the UNICORN.
All hands to repel boarders!

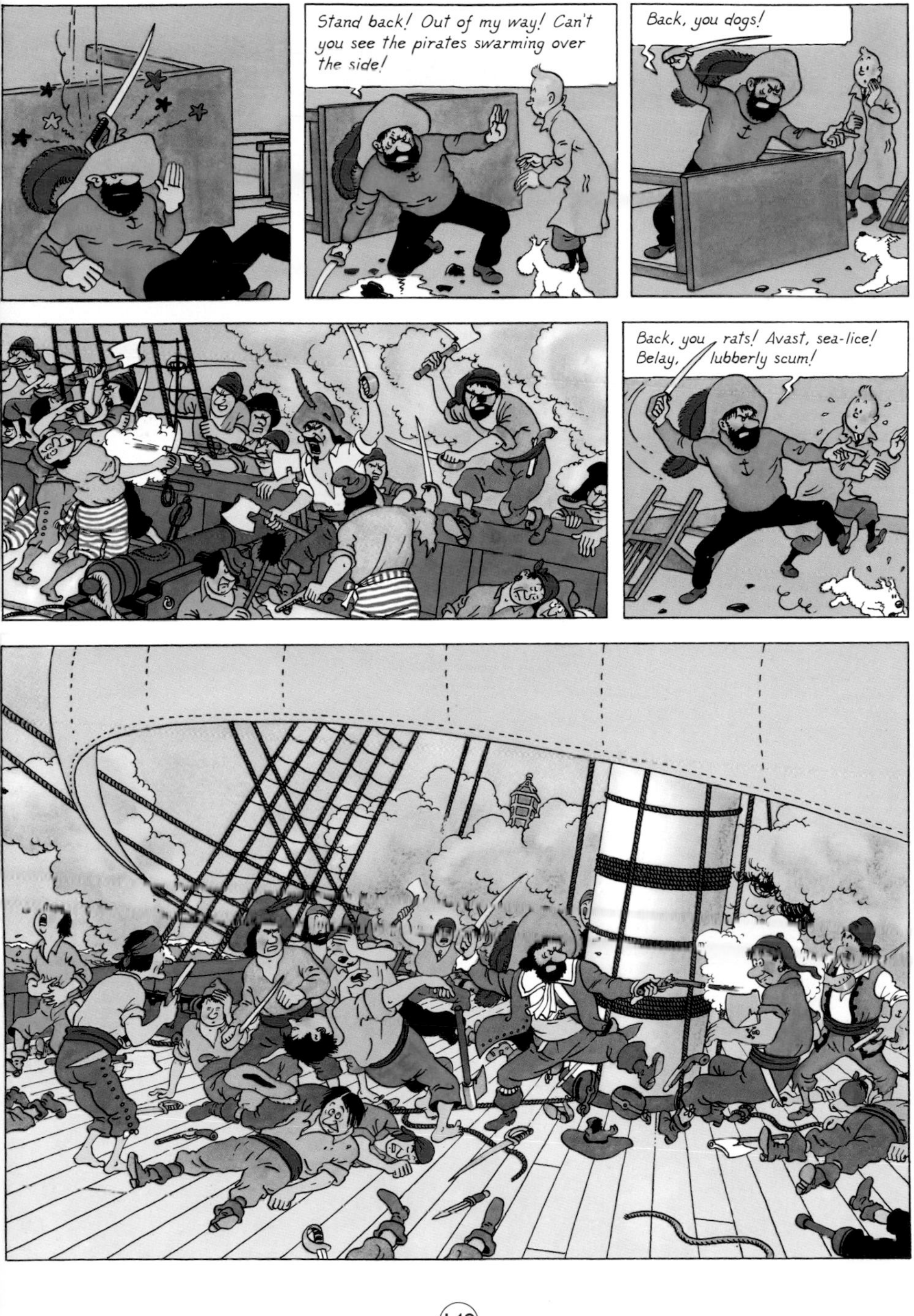

Stand back! Out of my way! Can't you see the pirates swarming over the side!
Back, you dogs!
Back, you rats! Avast, sea-lice! Belay, lubberly scum!

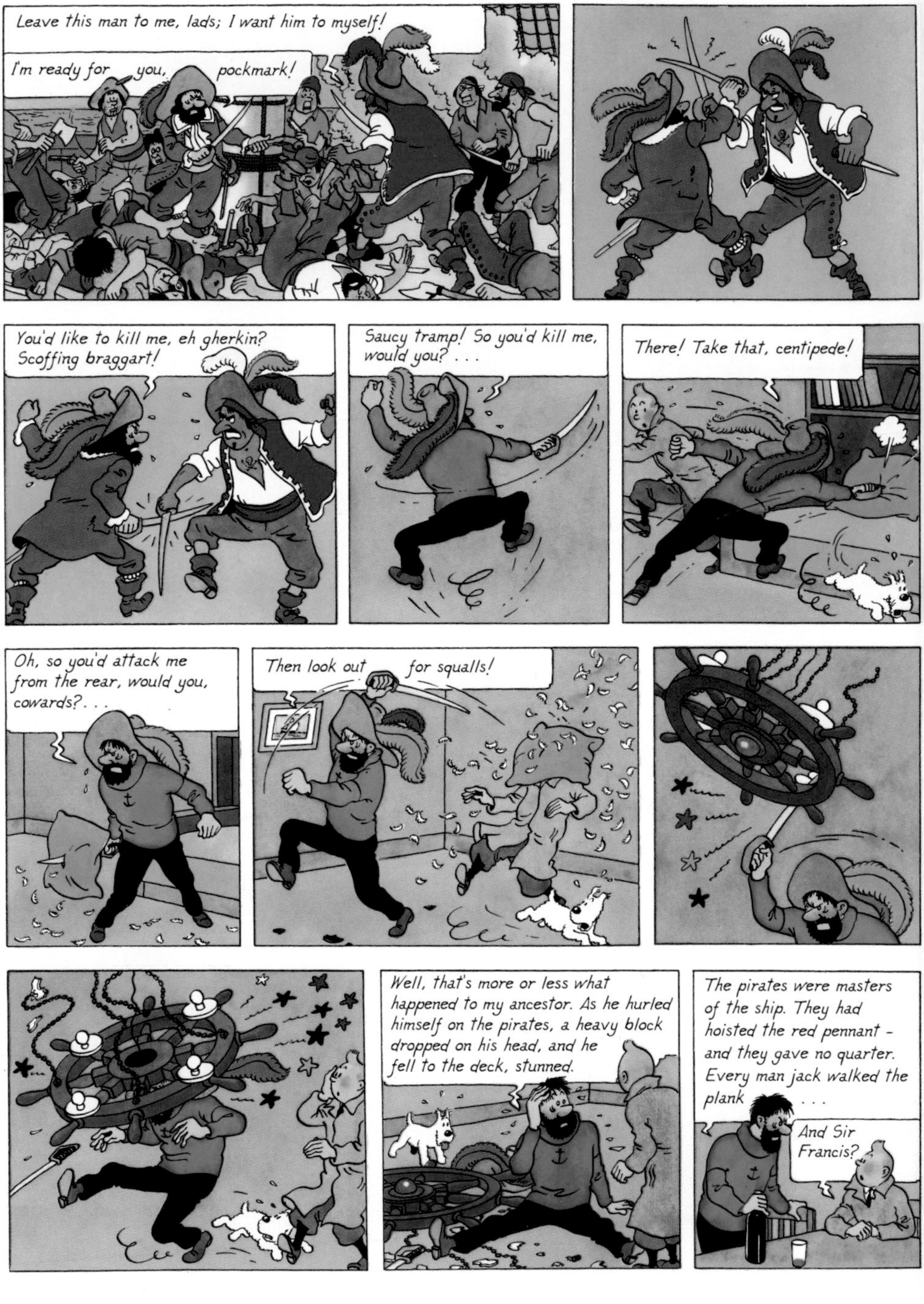
Leave this man to me, lads; I want him to myself!
I'm ready for you, pockmark!
You'd like to kill me, eh gherkin? Scoffing braggart!
Saucy tramp! So you'd kill me, would you? . . .
There! Take that, centipede!
Oh, so you'd attack me from the rear, would you, cowards? . . .
Then look out for squalls!
Well, that's more or less what happened to my ancestor. As he hurled himself on the pirates, a heavy block dropped on his head, and he fell to the deck, stunned.
The pirates were masters of the ship. They had hoisted the red pennant - and they gave no quarter. Every man jack walked the plank . . .
And Sir Francis?

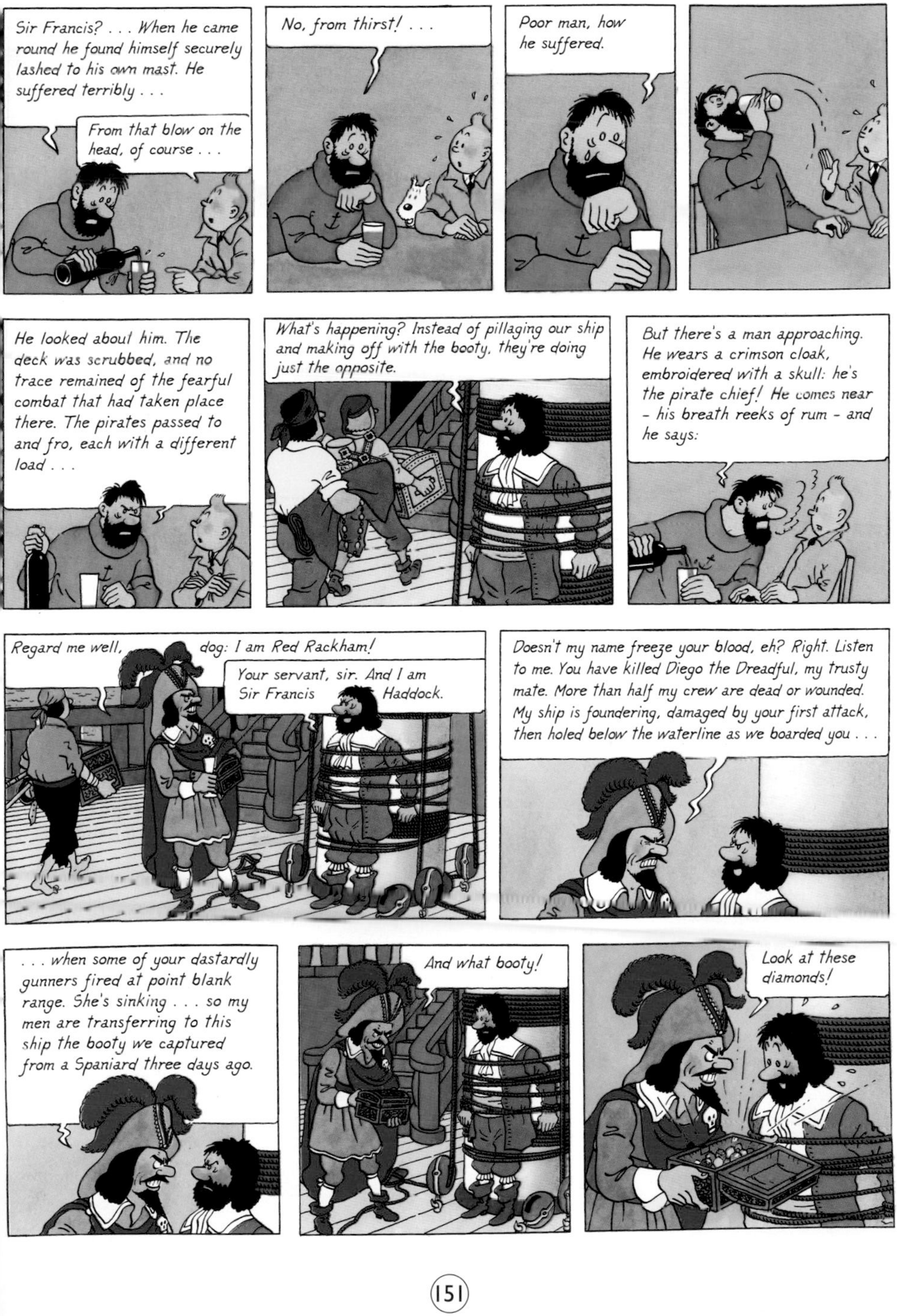
Sir Francis? . . . When he came round he found himself securely lashed to his own mast. He suffered terribly . . .
From that blow on the head, of course . . .
No, from thirst! . . .
Poor man, how he suffered.
He looked about him. The deck was scrubbed, and no trace remained of the fearful combat that had taken place there. The pirates passed to and fro, each with a different load . . .
What's happening? Instead of pillaging our ship and making off with the booty, they're doing just the opposite.
But there's a man approaching. He wears a crimson cloak, embroidered with a skull: he's the pirate chief! He comes near - his breath reeks of rum - and he says:
Regard me well, dog: I am Red Rackham!
Your servant, sir. And I am Sir Francis Haddock.
Doesn't my name freeze your blood, eh? Right. Listen to me. You have killed Diego the Dreadful, my trusty mate. More than half my crew are dead or wounded. My ship is foundering, damaged by your first attack, then holed below the waterline as we boarded you . . .
. . . when some of your dastardly gunners fired at point blank range. She's sinking . . . so my men are transferring to this ship the booty we captured from a Spaniard three days ago.
And what booty!
Look at these diamonds!

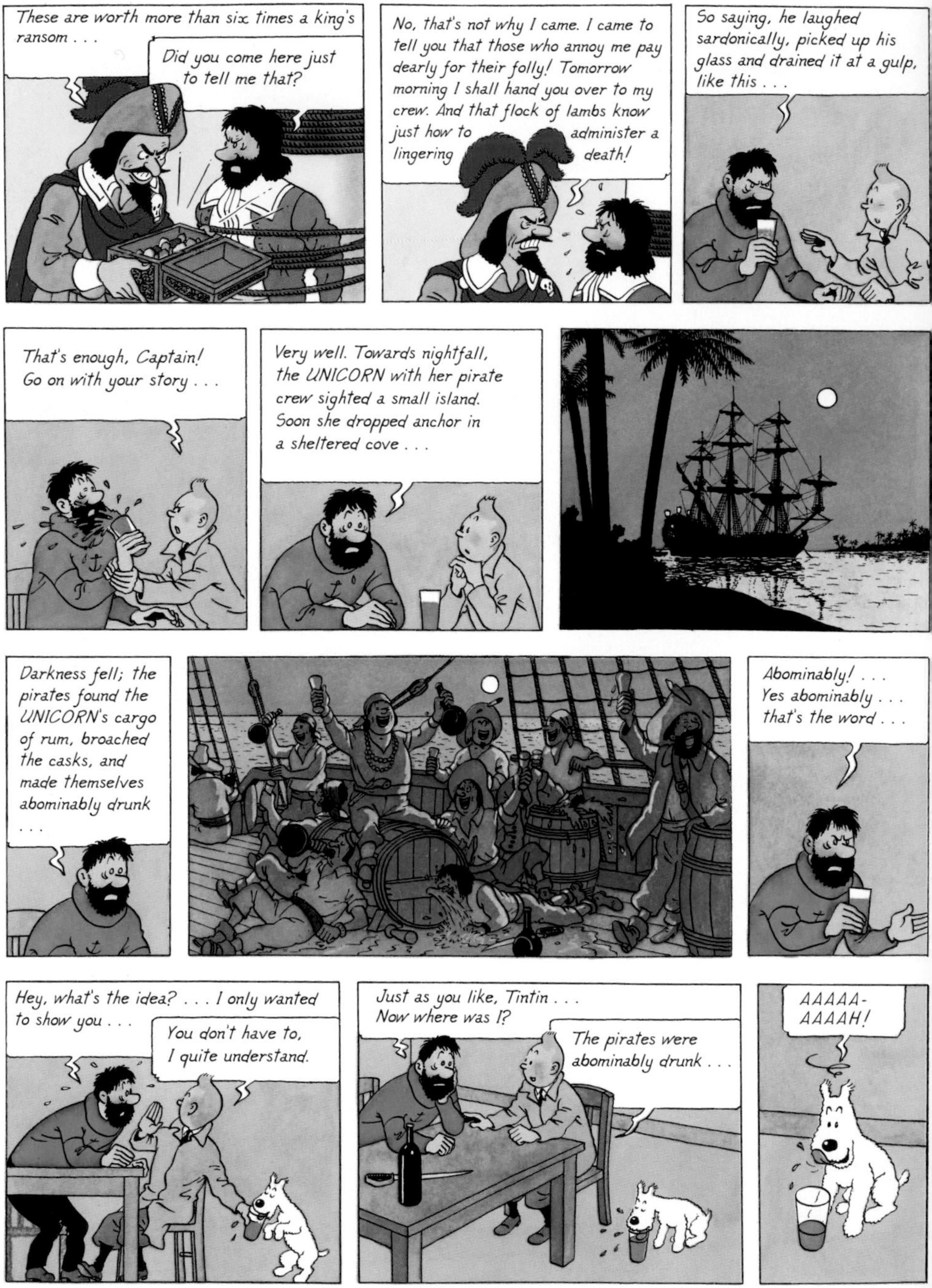
These are worth more than six times a king's ransom . . .
Did you come here just to tell me that?
No, that's not why I came. I came to tell you that those who annoy me pay dearly for their folly! Tomorrow morning I shall hand you over to my crew. And that flock of lambs know just how to administer a lingering death!
So saying, he laughed sardonically, picked up his glass and drained it at a gulp, like this . . .
That's enough, Captain! Go on with your story . . .
Very well. Towards nightfall, the UNICORN with her pirate crew sighted a small island. Soon she dropped anchor in a sheltered cove . . .
Darkness fell; the pirates found the UNICORN's cargo of rum, broached the casks, and made themselves abominably drunk . . .
Abominably! . . . Yes abominably . . . that's the word . . .
Hey, what's the idea? . . . I only wanted to show you . . .
You don't have to, I quite understand.
Just as you like, Tintin . . . Now where was I?
The pirates were abominably drunk . . .
AAAAA-AAAAH!

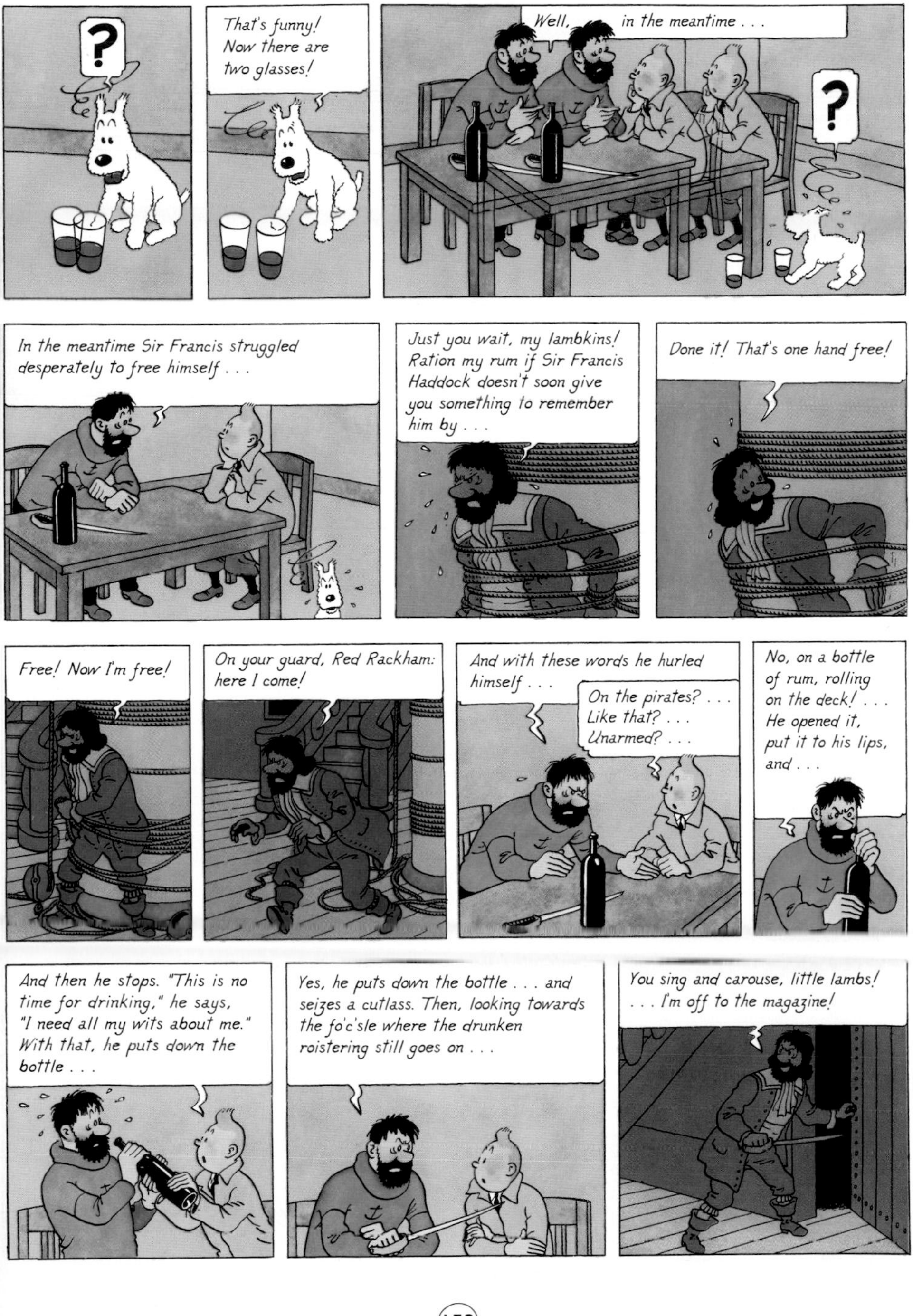
?
That's funny! Now there are two glasses!
Well, in the meantime . . .
?
In the meantime Sir Francis struggled desperately to free himself . . .
Just you wait, my lambkins! Ration my rum if Sir Francis Haddock doesn't soon give you something to remember him by . . .
Done it! That's one hand free!
Free! Now I'm free!
On your guard, Red Rackham: here I come!
And with these words he hurled himself . . .
On the pirates? . . . Like that? . . . Unarmed? . . .
No, on a bottle of rum, rolling on the deck! . . . He opened it, put it to his lips, and . . .
And then he stops. "This is no time for drinking," he says, "I need all my wits about me." With that, he puts down the bottle . . .
Yes, he puts down the bottle . . . and seizes a cutlass. Then, looking towards the fo'c'sle where the drunken roistering still goes on . . .
You sing and carouse, little lambs! . . . I'm off to the magazine!

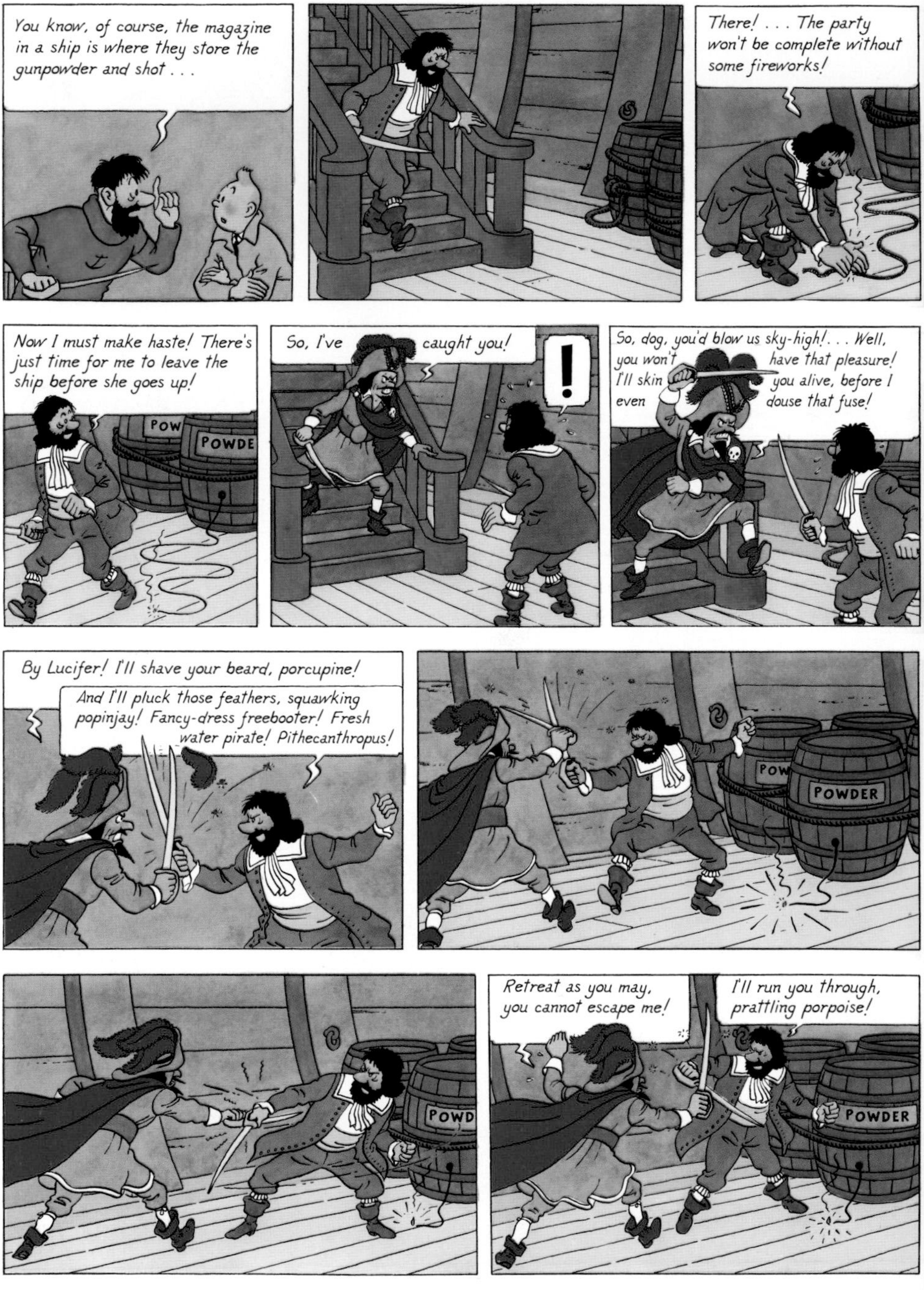
You know, of course, the magazine in a ship is where they store the gunpowder and shot . . .
There! . . . The party won't be complete without some fireworks!
Now I must make haste! There's just time for me to leave the ship before she goes up!
POW
POWDE
So, I've caught you!
!
So, dog, you'd blow us sky-high! . . . Well, you won't have that pleasure! I'll skin you alive, before I even douse that fuse!
By Lucifer! I'll shave your beard, porcupine!
And I'll pluck those feathers, squawking popinjay! Fancy-dress freebooter! Fresh water pirate! Pithecanthropus!
POW
POWDER
POWD
Retreat as you may, you cannot escape me!
I'll run you through, prattling porpoise!
POWDER

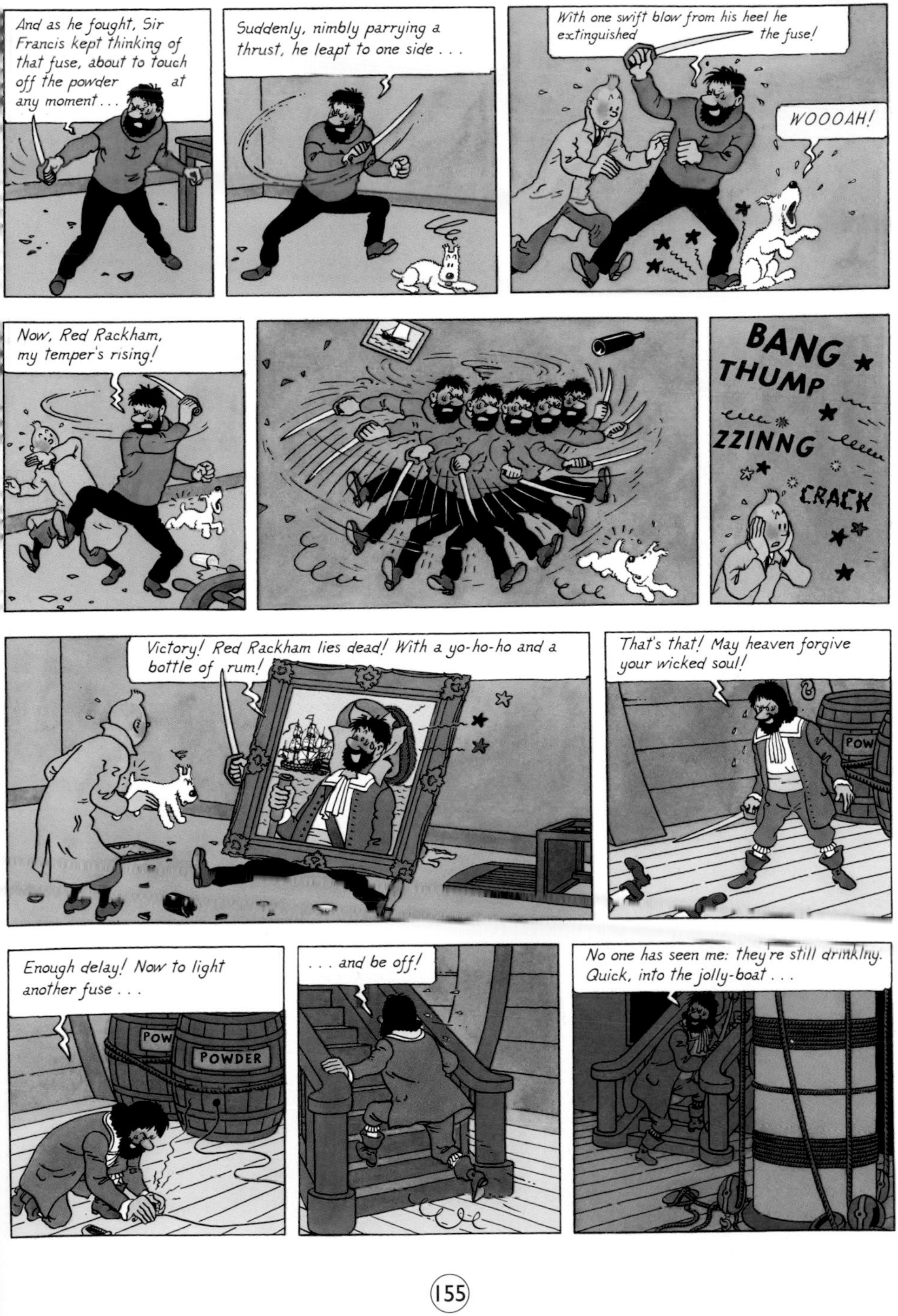
And as he fought, Sir Francis kept thinking of that fuse, about to touch off the powder at any moment . . .
Suddenly, nimbly parrying a thrust, he leapt to one side . . .
With one swift blow from his heel he extinguished the fuse!
WOOOAH!
Now, Red Rackham, my temper's rising!
BANG
THUMP
ZZINNG
CRACK
Victory! Red Rackham lies dead! With a yo-ho-ho and a bottle of rum!
That's that! May heaven forgive your wicked soul!
POW
Enough delay! Now to light another fuse . . .
POW
POWDER
. . . and be off!
No one has seen me: they're still drinking. Quick, into the jolly-boat . . .

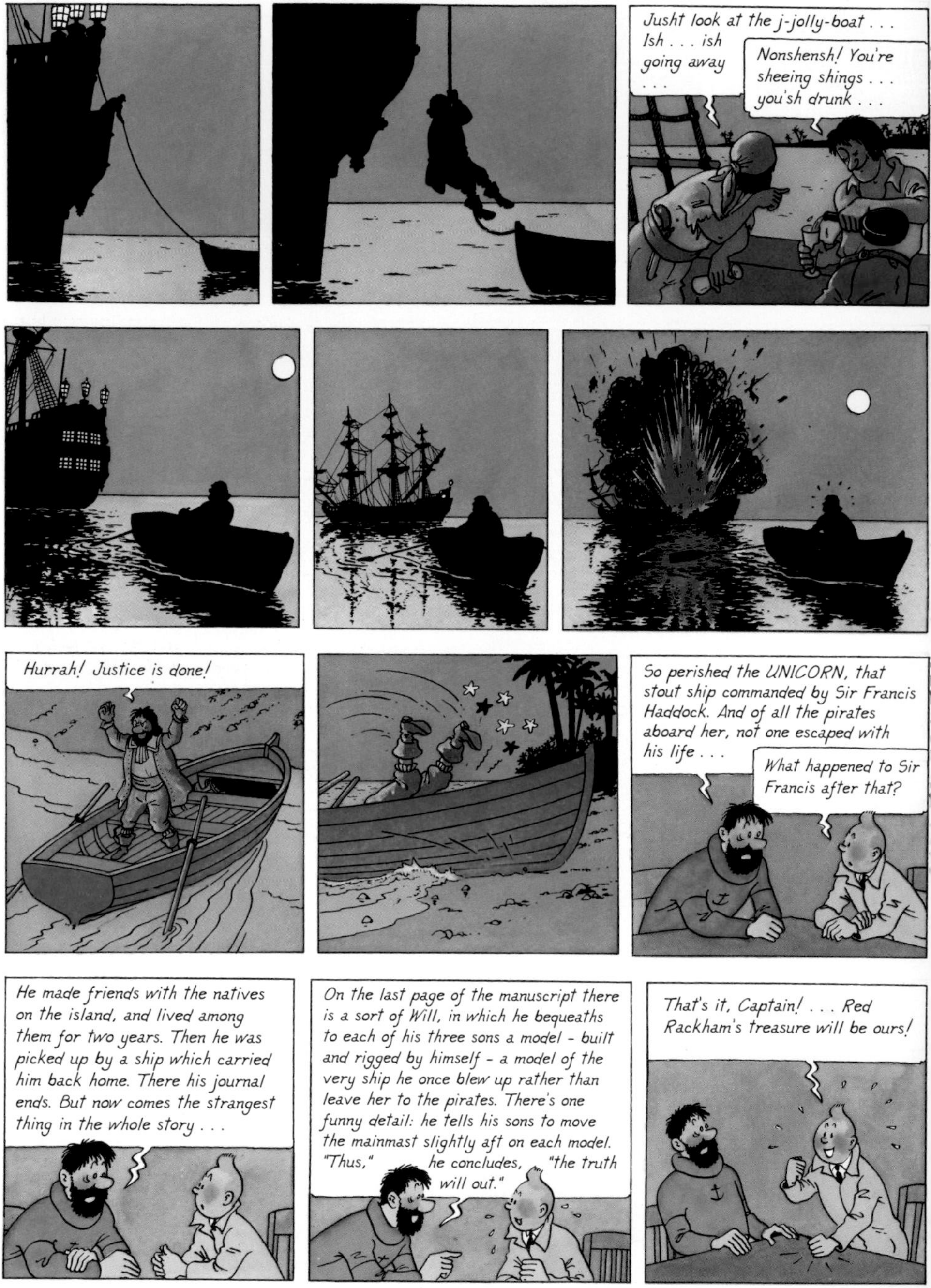
Jusht look at the j-jolly-boat . . . Ish . . . ish going away . . .
Nonshensh! You're sheeing shings . . . you'sh drunk . . .
Hurrah! Justice is done!
So perished the UNICORN, that stout ship commanded by Sir Francis Haddock. And of all the pirates aboard her, not one escaped with his life . . .
What happened to Sir Francis after that?
He made friends with the natives on the island, and lived among them for two years. Then he was picked up by a ship which carried him back home. There his journal ends. But now comes the strangest thing in the whole story . . .
On the last page of the manuscript there is a sort of Will, in which he bequeaths to each of his three sons a model - built and rigged by himself - a model of the very ship he once blew up rather than leave her to the pirates. There's one funny detail: he tells his sons to move the mainmast slightly aft on each model. "Thus," he concludes, "the truth will out."
That's it, Captain! . . . Red Rackham's treasure will be ours!

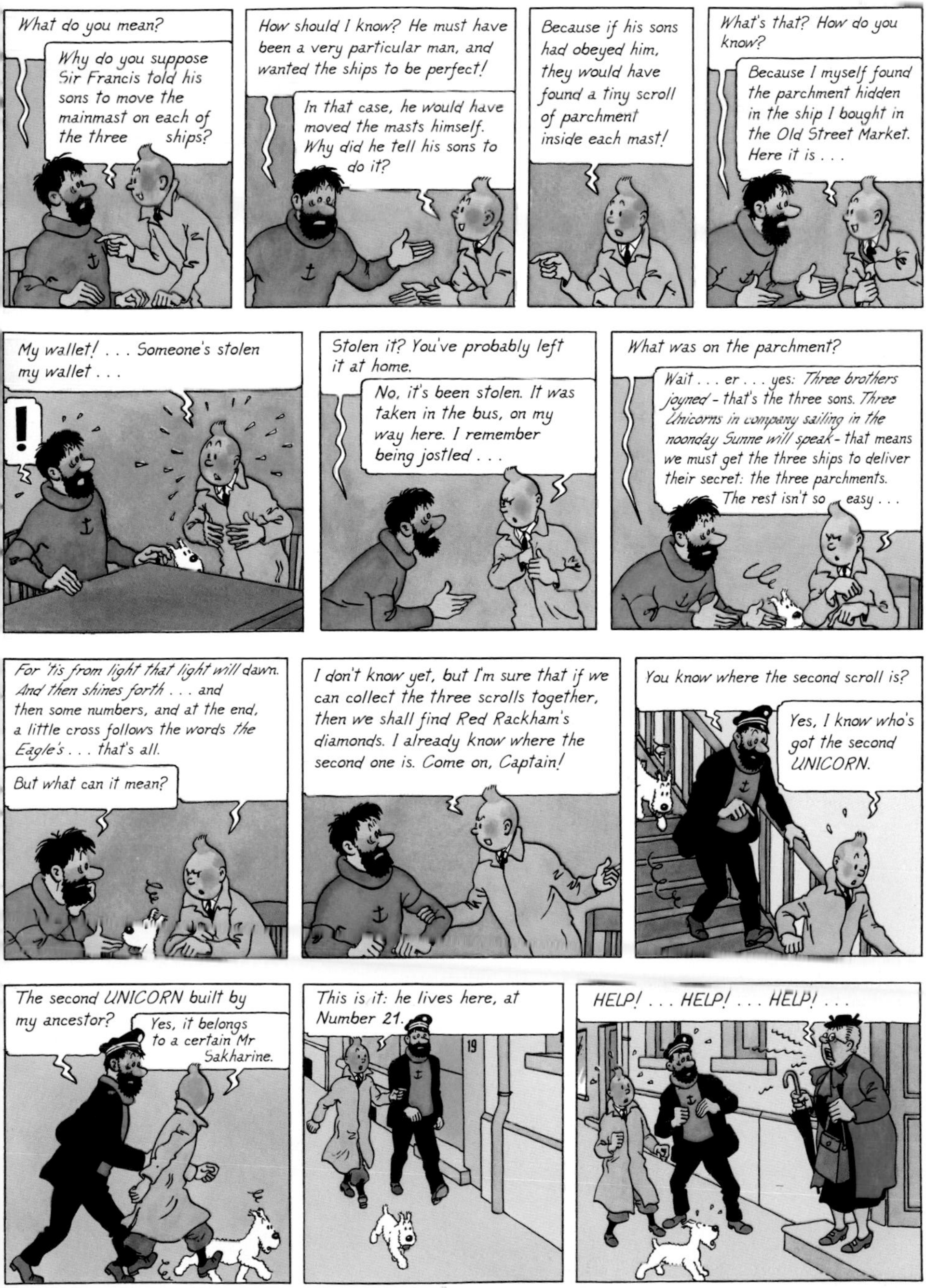
What do you mean?
Why do you suppose Sir Francis told his sons to move the mainmast on each of the three ships?
How should I know? He must have been a very particular man, and wanted the ships to be perfect!
In that case, he would have moved the masts himself. Why did he tell his sons to do it?
Because if his sons had obeyed him, they would have found a tiny scroll of parchment inside each mast!
What's that? How do you know?
Because I myself found the parchment hidden in the ship I bought in the Old Street Market. Here it is . . .
My wallet! . . . Someone's stolen my wallet . . .
!
Stolen it? You've probably left it at home.
No, it's been stolen. It was taken in the bus, on my way here. I remember being jostled . . .
What was on the parchment?
Wait . . . er . . . yes: Three brothers joyned - that's the three sons. Three Unicorns in company sailing in the noonday Sunne will speak - that means we must get the three ships to deliver their secret: the three parchments. The rest isn't so easy . . .
For 'tis from light that light will dawn. And then shines forth . . . and then some numbers, and at the end, a little cross follows the words the Eagle's . . . that's all.
But what can it mean?
I don't know yet, but I'm sure that if we can collect the three scrolls together, then we shall find Red Rackham's diamonds. I already know where the second one is. Come on, Captain!
You know where the second scroll is?
Yes, I know who's got the second UNICORN.
The second UNICORN built by my ancestor?
Yes, it belongs to a certain Mr Sakharine.
This is it: he lives here, at Number 21.
19
HELP! . . . HELP! . . . HELP! . . .

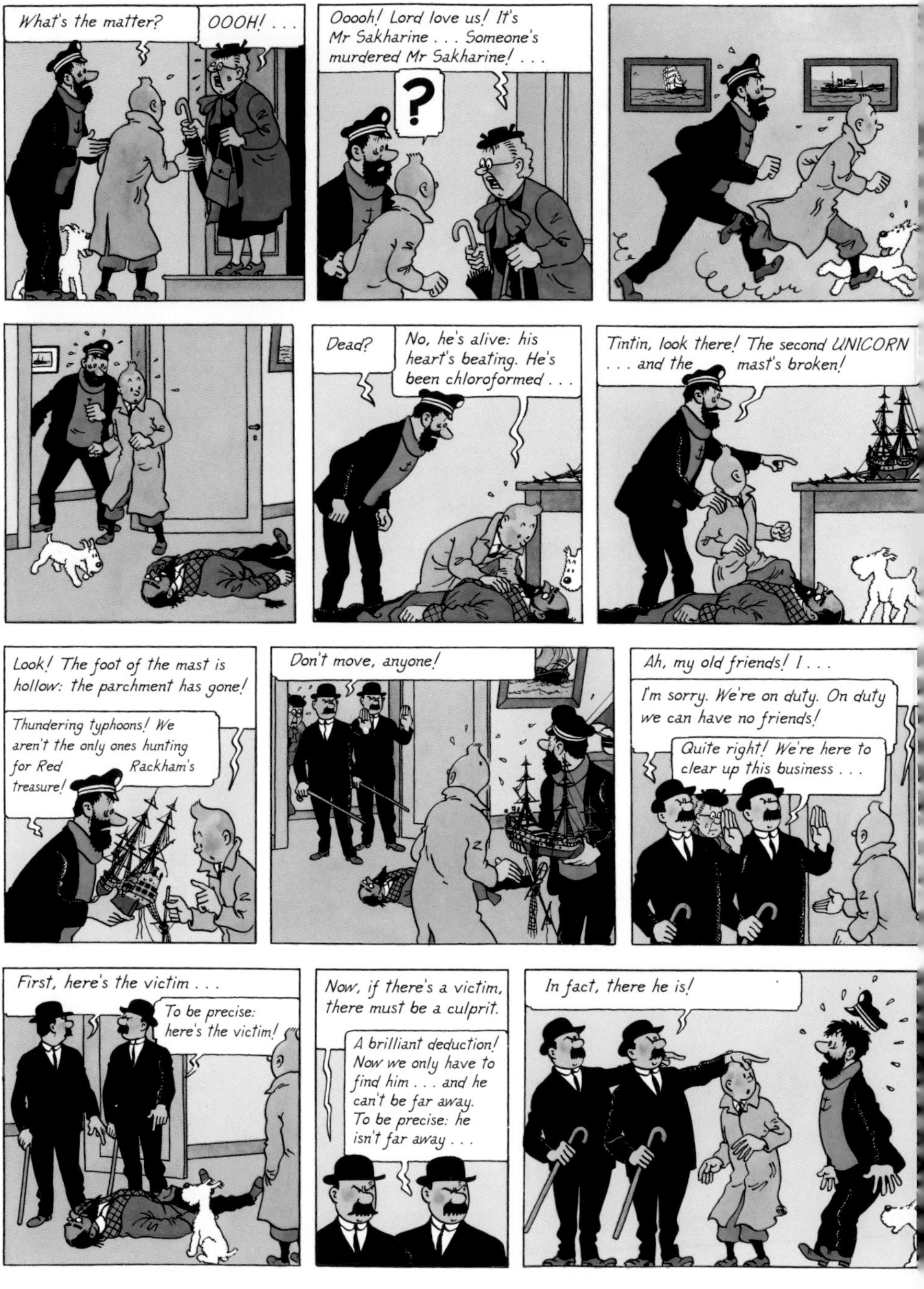
What's the matter?
OOOH! . . .
Ooooh! Lord love us! It's Mr Sakharine . . . Someone's murdered Mr Sakharine! . . .
?
Dead?
No, he's alive: his heart's beating. He's been chloroformed . . .
Tintin, look there! The second UNICORN . . . and the mast's broken!
Look! The foot of the mast is hollow: the parchment has gone!
Thundering typhoons! We aren't the only ones hunting for Red Rackham's treasure!
Don't move, anyone!
Ah, my old friends! I . . .
I'm sorry. We're on duty. On duty we can have no friends!
Quite right! We're here to clear up this business . . .
First, here's the victim . . .
To be precise: here's the victim!
Now, if there's a victim, there must be a culprit.
A brilliant deduction! Now we only have to find him . . . and he can't be far away. To be precise: he isn't far away . . .
In fact, there he is!

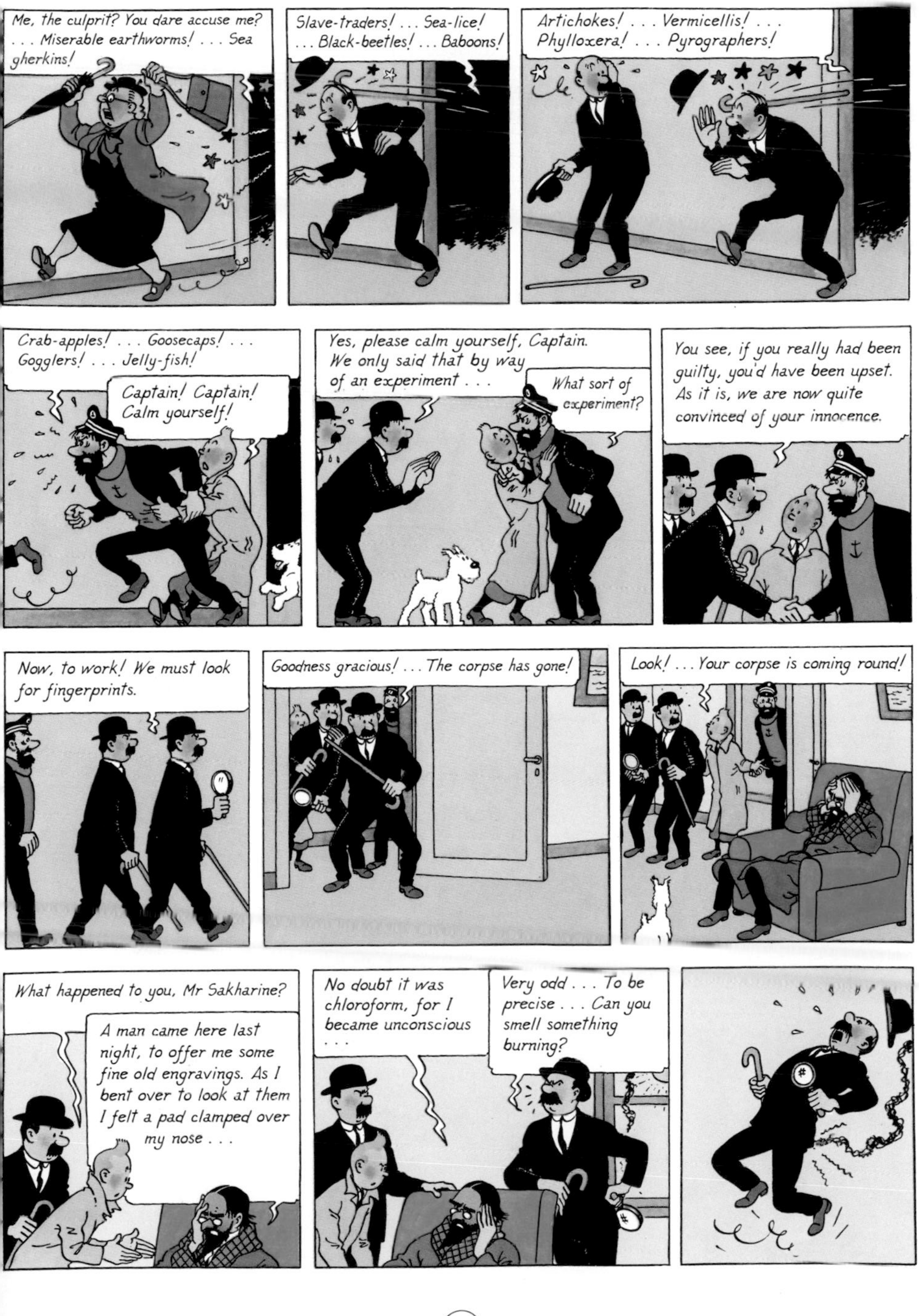
Me, the culprit? You dare accuse me? . . . Miserable earthworms! . . . Sea gherkins!
Slave-traders! . . . Sea-lice! . . . Black-beetles! . . . Baboons!
Artichokes! . . . Vermicellis! . . . Phylloxera! . . . Pyrographers!
Crab-apples! . . . Goosecaps! . . . Gogglers! . . . Jelly-fish!
Captain! Captain! Calm yourself!
Yes, please calm yourself, Captain. We only said that by way of an experiment . . .
What sort of experiment?
You see, if you really had been guilty, you'd have been upset. As it is, we are now quite convinced of your innocence.
Now, to work! We must look for fingerprints.
Goodness gracious! . . . The corpse has gone!
Look! . . . Your corpse is coming round!
What happened to you, Mr Sakharine?
A man came here last night, to offer me some fine old engravings. As I bent over to look at them I felt a pad clamped over my nose . . .
No doubt it was chloroform, for I became unconscious . . .
Very odd . . . To be precise . . . Can you smell something burning?

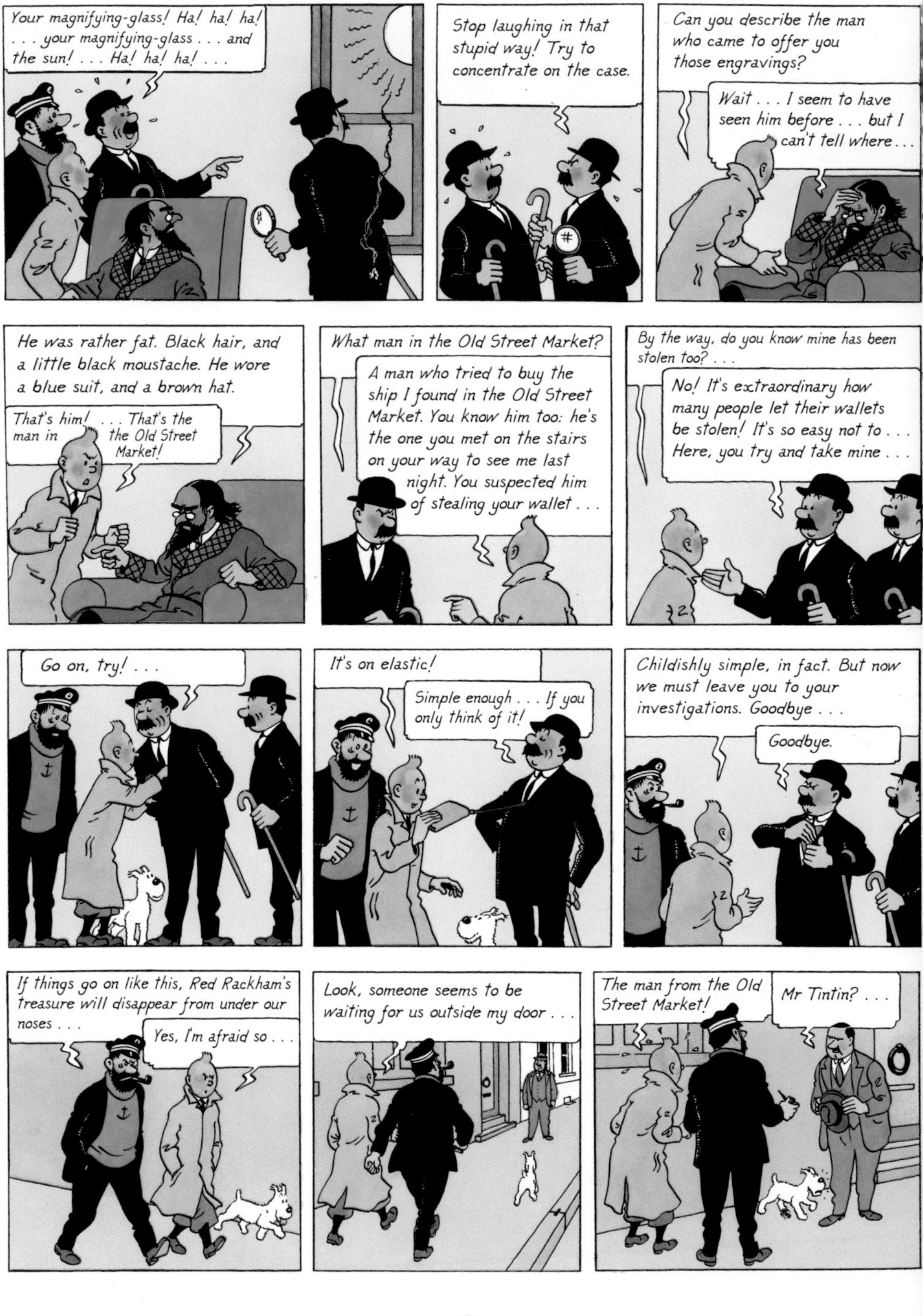

Your magnifying-glass! Ha! ha! ha! . . . your magnifying-glass . . . and the sun! . . . Ha! ha! ha! . . .
Stop laughing in that stupid way! Try to concentrate on the case.
Can you describe the man who came to offer you those engravings?
Wait . . . I seem to have seen him before . . . but I can't tell where . . .
He was rather fat. Black hair, and a little black moustache. He wore a blue suit, and a brown hat.
That's him! . . . That's the man in the Old Street Market!
What man in the Old Street Market?
A man who tried to buy the ship I found in the Old Street Market. You know him too: he's the one you met on the stairs on your way to see me last night. You suspected him of stealing your wallet . . .
By the way, do you know mine has been stolen too? . . .
No! It's extraordinary how many people let their wallets be stolen! It's so easy not to . . . Here, you try and take mine . . .
Go on, try! . . .
It's on elastic!
Simple enough . . . If you only think of it!
Childishly simple, in fact. But now we must leave you to your investigations. Goodbye . . .
Goodbye.
If things go on like this, Red Rackham's treasure will disappear from under our noses . . .
Yes, I'm afraid so . . .
Look, someone seems to be waiting for us outside my door . . .
The man from the Old Street Market!
Mr Tintin? . . .

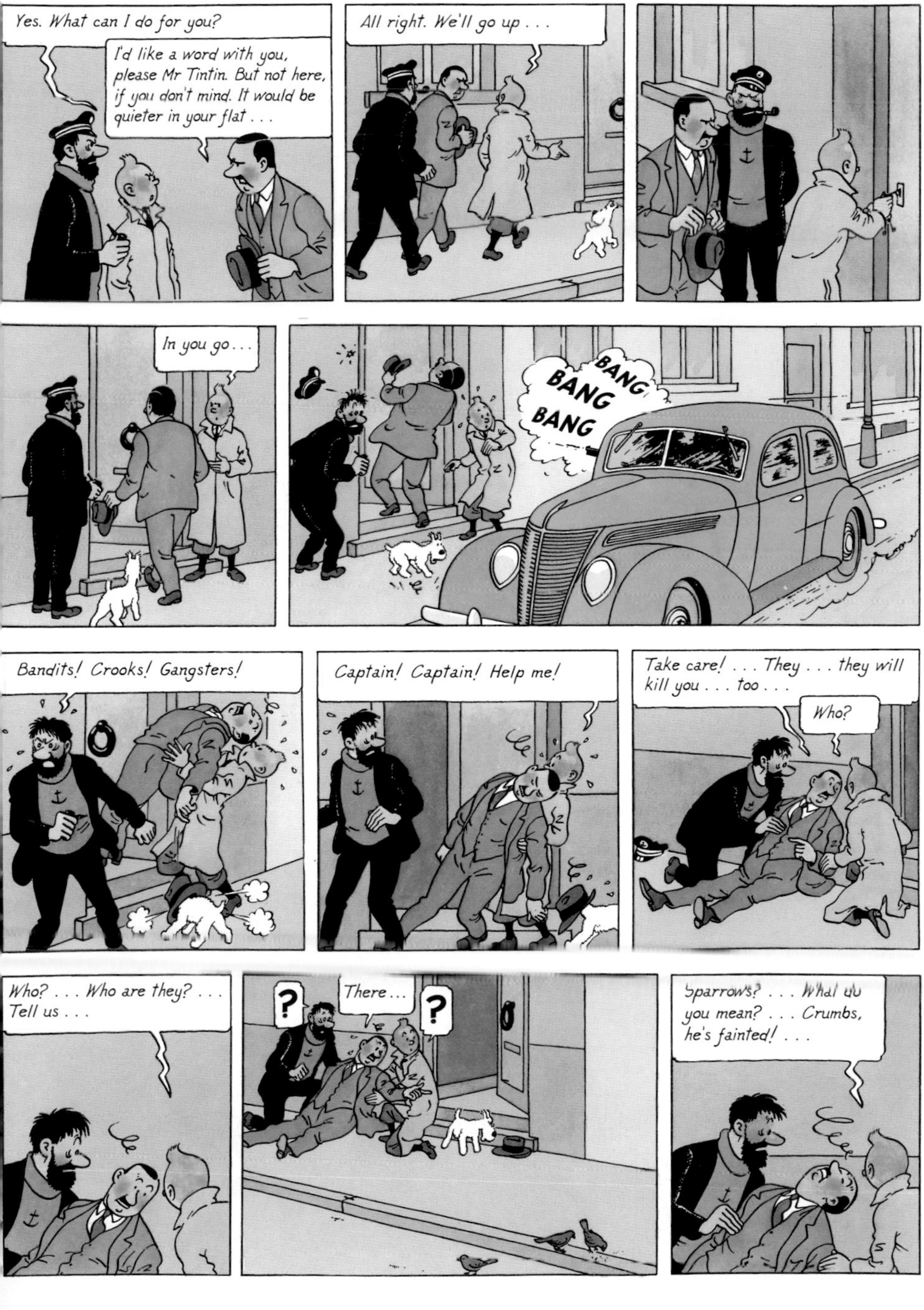
Yes. What can I do for you?
I'd like a word with you, please Mr Tintin. But not here, if you don't mind. It would be quieter in your flat . . .
All right. We'll go up . . .
In you go . . .
BANG BANG BANG
Bandits! Crooks! Gangsters!
Captain! Captain! Help me!
Take care! . . . They . . . they will kill you . . . too . . .
Who?
Who? . . . Who are they? . . . Tell us . . .
?
There . . .
?
Sparrows? . . . What do you mean? . . . Crumbs, he's fainted! . . .

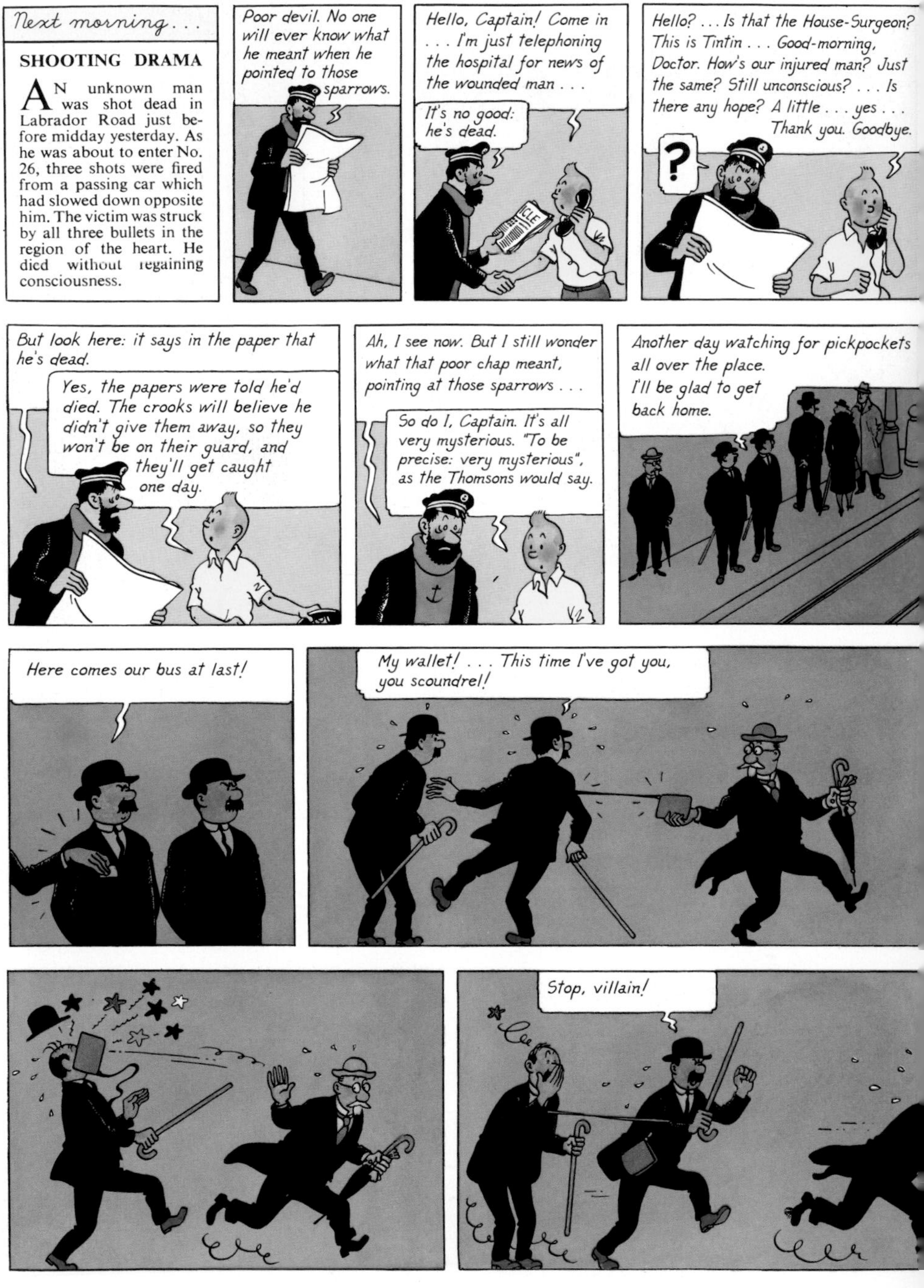

Next morning . . .
SHOOTING DRAMA
AN unknown man was shot dead in Labrador Road just before midday yesterday. As he was about to enter No. 26, three shots were fired from a passing car which had slowed down opposite him. The victim was struck by all three bullets in the region of the heart. He died without regaining consciousness.
Poor devil. No one will ever know what he meant when he pointed to those sparrows.
Hello, Captain! Come in . . . I'm just telephoning the hospital for news of the wounded man . . .
It's no good: he's dead.
Hello? . . . Is that the House-Surgeon? This is Tintin . . . Good-morning, Doctor. How's our injured man? Just the same? Still unconscious? . . . Is there any hope? A little . . . yes . . . Thank you. Goodbye.
?
But look here: it says in the paper that he's dead.
Yes, the papers were told he'd died. The crooks will believe he didn't give them away, so they won't be on their guard, and they'll get caught one day.
Ah, I see now. But I still wonder what that poor chap meant, pointing at those sparrows . . .
So do I, Captain. It's all very mysterious. "To be precise: very mysterious", as the Thomsons would say.
Another day watching for pickpockets all over the place. I'll be glad to get back home.
Here comes our bus at last!
My wallet! . . . This time I've got you, you scoundrel!
Stop, villain!

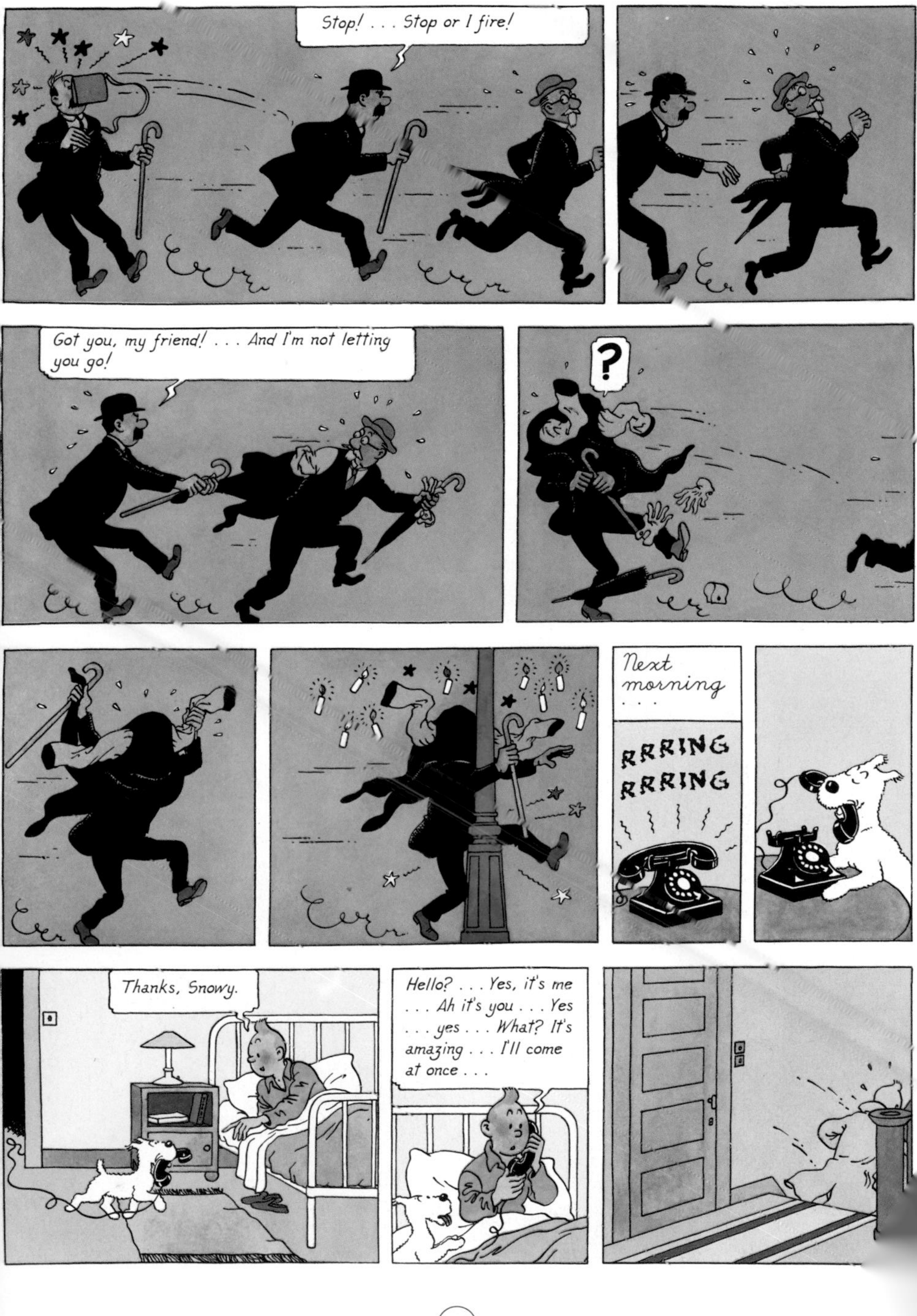
Stop! . . . Stop or I fire!
Got you, my friend! . . . And I'm not letting you go!
?
Next morning . . .
RRRING
RRRING
Thanks, Snowy.
Hello? . . . Yes, it's me . . . Ah it's you . . . Yes . . . yes . . . What? It's amazing . . . I'll come at once . . .

Ah, Captain! . . . Come with me . . .

Where? . . .

To see the Thomsons: they've found my wallet!

There's no mistake: it's mine all right.

He had seven in his pockets. The day's takings, no doubt.

?

Here's the parchment from the UNICORN's mast. Look, Captain . . .

Er . . . that's good . . .

Tell me: how did you manage to catch the thief?

Catch him? . . . Well, to be quite honest, we only managed to catch his morning-coat.

Yes, it's certainly a morning-coat. How odd for a pickpocket to wear a thing like this.

Isn't it?

The trouble is that the coat doesn't give us any clue about its owner's identity . . .

Doesn't it?

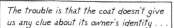

Look at these stitches; they make up a number. That means the coat has been to the cleaners recently.

Goodness, you're right!

So . . . to find the thief's name and address, we've only got to trace the cleaners who use this mark. Quick, we'll make a list of cleaners from the telephone directory, and start hunting for the thief at once!

CLEANERS

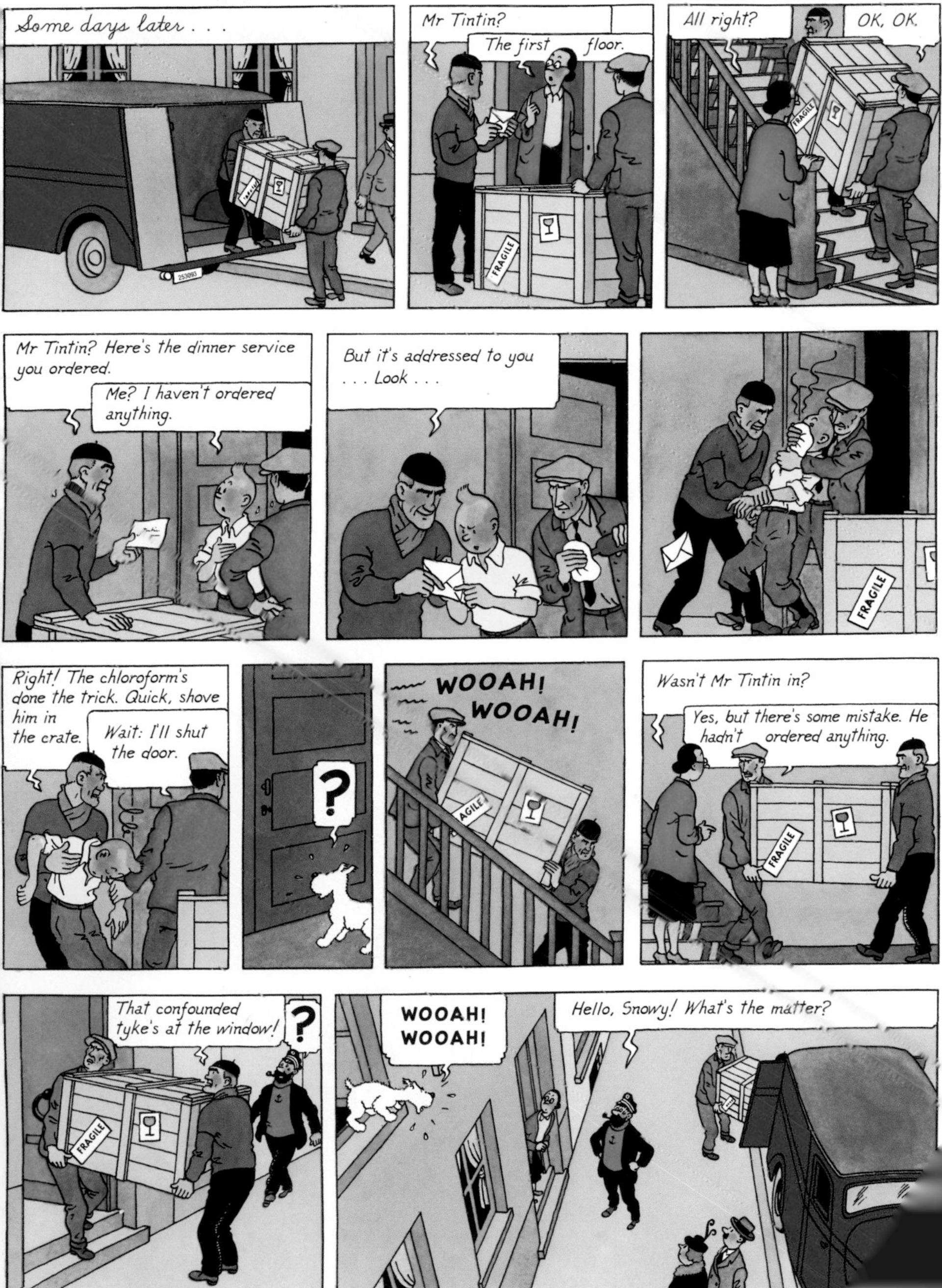
Some days later . . .
Mr Tintin?
The first floor.
All right?
OK, OK.
FRAGILE
Mr Tintin? Here's the dinner service you ordered.
Me? I haven't ordered anything.
But it's addressed to you . . . Look . . .
FRAGILE
Right! The chloroform's done the trick. Quick, shove him in the crate.
Wait: I'll shut the door.
?
WOOAH! WOOAH!
Wasn't Mr Tintin in?
Yes, but there's some mistake. He hadn't ordered anything.
FRAGILE
That confounded tyke's at the window!
?
FRAGILE
WOOAH! WOOAH!
Hello, Snowy! What's the matter?

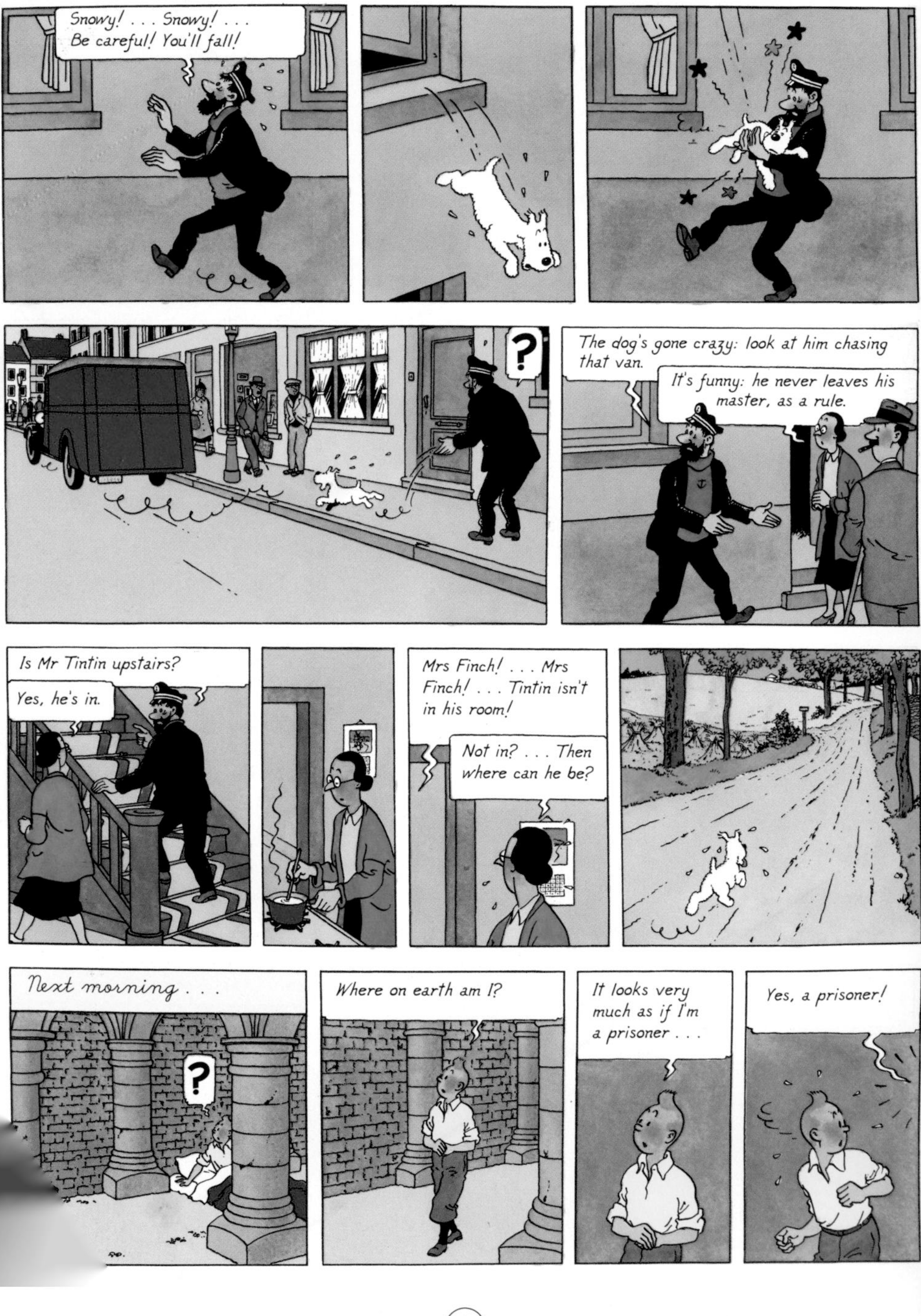

Snowy! . . . Snowy! . . .
Be careful! You'll fall!
?
The dog's gone crazy: look at him chasing that van.
It's funny: he never leaves his master, as a rule.
Is Mr Tintin upstairs?
Yes, he's in.
Mrs Finch! . . . Mrs Finch! . . . Tintin isn't in his room!
Not in? . . . Then where can he be?
Next morning . . .
?
Where on earth am I?
It looks very much as if I'm a prisoner . . .
Yes, a prisoner!

Nobody there! But I wasn't dreaming: someone spoke!
Yes, someone spoke!
Who . . . who are you? . . . And where are you?
Who am I? I am the ghost of the captain of the UNICORN!
Ha! ha! ha! ha! ha!
Ha! ha! ha! . . . That frightened you, didn't it? . . . Come over to the door . . . Come on.
Come nearer. Good . . . Now, can you see the speaking-tube?
Who are you, and what do you want with me?
Who am I? . . . You must allow me to remain anonymous . . . And why did I have you kidnapped? You have guessed that, no doubt . . .
I want to know where you have hidden the two parchments you stole from me.
Me? I stole two parchments? . . . But I never had more than one.
Come on now, let's be sensible! I'd collected two of the three scrolls: you took them from me. That night when I had your flat searched, only the third one was found . . . in your wallet. Where are the other two?
How should I know?
As you like. But I warn you: I know of several ways to loosen stubborn tongues . . . I'll give you two hours to tell me where you hid those scrolls, then if you won't talk, you'll soon see the sort of man I am!
But I tell you . . . Oh he's cut off, the gangster!
Now I'm in a fine mess! How do I get out of this one?

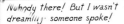

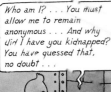

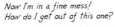

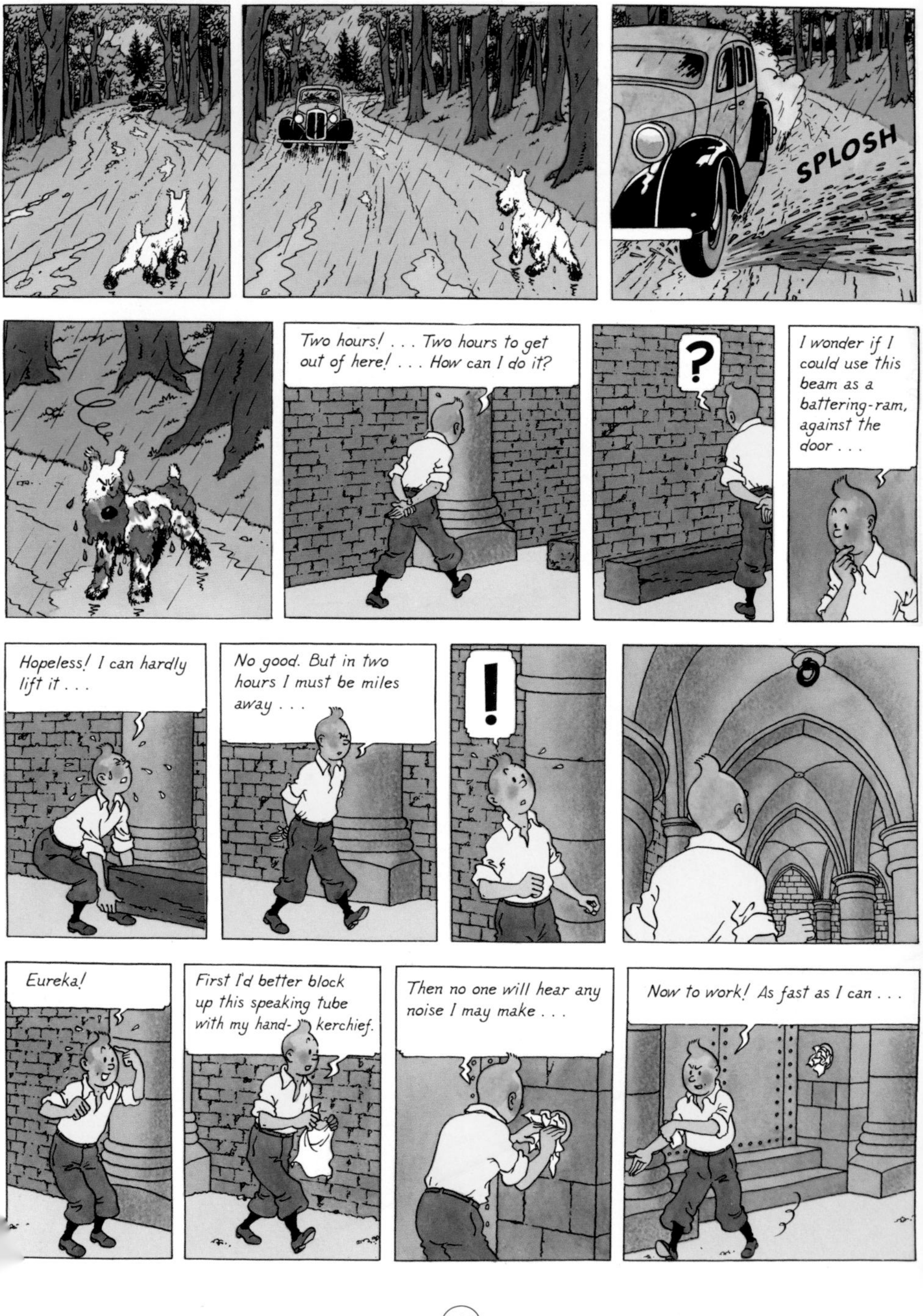
SPLOSH
Two hours! . . . Two hours to get out of here! . . . How can I do it?
?
I wonder if I could use this beam as a battering-ram, against the door . . .
Hopeless! I can hardly lift it . . .
No good. But in two hours I must be miles away . . .
!
Eureka!
First I'd better block up this speaking tube with my hand- kerchief.
Then no one will hear any noise I may make . . .
Now to work! As fast as I can . . .

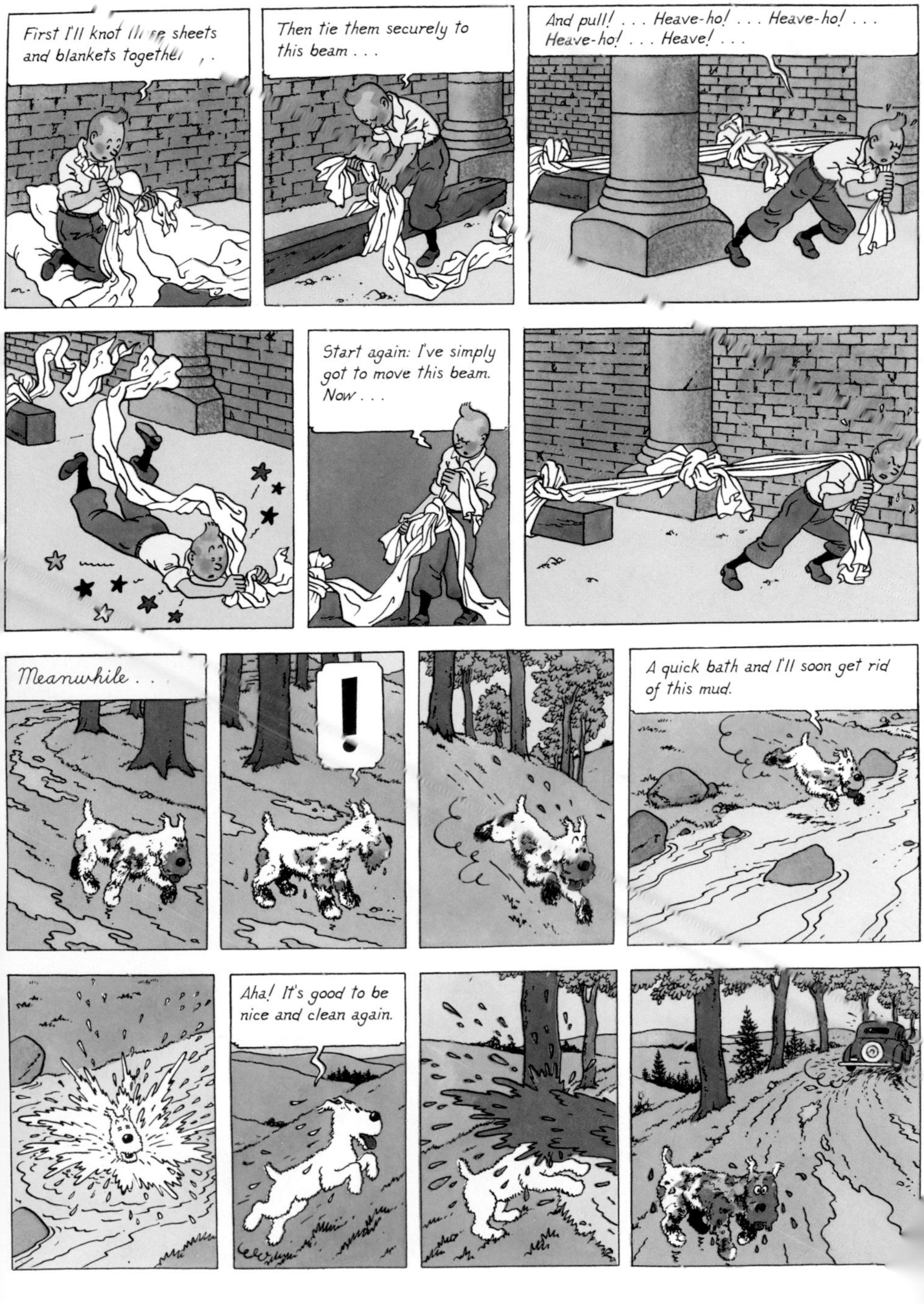
First I'll knot these sheets and blankets together . . .
Then tie them securely to this beam . . .
And pull! . . . Heave-ho! . . . Heave-ho! . . . Heave-ho! . . . Heave! . . .
Start again: I've simply got to move this beam. Now . . .
Meanwhile . . .
!
A quick bath and I'll soon get rid of this mud.
Aha! It's good to be nice and clean again.

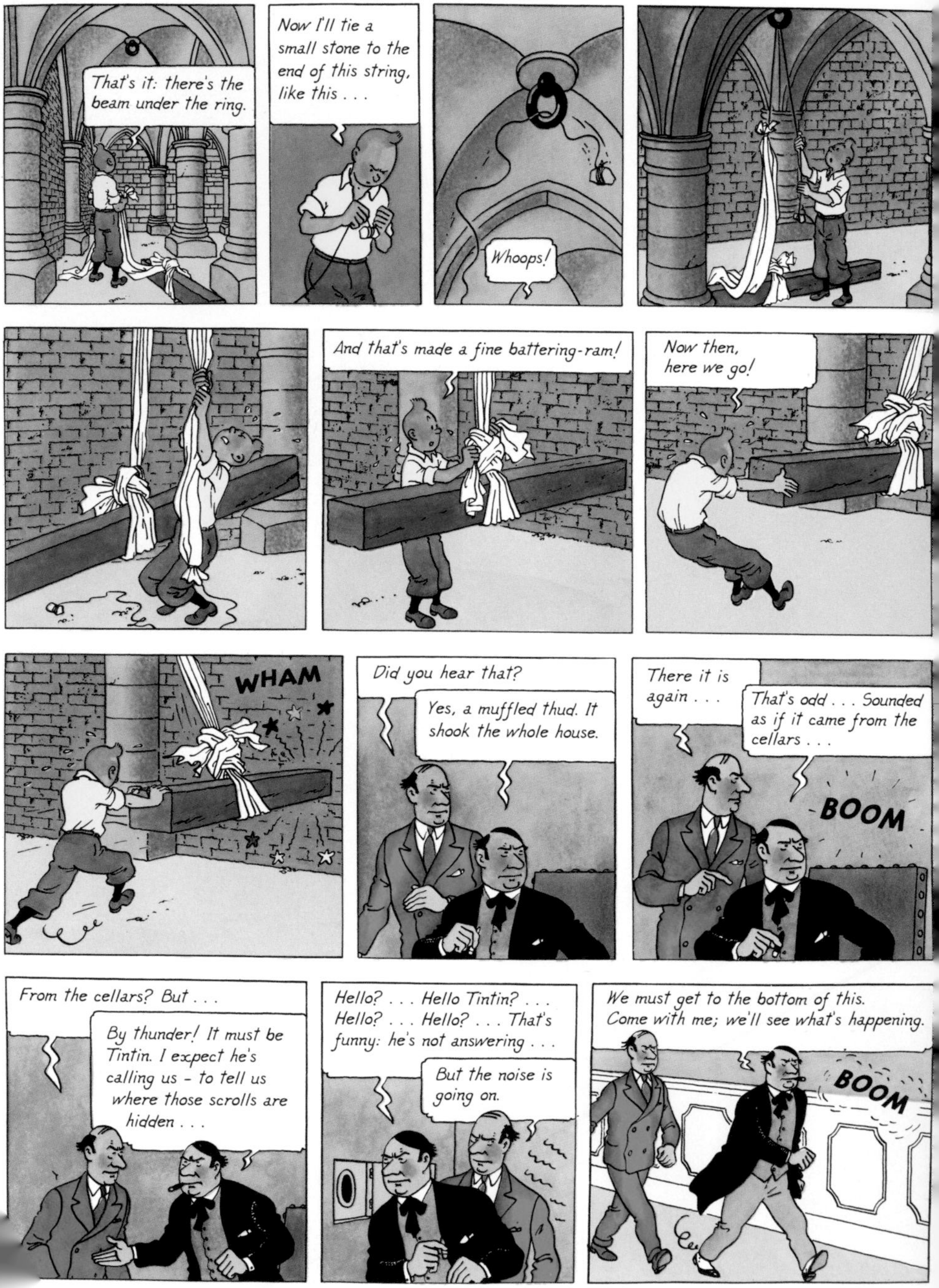
That's it: there's the beam under the ring.
Now I'll tie a small stone to the end of this string, like this . . .
Whoops!
And that's made a fine battering-ram!
Now then, here we go!
WHAM
Did you hear that?
Yes, a muffled thud. It shook the whole house.
There it is again . . .
That's odd . . . Sounded as if it came from the cellars . . .
BOOM
From the cellars? But . . .
By thunder! It must be Tintin. I expect he's calling us - to tell us where those scrolls are hidden . . .
Hello? . . . Hello Tintin? . . . Hello? . . . Hello? . . . That's funny: he's not answering . . .
But the noise is going on.
We must get to the bottom of this. Come with me; we'll see what's happening.
BOOM

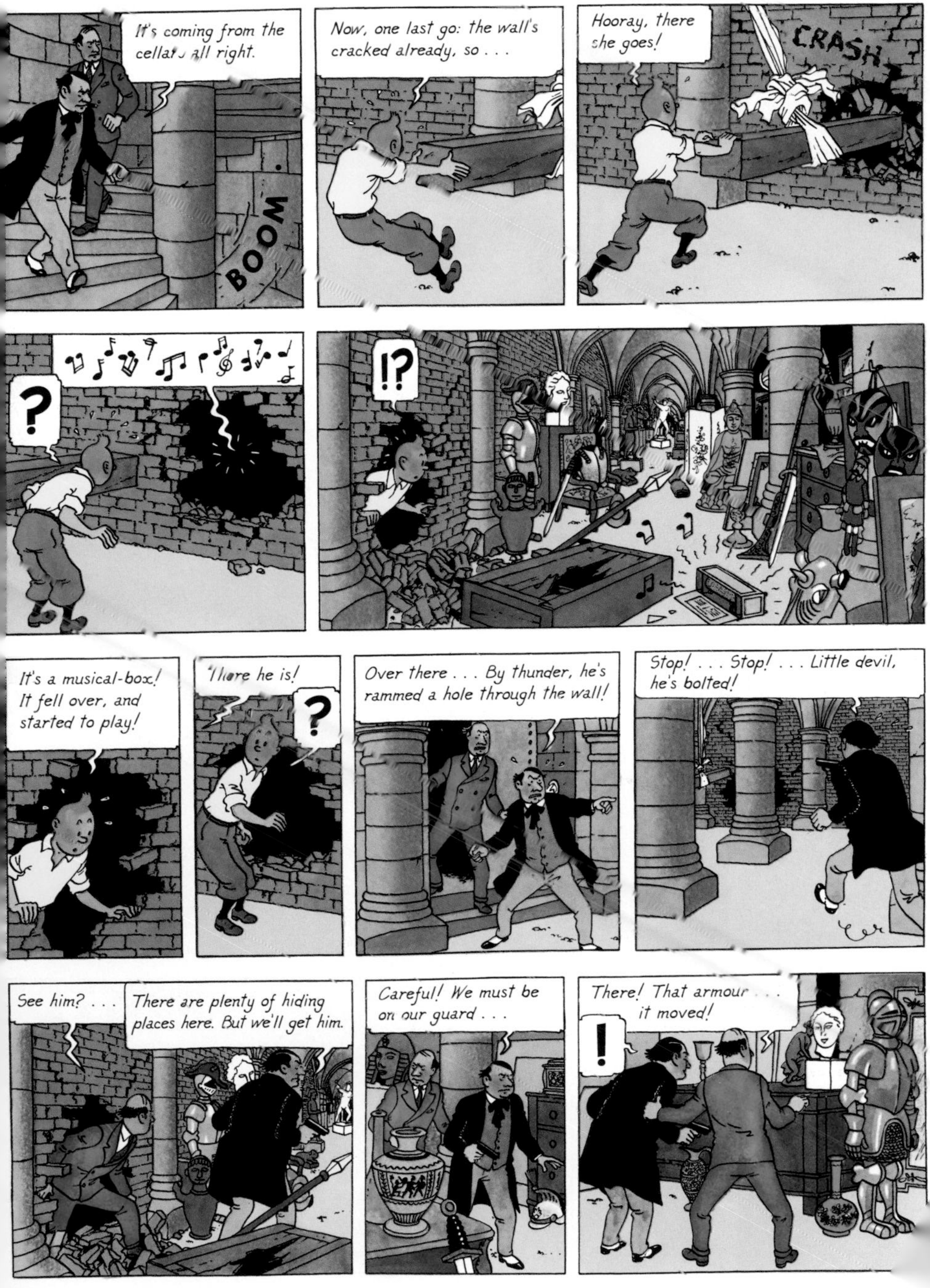
It's coming from the cellar, all right.
BOOM
Now, one last go: the wall's cracked already, so . . .
Hooray, there she goes!
CRASH
?
!?
It's a musical-box! It fell over, and started to play!
There he is!
?
Over there . . . By thunder, he's rammed a hole through the wall!
Stop! . . . Stop! . . . Little devil, he's bolted!
See him? . . .
There are plenty of hiding places here. But we'll get him.
Careful! We must be on our guard . . .
There! That armour . . . it moved!
!

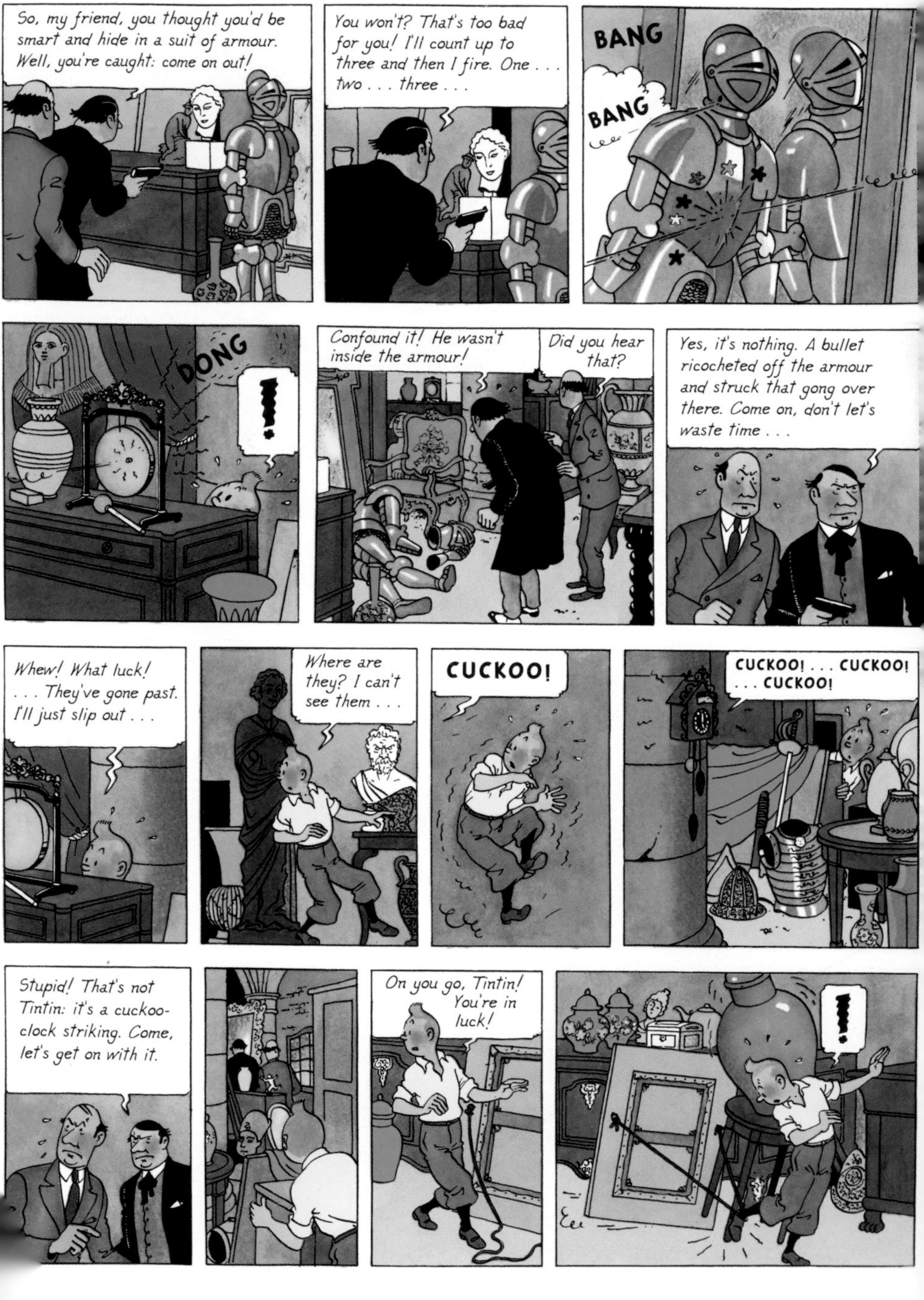

So, my friend, you thought you'd be smart and hide in a suit of armour. Well, you're caught: come on out!
You won't? That's too bad for you! I'll count up to three and then I fire. One . . . two . . . three . . .
BANG
BANG
DONG
!
Confound it! He wasn't inside the armour!
Did you hear that?
Yes, it's nothing. A bullet ricocheted off the armour and struck that gong over there. Come on, don't let's waste time . . .
Whew! What luck! . . . They've gone past. I'll just slip out . . .
Where are they? I can't see them . . .
CUCKOO!
CUCKOO! . . . CUCKOO! . . . CUCKOO!
Stupid! That's not Tintin: it's a cuckoo-clock striking. Come, let's get on with it.
On you go, Tintin! You're in luck!
!

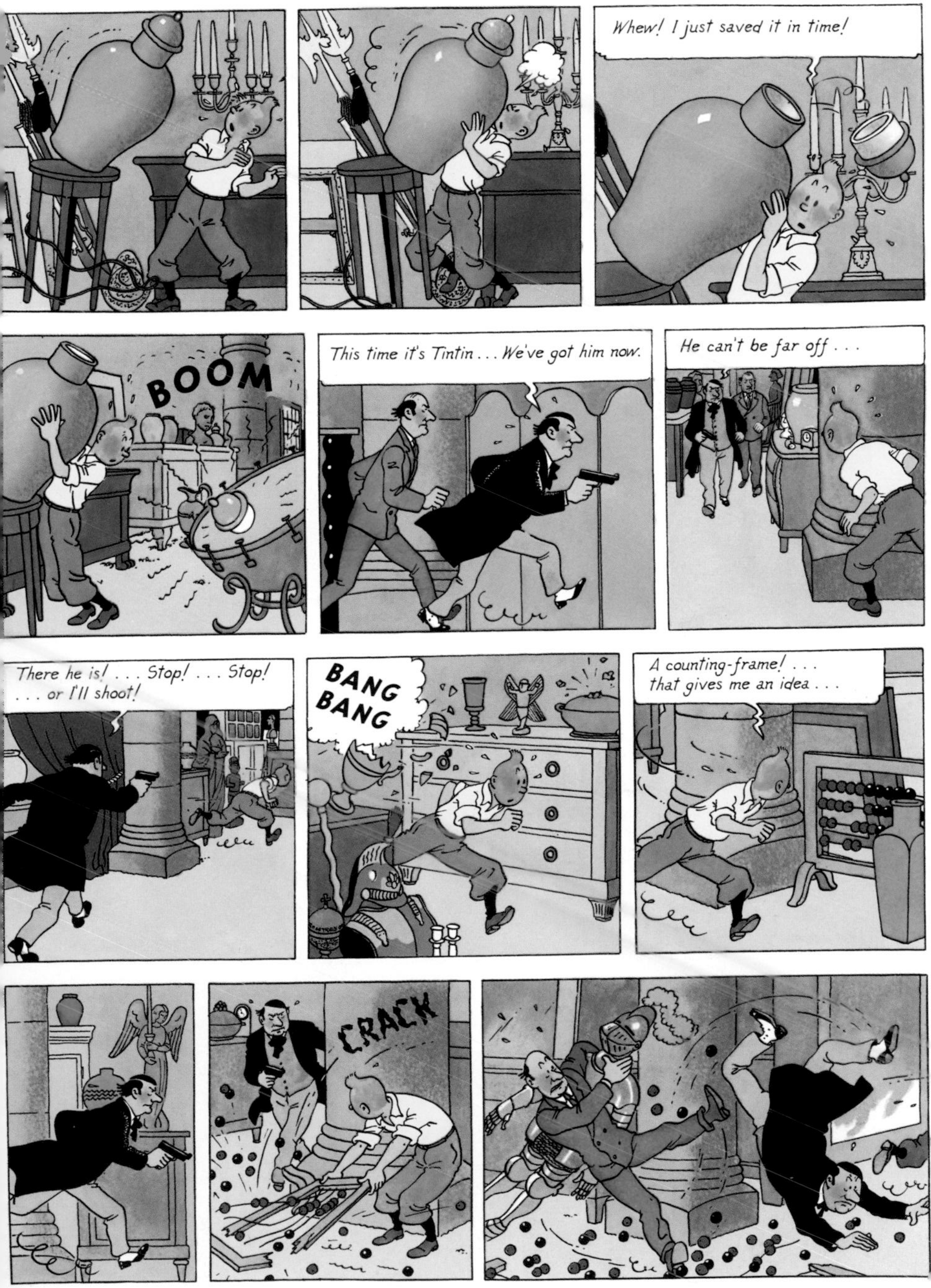
Whew! I just saved it in time!
BOOM
This time it's Tintin... We've got him now.
He can't be far off...
There he is! ... Stop! ... Stop! ... or I'll shoot!
BANG BANG
A counting-frame! ... that gives me an idea...
CRACK

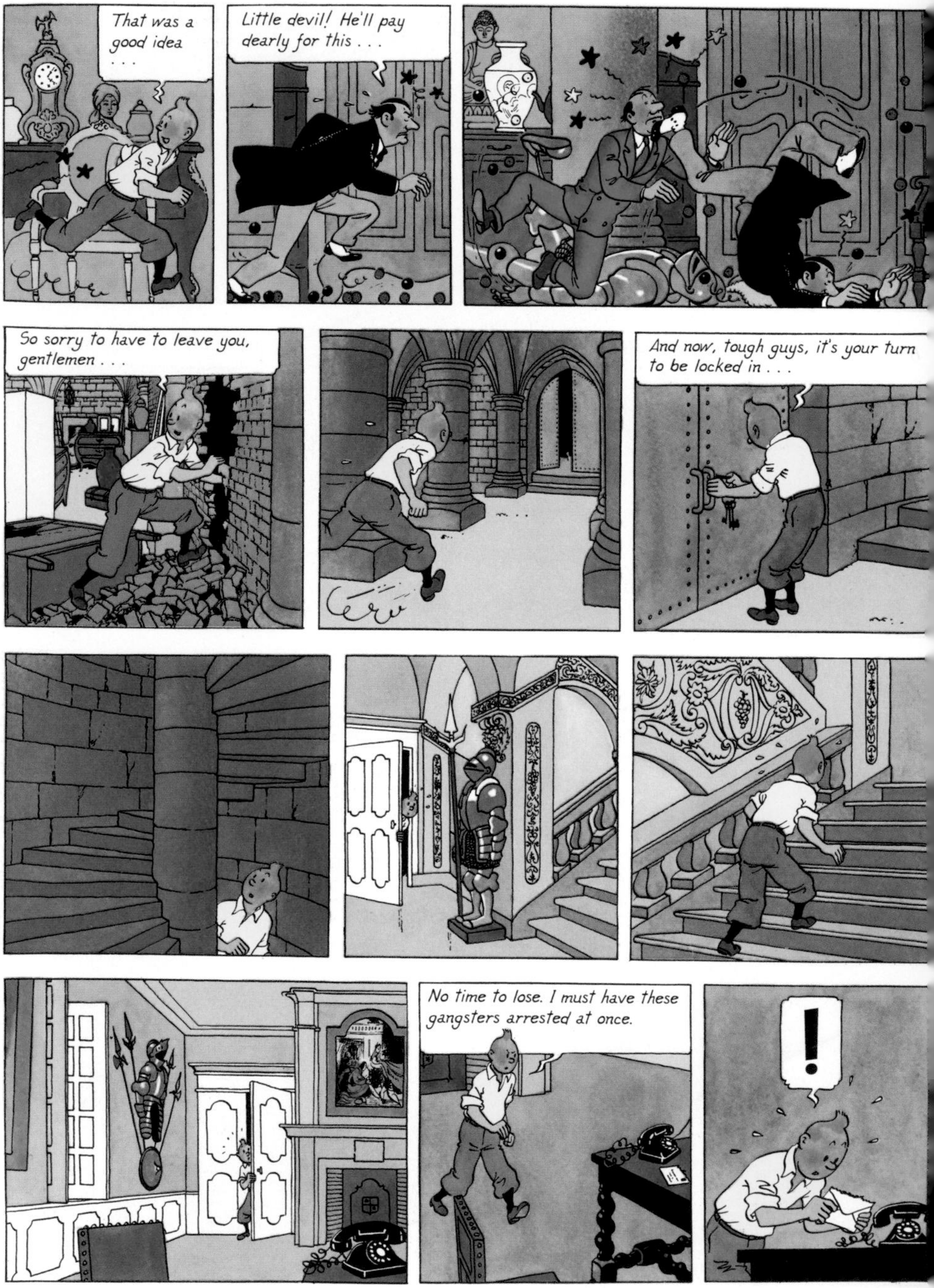
That was a good idea . . .
Little devil! He'll pay dearly for this . . .
So sorry to have to leave you, gentlemen . . .
And now, tough guys, it's your turn to be locked in . . .
No time to lose. I must have these gangsters arrested at once.
!

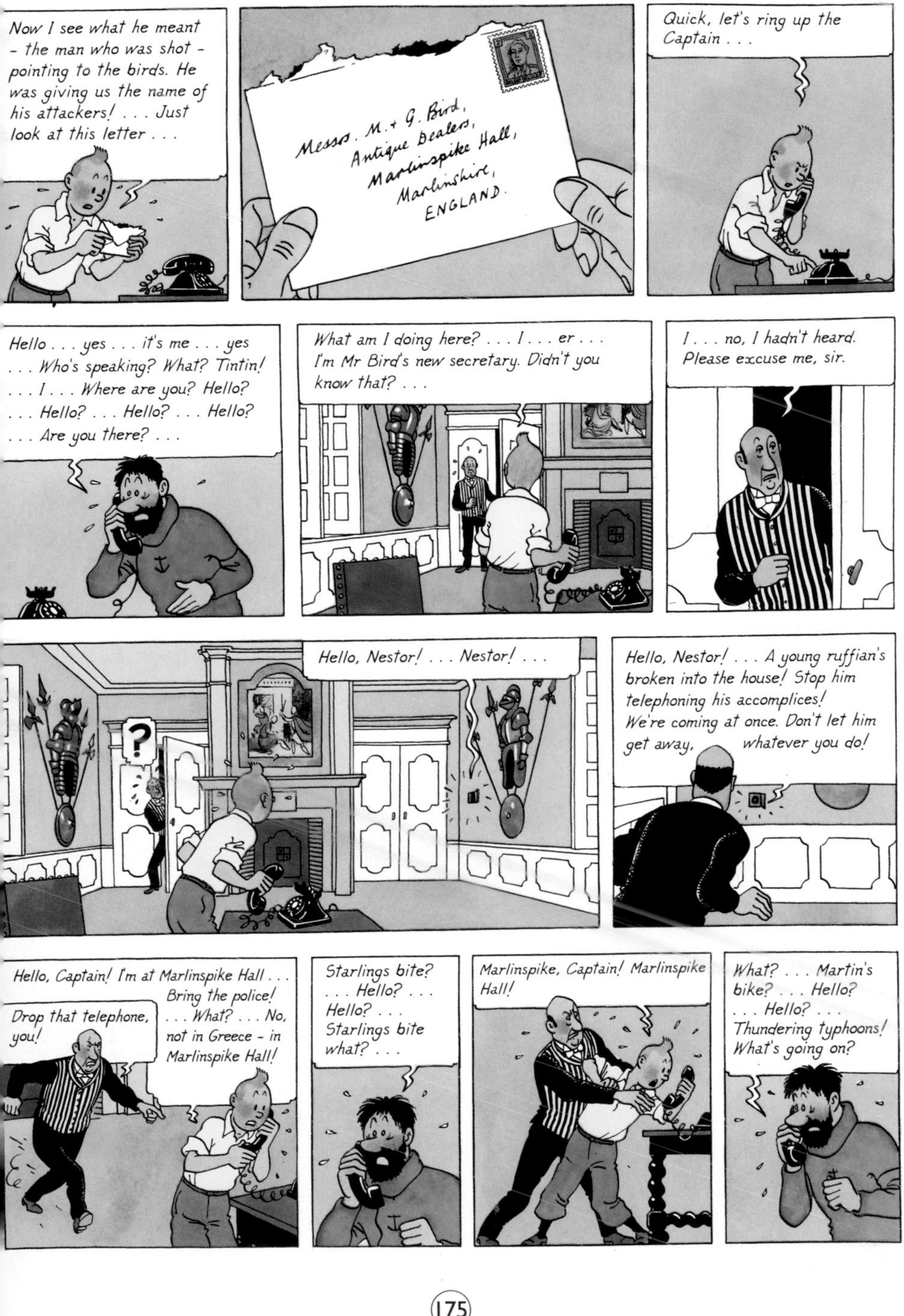
Now I see what he meant - the man who was shot - pointing to the birds. He was giving us the name of his attackers! . . . Just look at this letter . . .
Messrs. M. + G. Bird, Antique Dealers, Marlinspike Hall, Marlinshire, ENGLAND.
Quick, let's ring up the Captain . . .
Hello . . . yes . . . it's me . . . yes . . . Who's speaking? What? Tintin! . . . I . . . Where are you? Hello? . . . Hello? . . . Hello? . . . Hello? . . . Are you there? . . .
What am I doing here? . . . I . . . er . . . I'm Mr Bird's new secretary. Didn't you know that? . . .
I . . . no, I hadn't heard. Please excuse me, sir.
?
Hello, Nestor! . . . Nestor! . . .
Hello, Nestor! . . . A young ruffian's broken into the house! Stop him telephoning his accomplices! We're coming at once. Don't let him get away, whatever you do!
Hello, Captain! I'm at Marlinspike Hall . . . Bring the police! . . . What? . . . No, not in Greece - in Marlinspike Hall!
Drop that telephone, you!
Starlings bite? . . . Hello? . . . Hello? . . . Starlings bite what? . . .
Marlinspike, Captain! Marlinspike Hall!
What? . . . Martin's bike? . . . Hello? . . . Hello? . . . Thundering typhoons! What's going on?

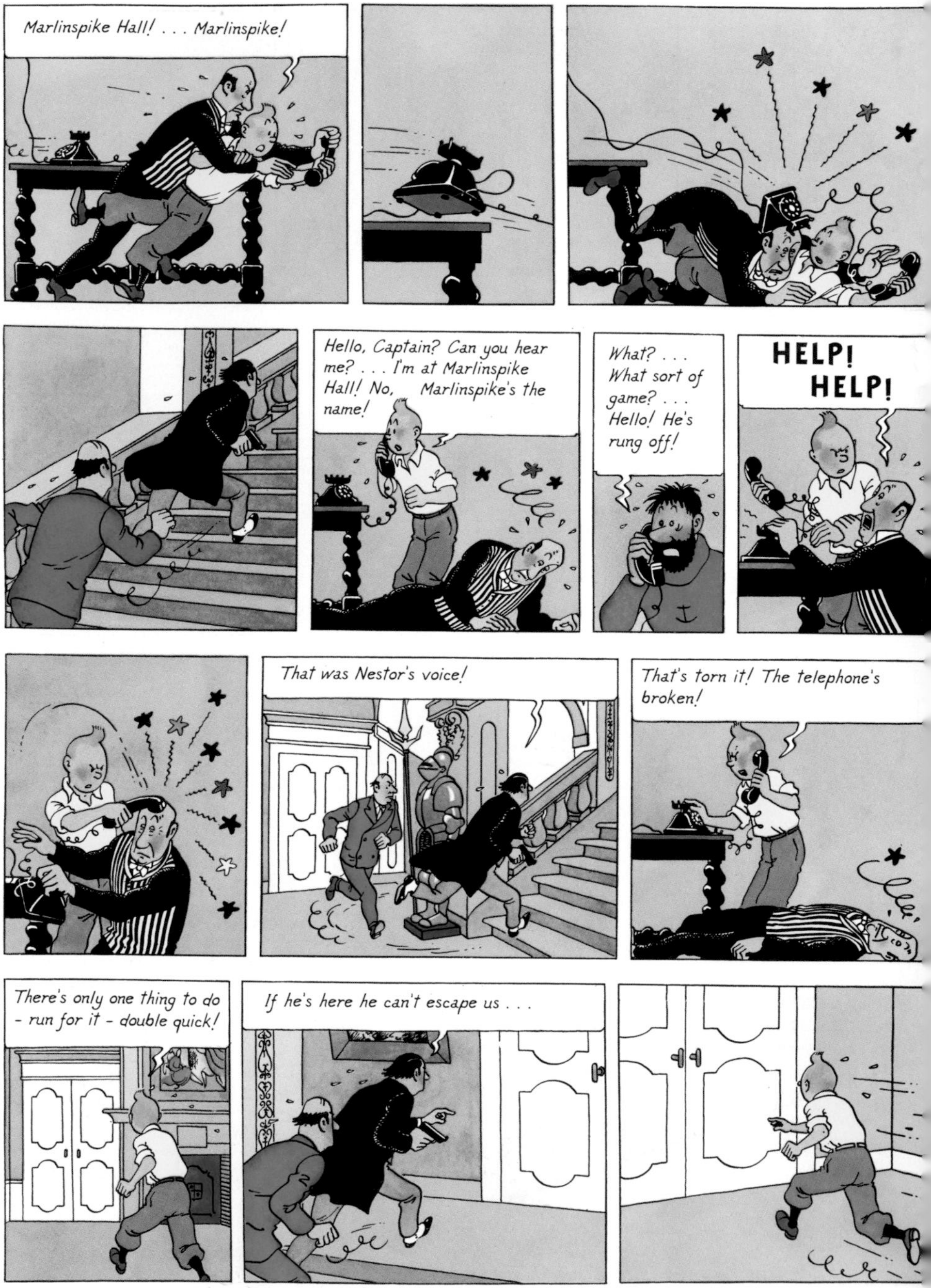

Marlinspike Hall! . . . Marlinspike!
Hello, Captain? Can you hear me? . . . I'm at Marlinspike Hall! No, Marlinspike's the name!
What? . . . What sort of game? . . . Hello! He's rung off!
HELP! HELP!
That was Nestor's voice!
That's torn it! The telephone's broken!
There's only one thing to do - run for it - double quick!
If he's here he can't escape us . . .

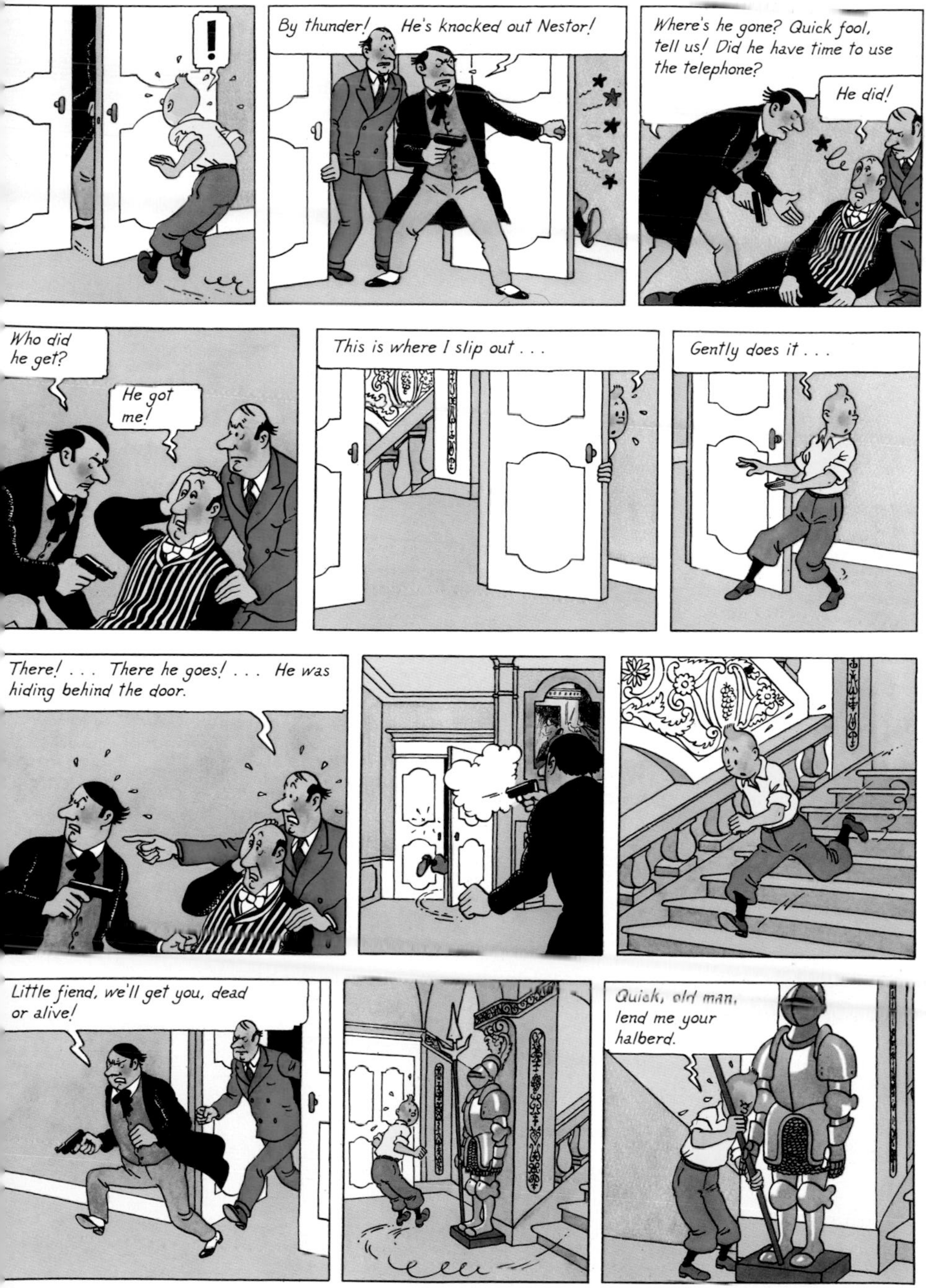
!
By thunder! He's knocked out Nestor!
Where's he gone? Quick fool, tell us! Did he have time to use the telephone?
He did!
Who did he get?
He got me!
This is where I slip out . . .
Gently does it . . .
There! . . . There he goes! . . . He was hiding behind the door.
Little fiend, we'll get you, dead or alive!
Quick, old man, lend me your halberd.

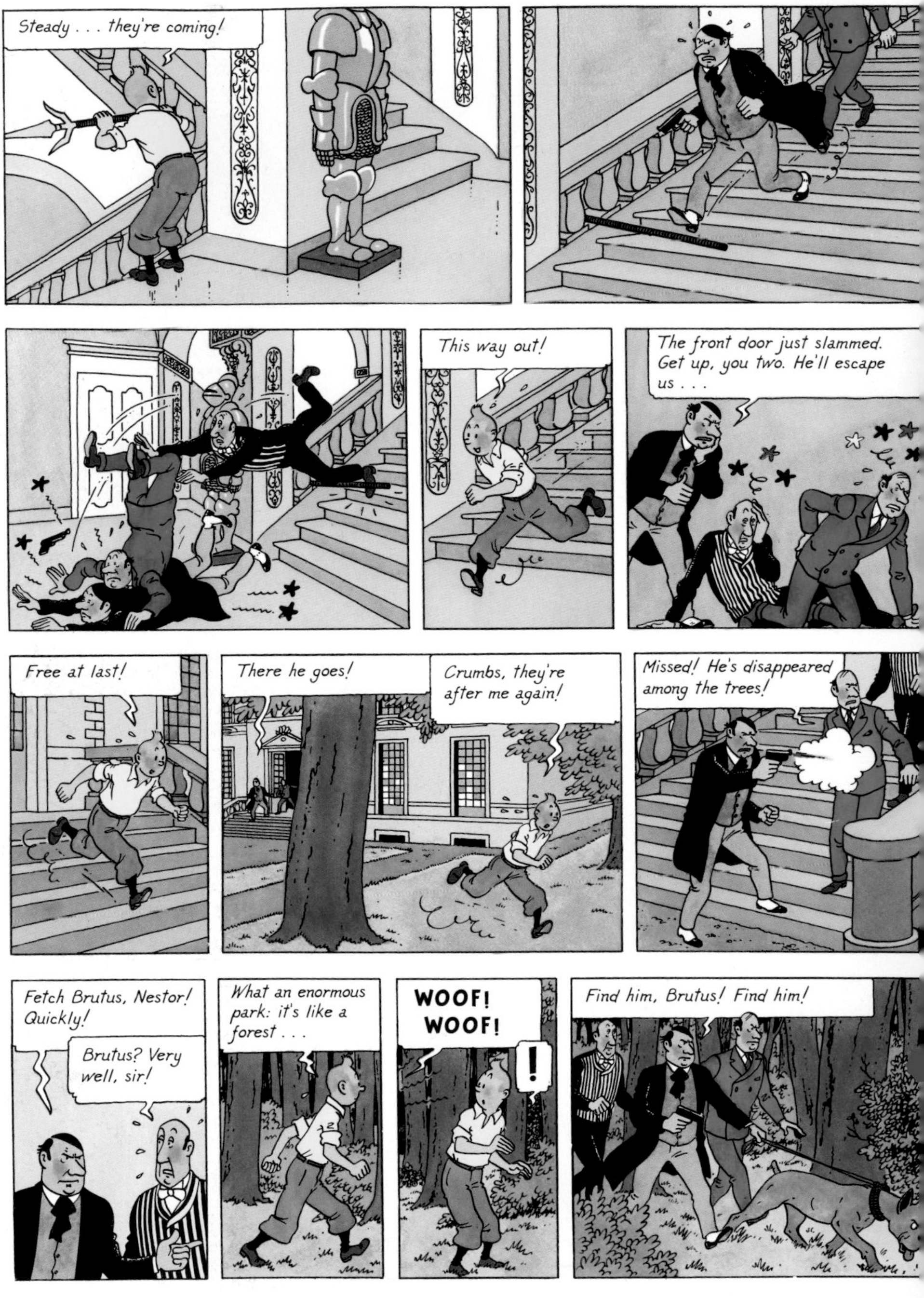
Steady . . . they're coming!
This way out!
The front door just slammed. Get up, you two. He'll escape us . . .
Free at last!
There he goes!
Crumbs, they're after me again!
Missed! He's disappeared among the trees!
Fetch Brutus, Nestor! Quickly!
Brutus? Very well, sir!
What an enormous park: it's like a forest . . .
WOOF! WOOF!
!
Find him, Brutus! Find him!

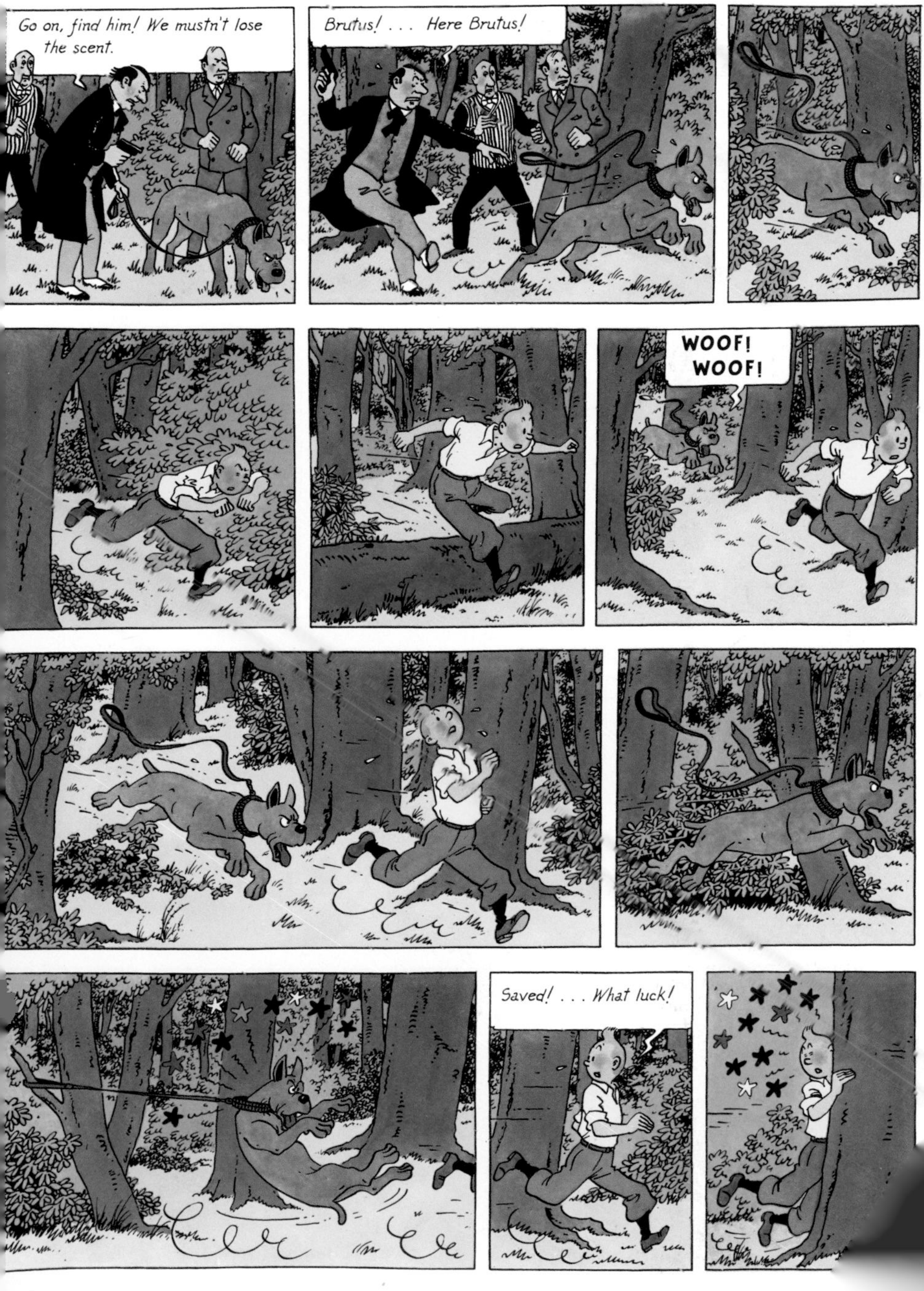
Go on, find him! We mustn't lose the scent.
Brutus! . . . Here Brutus!
WOOF! WOOF!
Saved! . . . What luck!

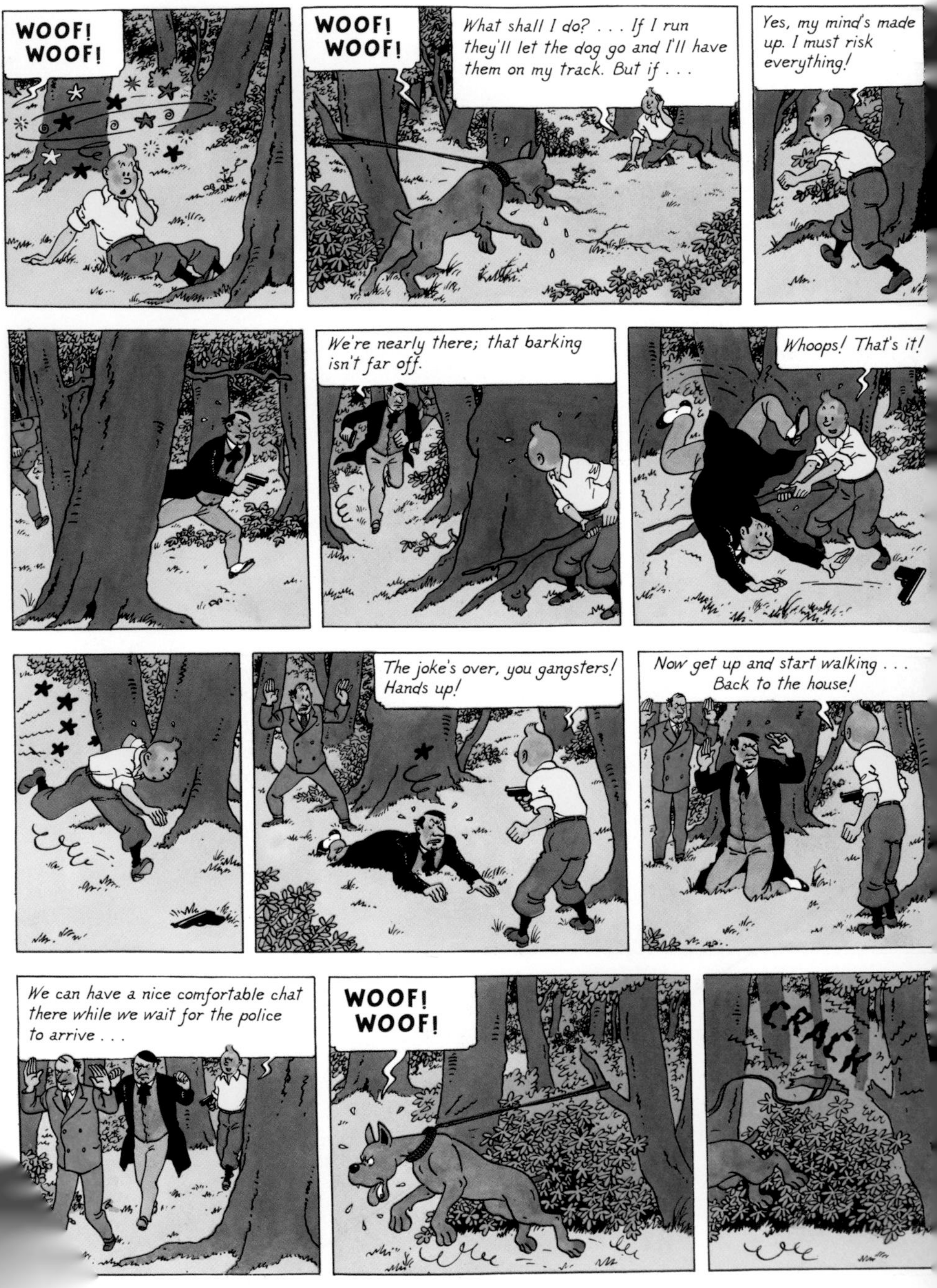
WOOF! WOOF!
WOOF! WOOF!
What shall I do? . . . If I run they'll let the dog go and I'll have them on my track. But if . . .
Yes, my mind's made up. I must risk everything!
We're nearly there; that barking isn't far off.
Whoops! That's it!
The joke's over, you gangsters! Hands up!
Now get up and start walking . . . Back to the house!
We can have a nice comfortable chat there while we wait for the police to arrive . . .
WOOF! WOOF!
CRACK

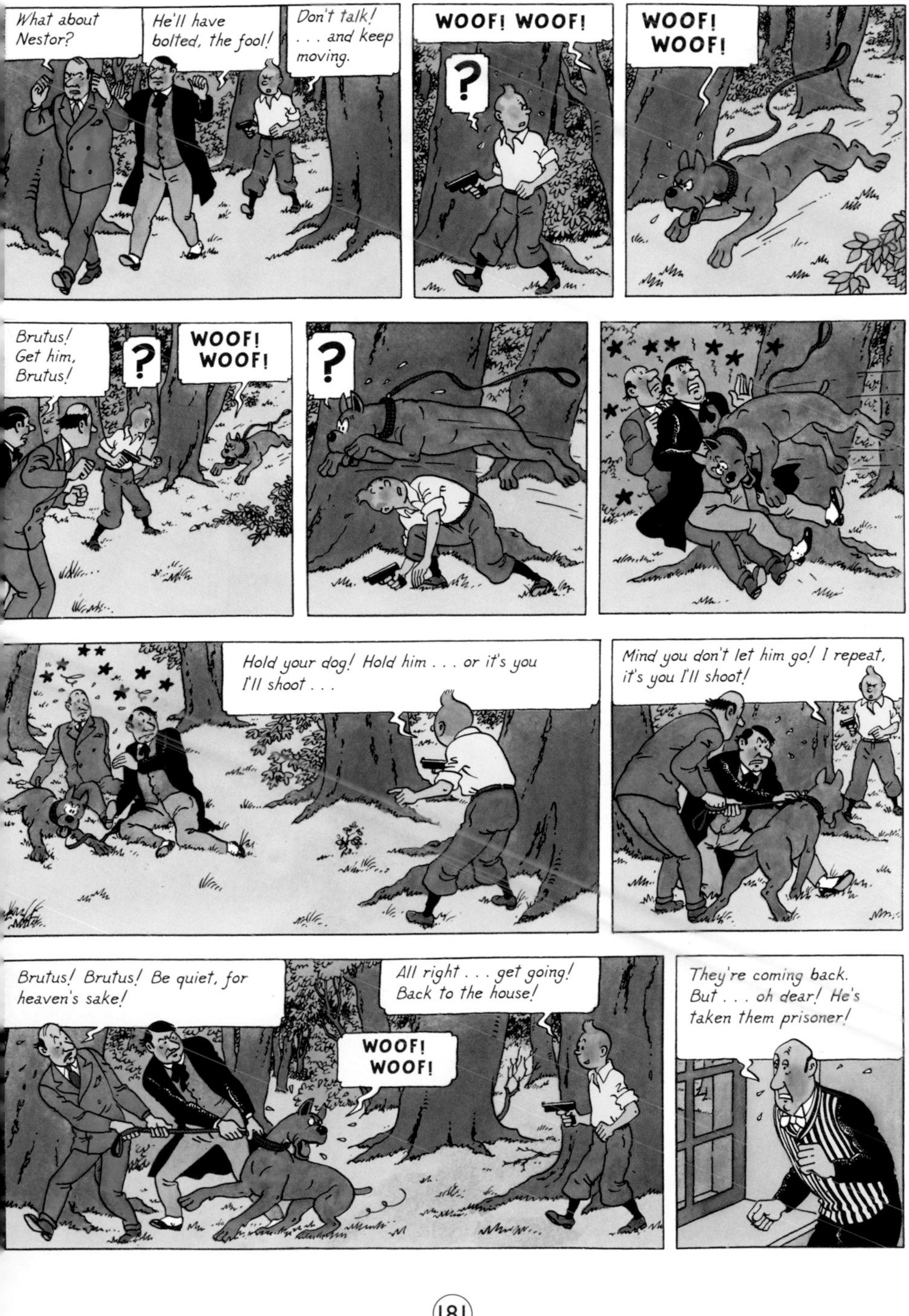
What about Nestor?
He'll have bolted, the fool!
Don't talk! . . . and keep moving.
WOOF! WOOF!
?
WOOF! WOOF!
Brutus! Get him, Brutus!
?
WOOF! WOOF!
?
Hold your dog! Hold him . . . or it's you I'll shoot . . .
Mind you don't let him go! I repeat, it's you I'll shoot!
Brutus! Brutus! Be quiet, for heaven's sake!
All right . . . get going! Back to the house!
WOOF! WOOF!
They're coming back. But . . . oh dear! He's taken them prisoner!

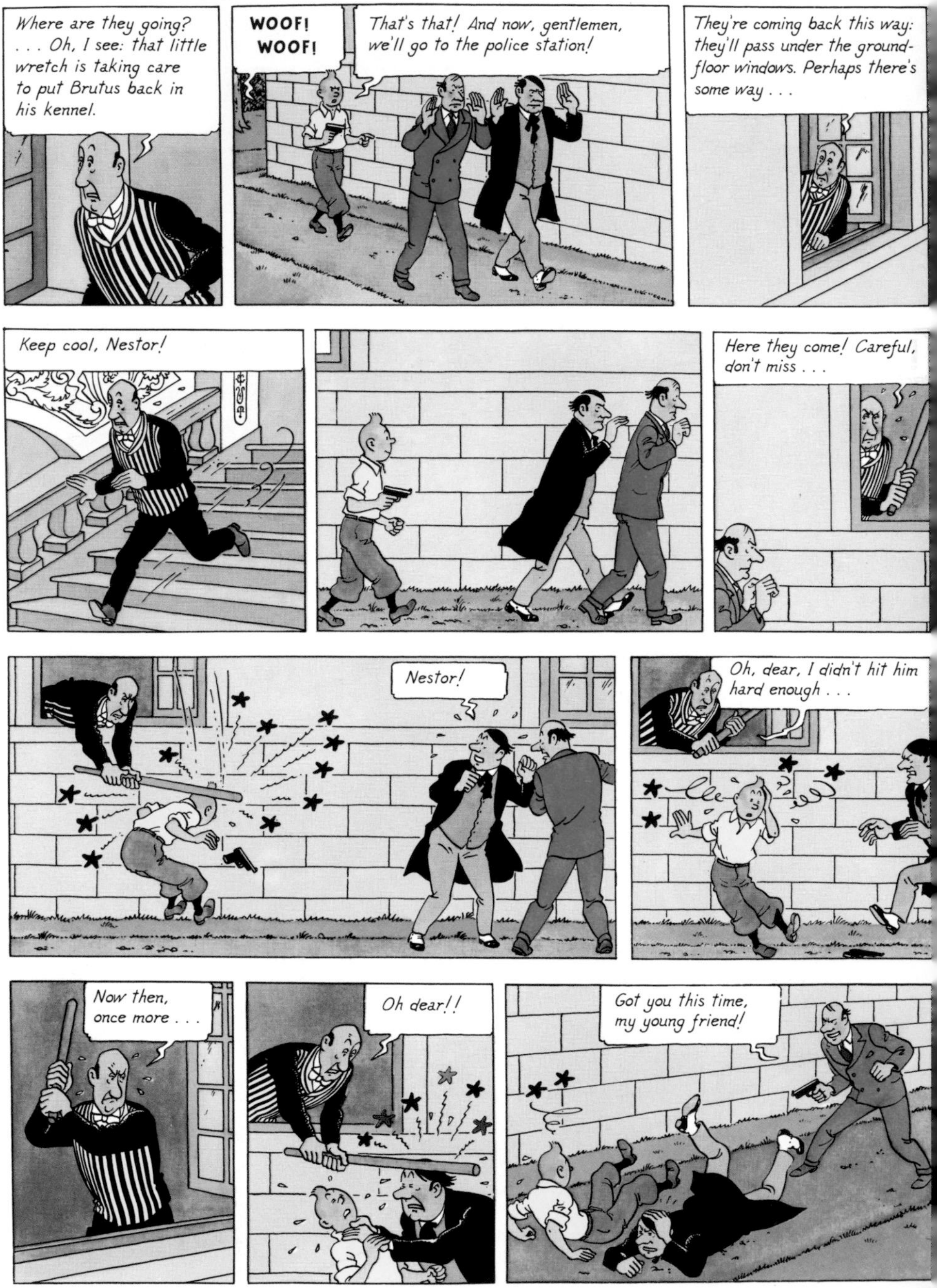
Where are they going? . . . Oh, I see: that little wretch is taking care to put Brutus back in his kennel.
WOOF! WOOF!
That's that! And now, gentlemen, we'll go to the police station!
They're coming back this way: they'll pass under the ground-floor windows. Perhaps there's some way . . .
Keep cool, Nestor!
Here they come! Careful, don't miss . . .
Nestor!
Oh, dear, I didn't hit him hard enough . . .
Now then, once more . . .
Oh dear!!
Got you this time, my young friend!

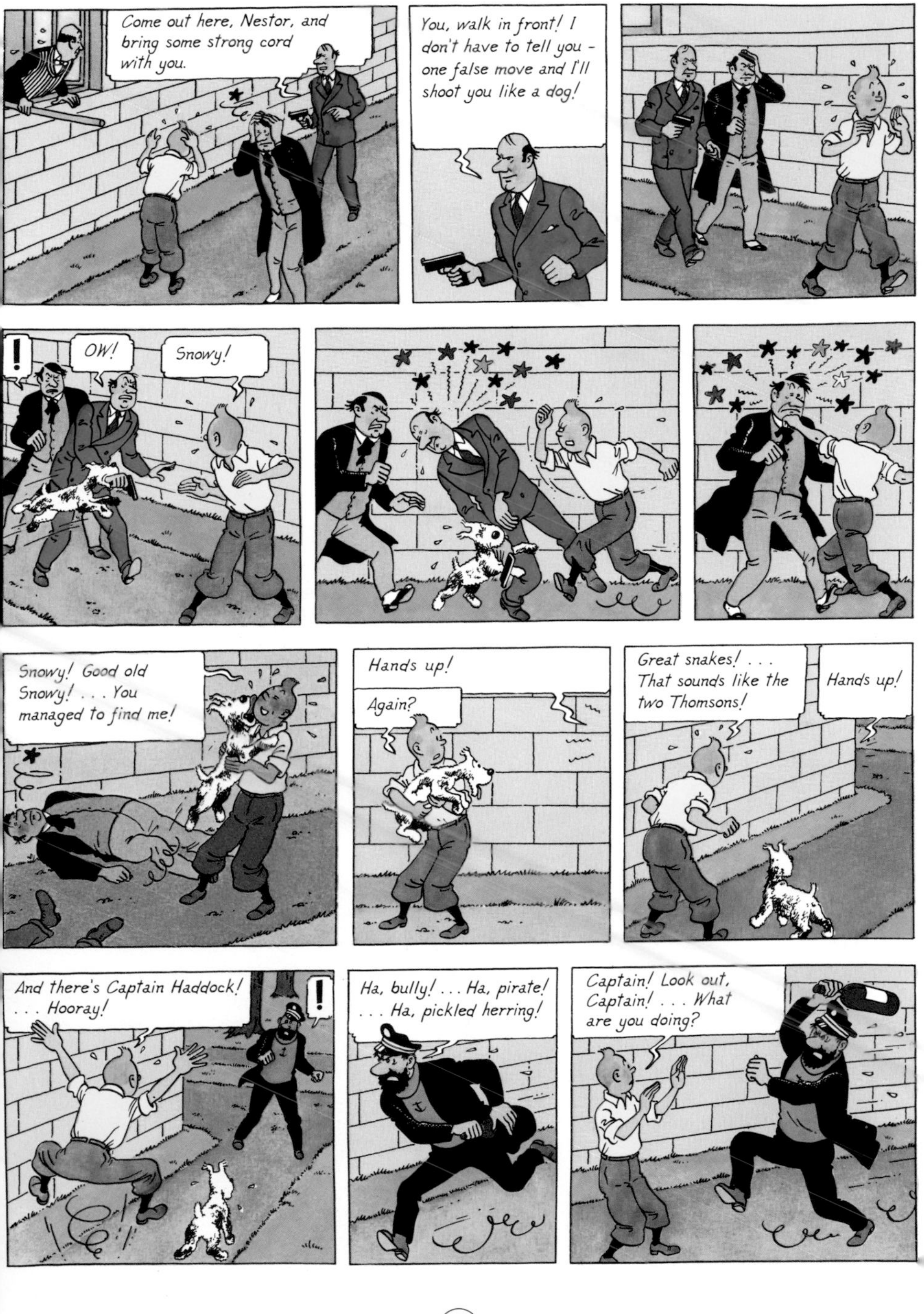
Come out here, Nestor, and bring some strong cord with you.
You, walk in front! I don't have to tell you - one false move and I'll shoot you like a dog!
!
OW!
Snowy!
Snowy! Good old Snowy! . . . You managed to find me!
Hands up!
Again?
Great snakes! . . . That sounds like the two Thomsons!
Hands up!
And there's Captain Haddock! . . . Hooray!
!
Ha, bully! . . . Ha, pirate! . . . Ha, pickled herring!
Captain! Look out, Captain! . . . What are you doing?

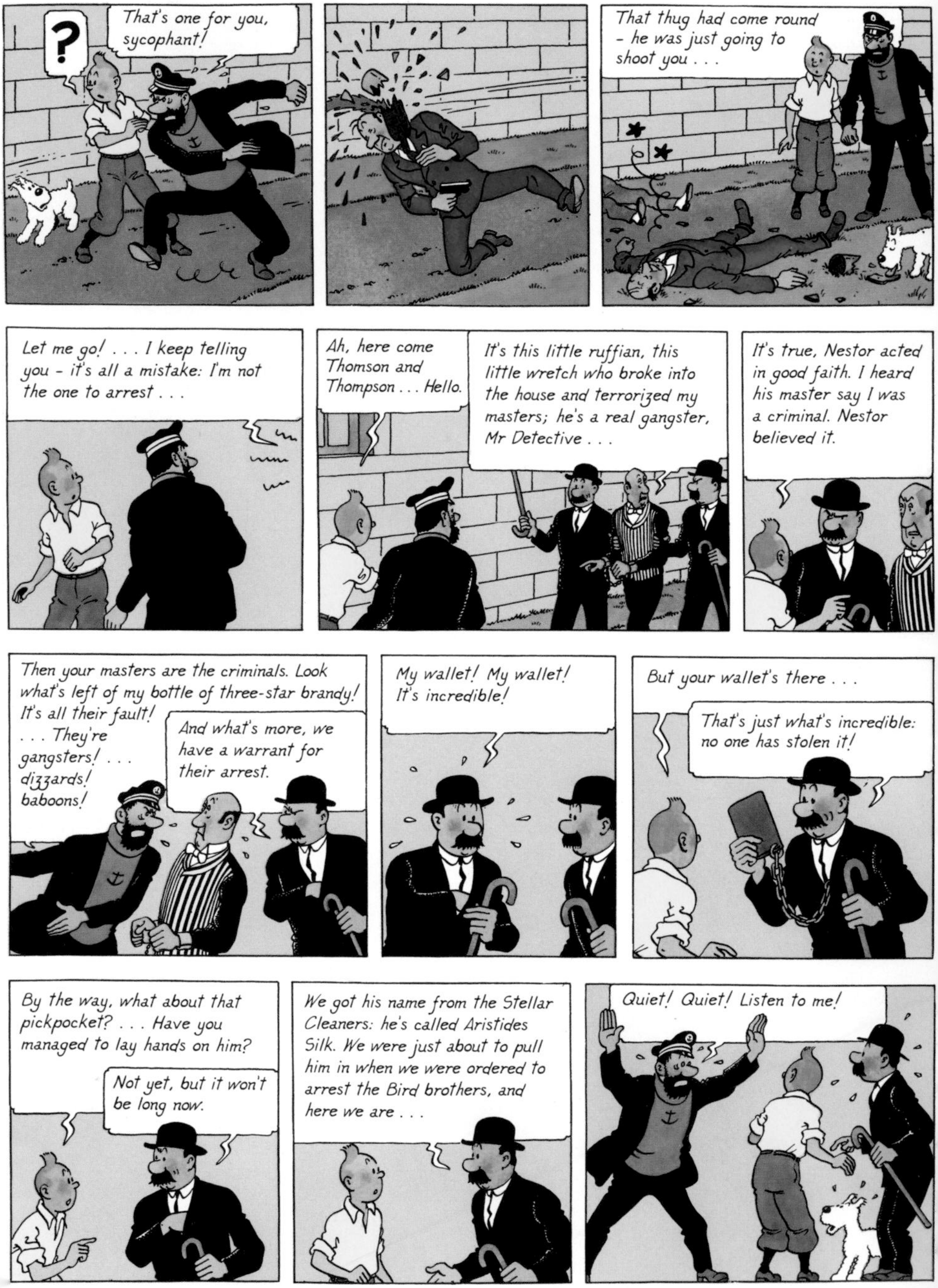
?
That's one for you, sycophant!
That thug had come round – he was just going to shoot you . . .
Let me go! . . . I keep telling you – it's all a mistake: I'm not the one to arrest . . .
Ah, here come Thomson and Thompson . . . Hello.
It's this little ruffian, this little wretch who broke into the house and terrorized my masters; he's a real gangster, Mr Detective . . .
It's true, Nestor acted in good faith. I heard his master say I was a criminal. Nestor believed it.
Then your masters are the criminals. Look what's left of my bottle of three-star brandy! It's all their fault! . . . They're gangsters! . . . dizzards! baboons!
And what's more, we have a warrant for their arrest.
My wallet! My wallet! It's incredible!
But your wallet's there . . .
That's just what's incredible: no one has stolen it!
By the way, what about that pickpocket? . . . Have you managed to lay hands on him?
Not yet, but it won't be long now.
We got his name from the Stellar Cleaners: he's called Aristides Silk. We were just about to pull him in when we were ordered to arrest the Bird brothers, and here we are . . .
Quiet! Quiet! Listen to me!

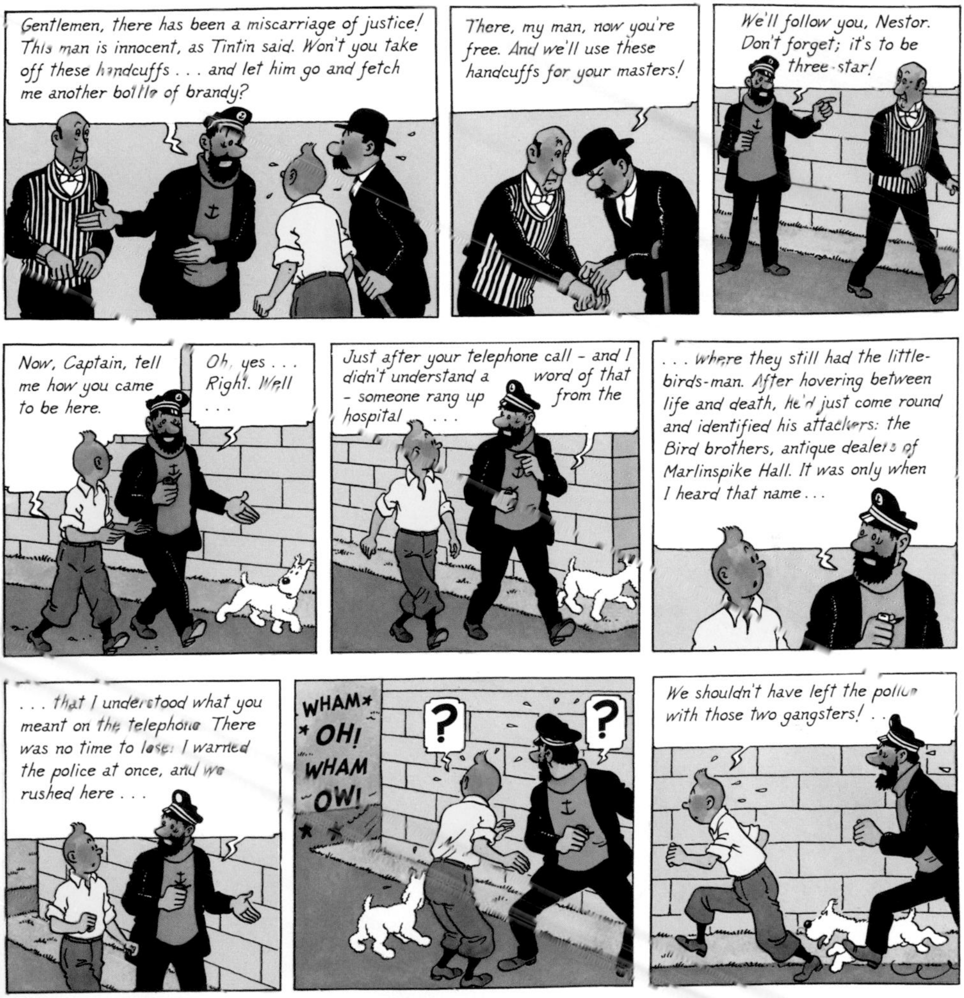
Gentlemen, there has been a miscarriage of justice! This man is innocent, as Tintin said. Won't you take off these handcuffs . . . and let him go and fetch me another bottle of brandy?
There, my man, now you're free. And we'll use these handcuffs for your masters!
We'll follow you, Nestor. Don't forget; it's to be three-star!
Now, Captain, tell me how you came to be here.
Oh, yes . . . Right. Well . . .
Just after your telephone call - and I didn't understand a word of that - someone rang up from the hospital . . .
. . . where they still had the little-birds-man. After hovering between life and death, he'd just come round and identified his attackers: the Bird brothers, antique dealers of Marlinspike Hall. It was only when I heard that name . . .
. . . that I understood what you meant on the telephone. There was no time to lose. I warned the police at once, and we rushed here . . .
WHAM
OH!
WHAM
OW!
?
?
We shouldn't have left the police with those two gangsters! . .
Look! . . . one's escaping! . . . there! He's just turned the corner!
He's the most dangerous of the two: he mustn't get away!
BRRRR
BRRR
A car! That's a car starting up!

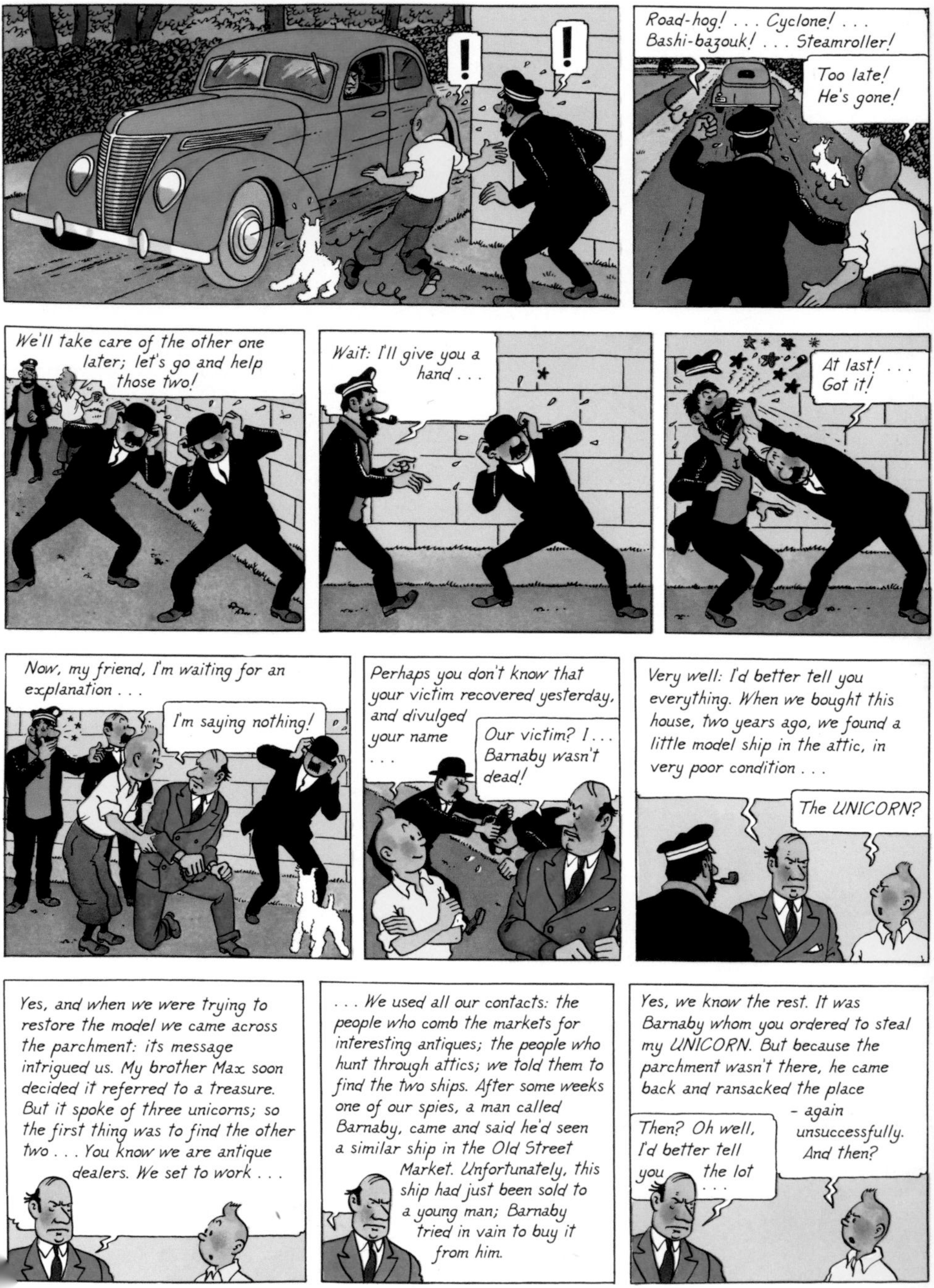
!
!
Road-hog! . . . Cyclone! . . . Bashi-bazouk! . . . Steamroller!
Too late! He's gone!
We'll take care of the other one later; let's go and help those two!
Wait: I'll give you a hand . . .
At last! . . . Got it!
Now, my friend, I'm waiting for an explanation . . .
I'm saying nothing!
Perhaps you don't know that your victim recovered yesterday, and divulged your name . . .
Our victim? I . . . Barnaby wasn't dead!
Very well: I'd better tell you everything. When we bought this house, two years ago, we found a little model ship in the attic, in very poor condition . . .
The UNICORN?
Yes, and when we were trying to restore the model we came across the parchment: its message intrigued us. My brother Max soon decided it referred to a treasure. But it spoke of three unicorns; so the first thing was to find the other two . . . You know we are antique dealers. We set to work . . .
. . . We used all our contacts: the people who comb the markets for interesting antiques; the people who hunt through attics; we told them to find the two ships. After some weeks one of our spies, a man called Barnaby, came and said he'd seen a similar ship in the Old Street Market. Unfortunately, this ship had just been sold to a young man; Barnaby tried in vain to buy it from him.
Yes, we know the rest. It was Barnaby whom you ordered to steal my UNICORN. But because the parchment wasn't there, he came back and ransacked the place - again unsuccessfully. And then?
Then? Oh well, I'd better tell you the lot . . .

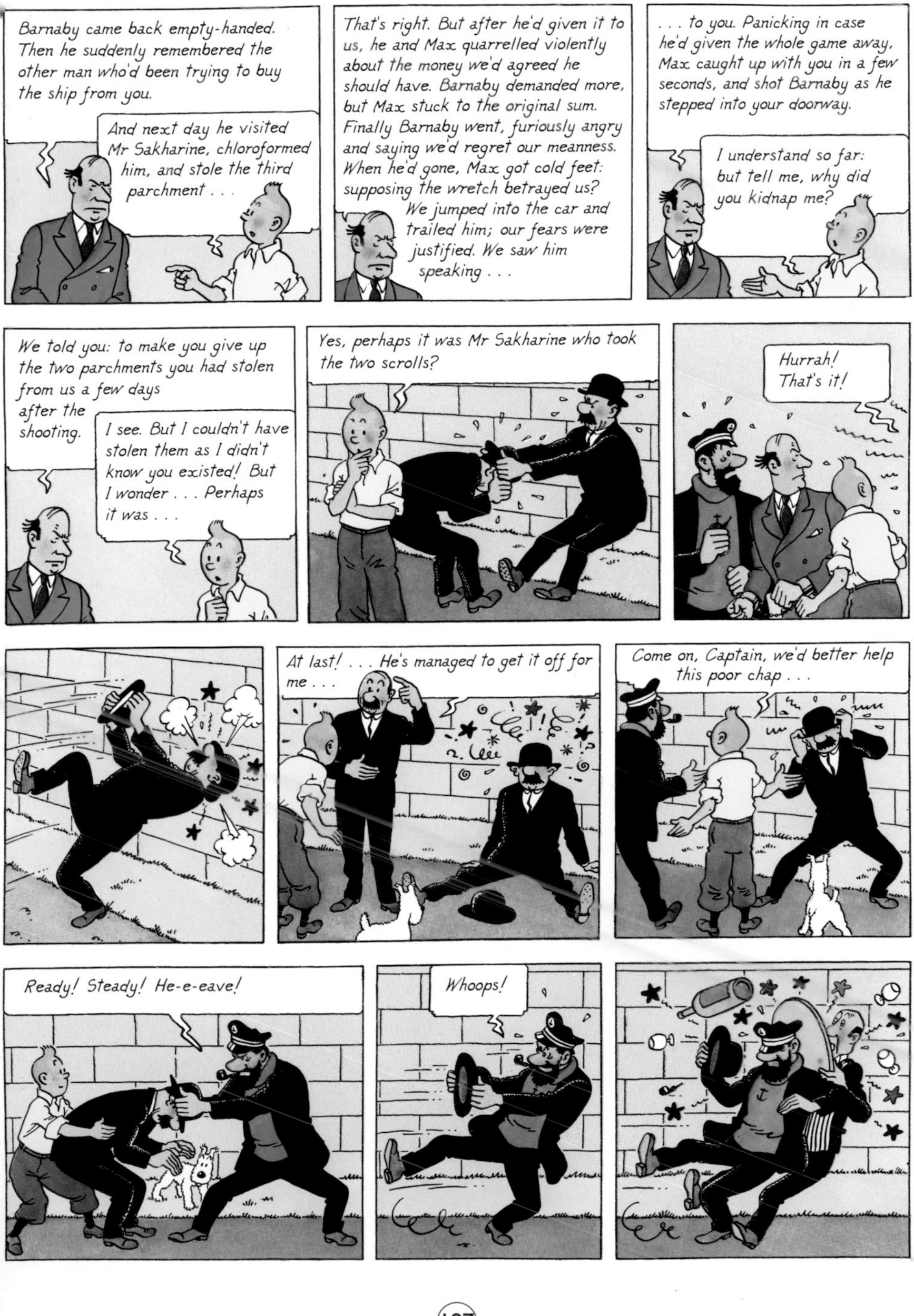

Barnaby came back empty-handed. Then he suddenly remembered the other man who'd been trying to buy the ship from you.
And next day he visited Mr Sakharine, chloroformed him, and stole the third parchment . . .
That's right. But after he'd given it to us, he and Max quarrelled violently about the money we'd agreed he should have. Barnaby demanded more, but Max stuck to the original sum. Finally Barnaby went, furiously angry and saying we'd regret our meanness. When he'd gone, Max got cold feet: supposing the wretch betrayed us?
We jumped into the car and trailed him; our fears were justified. We saw him speaking . . .
. . . to you. Panicking in case he'd given the whole game away, Max caught up with you in a few seconds, and shot Barnaby as he stepped into your doorway.
I understand so far: but tell me, why did you kidnap me?
We told you: to make you give up the two parchments you had stolen from us a few days after the shooting.
I see. But I couldn't have stolen them as I didn't know you existed! But I wonder . . . Perhaps it was . . .
Yes, perhaps it was Mr Sakharine who took the two scrolls?
Hurrah! That's it!
At last! . . . He's managed to get it off for me . . .
Come on, Captain, we'd better help this poor chap . . .
Ready! Steady! He-e-eave!
Whoops!

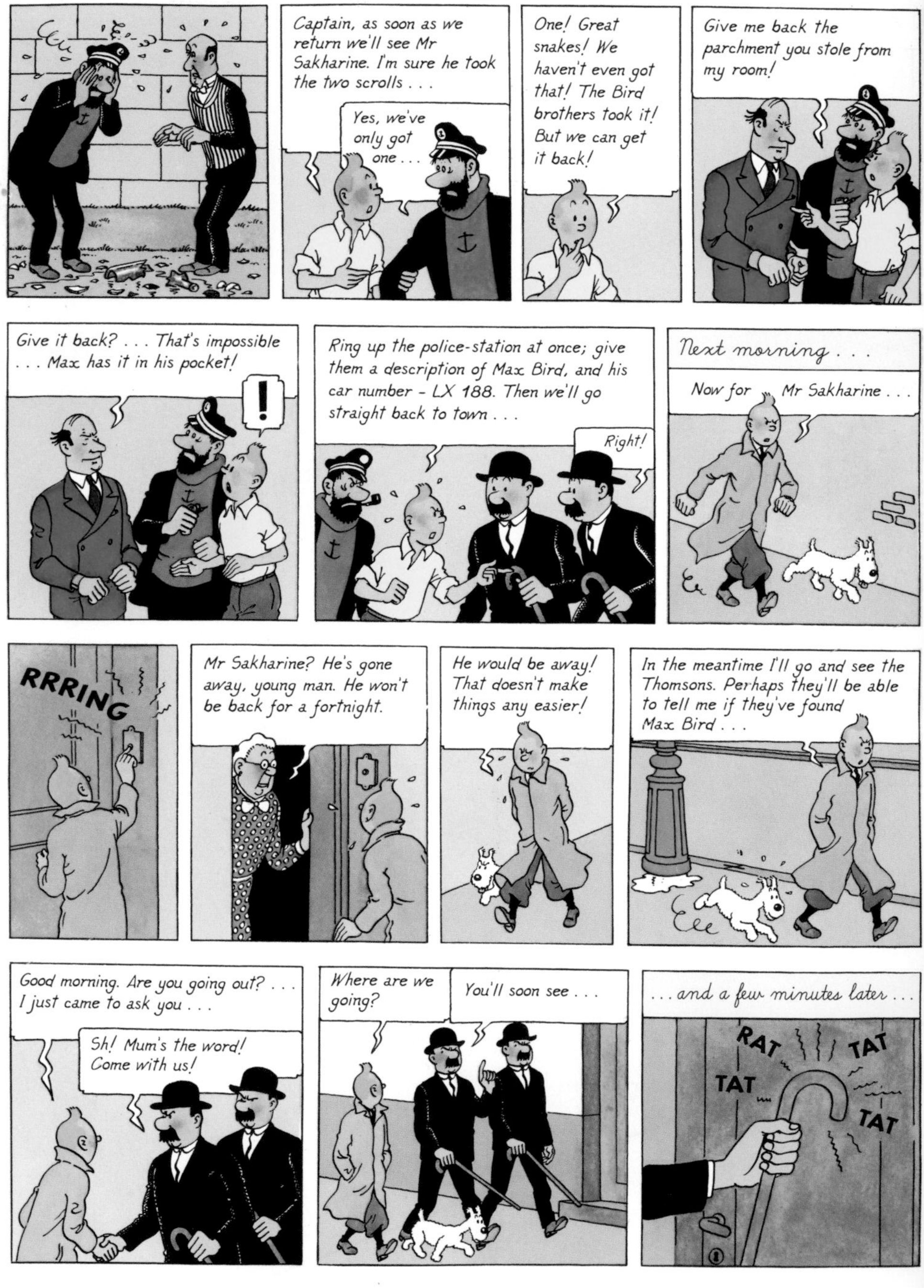
Captain, as soon as we return we'll see Mr Sakharine. I'm sure he took the two scrolls . . .
Yes, we've only got one . . .
One! Great snakes! We haven't even got that! The Bird brothers took it! But we can get it back!
Give me back the parchment you stole from my room!
Give it back? . . . That's impossible . . . Max has it in his pocket!
!
Ring up the police-station at once; give them a description of Max Bird, and his car number - LX 188. Then we'll go straight back to town . . .
Right!
Next morning . . .
Now for Mr Sakharine . . .
RRRING
Mr Sakharine? He's gone away, young man. He won't be back for a fortnight.
He would be away! That doesn't make things any easier!
In the meantime I'll go and see the Thomsons. Perhaps they'll be able to tell me if they've found Max Bird . . .
Good morning. Are you going out? . . . I just came to ask you . . .
Sh! Mum's the word! Come with us!
Where are we going?
You'll soon see . . .
. . . and a few minutes later . . .
RAT TAT
TAT
TAT

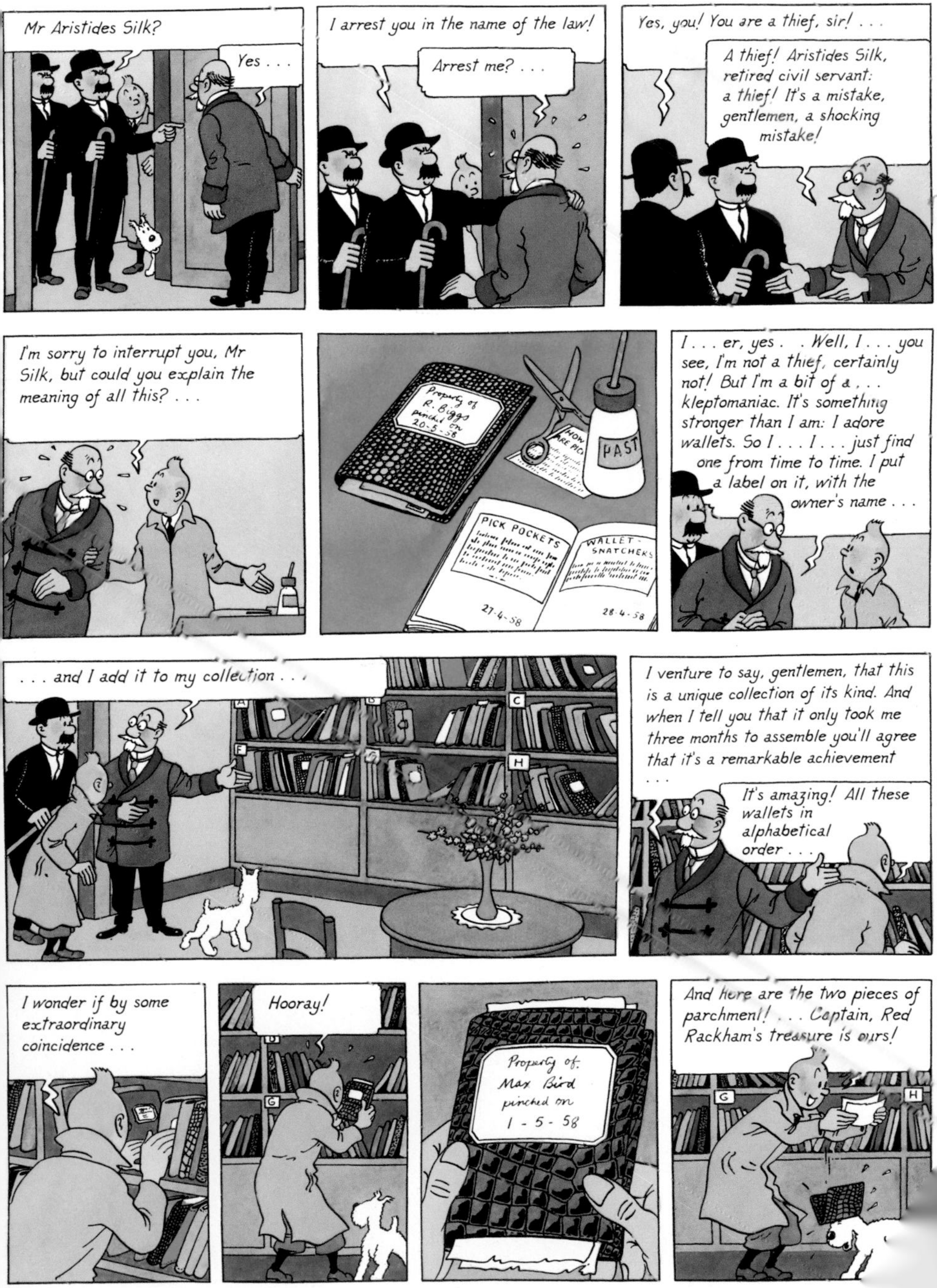
Mr Aristides Silk?
Yes . . .
I arrest you in the name of the law!
Arrest me? . . .
Yes, you! You are a thief, sir! . . .
A thief! Aristides Silk, retired civil servant: a thief! It's a mistake, gentlemen, a shocking mistake!
I'm sorry to interrupt you, Mr Silk, but could you explain the meaning of all this? . . .
Property of R. Biggs pinched on 20-5-58
PAST
PICK POCKETS
WALLET-SNATCHERS
27-4-58
28-4-58
I . . . er, yes . . . Well, I . . . you see, I'm not a thief, certainly not! But I'm a bit of a . . . kleptomaniac. It's something stronger than I am: I adore wallets. So I . . . I . . . just find one from time to time. I put a label on it, with the owner's name . . .
. . . and I add it to my collection . . .
A
C
F
H
I venture to say, gentlemen, that this is a unique collection of its kind. And when I tell you that it only took me three months to assemble you'll agree that it's a remarkable achievement . . .
It's amazing! All these wallets in alphabetical order . . .
I wonder if by some extraordinary coincidence . . .
Hooray!
G
Property of Max Bird pinched on 1 - 5 - 58
And here are the two pieces of parchment! . . . Captain, Red Rackham's treasure is ours!
G
H

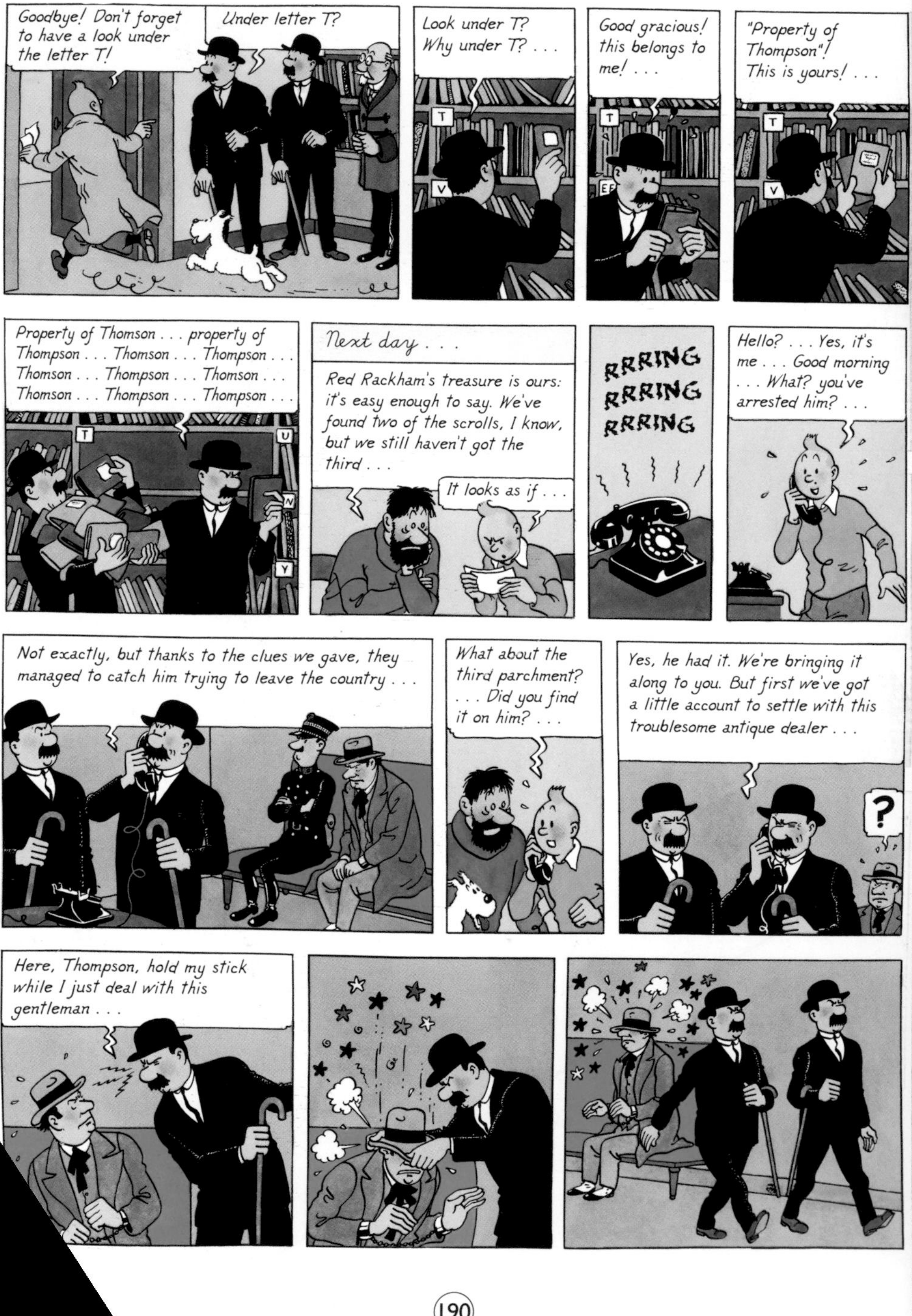

Goodbye! Don't forget to have a look under the letter T!
Under letter T?
Look under T? Why under T? . . .
Good gracious! this belongs to me! . . .
"Property of Thompson"! This is yours! . . .
Property of Thomson . . . property of Thompson . . . Thomson . . . Thompson . . . Thomson . . . Thompson . . . Thomson . . . Thomson . . . Thompson . . . Thompson . . .
Next day . . .
Red Rackham's treasure is ours: it's easy enough to say. We've found two of the scrolls, I know, but we still haven't got the third . . .
It looks as if . . .
RRRING RRRING RRRING
Hello? . . . Yes, it's me . . . Good morning . . . What? you've arrested him? . . .
Not exactly, but thanks to the clues we gave, they managed to catch him trying to leave the country . . .
What about the third parchment? . . . Did you find it on him? . . .
Yes, he had it. We're bringing it along to you. But first we've got a little account to settle with this troublesome antique dealer . . .
?
Here, Thompson, hold my stick while I just deal with this gentleman . . .

Three Brothers joyned. Three Unicornes in company sailing in the noonday Sunne will speak.
For 'tis from the Light that Light will dawn. And then shines forth
20 7 7 5 N.
the Eagle's +
No! No! and No! You can go on hunting if you want to, but I've had enough: I give up. Blistering barnacles to that pirate Red Rackham, and his treasure! I'd sooner do without it; I'm not racking my brains any more trying to make sense out of that gibberish! Thundering typhoons! What a thirst it's given me!
I've got it, Captain! . . . I've got it! . . .
The message is right when it says that it is "from the light that light will dawn!" Look. I put them together . . .
. . . and hold them, "sailing in company", in front of the light. Look now! See what comes through! . . .
Thundering typhoons! The numbers and letters are completed, and it gives us . . .
Three Brothers joyned. Three Unicornes in company sailing in the noonday Sunne will speak.
For 'tis from the Light that Light will dawn. And then shines forth
20 37 42 N. 70 52 15 W.
the Eagle's +

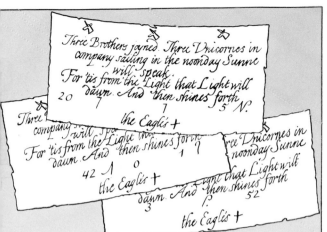

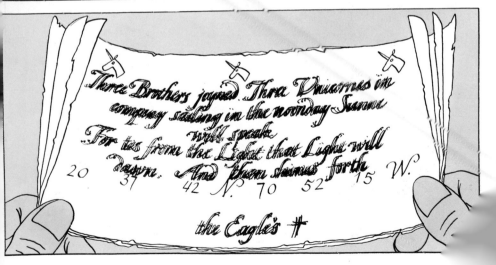

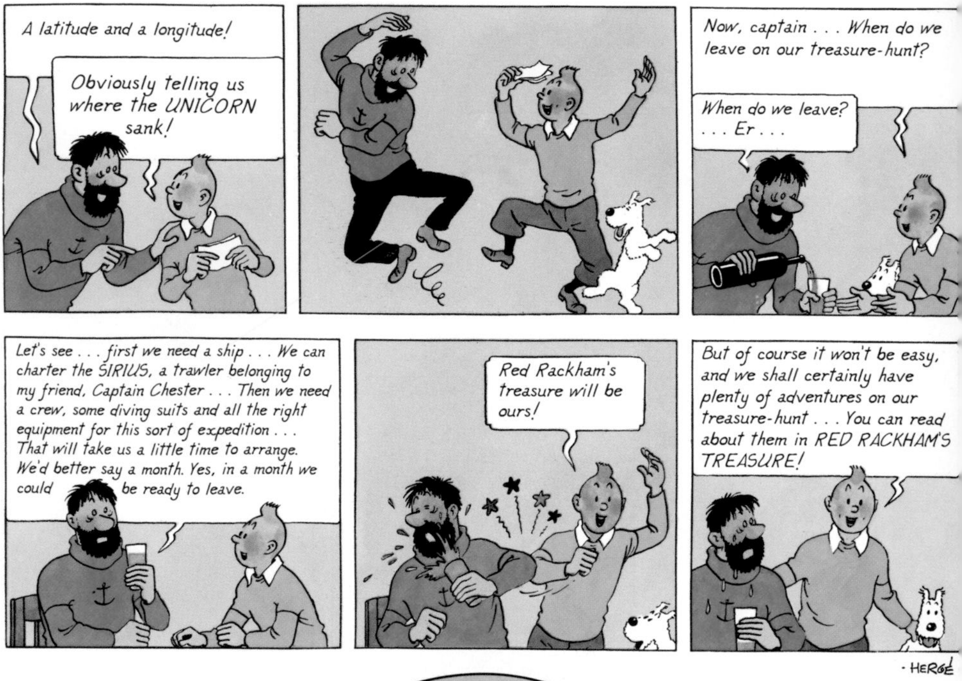
A latitude and a longitude!
Obviously telling us where the UNICORN sank!
Now, captain . . . When do we leave on our treasure-hunt?
When do we leave? . . . Er . . .
Let's see . . . first we need a ship . . . We can charter the SIRIUS, a trawler belonging to my friend, Captain Chester . . . Then we need a crew, some diving suits and all the right equipment for this sort of expedition . . . That will take us a little time to arrange. We'd better say a month. Yes, in a month we could be ready to leave.
Red Rackham's treasure will be ours!
But of course it won't be easy, and we shall certainly have plenty of adventures on our treasure-hunt . . . You can read about them in RED RACKHAM'S TREASURE!
HERGÉ

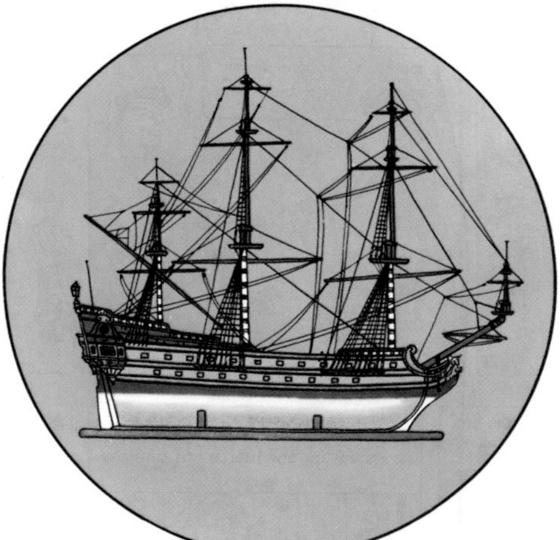